Mutt

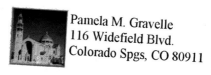

By

M.J. Brett

Blue Harmony Press

Blue Harmony  **Press**

528 Southern Cross Dr.
Colorado Springs, CO 80906
EbrettMBour@aol.com

First Printing, December 2003
Second Printing, December 2004

Dedication

Most war stories tell of heroes, of the bravery and sacrifice of soldiers, aviators, and sailors. Their glory is well deserved.

But this story attempts to present the equally heroic efforts of women left behind to take responsibility on the home front.

This book is dedicated to the *real* Mutti, who lived it and trusted me with her secrets, and to all other women like her, through all of the world's wars. They lived through Hell with the single-minded goal of protecting and reuniting their families. Some managed to do so, and many did not.

Acknowledgments

Though writing is a solitary endeavor, there are many people who put forth great effort on the author's behalf to bring any work to fruition.

Special thanks go to my husband, Eric, who checked my German spellings, and to our children, Kathy, Karen, Nina, and Walter who encouraged me. Kathy even bought a laptop computer 'as an investment in my writing future.' No pressure there!

Without the goading of my former students from Stuttgart and Patch American High Schools to 'get busy with the story,' I probably would never have actually taken my notes from the dresser drawer where they were hidden for years.

The German/Austrian members of Enzian Club were generous with explaining details, like wartime rationing, for instance, while friends in the Cheyenne Mountain Newcomers Club kept me moving, especially Dorothy, who read my first ten chapters and demanded more!

To my critique group, especially Sue, Cindi, Marcella, and Joan, thanks for being both brutal *and* loving until I found my direction. And special thanks go to Jimmie Butler, author and special mentor of the Pikes Peak Writers Conference, where any aspiring writer can go to get expert advice.

A Note on Pronunciation

Few German words have been used in this novel—mostly proper nouns, and all are explained or defined within the text. For those readers who speak no German at all, and feel proper pronunciation adds to their enjoyment, this is a "down and dirty" pronunciation guide for easily negotiating most differences between German and American speech.

Relationships: Mutti is pronounced 'Moottee' and means "little mother' or perhaps 'mama.' In German, it is the diminutive of 'Mutter,' (Mother). Hence, Regina is 'Mutti' to her children, but she calls her own mother by the more formal 'Mutter." 'Oma' and 'Opa' are 'grandmother' and 'grandfather,' respectively. The last name is frequently included as a sign of respect, as in 'Oma Reh' (pronounced Ray).

'I' becomes 'E' in most words: Thus Regina is 'Regeena,' not 'Regiina.' Her husband's nickname for her is Ina, pronounced 'Eena,' not 'Iina.' Elli is pronounced 'Ellee.'

'W' becomes 'V' when it begins most words. Thus poor Willi was tagged 'Valter, Vilhelm Vollf.' And Weida becomes 'Veida.' Ausweis becomes 'owsviis.'

The Umlaut is a vowel with two dots over it. It usually changes the pronunciation to add an 'errr' sound. Königsberg or Nürnberg would be pronounced as Kernigsberg or Nuremberg. Führer becomes Fuurhrer (or at least that is as close as English can get.)

Double vowels in English say the long sound of the first vowel. In German, it is the opposite—the second vowel is long. Therefore Rainer is not Raaner, but Riiner. Weida is not Veeda, but Viida.

E on the end of a word, which may be silent in English, will be pronounced very near to a short 'a' in German. Christine (e silent in English) almost becomes Christina in German. (perhaps closest would be Christin-eh. Many names end in 'a' as well.

That's all you'll need!

"It all began with an unexpected letter. As I think back, it all ended with an unexpected letter, as well. Had I known about the last letter, I might have responded differently to the first. But it would not have made any difference in the long run. Either decision would have brought change, and I have always detested change."

Regina Wolff 1911-1997

Chapter 1

The Russians were forty miles away and closing in on Königsberg. But no alarm had sounded, and no one seemed aware. German citizens who might suspect the Third *Reich* was losing the war dared not discuss it openly with their neighbors. This city in the extreme northeastern corner of Germany had been bombed frequently through the late summer of 1944, which made walking home through rubble-filled streets frustrating and difficult.

Regina Wolff sidestepped massive chunks of concrete that dwarfed her petite stature. With the practiced endurance of a delicate woman negotiating a world more attuned to brawn, she picked her way through broken glass, using her briefcase for balance and trying to protect her last pair of cotton stockings. Only another obstacle to be overcome, she thought, habitually keeping her mind on matters other than her worst fears.

As she approached the northern edge of town and turned onto her own street, her steps slowed. She dreaded conversation with her neighbor at the corner of Gustloffstrasse. It forced her to face unpleasant questions. But her neighbor was waiting near the gate as usual, balancing her young daughter on her hip.

"Guten Tag, Frau Wolff. Any news? Have you heard from

your husband?"

"Not yet," answered Regina. She didn't need reminding. He's been missing far too long with no word, she thought to herself for the hundredth time--but she quickly remembered to pretend he could not be dead. *Never! Don't think of it now.*

"And you, *Frau* Schmidt," she answered evenly. "Has anything come from your *Mann*?"

"Mail's been scarce since the war's so much worse. I'm afraid he may be lying dead in some frozen foxhole in Russia."

Regina saw tears form in the woman's eyes and immediately reached out to pat her arm "You mustn't say that. You mustn't even think it. None of the other women has heard anything either. The Russians can't have swallowed up all our soldiers. The war will end, and they'll all come home. You'll see." She forced a smile, waved, and moved away from their communal fear.

Regina shuddered to block out thoughts her neighbor might be right. Were their husbands dead, captured, or terribly wounded? The disasters at Stalingrad and Smolensk, with many casualties on both sides, had come and gone with no news. She sighed and walked on more slowly. She wasn't sure she believed her own words of encouragement? At first, after Gustav's last leave during Christmas, 1941, she had received his usual, loving letters--then nothing. She'd lived each day determined to lock her fear inside so the children wouldn't see it.

She approached the house where her three little boys and their young nanny usually waited, but this time they came running down the walk toward her.

Willi screamed, "*Mutti, Mutti! Vati's* alive!"

Regina reeled dizzily, grabbing a white picket fence to keep from falling. Elli scooped up little Franzi, while Willi and Rainer raced ahead.

Willi screamed again at the top of his lungs, "*Mutti,* didn't you hear? *Vati's* alive!"

"How do you know?" Regina gasped. "What's happened?"

Elli pulled a letter from her apron pocket. "There's no return address, but I think the envelope is in his handwriting."

"Please, let me see!" Regina dropped her briefcase into

Willi's arms and ripped open the letter. Yes, it was from Gustav. Her hands shook. She wanted a moment of privacy to read it alone, but the children danced around her.

Willi insisted, "What does *Vati* say? What does he say?"

She glanced at the opening line and froze. Then she answered slowly, without looking up, "*Vati* says he is well and he loves you." She felt guilty for making up the words, but she could not tell them what the letter really had said.

Shaking her head and unable to speak further, Regina turned pleading eyes to Elli.

The younger woman obviously realized something was wrong. Almost as an afterthought, Elli said, "This came today too." She handed Regina a telegram, and began herding the boys back toward the house. "Come boys, we must get our supper. We're already late. Your mother needs some time alone."

They skipped, chanting happily in singsong fashion, "*Vati's alive, Vati's alive!*"

Her husband's first words burned in Regina's mind. *"Destroy this letter as soon as you've read it, and tell no one of its contents. You must get the boys out of Königsberg, now!"*

Regina walked into the house, trying to control her explosive heartbeat. She climbed to her bedroom, and closed the door. Sitting on the edge of the bed, she lit a tapered candle. The flickering light brought familiarity and a measure of calm to the room she and Gustav had shared.

She had longed for her husband to come home and resume directing their lives, making all the decisions, pampering her, praising her delicacy, and calling her his 'little dove.' But now, she thought his protection might have been a mistake. She'd had no experience in managing alone, especially in wartime. She clung to the belief their lives would someday be the same as they'd been before the war. Always the dreamer, Regina spent her lonely nights remembering and analyzing.

Now, Regina held the thin paper tightly, trying to feel Gustav's presence in the silent room. As calm returned, she could finally read the whole letter.

"Dear Ina Popeena," it began.

Tears filled her eyes at the silly rhyming nickname with which he had teased her as a child. He had never called her by her real name. 'Ina' was always his pet name for her, even after their marriage. Regina steeled herself to read the strange opening lines again, and then continue.

"Use the telegram you should also receive to obtain an Ausweis at the city hall to take the boys on a train west to Berlin, and then south to Karlsbad, Czechoslovakia. You must do it now!"

Why so much emphasis on haste? What could be the rush to leave home, especially in wartime when travel was so difficult?

"Stay to the north," the letter demanded. *"Don't go south until after you pass Berlin, no matter what happens. Bring as much money and paperwork from the business and house as you can without attracting suspicion.*

"I'll be at the hospital in Karlsbad for thirty days. You must arrive before then."

She fought her anxiety. The hospital? Was he injured, or ill? She forced herself to read on.

"Don't tell the children more than you must because they might accidentally tell someone. We'll decide what to do once you arrive. Come immediately! Take care of our boys. As ever, Gustav."

There was nothing more, no personal thoughts, no explanations. Why were his words so brusque, almost like orders? He wanted the letter to be secret. Perhaps there was no time, or someone was watching. Perhaps he was injured too badly to write more.

As the room darkened into evening, she read the entire letter several more times. Then, as her husband had ordered, she tore it into pieces and burned it to ashes over the candle.

She had been afraid to open the telegram first, fearing it might be from the government with bad news. But now she knew it came from her husband. It simply requested an *Ausweis*—a pass-- for Regina Wolff and three sons to journey to Karlsbad via Berlin to the bedside of soldier Gustav Wolff for thirty days and return. Some unfamiliar signatures and strange letter and number combinations crowded the bottom, but that was all.

Regina gasped in disbelief. How could these simple words get her an Ausweis? Everyone knew East Prussia's district official, *Gauleiter* Koch, had become more ruthless as his Ukrainian territories were lost in the east. He allowed no travel permits to leave the city. Everyone was expected to stand his ground against any Russian onslaught. "Surely, I'll not be allowed to go to Karlsbad with such a telegram." she cried aloud. "It says nothing at all."

Questions and doubts overwhelmed her. Where had Gustav been missing, and what had he endured during more than two lonely years? Why had he been unable to write sooner?

Realizing her questions wouldn't be answered until she could talk to Gustav, Regina willed herself to consider more immediate matters. How quickly could she carry out his orders? What would she need to take along for her three boys? Were the trains still running to Berlin with all the bombing and strafing? She studiously avoided the most basic question of all--wouldn't they be safer staying in their own home?

She rubbed her hands together to dispel anxiety. Gustav was asking too much of her. She felt incompetent to make such rash decisions. But Regina could never consider disobeying her husband. Tradition demanded she would have to go to Czechoslovakia, somehow.

Besides, reality now overcame all questions and fears, and she collapsed on the bed, simultaneously laughing and crying with relief. Her husband was alive! Nothing else mattered. She would travel anywhere in the world to see him, war or no war. What were a few days on a train?

Memories of Gustav and their love invaded the room. She could almost see his gentle smile and feel his warm touch. Remembering the softness of his kiss, she touched her mouth with her fingertips, as he had always done. Regina had loved him from the beginning, when he had been her childhood hero.

Wreathed in smiles on their wedding day, Gustav had admired her figure in the soft, bias-cut, crepe dress, and softly called her his "beloved Ina, gentle Ina." She loved the warmth he brought into her life. Their days were filled with laughter and their nights with loving. Gustav was protective, gentle, and confident. Regina unconsciously rubbed her wedding ring and smiled to herself, remembering.

They had bought this elegant, three-story row house on the northern edge of town and started a flower garden. When the first blossoms emerged, they celebrated by building a stone terrace in the back yard so they could dine outside on fine days. Neither had ever wanted more from life than this.

And now he wants me to leave all this behind, thought Regina, dragging herself back to the problem of the letter. How can he think leaving our home will make this terrible war any better?

Chapter 2

Dusk had overtaken the room, and bedtime noises of Elli and the three boys drifted up from the kitchen below. Regina knew she must take some kind of action, but her reveries of Gustav and her naturally passive nature had slowed all movement.

Besides, what should she do first? She rose and walked to the window to gaze down at the terrace and their flower garden in the deepening twilight. There were only a few ragged, stubborn flowers left. She and Elli had long since dug up the garden and planted vegetables. War made food more important than flowers, but she still missed their color and fragrance.

Her moment of contemplation was loudly interrupted.

"Are you sure you got the boiler hot enough?" Willi's voice, busily questioning authority, reached her from downstairs. "This water doesn't seem very hot to me." It was the usual nighttime battle and Willi, at nine, was always ringleader. He was as mischievous as his father. Regina had already caught him drilling a hole through his bedroom wall in hopes of communicating with a boy his age in the next rowhouse.

"Yes, Willi, the boiler is hot and, if you're not kinder to your baby brother, I'll be sure he gets all the hot water." Elli, blessed with infinite patience, still had her hands full. Franzi shouted excitedly at being first for a change. Somehow the two older boys always seemed to stick together and little Franzi, proudly four just that week, could not compete.

"But then I'll have nothing but cold water, too," sniffled seven-year old Rainer. His feelings were easily hurt.

They're all so different, Regina thought. But this particular argument over who takes a bath first and gets the most hot water always finishes each day's quota of competitive spirit. Perhaps she should make a schedule for rotating the dubious honor since every night required the survival of the fittest. No time. Now there must be a more important plan. She walked downstairs.

Both the older boys missed their father's love and his games. Regina had exhausted her fabricated stories to keep them

reasonably content. "Yes, someday we'll all be together again."
"Yes, someday the war will be over and Vati will come home."
"Yes, someday we'll have enough food to fix a real dinner." But
the 'somedays' had now gone on for over two years.

Smelling fresh, well scrubbed, and with their squabbling
quickly forgotten, Willi and Rainer leaned, one on each shoulder,
as Regina told them how much their father loved them. Though
this was a nightly ritual, she sensed this time, they truly believed
her. Then she walked them upstairs and tucked them into bed.
They seemed satisfied. Little Franzi was already slumbering. She
was amazed the children had somehow sensed her unspoken fears
for their father's safety. 'He's alive,' Willi had said. She had
thought her feelings so well hidden. War made children far too
wise.

She told them a story while Rainer's breathing slowed, and
smiled as Willi picked up his favorite book to read by candlelight,
and crinkled his fingers in their secret goodnight. His innocent
smile at the end of a mischievous day always brought a catch to
her throat. It was so like Gustav's.

Regina walked from the room and down the stairs feeling
both happiness and anxiety that didn't fit well together. She hoped
she could calm herself enough to find some middle ground.

She discovered Elli singing in the kitchen.

"This is such wonderful news, Regina. I'm so happy for you
about the letter. Gustav must be alive and well, after all. You must
be so excited. I know you've been worried."

"I suppose it's all I was waiting for, Elli, except for him to
come home, of course. I miss him so very much."

"I know. I hear you crying at night. It must be hard to love
someone so much."

The two settled at the kitchen table and Elli poured their
nightly cup of tea.

"I wish I loved someone like that. Tell me how you two met.
Did someone introduce you?"

"Gustav's little sister, Erna and I were great friends, seven
years younger than Gustav. We spied on him with his teen-aged
girlfriends. In return, he teased us constantly, taunting us with

rhyming nicknames for fun."

"Like what?" Elli good-naturedly prodded the more reserved Regina.

Regina laughed. "You'll never believe this—Ina Popeena and Erna Scherna. He always made us laugh. I guess I dreamed he'd marry me when I grew up, but he only noticed girls his own age." She moved her fist over her heart in an elaborate gesture. "I felt stabbed in the heart when I saw him with each different girlfriend, and I wanted to grow up quickly before he married one of them."

"Well he is sort of handsome, I guess. He has those strange eyes."

Regina smiled and rested her chin on her hand.

"I always imagined those lovely almond eyes proved him a descendent of medieval invaders from the east, like Genghis Khan. The men in his family all have that Oriental look. Why, Gustav's father was actually arrested as a Russian spy during the Great War. But they had to let him go when they discovered his family had lived in East Prussia absolutely forever."

Both young women laughed at the family folklore.

"His family always joked about their 'barbarian' strain, but the men did seem more aggressive and adventure-oriented than most. I thought Gustav quite mysterious and wonderful."

"But how did the reluctant Mr. Wolff wind up asking you to marry him?"

"He always jokes that we caught him by surprise. One day, when Erna and I had grown to our teens and Gustav was in his twenties, we tried to get him to notice me. She bobbed my long coiled braids to look like his fashionable girlfriends. He noticed, all right!"

"That sounds bad."

"He seemed angry and he yelled, 'What have you done to yourself? Your hair's all gone.'"

"I said I thought he'd like it since he liked all the big girls with their hair like that."

"'But you don't look like yourself,' he roared. I asked if it made me look old, or ugly, or something? I knew I'd made a terrible mistake, but I was determined not to let him make me cry. I just stood still while Gustav walked slowly around me, rumpled my short hair, and seemed to be studying my profile. It seemed an eternity before he answered."

"How embarrassing. What did he say?"

Acting out the part, Regina imitated Gustav's gruff voice. "'You *do* look older...I never noticed before if you were ugly or not.'"

Elli clapped her hands to her mouth with a giggle. "Oh. How awful."

"I was so embarrassed. Then suddenly, Gustav laughed and took my hands in his two big ones and said, 'Now that you're so terribly grown up, I guess you'll have to marry me. After all, I've waited a long time for you.' I was so shocked I thought I hadn't heard him properly.

"And obviously your answer was 'yes.'"

Regina nodded, with a grin. "I didn't even think it over. And he didn't seem surprised. I've always wondered if he'd known I loved him from the beginning. We were married two years later, in 1931"

"You're lucky, Regina. With my luck, my beau would have just told me to go away." Elli laughed heartily. As their laughter and girl talk died, Elli rose to start the dishes.

Regina sobered. What should she tell Elli about the letter from Gustav?

Her husband had said to tell no one, but much had changed in Königsberg since he left. No one talked anymore. Regina couldn't explain how or when she'd realized it wasn't a good idea to discuss her suspicion of problems within the German government with the butcher, or druggist, or even a stranger on the *Strassenbahn*—the streetcar. There were knocks on the door in the night and people were gone the next day. Sometimes they came back, silently, with teeth missing and bruises, or sometimes they didn't come back at all. She was sure uncertainty and terror kept everyone following the rules. Gustav couldn't know of the sense of isolation this secrecy generated.

Gustav had hired Elli in 1937 to join their live-in maid,

Christa, to give Regina more time for him and the children. He said it was so Regina "...wouldn't get her pretty hands all rough." He saw a broken fingernail or mussed hair as a tragedy. He expected everything in their home to be perfect, and everything in their lives to be elegant and refined. He was a 'candlelight and wine' person, with a need for luxury, and Regina loved providing him such a home. Just before war came, Gustav was called into the Army. She had been needed to help at his business, something unusual for a female in their privileged family. But when Christa went home to help her own family, Elli had quickly become indispensable.

Squaring her shoulders and taking a deep breath, Regina made her first decision alone. She would confide in Elli, no matter what Gustav had said.

Regina picked up a dishtowel and joined the younger woman at the sink. "Elli," she began slowly, "You've been with us a long time now, and..."

"Seems like always, doesn't it? Long before Franzi was born. What was I, nineteen? I thought I was escaping the chaos of life with my stepmother. I sure didn't know I was just starting the chaos of wild toddlers--the team of Willi and Rainer." Elli laughed.

Regina smiled, knowing Elli loved the boys. She began again the difficult task of disobeying her husband. How should she broach the subject?

"Elli, you've always been so good in a crisis, like helping me keep the boys calm in the bunker during air raids and I..."

"You know how much they like the shadow plays on the wall in the candlelight? I've thought of a few more animals for them to guess. That game seems the only way to keep Rainer's mind off the bombs falling. I can always get him started by telling him he's the best at guessing. He gets all puffed up with his own pride, but then I know the others will compete, too."

"Especially when the plaster falls on our heads," said Regina. "Sometimes those nights seem endless." She chuckled, realizing it was sometimes hard to get Elli to listen instead of chattering on. She tried again. "Elli, the letter and telegram I received today had some strange news. Gustav wants no one told, but I know you love the boys, and I trust you not to speak to anyone who might jeopardize their safety. I need your help."

"What can I do?" Elli was instantly sober and attentive.

"Gustav wants me to get the boys out of Königsberg immediately. There seems some urgency, so I want you to come along too. We can say you're my younger sister so I can get your name on the *Ausweis.*

"I couldn't ever leave Königsberg, Regina. It's my home, and my aunt is alone here. Gustav must be crazy to ask you to do this." Realizing she may have overstepped the bounds of an employee, she added quietly, "You'll be back soon, and I'll be just fine here. You mustn't worry about me."

Regina tactfully ignored the breach and explained the contents of the letter, showing Elli the mysterious telegram.

Together, they decided Regina would go downtown in the morning to get the *Ausweis* while Elli prepared the boys for the trip. Sure enough, it was easier to plan with two heads working on the problem. They quickly finished the dishes and set to work dumping emergency supplies out of knapsacks each family member normally kept beside the door for fast trips to the air raid bunker. Then they discussed what the boys and Regina would need for a thirty-day round trip by train.

"I assumed the Russians were still far away," Regina mused, "but now I'm beginning to wonder if Gustav knows of some urgency on the eastern front."

"We would have heard something by now if the Russians were close. Our *Führer* would've warned us if there were any danger."

"I don't know," answered Regina, slowly. She no longer shared Elli's confidence in Hitler, but this was another thought best left unspoken. She realized Elli wouldn't accept any possibility of German defeat, and would not be persuaded to leave Königsberg.

Seeking to reassure the younger woman, Regina added, "My father always tells stories of how he and his fellow soldiers stopped the Russian Army in the south, by the swampy Masurian Lakes. That was when they tried to cut off our city during The Great War of 1914 to 1918. Father calls Königsberg the fortress of Prussia that will always protect us. Perhaps he's right."

"So it's not right for Gustav to demand that you and the boys leave the protection of the fortress," said Elli emphatically.

Her comment gave voice to the logical question Regina had deliberately refused to let surface.

"I don't know, Elli. At this moment, it's his emphasis on '*now*' that scares me most."

Regina could tell Elli disapproved of her leaving. The younger woman fussed and stomped as she gathered a few of the children's clothes.

"This suitcase weighs too much, Regina. You're too small to carry it and still handle Franzi on the train. How can you manage a trip like this by yourself with the war going on? Whatever could Gustav be thinking?" She sniffed, as though disgusted or angry, yet there were tears in her eyes.

Regina had been so happy she would soon see Gustav that she deliberately ignored possible difficulties. Neither had she thought what it might mean for Elli to lose the only family she'd known, even for thirty days. She touched the younger woman's shoulder and said softly, "I must manage it, Elli. And I need you to understand. Gustav says to come to Karlsbad. I must go."

Elli pursed her lips in silence and turned away, stitching up some of the household money into the hem of the sturdiest *Dirndl* Regina had left. It was a brown dress formerly used for special festivals, now indestructable for everyday tasks and as a traveling outfit.

They left space in the bottom of Regina's knapsack for the papers that licensed the family business. She felt sure she could sneak the papers out of the office without attracting suspicion.

Regina made a mental note of her tasks for the next day-- picking up money and papers from the business and round trip tickets for the train to Karlsbad. Everything would depend on getting the *Ausweis* first. She hoped she'd have an idea for obtaining one by morning, because both she and Elli agreed the telegram would not be convincing enough.

Regina hated the thought of leaving home. She'd never liked change and she knew she lacked the confidence to venture new ideas alone. She leaned her head against the windowpane and imagined her dearest dream. The war would be over, and she would be sitting in her own garden waiting for her loving husband to come home and reunite the family. She would be wearing Gustav's favorite frilly dress, his favorite perfume, and the last pair of silk stockings she had hidden away for the occasion. He would whisk her into the air and whirl her around, kissing her tenderly. She had dreamed of the moment a hundred times...to again be in his arms as 'his little dove.'

Elli's noisy bustling broke into Regina's reverie.

Now she feared the necessity of this journey would destroy her dream. She sighed and resumed her work. It never occurred to her that the family might not be able to return to their home, ever.

Chapter 3

With the dawn, Regina boarded the *Strassenbahn* for downtown. Estimating the damage from last night's air raid, she noticed most seemed centered near the harbor. Their office was in that district.

At the *Rathaus*, Königsberg's ornate old city hall with its beautiful 'Little Maiden' fountain in the front, Regina steeled herself to tackle her first and most difficult problem--obtaining the *Ausweis*. She needed this pass before she could buy tickets or get on a train.

She found the proper office, filled out forms required for requesting a pass, and presented her papers to the morose clerk behind the reception desk. Contorting her face into a scowl, the clerk screamed at Regina, "What can you be thinking? It's impossible!"

Normally, Regina would have accepted any authoratative decision and left humbly, but now she was following the orders of her husband, and that fact gave her strength. Pulling herself up as tall as she could manage, she said in an even tone of voice, "I demand to see the *Bürgermeister* at once."

The clerk angrily flicked her hand at all the other people waiting in the next room. "You're wasting your time. It'll take months to process all your forms, and even then, you'll not be allowed to leave the city. There's a war on, don't you know?"

Regina felt she had no choice but to stubbornly wait in the next room anyway. Hours ticked by on the old clock kiosk as she casually observed the rococo decor around the room and daydreamed.

Finally, a woman called her name and led her to an ostentatious office. An elderly man with thick spectacles motioned her, not to sit, but to stand in front of his desk. She noticed his rumpled, indiscriminate uniform bulging around its buttonholes.

"What do you want?" he growled. Regina's natural shyness paralyzed her tongue, so she simply handed him the telegram. He didn't look at it right away, only stared through her as though she weren't there. Finally, she forced out words.

"I must have an *Ausweis* to see my injured husband in Karlsbad," she blurted, more forcefully than she had intended. The man nodded, read the telegram, and handed it back to her with a motion of dismissal.

"*Herr Bürgermeister*," Regina hurried to continue before he could send her away, "I thought my husband was dead on the Russian front and now I find he's hospitalized in Czechoslovakia. My children need to see their father in case anything bad happens. I must have the *Ausweis!*" Belatedly, she remembered to add "*Bitte*"--please.

His eyebrows flew up, but the *Bürgermeister* at last looked straight at Regina. He moved his round little spectacles down over his nose, staring more closely, then said in a softened tone, "What makes you think I'd let you go? Every woman in Königsberg wants an *Ausweis* because they think the Russians will be attacking soon, and they all want to find their husbands. At least you know yours is alive. Be grateful for that and go home."

Regina felt rather selfish asking for a pass if so many others wanted one too. "Are the Russians really so close?" she asked.

The simple naiveté of her question must have caught the *Bürgermeister* by surprise, because he answered just as directly, "They're about seventy kilometers to the east and south." Then he apparently thought better of it and added, "…but the *Führer* already has plans to stop them. There's no need for you to go running back to Central Germany and panic our hard-working Berliners into a defeatist attitude. No one is authorized to leave East Prussia now except special cases."

"Would it matter so very much if my little boys and I went to Karlsbad and came back within thirty days?" Regina asked quietly.

"Those trains are needed for supplying our troops. They must defend the Front," he said, beginning again to bluster. "We have no room for women and little boys, and we might be cut off and under siege within those thirty days!"

Persistence bothered him, Regina thought. He seemed angry, but was his anger directed at her? Perhaps he was more afraid of *Gauleiter* Koch, the eastern defense area's supervisor. She decided to take a chance.

"*Herr Bürgermeister*, I'm sorry you have so many applicants. It must be difficult for you to solve your many problems with the Russians so close. But my father always said our city walls and gates and fortresses could withstand any siege. Perhaps you don't need to worry so much."

"Those walls are hundreds of years old," he snapped. But, just as suddenly, he shook his head and softened his tone. "Who's your father, young woman?" he asked, motioning Regina to sit down after all.

She told him the name.

He again picked up the telegram, this time noticing the strange numbers and letters at the bottom and staring at them a few moments. His brow wrinkled. Then he dug, rather frantically, Regina thought, through his desk drawer and drew out a small green book hidden under a panel. He checked the numbers on the telegram again and compared them to one page. Beads of sweat appeared on his crimson forehead.

Regina didn't realize until he finally spoke that she'd been holding her breath.

"I can give you the *Ausweis* for thirty days only," he announced suddenly.

Regina jumped up quickly, before he could change his mind. "Thank you, *Herr Bürgermeister*."

He scratched out something on her application and scribbled his signature at the bottom. Then out came not one, but two official stamps, which he applied with a satisfied flourish.

"You may go," he said, with a strange emphasis.

Regina searched his face, confused. What had changed his attitude?

He rose and gave an almost imperceptible bow. "I can understand you want to see your husband before he goes back to the front. Because of his, and your father's, exceptional service to the Third *Reich*, I'll accommodate your wishes. You must understand, of course, I cannot allow the little boys to go with you. You might not then wish to come back to us." He smiled, looking relieved. With that, he handed Regina her signed documents, saluted, and abruptly left the room.

She was stunned by both his statement and by his sudden departure. What had he meant by 'exceptional service' rendered to the German government? What kind of service? After all, Gustav was only a common soldier, and her father just another civilian.

But how, then, from his far-away location in Czechoslovakia, had her husband known the Russians were so close to Königsberg that he wanted her to leave the safety of their home immediately? For a moment, Regina pondered this new question.

She looked again at her application. The man had scratched out the words, '... and three sons' leaving her name alone on the document.

"He knew," she thought angrily. "He knew I couldn't go away and leave my sons behind, not with the Russians so close."

"Oh Gustav," she whispered, "How I wish you were here to tell me what to do now."

Chapter 4

But for all her wishing, Gustav was not there. Regina would have to find a solution to save her boys, alone. *She was no good alone. She'd always known that.* She reluctantly walked back to the waiting room, sat among the remaining petitioners, and tried to consider her options.

The only two choices were to go without the boys, or stay behind with them and hope they could wait out the Russian siege safely. It was like choosing between her husband and her sons, and both choices were unthinkable. She needed an alternate plan.

Regina was confident the *Bürgermeister* would never have confirmed, even inadvertently, both the Russian advance and its speed, if he weren't sure. Besides, if it were true that her husband and her father had helped the Third *Reich* in some way, as the *Bürgermeister* had indicated, the Russians might deal harshly with her children if they were left behind.

Those strange letters and numbers must have meant something... but what? *Stop wondering--no time for that now.* She could still cancel her own trip if she couldn't find a way to take the boys, couldn't she? Regina decided to get the first pass in her hands. Then she would work on a better solution.

Sighing in resignation at having made another decision alone, Regina waited for a clerk to type her own *Ausweis* out of Königsberg.

It was obvious she would have a long wait. So many desperate people were sitting there, just as she was. Why had their right to travel about the country been denied? When had leaders of the country become so uncaring? When had the chance to change the outcome slipped by? Or had she simply been too naïve to understand the problems before?

As usual, Regina passed the time in day-dreaming, trying to probe the beginning of the terrible changes in Germany. She believed it had started long ago. She'd been too young to remember the beginning of the Great War in 1914, except that her father was away as a soldier. She was, however, old enough to remember its end in 1918, and his disgust with the Versailles Peace Treaty that followed. Closing her eyes, she could still see her father and his neighbors arguing about it constantly.

"This will be devastating to Germany," he had shouted. "How can we stop all production of airplanes when they'll be the transport of the future? We can't compete, and it'll drive us into depression. We can't destroy all our industry. Do they want us to weave baskets for a living?"

He had tapped out his pipe, not even noticing the ashes drifting to the floor. No one dared to interrupt.

"We can't allow a corridor through our country to be given to Poland, either. It'll isolate East Prussia from the rest of Germany, plus our countrymen trapped there will be persecuted. The traitors of Versailles have stabbed us in the back! Germany must get back a nationalist government to avoid chaos. You mark my words. We'll no longer survive as a nation if we allow this travesty of justice to stand."

His neighbors nodded, perhaps in consternation and perhaps in fear of the future he painted.

During these heated conversations, the young Regina would try to tease her father back into his normally good mood by sneaking up and twirling his long, thick mustache from behind his chair. But even her little girl pranks couldn't gain his attention or stop his frustration.

"I hate the Russians." He struck the table with his fist. "This so-called democratic government being forced upon us will open the door to the Bolsheviks who've brutalized our people in every part of East Prussia they've occupied. Someday, they'll pay!"

His violent talk scared Regina. She hadn't understood his anger. After all, the little girl had never seen either a Depression or a Russian, and she certainly hadn't known then what bitterness this Peace Treaty would bring her people.

Herr Reh, Regina's father, was a prosperous pharmacist. He owned his own pharmacy and their whole city block of apartments downtown, near the university, as well. Over the next years, as the inflation her father predicted became reality, it took wheelbarrows of money to buy even bread and milk. And if the years of inflation were destructive, the Great Depression of the early 1930's was more so. Though *Herr* Reh had money to buy what his family needed, Regina discovered shortly after her marriage that many people did not.

Regina shook her head, remembering how Gustav held her hand as they walked along the harbor's stone retaining walls almost every evening. By 1931, a continuous line of idle businesses stretched along the waterfront near the tobacco import/export business they'd inherited from Gustav's father. Though their city was far from the center of activity in Berlin and separated from it by the new Polish Corridor through Danzig, the Depression had gradually seeped into Königsberg as well. Gustav drove further into the countryside each day for his business. He was often paid only with the root vegetables grown by surrounding farmers. Thousands of men had no jobs at all. Their gaunt faces haunted Regina as they stood on street corners with their tools, begging for a few hours' work to feed their families.

One day in late 1932, Gustav had rushed in, breathlessly telling of bloody riots between the communists and a group of men who called themselves National Socialist Workers. Others called them *Nazis*, for short. "Fighting forced everyone off the street. I drove blocks out of the way to get home," he said.

Gustav had strong opinions about the cause of these latest clashes. "Our so-called 'Republic' was supposed to replace the monarchy, but it was doomed from the beginning," he said emphatically. "Oh, it sounded good on paper but, in actual practice, it was only able to function with help from America. Our weak leaders have been plagued with *Putches*, coups, and riots from every demagogue trying to start his own political party, and the leadership has done nothing about them."

Regina hadn't understood politics, nor had she interrupted when he continued.

"Why, we've got everything from Bolshevists to Monarchists to extreme right wing Nationalists, and our Army tends to back first one group and then another. No one takes notice of these riots, and no one knows how to stop them. And candidates haven't addressed the problem of communist insurgents harassing

German citizens to join their party." He added confidently, jabbing his finger for emphasis, "These Brownshirt *Nazis* are at least doing something to stop the communists. That's a step in the right direction. And they're gaining power in the *Reichstag*."

With such unrest in the cities, the political party with the most persuasive speaker was bound to take power that year, though with so many political parties, no one group could gather enough votes for a clear majority. Like Gustav, others seemed fed up with weak leaders and the democratic process, especially Regina's father.

"A republic hasn't worked in Germany!" her father shouted out with his usual exuberance. "Only strong leaders like Frederick the Great, Bismarck, and Hindenberg have made Germany great. We need a strong, nationalist leader to get back our prosperity."

Yet the Great Depression didn't seem the biggest problem on Gustav's mind.

"I'm more concerned about safety from mobs rioting in the streets," he had said. "I fear we're close to a civil war if someone doesn't take charge forcefully, and soon."

Regina's father and her brother agreed, as they discussed the news over dinner. Regina thought they talked too much about politics. It seemed men's only interest.

Mother Reh and Regina spent their time in the kitchen, where they tried to fashion the only vegetable available at the *Marktplatz* that day, beets, into a palatable dinner by adding vinegar, onions and spices. What did they care of political change? Women had enough to do just to keep food on the table.

Her father said, "Well, at least this one candidate, Adolf Hitler, promises to reverse the injustices and indignities of the Versailles Peace Treaty. That would be a great feat. If he also can, as he promises, deal with the communist threat, put people to work, feed the hungry, and restore peace and prosperity to Germany, we should vote for him."

"Aren't those too many promises for one man to keep," ventured Regina.

"You women know nothing about it," said her father bruskly. "In cinema newsreels, thousands of people cheer enthusiastically everywhere Hitler goes. He's the answer to every good German's prayer."

Perhaps, Regina admitted, she had not fully understood that election. Citizens were to vote 'yes' or 'no' to the National Socialist program. Only those two choices--and all the radios and posters prodded, "Vote 'yes' for law and order. Defeat the Communists." A yes vote would also mean the dramatic Hitler would be Germany's new *Chancellor*, and Hindenberg, whom they revered, seemed to sanction the man. Everyone she knew voted 'yes!'

Now, in 1944, Regina felt Hitler had been perhaps too knowledgeable about appealing to every segment of society? And perhaps weak old Hindenberg, their president, had been used to bring along Army backing for the *Nazi* party. It hadn't been apparent to her then. How was she able to see it now?

Back in 1933, however, everyone had anticipated the wonderful changes promised once Hitler took power as *Chancellor*. When shortly after, a fire destroyed the legislative hall, the *Reichstag*, Hitler consolidated all power behind himself to ward off what he said was a communist plot. With the loss of their legislative forum, however, there was also the loss of any further realistic attempt at democracy. The strong-arm SA members walked out to force their own legislation, and Hitler assumed supreme lawmaking power under the Enabling Act.

"I don't see any problem with his handling *all* the power," her father had said then.

Gustav had added, "Nor do I see anyone questioning our *Führer's* sincerity. His assumption of power is necessary for greater security. He seems a good man for the times."

Regina wondered now if the *Reichstag* fire hadn't been a little too convenient. Shouldn't the German people have questioned that act? But she had never questioned her husband's judgment at the time.

Even the most non-political citizens could see the Depression ended when Hitler built new *Autobahns*--super highways linking far-flung parts of Germany, employing over 350,000 men on that project alone. He also promised Volkswagen cars in every garage and money for each family to feed their children, called *Kindergeld*. His forceful and mesmerizing speech spun dreams for the German people. Was it actually what he said, or perhaps only the way he said it? Regina had never been sure. But he gave everyone hope? He was a real showman, creating fantastic spectacles with red and black banners and fiery torches at each rally. People were impressed.

"Now, isn't he handsome," said Regina's docile mother, enthusiastically. "He must be a great leader." Her father had laughed at his wife's naiveté, but he had not bothered to enlighten her. She was, after all, only a woman. 'Handsome' was good enough to ensure her loyalty.

But though those first years improved German lives, strange ordinances soon appeared. Hitler screamed against Jews with the Nürnberg Laws. He even purged his own Brownshirt SA supporters, claiming their leaders had become traitorous. By 1939, many Germans had some misgivings about the possible consequences of the new alliances and new war Hitler seemed determined to force upon them. Yet Regina knew neither her husband nor her father had seen any problem with his leadership. Her husband had gone willingly into the Army, which had sworn its personal allegiance to Hitler, not to the now defunct Constitution. Had they all blindly followed a Pied Piper with his own personal agenda? She had never understood it, then.

But now, in 1944, even Regina, with no interest or comprehension of politics at all, had become disillusioned by the cruelty, fear, and multiple regulations that dominated German lives. Could anyone have seen disaster coming and stopped it? Regina had often wished so, but women weren't expected to express opinions. Could she, as one shy housewife, have made a difference?

Over time, she had seen good German citizens polarized into bitter fanatics or fearful and silent prisoners through governmental terror. She now had time to look at the misery in faces sitting around her, waiting in this office, and she felt they'd all been betrayed.

It was already afternoon when Regina's reveries were

interrupted by the calling of her name to see a clerk who would type her *Ausweis*. All the clerks looked busy, bored, and extremely tired.

A middle-aged, mousy little woman glanced at her application, noted its signature and stamps, and started typing. When she got to the scratched out part, she looked up at Regina and asked, "Who will look after your little ones?" There was a note of concern in her question.

Regina sensed the woman might be sympathetic to her dilemma, but since everyone had become so restrained and secretive, she couldn't be certain. One could never tell whom to trust.

"I...I'll try to get someone," Regina said, cautiously.

The clerk didn't answer, but she pursed her lips in concentration and stared at the wall for a moment. Regina hoped fervently the woman would say she could change the wording to include the children. The pause hung heavily between them. Regina could see the clerk was thinking, but she seemed afraid to change the order. She started typing again.

"Perhaps our nanny can stay to look after them," Regina added. The hope was gone.

"Tell her to keep them indoors, as this August daytime heat is hard on children," the woman commented quietly. She glanced around behind her at the armed guard sitting in a corner, and then locked her eyes to Regina's. "It would be nice if you could take them out after dark to play when it's cooler," she added. "Too bad there's curfew after we close our office." She adjusted her glasses and again began typing.

The exchange sounded like idle chatter, but Regina couldn't be sure. Was the clerk trying to tell her something? Or was her hopeless situation making her search for meaning even when there was none? Regina's brain raced to find some missing connection. She scanned the clerk's face for meaning, but it was void of expression. Regina could only nod her thanks as the woman handed her the legally stamped paper.

Then the clerk surprised Regina by rising to shake her hand, saying quietly, "It's sad that the '...and three sons' addition could not be typed right after your name, on the same typewriter, of course." She paused and peered at Regina again, rather intently. "Perhaps for your next journey."

Somewhere someone coughed. The clerk turned abruptly and called for the next person in the waiting room.

Somehow that cryptic exchange helped Regina develop a plan, though she felt ashamed to even consider it rationally. She tried to imagine how she could find the courage to break a law. She had never been considered an innovator.

But she sat down in the outer office and carefully sketched the layout of the building. Anxious, self-absorbed people did not seem to notice the shy woman. In the lady's office were nine desks in three rows. Each had a typewriter and a filing cabinet on the left, always in the typically German, well regulated, and orderly style.

The kind clerk was in the middle row, left desk. Could Regina find it in the dark? She would need to use the clerk's modern machine to match the type. Her own typewriter at the office had an old-fashioned, ornate script that wouldn't do. She also knew, from the experience of others, that penalties for tampering with official documents could be catastrophic. Yet, even with her passive nature, Regina felt sure this would be her only chance to get around *Nazi* restrictions on travel. Above all, she needed to keep her children together and get them safely to their father in Karlsbad.

She counted every step as she descended from the second floor office and carefully memorized all the twists and turns of the rotunda. She would find a way to come back, after curfew, as she hoped the clerk had been hinting.

Chapter 5

"I'll be out of town for about thirty days, *Herr* Busch," Regina explained later that afternoon to the elderly accountant who helped manage Gustav's harbor business office. They shook hands with the usual Prussian formality. "Can you manage here alone?"

"Of course. The bombings have been heavy on the harbor, but they haven't hit us yet. Will you need anything for the trip, *Frau* Wolff?" He added with a hint of concern, "This is rather sudden, isn't it? Can I help you in some way?"

"I'll need to take some money from the bag you're readying for the bank. Will that be a problem?"

He stooped immediately to retrieve the bag, groaning unconsciously from his rheumatism.

"Oh, no, *Frau* Wolff. It's never a problem. Will the boys and Elli be going along?"

"No. They'll stay here until I return." The old man glanced away, but said nothing. Had she replied too quickly?

What if *Herr* Busch were a *Nazi* loyalist? Or could he be only another simple citizen caught in the web as she was? Had he already known something? Was her face betraying some concern? On the other hand, he might secretly be offering his support, just in case she needed it. How many people would like to help each other if they only dared? The thought gave Regina a bit of hope.

While *Herr* Busch was rewriting the deposit slip, Regina pulled the business ownership papers and licenses from her file drawers and put them carefully into her purse. She felt no concern, since they wouldn't need renewal for another year.

When *Herr* Busch returned, he smiled broadly. "Have a wonderful trip," he said, "and don't worry. Until I hear from you, I'll continue to send money to your home for the boys and Elli and the usual bank draft to the Swiss account."

Regina couldn't remember any Swiss bank account, or anyone she knew in Switzerland, but she didn't want to ask questions that might cause suspicion or slow her departure at this crucial moment. Then she suddenly remembered, and it took all her restraint not to show the excitement she felt. Only one family might be in Switzerland. Long ago, Gustav had promised he'd send a monthly check to the Minslov's account once those long-time Jewish friends and partners were reestablished in another country. They must have arrived safely in Switzerland after their hurried departure from Königsberg. She wanted to laugh out loud with relief, but she struggled to keep her face registering only business efficiency.

"Thank you, *Herr* Busch. That will work perfectly," she said. Why hadn't Gustav told her that their friends were safe? Surely he knew she would be worried about Gudrun and her family. This was another strange piece of information she forcibly put aside to think about later, when she was alone. *Now was not the time.* Relief at the knowledge of the Minslov's safety was tempered by her anxiety to escape quickly. She wished neither to endanger *Herr* Busch nor to arouse his curiosity with further questions.

"*Aufwiedersehen, Herr* Busch. I'll write you if there are additional instructions. Right now, I barely have enough time to get to the *Bahnhof* and buy train tickets." Regina gasped, instantly realizing her mistake in using the plural, but *Herr* Busch only shook hands again, and patted her arm--an uncharacteristic gesture. She shrugged helplessly, smiling at this kind old man, and hurried out. She appreciated his quiet encouragement.

The East Train Station, rather than the main *Bahnhof*, was her best chance to buy tickets without being noticed. It was her usual station for catching the *Strassenbahn* home.

Gustav had said to stay north as long as possible. She presumed this was to avoid any Russian advances from the southeast. The northernmost train leaving Königsberg went to Berlin, via Stettin. Regina decided to buy four full-fare round trip tickets hoping adult fares would not cause as much notice as buying tickets for three children.

She wiped her perspiring palms in near panic. What would she do when the ticket agent asked for her *Ausweis*? The long line moved slowly ahead and soon it was her turn. Several men in uniform were standing at kiosk tables chatting and eating sausage sandwiches with their beer. She hoped they were not close enough to hear her quiet request for four tickets to Karlsbad by way of Berlin.

Then came the dreaded demand from the matron in the ticket window, "*Ausweis, bitte.*"

Regina took a deep breath and rushed ahead. "They told me at the *Rathaus* the paperwork would take another day, but I need to get tickets today for tomorrow's departure, so we can leave right away." She lied. She dared not show her *Ausweis* naming only one person. The matron would ask about the other three tickets.

"This is very irregular. I'll need to call my supervisor." The woman tucked dirty wisps of hair up under her uniform cap and started to turn away.

"Oh please," Regina begged. "Please help me see my husband in the hospital. He's very sick. Two of his brothers and his sister are going with me. None of them has time off to buy the tickets. They're all working for the Fatherland. We must leave from the *Hauptbahnhof*—the main train station, and I'll be meeting them there, so I need the tickets now!"

Please God, she prayed silently--it's not so important a lie.

The matron looked at the impatient line of people behind Regina, glanced at her watch, and said with a tired sigh, "Oh, all right. Here." She slammed the tickets down on the counter.

Regina handed her the money she already held in her hand and slid the tickets into her purse. She thanked the matron, automatically adding the required "*Heil Hitler,*" and hurried out onto the platform.

Her *Strassenbahn* was ready to leave. Thank goodness, she didn't have to wait while wondering if she looked as guilty as she felt. She had never been able to lie convincingly. It filled her with a desperate, conflicting sense of shame to have to do so now.

Once home, Elli examined the *Ausweis* many times, as they talked over Regina's plan for the night. Elli paced the kitchen floor with her hands on her hips and scolded, "Regina, what if you get caught? Wouldn't they come for the boys and take them away from me? They'd send you to a work camp and I wouldn't know what to do."

Regina tried to give clear instructions, even as she struggled to keep her voice steady. "If I'm not back by eight in the morning, take the boys to my parent's home. Stay there with them until you see what the authorities do. Sometimes they question people and send them home after a few days." And, Regina admitted to herself, sometimes not. "Leave the terrace door open for me in case you go to the basement for an air raid. And please let me borrow your black coat." The words tumbled out all together.

Elli stopped pacing the floor and nodded hesitantly.

"Don't worry, I have this all planned out," Regina continued, pleased she sounded more confident than she felt. "If too many police are out, I'll stop at my friend Magda's, downtown, and tell her I got caught out after curfew. I can get home when people are going to work in the morning. I've done that before when my *Strassenbahn* was late, so Magda won't be surprised."

Regina shifted her position away to hide her shaking. *Who am I trying to convince?*

She could feel Elli's skeptical glance on her. Elli's hands still rested on her hips.

Regina tried again. "I'll be home in time to get the boys and we'll catch the afternoon train at the *Hauptbahnhof.* Can you have them ready? Don't tell them yet that we're leaving, just in case…"

"I'm afraid, Regina!" Elli said. Her solemn eyes darkened. She clearly understood the consequences. "But I can see you're determined. I'll do as you ask." She bit her lip and was silent.

While Elli fed the boys, Regina packed their small knapsacks, adding to each a few extra pieces of clothing, a small packet of money hidden in the bottom, and a piece of her silver wedding tea service. *If we get separated, they'll need to barter, as they've seen me do in the Marktplatz,* thought the young mother.

The reality of the thought started her shaking again. *What if we did get separated? What would my little boys do if they were lost with a war going on?* Regina tried to think in practical terms and wrote out names and addresses of all Gustav's brothers and his sister. She added her own brother and his wife who had moved in 1938 to Weida in central Germany, south of Leipzig. Her brother, Hans, was also away at war, but she hoped his wife would help her children, should they be lost and alone.

Regina copied the list five times, sewed one in each of the boys' small knapsacks with the money, and put one inside her own larger one. That left one for Elli. Surely someone would be kind enough to help lost children find family members. Everyone who survives the war must somehow get back together again.

She realized she was again thinking the unthinkable... that someone might not survive. The war had already killed many people. She knew she was more realistic this day than she'd ever been in her life. Her plan wouldn't be child's play and, if she failed, she could lose everyone she loved.

Understanding completely the implications of her action, Regina brushed away tears, took a deep breath, and folded her palms together tightly to gain control over her fear. *She had to try.* For her, there could be no other option except to follow her husband's orders, though surely he could not know how difficult it would be for her.

Regina studied her crudely drawn floor plan of the *Rathaus* several times more, then tore the paper into bits and burned it so Elli would not be blamed if she were caught. As an afterthought, she tossed the oiled packet of matches and Gustav's old pocketknife into her knapsack. For her own reasons, she rolled into a small bundle her last pair of silk stockings and a soft, ice blue chiffon dress--her husband's favorite of what he called her 'delicate, elegant dresses.' It was the only one she had managed to save when she bartered away her extensive wardrobe for supplies needed throughout the war.

Chapter 6

Elli was crying as she tidied the kitchen after dinner. Regina wondered what she could say to the nanny that wouldn't betray her own fear? "I know you'll do your best for the boys and yourself, Elli. God bless you."

Regina tucked the children in, left Elli to read them a bedtime story, and ran to catch the last *Strassenbahn* downtown. She hoped it would arrive about forty-five minutes before curfew. As darkness closed in, she wondered if that would be enough time.

It took forever for the twenty-minute ride, or perhaps it was only her nervousness that made it seem so. Regina got off and walked the last three blocks to the *Rathaus*. She forced herself to maintain an unhurried pace as she circled all four sides of the building, casually stroking each of the basement windows with her fingers as she moved along, as innocent-looking as a child clicking a stick between the stakes of a picket fence.

Only three windows appeared unlocked. One was blocked by a large piece of furniture on the inside. In front of another, two watchmen were leaning against the wrought iron railings on the grandiose double staircase floating up to the entrance. They were smoking and talking, perhaps killing time before they would change shifts to patrol inside, but they paid no attention as she strolled by.

That left only the window at the back of the building. Regina looked up and down the street and saw no one. Most sane people were already getting home before curfew began. She knew being out on such a mission placed her among the insane ones. The window moved a little with her push. She was tiny, but so was the window. Could she get through it?

Wiping her sweaty palms on a handkerchief and stuffing it back in her pocket, Regina walked to the corner to take another look at the window under the staircase where the watchmen had loitered. They were gone. Home? Inside? How would she know who was still in the building? *Slowly... control those shaky knees. No time for second thoughts. Just do it!* She inched forward, glancing in each direction.

The low basement window was partially hidden behind the double stairway on the main street. Perhaps it would be even better for her purpose since it was in shadow. The frame leaned inward with an easy push, and Regina scrambled through before she could change her mind. She stood frozen in the dark to avoid stumbling over something unseen. A light would have been helpful, but too dangerous. Never having been in the basement, she moved painstakingly, trying to guess where she might be.

As her sight gradually adjusted, Regina could see shapes of furniture stacked nearly to the ceiling. A dim light outlined a door across the room. Did the door go into an office? Would someone be there? Did it go into the hall or to the stairwell? She tested each step, feeling her way toward the door. She stood behind it, listening. She heard nothing.

The *Rathaus* offices had closed over an hour before, yet Regina hesitated, worried someone might be working late. What could she say if she were caught in the building after it was officially closed? She couldn't think of an excuse that sounded plausible. She plunged ahead, opening the door a crack, peeking out, and stepping into the basement hallway.

The old stone and wooden structure creaked and groaned with night sounds. Was it from the weather? Musty smells filled the hallway, reminiscent of centuries of dampness. For a giddy instant, Regina actually wondered just how old the *Rathaus* was. She could not remember. How bizarre that it should matter at a time like this, she thought, stifling a nervous giggle. It would have been helpful to know the inside of the building better but, with their current government, it had become a place to avoid. Almost everything that happened here seemed either suspicious or dangerous.

On tiptoe, Regina reached the stairwell, moved the door open a crack, and listened again. She felt sure she could climb to the second floor and find her way to the correct office, once she reached the main rotunda. But, for now, she would need to climb the basement stairs blindly and slowly to avoid creaking the ancient wooden risers. She was confused about where in the rotunda she would be arriving since, in her nervousness, she had neglected to check which way she had turned from the entry window. How stupid of me, she thought, realizing she was not adept at this type of activity.

At the top of the stairs, Regina found a small gate. It wasn't locked, and she folded it quietly against the wall long enough to pass through. A light from behind the main desk showed her where she was in the rotunda, and she moved to the more familiar wide staircase leading upward.

Entering the second floor, she noticed a dimly lit office at the end of the hall. The watchman inside was reading a book. Regina pressed against the wall and waited. The man seemed absorbed and had apparently not heard her. Hoping it was an engrossing book or that he was particularly lazy, she stepped across the light's path into the shadows at the opposite wall. The watchman didn't move. She edged her way down the hall to the open waiting room and through it to the clerks' office.

Counting the desks, Regina crept to her clerk's typewriter and felt the wooden cover. The lock was hanging loose in the hasp, not locked. A thrill of relief brought her smile in the darkness. The clerk had known she would come, then. She really *had* been trying to send a signal. There were still good people trying to help, after all. It was a comforting thought.

Lifting off the cover, Regina set it aside. Then she pulled the *Ausweis* from her coat pocket and tentatively began to insert it into the machine. She had measured to her name's line with her fingers many times but, now, in the darkness, she was not even sure she had the paper right side up or that her shaking fingers were measuring the space correctly. It seemed a risky chance that she could insert it properly.

Praying the paper was straight at the top, Regina held her breath and typed. One letter at a time, "…and three sons" clicked from the machine after what she hoped was the correct line for her name. The clicking of the keys sounded thunderously loud and she stopped after each letter. She unrolled the carriage, flinching with each soft sound it made.

It was done now. She had no way to undo it. She folded the

incriminating document back into her coat pocket and covered the typewriter. Her brow was damp as she realized the enormity of what she had done. "I, Regina, my father's good little girl, have lied, broken into a public building, and forged an official document. I cannot believe it myself," she confessed... to no one in particular.

At that moment, the last of the dimmed lights were extinguished, leaving each watchman with only the red glow of fire exit lights and a hooded flashlight. Now, she had broken curfew and blackout as well. *Whatever was she thinking? However could she get away with this?* She found herself frozen to the floor in panic.

Shaking in the dark, Regina tried to think straight and keep control. She ran her hand over the typewriter and the desk, making sure she hadn't disturbed anything noticeable. She clicked the lock shut on the cover. Nothing in the morning should cause suspicion or put her helpful clerk in danger. She'll know I was here, though, and that she helped me. God bless her, thought Regina.

Feeling her way to the darkened door, she stepped into the waiting room and moved down the hall. The red fire lights were no help. Regina could see nothing at first. What if the watchman had heard a noise from the clerk's office and was waiting in the dark to catch her and take her away? Fighting the temptation to run, she barely managed to restrain herself. *Think, Regina, think. Running will get you caught.* Holding her breath, she listened again. Silence. Was the watchman still reading by the flashlight in his office?

Regina searched for the strength to leave as her heart pounded loudly in her ears. Surely anyone else could hear it too. Her feet would not move. *Slowly--breathe slowly. You can't stand here all night. Why am I doing this? Hold onto the thought. My family must be together. I cannot let Nazis take my children or separate me from my husband. That's important.*

Slowing her breathing by force of will, one step at a time, she crept toward the staircase.

She would be in sight of the watchman's room while crossing the hall. Startled, she realized he wasn't there. Where was he?

Not waiting to find out, Regina slid across the hall to the stairwell door, opened it, and inched down the curving stone stairway to the first floor. As she reached the last steps to the rotunda, she saw the watchman's flashlight, shining around the walls of the main foyer to the right of the stairway. He would have to go back up these very stairs to get to his room. She couldn't stay there. She stepped around to the opposite side of the staircase, crouched down, and prayed he had already checked her side of the rotunda.

She could not see the man, only streaks from his flashlight shooting around the ornate room in wide arcs. If he had heard anything, wouldn't he keep looking until he found her? To fight that fear, she tried to convince herself this was his routine, periodic walk around the building to check security. She waited. Her knees ached as she continued to crouch low.

The watchman flashed his light behind the main desk and jiggled a lock of some kind--a safe or file drawer? Perhaps he suspected a burglar.

Please, please, please let him go back upstairs. Regina hoped God was listening. She could no longer see the flashlight moving behind the big desk. Where had he gone? Suddenly, she heard his footsteps almost at her ear. He must have either walked without his flashlight to the stairway behind which she was hiding, or she had closed her eyes in fear and hadn't seen him move.

She ducked her head down, froze in place, and held her breath, thankful she was wearing Elli's dark coat. The guard stopped, apparently listening for something. Her numb, aching knees measured a lifetime. Then, with a curse, he turned and thumped up the stairs, singing a bawdy *Nazi* song as he neared the top.

Regina had trouble breathing. She couldn't stop the shaking of her knees and hands. *Please don't faint. Hang on.* She wondered why panic sets in after the real danger is over. Given a few moments, a relieved sort of control returned. She pulled herself to her feet using the centuries old stairway newel posts for support, slipped to the little gate, slid it open, then closed, and crept softly down to the basement. She wondered if there might be more than one watchman, but she had no time to worry about that possibility. A moment of confusion--which way had she come to the stairwell? Which was the door to her escape window? She was so near now. She scolded herself for taking chances by hurrying.

She found the window and pulled it open, squeezing her head and shoulders out to look and listen. She heard the quavering two-note sound of a police siren coming up the street, and pulled back inside. Had the guard called the *Polizei*? Even the most respectable citizen felt limp with fear at this ominous 'neener, neener' sound, more frightening than any air raid warning siren. Regina's fear was stifling after what she'd done. She felt guilty and frightened, yet she knew waiting inside a moment longer was her only option.

The police siren passed by and stopped two blocks away. She said a silent prayer for whoever the authorities were after. Since she could see no one in such darkness, she hoped no one would be able to see her either, and climbed out onto the street.

Once outside, Regina pulled the window closed as far as she could without nipping her fingers, and rested under the grand entry staircase to catch her breath. Then, slipping from shadow to shadow, she crept the two blocks to Magda's row house.

Regina knocked softly. She could hear her friend's footsteps padding to the door.

"Who is it?" Magda whispered in a trembling voice. A knock in the night these days always meant trouble.

"It's only me, Regina."

Immediately, the door opened, Magda pulled her in, and shut the door behind her. She was in her nightdress and old slippers with the fuzz rubbed off. She had not yet been to bed.

That fact surprised Regina. Perhaps it had not taken her as long to do her illegal work as the many hours it had seemed.

"What did you do, Regina; get left behind by your *Strassenbahn* again? You know they stop running after curfew. You must be more careful," Magda scolded as she shuffled toward the hall closet. "What would your boys do if you got yourself picked up?"

Regina nodded. Magda gathered her only spare blanket for

Regina to use on the faded couch. "You'll have to stay here until curfew is over in the morning," she clucked on in her motherly tone. Regina nodded again and curled up in the ragged blanket and her borrowed coat.

As Magda climbed the stairs, she called out cheerfully, "I'm too tired for talk tonight, but I'll make some tea in the morning."

Regina was relieved she would not have to talk, and wouldn't need to tell more lies. She didn't say she would be leaving early. She knew Magda had no extra tea.

Though Regina could feel the *Ausweis* in her pocket, with blackout conditions, she would have to wait until morning to see if it was completed properly. Her heart was pounding so hard she feared it would wake Magda, even far away upstairs.

Magda was almost ten years older than Regina, and fiercely protective. Regina believed her a good person. There were rumors she met with other men after her husband was reported missing near Minsk on the Russian front. But the younger woman knew Magda loved Manfred. However, Magda's loneliness was understandable too. Perhaps she couldn't bear the uncertainty alone, and was trying to drown it with 'company.'

Regina didn't want to know if the rumors were true or not. Magda had always been a friend, and she would help anyone in need, though she had little herself. I certainly would not cast the first stone, thought Regina. After all, I have my boys and Elli to help keep away what Willi always calls the *Buschi-bau-bau*, or old scary boogiemen. Magda has no one--not since her only child, a boy of four, died of tuberculosis in the early days of the war. If war made changes in even loyal Magda's confidence and behavior, it could make changes in anyone. There must be many people suffering as Magda had, and perhaps turning to others for comfort. What a terrible time a war was for families.

Gradually, lying in the dark, the realization set in. She had done it! Her very own plan had worked. Gustav would be proud of her, and she would soon see him *with* their boys. They would travel four or five days by train, but she would not need to abandon her sons in order to reunite with her husband. She would not have to choose between them.

Chapter 7

By the time Magda's grandfather clock struck midnight, Regina knew she couldn't sleep. Whether from excitement or fear, she found herself with time to ponder what she had tried not to think about before--the question of why Gustav hadn't told her about the Minslov's safe arrival in Switzerland. *Why would he keep something so important from her when he knew how worried she had been about Gudrun and Jakob?* Sneaking through the darkness of curfew to Magda's, and wondering at *Herr* Busch's strange revelation about a Swiss bank account had made Regina think of their friends and remember the last time she had seen them, slipping through the shadows to escape. Had she unconsciously followed their example last night? If so, it had saved her. Gudrun would have laughed, and Gudrun's smile had been missing since 1938.

Gudrun had been Regina's friend since they competed in elementary school footraces. They shared adventures and secrets as teens, and picnics and hikes as they grew up. Gudrun's parents had given her a very German name, even though she was Jewish by both birth and religion. Was there some historic European anti-Semitism from which they were trying to protect her? Neither of the girls thought of such things. Gudrun's infectious laugh made all their pranks fun.

At Regina's wedding, Gudrun met Gustov's partner--a fine Jewish man, serious and contemplative, named Jakob Minslov. Six months later they were also married, and the friendship continued. They shared good jokes and fine evenings together, even as supplies became scarce during the worst of the Depression, in 1932.

The young women shopped together at the *Marktplatz*. They couldn't help noticing how many mothers bargained for bread, counting out each *Pfennig* while their hungry children clung to their skirts. Gudrun and Regina bought extra groceries and secretly left them on doorsteps of troubled families. Of course, the two needed their husbands' approval for such projects, but neither of the men seemed to mind. They were thankful that they did not yet have children of their own to worry about. That would come later.

If Gustav had been worried about business then, he never said so. Always he placed his hand on Regina's cheek and said, "Don't fret, Ina. This Depression will end soon, perhaps after the new regime takes over. I promise I'll always be beside you to protect you. Keep smiling for me." She never worried when he was near.

And things did get better as the Depression ended, the communist hooligans were arrested, and young couples could again stroll safely along the harbor. Big ships of the world were again bringing spices and woolens, and prosperity had returned to the *Marktplatz*. Both couples started families, and Regina assumed all was well.

But just as their business again grew prosperous, early in 1938, Jakob and Gudrun knocked at their door late one night. Both seemed nervous as Gustav drew them into the house. Each had one of their two small children strapped on their backs. The baby, three-month-old Sarah, whimpered as she slept against Gudrun's shoulder.

"We must get our children out of Germany," Jakob announced. "I've changed all our business papers to reflect your name alone as owner. Here, take them. The authorities must not think I had anything to do with the business."

"Why would you do this?" asked Gustav, staring at the papers in astonishment.

Jakob looked grim as he glanced at his children. "Germany is changing. Surely you've noticed Jews are being excluded from public life, and fewer jobs are allowed to them? Our boy won't be able to go to school with yours next year." He continued angrily, "Damn it, we're German too!" Jakob tossed his hair from his eyes and resumed in a more controlled voice.

"Many of our people are leaving the country. We're convinced Himmler and the *SS* will soon enforce the Nürnberg Laws more stringently. New rules come daily, and even our lives may be threatened. We don't want you to lose your share of the business because of us. You'll have to run it alone, at least until after the war our Rabbi says is coming."

Regina was shocked at their quiet friend's outburst, and she could tell from Gustav's startled look that he didn't understand either.

"Why, business is good. Germany is becoming a better and safer place all the time. Whatever gave you such ideas? There'll be no war."

This attempt at reassurance didn't change the strained look on Jakob's face. Gustav's smile flickered and died as he realized Jakob was deadly serious. "If you feel you must leave, my friend, what are your plans?"

"A few ways are still open to get out legally, though I fear not for much longer," said Jakob. "At Synagogue, they think the latest restrictions are designed to force us to emigrate. But there's a price. That's why I prepared these papers beforehand. Otherwise, they would've taken our joint business too." He put his hand to his brow, as though to wipe away his disbelief. "We had to sign over all our property as an exit tax in order to obtain visas and tickets on a steamer. We leave tonight for Denmark and then on to Portugal. A 'repatriation fee,' they called it. Repatriation to where? We're German citizens!"

At Gudrun's soft tug on his sleeve, Jakob quieted and slowed his next words.

"I have a cousin in Switzerland who may help us. We'll write when we find a safe place."

"Must you go now?" Regina asked, scarcely able to take in such alarming information.

"There are rumors the authorities have blocked some from leaving even after they've signed over all their property," answered Jakob. "We can't take the chance of waiting." He moved to the front window and peeked around the curtain. "And we shouldn't be seen leaving your home or traveling to the harbor. It wouldn't be safe for you either. We'll take the long way around on the forest path."

Gudrun sobbed, her pale hands clinging to Regina's arm.

Regina felt some foggy sense of disbelief at the whole scene, and it made her angry to see her normally bubbly friend so sad.

"This isn't fair. You shouldn't lose everything to such injustice. Which authorities are responsible? To whom should I write a letter to complain?"

Gustav looked at her sharply and shook his head. "It's not for you, Regina. I'll take care of it." Then he brightened. "I have an idea. As soon as you find a safe place, open a bank account and send me the number. I'll send you profits for your share of the business. I want to be fair about all this. And if it's Switzerland, their accounts are secret, so your money should be safe."

Gustav strode to his desk and emptied an old leather pouch, folding a stack of bills and pushing it into Jakob's hand. "Take this for extra travel money. You may need to do some bribing along the way."

The intensity of their stare into each other's eyes made Regina aware there was something the two of them were not saying aloud. Overwhelmed, she ran to get her hand-knitted shawl, the one her friend had always admired. Tearful goodbyes were exchanged as Regina wrapped the shawl around Gudrun's shoulders. Gustav extinguished the inside lights before opening the door, and the Minslovs moved into the night, creeping from shadow to shadow of the buildings nearby, disappearing into the darkness of the forest.

Gustav and Regina had watched from the window until they could no longer see their friends. They held hands in the darkness as tears ran down Regina's face. It was all too strange.

"Why were Jakob and Gudrun so secretive? What danger do they fear that I didn't even know about? Is their fear rational?"

Gustav gave no answer.

"Have you heard anything about all this?"

He was slow to give his usual reassuring comment, "You mustn't trouble your pretty head about it, Ina. I'll check into everything tomorrow."

He had seemed beyond her reach. He understood more than he was saying, Regina realized. He was holding something back. His reticence had seemed a warning not to ask further questions. She hadn't.

She thought about the situation in the days that followed,

though. The ordinances hadn't seemed dangerous at first, but they were annoying and unfair. She had heard some vicious propaganda against the Jews, but the majority of citizens would never believe such lies, would they? In 1938, Regina had still believed mistakes could be rectified, and that someone in the *Nazi* hierarchy would care enough to rectify them.

Shortly after Jakob and Gudrun left, however, the *SS* enforced new edicts that Jewish people were no longer allowed to own businesses or cars, go to public movies or concerts, or travel on streetcars. Jewish teachers, doctors, and religious leaders lost their licensing documents. Radio broadcasts and kiosk posters in the street proclaimed Jews 'enemies of the people,' just as the Bolsheviks had been the 'enemies' when Hitler first took office. Jews were singled out for mistreatment. Jakob's words had been prophetic, after all. His fear of persecution had been real.

Later, in November of 1938, Regina and Gustav had been walking home from the cinema when they saw storm troopers with *Nazi* armbands and young hoodlums on a rampage. They were breaking windows on Jewish-owned stores, setting fires, painting horrible signs on buildings, knocking down citizens, beating them, and loading them forcibly into trucks.

"Stop it," Regina had screamed. Her voice couldn't rise above the chaotic violence.

"Hush, Ina," Gustav said, pulling her into a side street. "They've gone mad, and you can't reason with a mob. I must get you away from here. They're even attacking bystanders who try to help." He led Regina down back streets toward their home, as she cried over those she had seen hurt and arrested.

"What can it be, Gustav? This doesn't make sense."

"I don't know, but I'll try to find out once you're safe."

"It was called *Kristallnacht*," Gustav had said the next morning after spending the night out trying to find answers. "Don't worry. These were just a few isolated incidents perpetrated by delinquent boys. When the *Führer* hears about it, they'll be punished."

But punishment never came, and Regina had seen men in uniform alongside the young hoodlums. By the time 1941 came and Jews were further isolated by the requirement to wear a Star of David, she knew hatred of Jews was no longer a temporary aberration by a stupid few, but government policy. The *Führer* shrieked his rage over the radio again and again, "*Deutschland muss Judenfrei sein!*" "Germany must be free of Jews." Soon after, the first convoys of Jews were sent to work in Poland and the east.

When Regina objected to Gustav, he had said, "You don't understand the overall situation, Regina, so don't speculate on the *Führer's* plan."

She couldn't understand how his views had changed so between 1938 and 1941.

Soon, no one was immune from arrest. Regina heard of a Christian pastor who wrote a letter condemning persecution of churches and synagogues. He was arrested, called 'subversive' by the *Nazi* Party, and put on trial. When international newspapers said the pastor had been a heroic U-Boat commander of the Great War, the Party was embarrassed. "He was good enough for a medal in 1916," announced the editorial. "Why is he not good enough to speak his mind now?" The *Nazi* Party's solution had been simple--forbid press coverage of the trials and exclude international newsmen from Germany. It was obvious the pastor disappeared after his letter of complaint. Regina felt intimidated. She had prepared just such a letter, though Gustav had forbidden her to mail it.

"Ina, promise me you won't speak of it again or write letters that could get you in trouble," he had whispered in her ear as he held her that night. "You must trust my judgment in these things. Please promise me you'll concentrate on keeping our boys together until all this is over. I need to know you'll be safe when I return to duty." He kissed her shoulder and begged her to understand.

Of course, Regina had obeyed her husband but, for the first time, she felt he was out of touch with her feelings and was misunderstanding important changes in the life of their country.

Magda's clock struck three.

Lying restlessly on the sofa, Regina remembered the climate of fear that had come with each new pronouncement by the government. A definite and noticeable social change had gradually taken place, as more and more people kept their opinions to themselves. She now realized it was the Jewish question that had awakened her sense of outrage. It was the catalyst for her questioning of *Nazi* authority, though she had not fully realized it at the time.

She began to ponder questions Gustav had never answered. What reason could he have had for not telling her he was in contact with the Minslov's and sending them money as he had promised? Was it to protect her... or them... or himself? He knew she wouldn't have betrayed their friends. Regina was confused. There would be many questions to clear up once she and the boys reached Karlsbad.

If we ever reach Karlsbad, she added in her anxiety. She feared this might be the more realistic assessment. But in spite of her new questions, exhaustion overcame Regina, and she dozed fitfully.

There was no air raid that night. She woke at dawn, noting from the clock that curfew had ended. She left a note thanking Magda for her help on previous occasions and for her friendship, and promising to contact her in a month. Regina slipped from the house into the anonymous stream of people heading to work for the *Führer's* war effort.

When she entered her own home through the terrace door, she pulled out her *Ausweis*, unfolding it carefully. She gasped and began to cry helplessly. Below the line that said: "Regina Wolff" and scraggling above the line that said, 'of Königsberg, Ost Preussen,' was a noticeably crooked line. It read, "...and three sons."

Chapter 8

"But I broke so many laws to get this done," Regina sobbed in despair, as she showed the *Ausweis* to Elli. "If anyone looks at this pass, they'll see it's been altered and take us away to the camps. I'll be considered a criminal, a forger."

"You felt you had to do it." Elli examined the *Ausweis* and wrinkled up her freckled nose. "Perhaps no one will look at it too closely," she added lamely.

Regina struggled to hide her fears as the boys came down the stairs.

They prepared breakfast of bread and milk. Elli added a few precious apples from the tree in the garden to each of the knapsacks. The tree was getting bare since they had stored each ripening apple in the cellar for the coming winter.

"Elli, can you make sure the boys are dressed and fed while I get a few last minute things in my room? I'm too nervous to eat." When Elli nodded, Regina fled to her bedroom with her knapsack.

Safely in her sanctuary, Regina wondered if she had really done all those insane things the night before. It felt like another person--someone else with more decisiveness and, certainly, with more courage. She looked into her grandmother's antique mirror. Frightened blue eyes stared back. She didn't know *that* woman at all.

It wasn't only her rash actions in getting this potentially dangerous *Ausweis* that made Regina nervous. She now wondered if it had all been for nothing. *Some revolutionary I'd make, bungling a whole forgery*. Should she even try to use the paper, given the increased brutality she had witnessed within Germany in recent years?

She was both frightened and angry. Why shouldn't she be able to travel freely in her own country, with her own children? Why should she have to be afraid? It wasn't right. Who had such power as to make her feel like a criminal? Germans had allowed themselves to be manipulated, she realized. Why had she not seen it before? Why was she afraid to say it, even to herself? The answer was right in front of her, though--a forged paper in her shaking hands. Everyone was afraid.

Her reverie of the Minslovs the night before had reminded her of the whole Jewish question that had so enraged her in 1938. Now here she was again, feeling angry and helpless that she couldn't stop the course of events. Increased restrictions and full mobilization had come after the Americans entered the war. By 1942, all citizens were working wherever they were told, and somehow Jew and Gentile alike had accepted that they had no choice in their future. No one had time to philosophize. Regina and her neighbors did as they were told without question. Penalties for not doing so had become painful.

"It's stupid that Hitler doesn't allow Jewish men to serve in our Army," Regina had once said to Elli, in 1942. "They served honorably during the first Great War. It's even more stupid they're being taken away from their trades when they could be working for Germany. We're already having shortages of soldiers, workers, doctors... all the same people the *Führer* is shipping off to work in factories in Poland or the east."

"It's Hitler's will to send away those who are disruptive to our war efforts. They can work elsewhere," Elli had responded, with a firm toss of her head.

Her comment was enough to make Regina realize Elli still didn't understand what was happening in their country. It made her more cautious about what she confided to the younger woman.

Gustav had been changing before he left as well. She realized now there were many things about his ideas she had gradually become afraid to ask. Why should she have been afraid? They loved each other. Shouldn't he have told her what was important to him and what he truly believed? Had he perhaps wondered if she still believed the same things?

Regina glanced back at the frightened woman in the mirror and straightened her shoulders. She had no time now to worry about all that. Right now, it was more important to decide if she should still try to take her sons on this trip, risking that someone might check the *Ausweis* carefully and discover her forgery? If discovered, it would mean forced labor camp, or worse. *Was there any other option?* She could think of none. The matter was settled. She could not change her single-minded goal of finding her husband and reuniting her family.

Regina glanced around the familiar room for anything else needed in her knapsack. She wished she could take her favorite books, but they were too heavy. Besides, books were replaceable. *What was irreplaceable?* Pictures.

She quickly picked up the family album and tore out a few beloved photos. A portrait of her father and mother with their two children showed how beautiful her mother had been as a young matron. And Regina loved them both so much. How could she leave them now? Yet, if she told them what she was trying to do, they would be afraid and try to stop her. She scribbled out a loving note which Elli could deliver after she had gone. Her father would feel hurt, but he would understand that she must obey her husband's wishes.

Holding the portrait in her hands, Regina thought of the life they had provided her as a young child.

Her parents had enjoyed taking the family to Cranz and Rauschen, nearby resorts on the Baltic or *Ost* Sea. Regina had loved their weekends at the seashore, watching gulls floating and soaring offshore while she and her brother, Hans, shivered in the cold morning air. Father was convinced Regina's 'delicacy' needed a great deal of fresh sea air, so the family walked on the beach every morning near their vacation home. She noticed it didn't make her grow any bigger.

Their childhood in Königsberg had been a pampered one, but Regina and Hans were expected to dress and behave properly, whatever the occasion. Because the family had servants, Regina's mother had time to take them on long walks. They particularly enjoyed the animals in the zoo. Young Regina loved the bears most, and made up pet names for each of them as she walked over the stone bridges above their pens. The nearby coastline was famous for strange blue sand containing amber, and Königsberg even boasted a museum containing rare specimens of the ancient mineral. Regina could feel their smooth, golden beauty. Sometimes the children's nanny also allowed them to sneak out to see an

American Charlie Chaplin film for a special day.

Most exciting of all was to walk along the *Hafen*—the harbor. There were hundreds of ships from every country. Her father helped the children recognize all the flags. Though inflation in those days had made everything very expensive, if one had enough money, he could buy many luxuries--even an ice cream dessert to follow the tiny fish sandwiches on *Brötchen* buns and the leaky paper cones of sauerkraut from huge salty-smelling wooden barrels. The young Regina had felt special when her father took her to the harbor.

She had never wanted anything more from life than to have a loving family like that in which she had grown up, and to live forever in Königsberg. She relished the security of having her own home where her own dear Gustav could return after the war.

"And now look at me," Regina said aloud to the empty bedroom, feeling the painful irony of having to leave that security.

With a tired sigh, she continued her quest, quickly adding to the small stack a photo of her brother on a high-wheeled bicycle, small pictures of her husband's parents, the garden in full bloom, and a few baby pictures of the children. She was especially fond of one Gustav had snapped in the attic playroom when Wilhelm and Rainer were toddlers. They were playing with a large stuffed elephant he had brought as a gift on one of his early trips home from the Army.

Tracing the outlines of the photo with her finger, she could almost hear their giggling and picture them wrestling on the floor. Gustav had laughed and encouraged their mischievous and adventurous behavior, even while Regina had tried to subdue them.

"You're both ragamuffins!" Gustav had roared as he joined them in their wrestling. He was so proud of them--Willi with his dark hair and almond eyes so much like his father's, and Rainer, as blonde as Willi was dark. What a happy time it had been.

Her fingers touched their simple wedding picture, as she thought of the champagne her father had managed to find in spite of the continuing Depression in 1931. Gustav had been so handsome and wonderful. "I'm thankful you're all mine now," he had said in their quiet moments. "We'll be together always." He made her feel beautiful, inside and out. He had a special talent. She smiled, remembering.

She gathered her selection of pictures into an oilskin pouch to keep them dry, and put them on top of her knapsack. Then her eye caught the lovely portrait of Willi on the wall. A Russian prisoner-of-war had painted it in 1941 from a small miniature her husband carried in his billfold. Regina had asked why Gustav would need to visit the POW camp at Riga.

He had answered, "Army business," and the matter was closed.

Now she wondered anew why there never seemed to be any answers. However, the likeness of the child was wistful and poignant, and so like Willi when he was seven. It was a family treasure Regina couldn't leave behind. She cut it from its frame and rolled it up into the pouch.

Satisfied she had saved a few memories, Regina closed up her knapsack. She could hear the radio downstairs with its customary mixture of screaming speeches and popping static. When had that screaming voice become a liability instead of an asset?

She believed she could see the problem more easily in 1944 than she had before. In 1934, when President Hindenberg died, Hitler had suspended elections and proclaimed himself *Führer*. He gave a small radio to every family, so each could listen to his speeches and hear new ordinances. Later, listening to the speeches became mandatory. Regina had ignored most ordinances. There were so many, and she had no interest in politics anyway. But Gustav had become quite interested, discussing policies with her father and the elderly man next door.

If she voiced concern about some new edict, Gustav laughed away her fears?

"All will be fine, Ina. I'll protect my lovely wife. I could do nothing without you?"

His kisses could always distract Regina from her questions. Besides, if her husband felt Germany was a better place under Hitler, she would loyally agree with him.

But politics had seemed unimportant in 1934 anyway. In late

August, their baby boy, Walter Wilhelm Wolff, filled their lives.
He even had Gustav's 'barbarian' eyes. They laughed together as
little 'Willi' giggled so much he wriggled off his blanket onto the
floor.

"He's already conquering new lands," Gustav had said with
obvious pride in his voice. "Things are perfect, Ina," he said softly,
as they listened to American dance music on the radio and cuddled
their baby.

Regina had believed it too. She was having far too much fun
making baby clothes and caring for their little boy to worry about
what was happening far away in Berlin.

It was an active and busy life in those prewar days--perhaps
the happiest Regina was ever to know in her whole lifetime, before
all the changes slipped in. She didn't want to think about the
changes anymore. They frightened her. She needed Gustav beside
her to laugh away her fear, and she loved him desperately. Now, as
she prepared to leave their home in 1944, she felt a cold shudder
through her body. Would they ever be as happy again?

Chapter 9

A precious hour had slipped by when Regina snapped herself out of her reverie. She had no time to drift and dream the morning away. She was sure Elli would be having a hard time by now trying to calm the boys. They would want an explanation of their traveling clothes. Regina hurried down to the kitchen and gathered her children around her.

"Boys, I have a surprise. We're going to see *Vati* for a month and then come back home."

Their stored up excitement spilled over into shrieks of laughter and chatter.

Elli wrinkled up her serious face and tried to reassure Regina about the typing on her *Ausweis* not being aligned. "The *Gestapo* probably won't notice it unless they take a really close look, Regina," she whispered, so the boys would not hear. "You'll have to try. In case the Russians come soon, you must get the boys out now. You may not have the choice later." Elli had apparently decided to back Gustav's orders after all.

Regina nodded, allowing her determination to deepen. There was no sense in rehashing the decision. "In a few days, we'll be safe with Gustav and he'll help us decide what to do next."

Both women were aware this might be a desperate hope, but Regina forced herself to dismiss the foreboding. If she thought about it now, she might not have strength to act at all.

Perhaps Regina's premonition showed in her face because Elli announced in a tone a bit too perky, "You mustn't worry. Everything will be fine here. The *Führer's* secret weapons will drive back the Russians. He said so on the radio this morning."

Regina shouldn't have been surprised. Poor Elli still believed in the statements from that radio which, to Regina, had now become ridiculous. She didn't want to insult the younger woman, so she couldn't reveal her worst fears. What was this element of blind faith that Elli still retained in the *Führer*, when it was becoming obvious to Regina that he had betrayed his people? How could Elli reconcile her exalted view of *Nazi* leadership with the fact that Regina had been forced to break laws to escape the city and would have to fear Hitler's *Gestapo*—his Security Police's imprisonment, in case her *Ausweis* came under close scrutiny? What would it take to make Elli see?

Regina knew Elli would never betray the children, though, no matter what mixed political views she seemed to hold.

But she also knew she had outgrown her own original innocence and wondered what Gustav would think of her new awareness?

"If the worst happens," Elli broke into Regina's thoughts, "my aunt and I will get out of Königsberg somehow. We know all about the Russians and we'll certainly not wait around for them." She laughed, grimly.

"I'll write you when we arrive. If anything happens that we can't get back, contact us at one of these addresses." Regina gave her the handwritten list. "It's the whole family. The best choices would be my brother's wife in Weida or Gustav's sister in Nürnberg."

Regina couldn't hide her sadness and worry. The moment to leave her home and her young friend was approaching far too fast. "Who knows when this war will be over or where we'll all be by then, Elli? You must keep in touch so we can hope you're safe."

Hope, to Regina, had become a translucent thing when the leader steering their course seemed out of control. Of course, she had to sound hopeful, if only for the children. She could not risk the boys telling someone they were leaving. Leaving would be seen as defeatist, a word used for many reasons in these chaotic days. Those to whom the term was applied were suspect and, at some point, their freedom was threatened. Regina didn't want to fall into that category, especially not now.

The children could barely suppress their giggles of delight to believe they were going to see *Vati* and then come back home. Regina prayed it was the truth.

Franzi's sudden shrieks interrupted her thoughts. The two older boys were teasing him. "You won't even remember *Vati* when you see him," Rainer jeered.

"You were too little when he left," added Willi.

"I will too, I will too. I'll be big by then too," cried Franzi, stomping his feet on the kitchen floor as Willi and Rainer pressed their advantage. The two were close and their sibling rivalry was not cruel, but they lost no chance to remind Franzi he was the baby of the family. He was usually left out of most of the older boys' activities as being 'too little.' This was a designation Franzi loudly resented.

Regina and Elli glanced at each other suppressing their laughter behind cupped hands.

"Oh goodness. I can see disaster coming," Regina said.

They diverted the children's attention by asking all three boys to select a few pieces of their rationed cheese and sausage to take along for snacks on the train--enough to last them about four days, she assumed. Regina would buy their regular meals at stops along the way.

Regina needed to be practical for a moment. She packed birth certificates, marriage license, business certificates and financial records, the house deed, a city map of Königsberg, and their bankbooks, all so they could prove ownership after the war. Who knew what might happen?

Then she began thinking as a mother. Was there anything she had forgotten that her boys would need for a month's journey? She added Franzi's small enamel washbasin to the pile of knapsacks. It was an awkward square shape, but he was never content without it and she knew it would ease his journey. Why it was so important to him, no one could understand, but he claimed that he '...needed it,' as some children insisted on keeping a favorite baby blanket.

Willi ran up to his room and returned, tucking some object into his knapsack. Regina didn't ask him about it. Willi habitually squirreled away his little treasures.

Sweaters and coats were added, even though it was still warm in August. They might be needed at night to cover the children on the train, which, like hotels and homes, no longer had the luxury of heat. It would become a valuable decision.

With a mischievous grin, Elli slipped into Regina's knapsack a luxury they had saved--a small can of sliced peaches. "You can use it for a special occasion," she said. "I hope you can manage to *look* as though you're just away on holiday with only your packs, a tiny suitcase, and the little washtub. I suppose even that's bizarre because holidays aren't exactly logical anymore with enemy troops closing in on all sides, but you must try to *look* casual. You're not a good actress, *Frau* Wolff...work at it!"

"I'll try hard, believe me," said Regina, laughing at Elli's reversion to the old formality of mistress and servant. They had discarded it long ago.

The exchange reminded Regina of one more task. She excused herself, slipping down to the *Keller* to smash her tiny shortwave radio with a hammer, and sweeping up the pieces. She had built it from scraps when foreign radio stations became forbidden, and the official German radio broadcasts became unbelievable. Directions for building such a receiver to hear foreign broadcasts were secretly circulated among people assumed to be trustworthy. Magda had built one, so it became a matter of pride that Regina could build one successfully, if Magda could.

The radio was hidden in the basement where she could sneak downstairs and listen to BBC when Elli and the boys were asleep. This English radio station, relayed, she thought, from somewhere north, perhaps Finland or Sweden, was translated into the German language. Sometimes it played a bit of American band music, to which Germans were now forbidden to listen. Memories of Gustav seemed closer, since they had danced to these orchestras on the radio many evenings before the war.

BBC was where Regina learned of German defeats in North Africa, Italy, and Russia, the destruction from bombs on both friends and enemies and, most recently, that the Americans and British had landed in France and were fighting across Europe toward Germany.

Magda told her that the occasional lists of cryptic statements interspersed with news were coded for underground fighters, though her friend never elaborated on who or where they were. It had seemed curious to Regina that Magda would know about such a thing. There was also information about several German officers who had tried to kill Hitler in order to end the war, since there was no option of having an election. Hitler had been injured, the BBC said. The official *Nazi* broadcasts claimed the *Fuhrer* was uninjured. Regina believed the *Nazi* officials were hiding the attempted coup. It made her wonder what else they were hiding. Of course, she said nothing about her feelings, or the radio, to Elli.

Perhaps the dustpan full of smashed pieces held the secret to why she no longer believed Hitler's explanations of happenings within the country. There was far too much discrepancy between the two radio broadcasts, and she could do nothing either for or against any of it.

As she listened each night, hidden under blankets to muffle any stray sound, she imagined her radio as a small connection with other secret listeners all over her city. But the fact that she could share her questions with no one else made her feel more isolated as well.

She could only listen for a short time. Rumors said such radios could somehow be traced. Building and listening to that radio had been the first time in Regina's quiet life she had ever violated a rule. But she had found obeying *Nazi* rules was not an easy task. It seemed now that the *SS* and *Gestapo*, and even the civilian police, had become thugs instead of watchmen. The people they randomly arrested on the street were no longer just criminals and rioters, but normal citizens as well, so she no longer felt safe in the streets. Violating rules had become infinitely dangerous. Regina held the radio's pieces and accepted the danger.

As she tiptoed up the stairs and scattered the smashed pieces under dirt in the garden, Regina was protecting Elli. Had Elli known about the radio, she would never have understood. She still believed Hitler would save the nation, as the posters in the street said, "*Hitler, the letzt Hoffnung*"—the last hope. By this day in 1944, Regina had begun to believe he was the cause of her nation's hopelessness. The radio was too large a liability should Elli find it or be found with it.

Moving about in the garden, Regina could not help smelling the earth in her hand one last time. Tears fell as she stooped to pull a few weeds from the little terrace where she and Gustav had planted all their hopes and dreams with their garden's flowers.

Where had they all gone?

Then, dusting off her hands and hanging up the dustpan on the porch, Regina made a final trip through the house, touching everything as she passed. Little scenes and private jokes flashed from each painting, corner, and piece of furniture as she impressed them on her memory--the warm smell of *Lebkuchen*—gingerbread, when neither Willi nor her husband could let it cool before snitching pieces from the corners--the shrieks and shouts of the boys as they played in their snow fort or skied with their father in winter, or climbed the triple-trunked apple tree in summer twilight. She knew she must close the door on all her memories and simply walk away. Would she and Gustav be able to return and rebuild their lives after her thirty-day trip, or when this mad war was over?

It was time to dry tears so the children wouldn't see them. So many things she was hiding lately. It was painful to hold in all grief and anxiety.

Arriving at the *Bahnhof* in the afternoon, Regina and Elli found near panic as people crowded through windows and got stuck in doors of trains.

"I expected nothing like this mob," said Regina. "How ironic, after all the illegal things I did, that so many others have found a way to get an *Ausweis*, also."

"I don't see any other children though, Regina. You may be the only one to get your children out."

"Then it's worth it," Regina replied thankfully, as they searched for the train to Berlin. Even after they found it, there seemed no way they could get the boys on board in such a crush. The crowd pushed indiscriminately, with no sense of direction. The engine was already belching steam, but the women were torn between risking the boys' safety trying to get on, and just holding them tightly to keep them from being swept away in the crowd.

The people standing in doorways could go in no further, and there was no room in any of the cars. A sudden surge of the crowd shoved them dangerously close to the huge wheels of the third carriage, and panic sickened Regina. Snatching Franzi up in her arms and screaming at the other boys, she had no idea where to turn next.

Suddenly, a round, bearded face appeared in the window above her, and arms reached out for Franzi. Hesitating only a second, Regina pushed the child up, and one by one, the heavy-set man pulled Rainer and Willi through the open window as the women boosted them. Regina wondered how she could join them, but Elli bent her knee as a step up while the man pulled on her arms, and she struggled over the windowsill and fell to the floor in a quite undignified manner. They all huddled on top of each other in the little bit of room at the man's feet, but at least they were on the train. The man smiled kindly as Regina struggled to straighten out her clothing and the belongings Elli tossed to her through the window.

Because of the lack of space, Regina tried to hand Franzi's little washtub back out the window to Elli as the train began inching forward.

But Franzi wailed at the top of his lungs, "I can't go see *Vati* without washing. You can't make me!" He banged his head and flailed his hands and feet on the floor, screaming uncontrollably.

Regina's face turned crimson as people around them drew away with glances of disgust. She would have swatted Franzi's bottom and thrown out the washtub for such behavior, except that an *SS* officer entered the car at that moment to check each *Ausweis*. She was paralyzed with fear when he examined one woman's papers, threw her suitcase out the open door, and ordered her briskly, "*Raus*," to follow after it.

If Regina had wanted to be unnoticeable so no one would look too closely at her misaligned, forged *Ausweis*, this was certainly not the way to do it. Franzi's continuous screams far outweighed her urgent pleas for him to be quiet.

The officer turned to come their way, and Regina became frantic. Dumping the contents of the tiny suitcase into the washtub, she tossed the suitcase out the window, hoping Elli could retrieve it.

Franzi stopped his tantrum as suddenly as if Regina had strangled the little boy. She felt her heart constrict in her chest as the angry official demanded her *Ausweis*.

This officer was having difficulty maintaining both his

footing and his dignity while pushing himself through the closely packed car. Regina held up her *Ausweis* from her place on the floor. Between the jostling of the passengers, and the lurching of the train, the guard could barely give a cursory glance at Regina's pass to check the all-important stamps. He seemed all too glad to get away from her misbehaving and unruly child. He focused a scathing look on Franzi as he moved to the next group of people, grumbling as he stepped over miserable individuals crowded on the floor. He seemed to move in a sort of bubble, as people offered their papers for scrutiny and parted fearfully for his footsteps.

Naturally, Franzi now smiled sweetly as though there had never been a problem. He climbed atop his beloved washtub and its disorganized contents on Regina's lap and snuggled against her shoulder. As the guard closed the door and disappeared, cursing all the way into the next car, her relief dissolved into quiet tears and she buried her head in the little boy's neck. Torn between her own efforts to control panic, and thankfulness for the diversion Franzi had unwittingly provided, Regina could not stop her shaking except by clutching him so tightly he struggled to loosen her hold.

How did this little monster of hers know he was now appreciated? He began patting her head and playing the big shot, comforting his mother, while Regina struggled to hide her emotions so those around her would not be suspicious.

Regina's sighs of relief must have been interpreted as fatigue, because the kind man who had helped them aboard tapped her shoulder and shifted his position so she could sit on the edge of the seat. The boys took turns sliding up from the floor to press their noses over the windowsill. Regina sat with the stuffed washtub on her knees, feeling rather stupid. She wondered how she could possibly manage carrying it in this fashion, instead of a normal suitcase. Yet the whole scene had happened so fast, and Franzi's washtub had saved the closer look at the *Ausweis* she had so feared. She reminded herself that this trip would take only a few days.

"Look, Mutti," cried Rainer, in alarm. "Can that happen to our train?" Regina looked out the window following his pointed finger to several burned passenger cars piled at the side of the track like carelessly stacked firewood. Rainer was puckered up, near tears of panic, when their bearded seatmate distracted him.

"We have adapted quite well to the war-time bombings of our railroads because we Germans need our trains," the man said in a scholarly voice.

The boys quieted and listened. They loved stories.

"Crews of men come immediately after bombs have caused damage with a flatcar carrying railroad ties, spikes, and even a crane mounted on top. Tracks can be replaced, and the crane can lift damaged cars off the tracks so other trains can pass them up and keep going. What you see here is what the crane did to get those old, burned cars off the track so you can go to wherever you are going."

"We're going to see *Vati*," piped up Franzi before Regina could stop him. How can one ever know what a young child will say?

She was frantic the child might say too much, and this man could be anyone. He could be simply interrupting the children's panic to help her calm them, or he might have guessed they were running away and was not willing to ask, or he could be *Gestapo*, quietly gathering evidence to have them arrested at the next station. Regina hated the necessity of feeling such terrible suspicion about a man who, thus far, had shown the family only kindness.

But the man smiled and asked the boy's names and ages. They all introduced themselves and shook hands. At such close quarters, it was impossible to remain aloof, anyway. About that time, the train slowed, braked noisily, and came to a stop. They were parallel to the *Frisches Haff*, an enclosed bay just west of Königsberg, so they had not yet gone far.

"It's probably only to repair the track," said the man. "Nothing to worry about. I ride this line frequently on business, and there are many delays these days. Sometimes one can get right through, and sometimes one must wait. Up ahead there's also a bridge over the Passarge River that was bombed this week. I'm not sure if they have it repaired just yet. We shall soon see."

The boys couldn't see up ahead, even hanging out of the open window. Regina realized then that the train's windows were not simply down--they had no glass in them. There were other signs of damage to the passenger car she should have recognized sooner--holes through the once-elegant roof, smashed glass in the lamps, red plush seats that were ripped and dirty. It all added up to the fact that this once grand train had been strafed by airplanes-- and very recently.

However dangerous it now seemed to be riding such a train, Regina reminded herself forcefully, this is our transportation to see Gustav. There's no way now to change the decision and go back.

Chapter 10

It was dark by the time the railroad cars again inched ahead, and the cars had no light inside. Passengers climbed over others packed on the floor to get to the toilet at the end of the car. Its filth and stench turned Regina's stomach, but they had no other option. When the family returned, each boy ate an apple and a piece of salami from his knapsack and dozed off, Franzi with his head in Willi's lap and Rainer leaning against Regina's knee. Even the man sharing their space had dozed off and was snoring softly.

As the cars thumped over patched seams in the track with hypnotic rhythm, the slow rocking lulled tired passengers into drowsiness or reverie. Regina felt quite alone, and her thoughts drifted to other trains on which they had traveled, to Cranz or Rauchen on the Baltic Sea, or even happy peacetime vacations in the Black Forest or Harz Mountains. She wondered what it would be like to see Gustav again after almost two and one-half years of separation and war. Had he changed? Had she? Perhaps a war forced some changes. Yet she ached to collapse safely in his tender embrace--the one place she felt secure and loved.

It had been a long time since Gustav, his brothers, and all the men in the neighborhood had received orders for the military reserve. They each had thirty days to report for training. Regina feared her husband's call up for the Army, though in early 1938, no war seemed likely.

Gustav had reassured her. "The *Führer* only wants a show of force in case some old enemy objects to our rise from the ashes of Depression. We should be proud to serve our country." He paced about with an air of importance in his new uniform, turning from side to side in front of the mirror. Their toddlers giggled as they imitated his every move.

Regina tried to smile and support his pride, because it seemed what he wanted, but he sounded more like one of the many posters on the street than like the man she loved.

She had slipped into their bedroom to sob out her anxious forebodings.

"It will be all right, you know." The soft words had come from the doorway. "Nothing terrible will happen. You'll see." Gustav came to sit on the bed, gathered Regina into his huge arms, and rocked her gently while stroking her hair. "You'll take care of the boys wonderfully as always, and I'll be home as often as I can be. I promise you nothing will ever change."

What could she have said? Perhaps the words were what she wanted to hear, so she had smiled to reassure him she was his for always. After he left for his initial training, Regina found she hated being alone. She didn't want to live without her husband. He was her life.

But following Gustav's reserve training, Regina did sense small changes. He was again home part time, working at his business as usual, and donning his uniform for occasional meetings. These meetings were held at a local *Gasthaus*, or restaurant, and always ran late into the night. He rarely said anything about them.

The man sleeping on the seat next to Regina shifted position, startling her from her reverie. He turned to face the wall and resumed his muffled snoring.

Regina again relaxed and escaped to her thoughts. But as though clarity was suddenly forced upon her, she realized, even all these years later, she hadn't known what Gustav thought about the war, or why those evening meetings were held. Were they important? Should she have asked more questions?

Approaching a small town, the train stopped on a siding while an eastbound train laden with tanks passed by. With eyes now accustomed to the darkness, Regina could see more burned out passenger, cattle, and freight railroad cars on both sides of the track and wondered how many usable train cars remained in Germany. There could not be many, it seemed. She supposed a moving train presented a tempting target to enemy airplanes above. It was not a comforting thought.

The train sat a long time on the siding. In the dark, flat countryside, Regina could see flashes of artillery somewhere far to the south. What town could it be? She thought about the frantic people receiving that artillery barrage, whoever they were.

Her brooding reflections wandered again to her husband and his plans to protect his family from artillery and bombs. Had he known while home on leave, in fall of 1941, that he would be sent immediately afterward to the Eastern Front? He hadn't mentioned his assignment. The war with Russia was expanding dangerously, so Regina was frightened for his safety, but it had seemed far away from Königsberg. Yet, as the couple walked their favorite route along the waterfront, Gustav had held her hand and offered suggestions for keeping the boys safe.

"Safe?" she had echoed. "Surely we aren't in any danger here at home. The *Führer* said…" But she had stopped in mid sentence. Did she believe what Hitler said by then?

Gustav had interrupted her. "I've arranged to have a bunker built in the back garden," he said. "There'll be a crew of Russian prisoners coming with a German guard to build it. *Gauleiter* Koch has ordered bunkers for civilians because of the possibility of enemy bombing or shelling. Sirens are being installed all around the city as well."

"But the boys…"

"I want you to train the two older boys to grab that elusive baby of ours and run to the bunker whenever they hear these new sirens. They must know to hurry, whether you're with them or not." The tone of his words sounded like an order. This was new. Flashing through Regina's mind, mixed with her fear of war, was an awareness of a subtle change in her husband. That awareness was even more frightening.

Regina had choked back tears. "I thought I only needed to pray for your safety in battle, but now you're saying the war could come here, too." She wanted him to refute this information, but he didn't.

"Königsberg's already close to Russia and, though our Army is doing well now, the battle lines can change at any time. You need to help the boys see this as a great adventure. You must be the brave one, Ina." He stopped and turned her toward him, searching her eyes to make sure she understood. The autumn wind blew his hair at the edges of his uniform cap.

Regina noticed he was not wearing any insignia on his

uniform and vaguely wondered what this might mean. She had not noticed the omission before. But she also sensed he was waiting for her promise to abide by his demand. She nodded, confused by her dichotomy of feelings. But all confusion dissolved as he kissed her on the nose, laughed, and then kissed her again, warmly, on the lips. She melted against him as always.

He had left for Russia soon afterward, and she had only seen him once more before he disappeared.

Sure enough, a few months after Gustav's departure, the Russian prisoners of war had arrived to shore up all *Kellers*—basements, and build an underground bunker with huge timbers under the garden. Regina feared these disheveled enemy prisoners might harm her boys.

"Elli, please keep the terrace doors locked and the boys inside whenever those men come to work," she had ordered.

The next day, however, Regina couldn't help noticing how these gaunt men, with their hollow eyes, stared at the garden's few remaining vegetables. She prepared a large pot of potato soup, and took bowls of it out to them at midday and again in the evening before they left for their POW camp. The strangely silent prisoners worked several days in the neighborhood, and the Wolff's supply of potatoes diminished considerably.

"Why are you giving them all the potatoes, Regina?" Elli had asked. She seemed angry. "Do you think they're treating our German prisoners in Russia so well as this?"

"I want to believe so," Regina answered. "The look in their eyes is that of any hungry man anywhere in the world, and I can't bear to see even an enemy live like that. Somewhere Gustav could be captured, and he might also be hungry."

Elli bit her lip and didn't speak of it again.

Through the end of 1943, the family had gathered around the legal radio to hear of all the victories, never of any defeats. However, Regina craved more information than its one-sided propaganda, so when everyone was asleep, she crept down to the clandestine radio in the basement to compare what, if anything, was true in the German broadcasts. If Germans were officially 'winning the war,' they were also being shelled at home.

Airplanes flew over and dropped bombs rather haphazardly. The women assumed the bombers were on their way back from some other, more important, target, but they spent more and more nights in the little bunker in the back garden. When this underground bunker became too damp, they would sometimes have to retreat to the *Keller*.

Elli was always afraid of this shored-up basement under the house. "The house makes a bigger target," she said. She much preferred the dampness of the bunker out in the garden and didn't seem to mind the bugs there. Soon, however, so much water seeped into the garden bunker the boys used it to sail their miniature armada of boats made from leaves and sticks. Since electricity to pump it dry became more intermittently damaged, the *Keller* in the basement was soon all that was left to them when the sirens sounded. Elli adjusted reluctantly.

Willi and Rainer had, indeed, learned to capture the baby, Franzi, and run for the basement, though they seemed to regard it as a game. "We should just leave him for the Russians to carry away," joked Willi. Regina did not find the suggestion funny, but Willi and Rainer would squeal in enjoyment of their own brand of humor.

Only occasional bombs had found their neighborhood on the outskirts of town, but the harbor received more than its share of damage. Even as they sat with their shaded oil lantern dangling in the *Keller* and shivered when they heard the bombs falling somewhere in the city, Regina still did not think Elli ever lost faith in the *Führer* or in doing all they could do for the Fatherland.

Regina had lost confidence by then, but what else was one to do except pray, and hope, and take first one day and then another. There was no way to see ahead. They fell into bed exhausted every night, then hurried down to the *Keller* bunk beds when alarms sounded, or planes flew over, or the shelling began. Franzi had terrible nightmares. The women became accustomed to his plaintive voice, "*Mutti*, can I climb into your bunk bed? I'm afraid the Ruskie bombs are coming. Why don't they like us?"

Regina had no answers for his questions. They had all forgotten what it was like to sleep the entire night in their own rooms. Weariness and fear dominated their lives. Regina often wondered if the same were true for the women of their enemies? She was sure this must be so.

She could no longer pretend everything would get better. What cheerful thing could she say when sirens wailed, electricity or water failed almost daily, bombs whistled down, and even jokester Willi began to ask in a serious voice, "If we die, will we get to see *Vati* in Heaven?" How could she protect her boys through a war? Gustav's protection and pampering seemed so long ago. She had no survival skills. But her children became a huge incentive to learn some, and quickly.

The train at last chugged ahead more slowly, disturbing Regina's thoughts. The far off thuds and booming had ceased now, and perhaps the sudden silence had wakened her. Had she been dreaming? Fires still burned on the ground. Bombs had done so much damage already. Would there be anything left to rebuild after this stupid war was all over? Of course, she asked herself, who was she to think it stupid? Perhaps, as usual, she didn't really understand it all. Gustav had always said, "Women cannot understand war. Women have no interest in politics, and that's as it should be." But war and politics were certainly now affecting the women of the world as much as it did the men.

Regina thought of the traditional German *"Kinder, Küche, Kirche"* view of the *Hausfrau*. Children, kitchen, and church were expected to fill the life of any good housewife. She had been content at home with her little boys and her garden. Her happy home, husband, and family were everything she had dreamed they would be, but had she missed something? She had not thought so before this moment. She had always rejoiced at how fulfilled she felt in reaching her cherished goal.

Now she was being forced to change her goal, even as she tried to protect it. National and international politics had entered her perfect little world whether she understood anything about them or not. Her new goals were simply keeping her children alive and finding her beloved husband. Rejoicing had nothing to do with it.

Chapter 11

Regina strained to read the village signs as the train huffed by each station, but they were dark. She could see only a few letters. They were passing a road sign pointing to Bladiau when the train again stopped for some time. Then it backed up, and everyone woke. It was near dawn, and there was no explanation for this reversal of several kilometers.

"What is it? What's happening?" Even their kind gentleman sounded surprised, and others sounded frightened. No one answered the questions. "Perhaps they've backed up because a bridge over the river was damaged," he said. "We'll just find another track."

He must have been right because, after a while, the engine again puffed forward and they seemed to be going a bit further south.

Gustav's instructions were, "Don't go south, stay north." This switch seemed only a little to the south, but Regina watched more closely and was anxious to see the next station's sign. Her legs had grown numb from sitting still in such a cramped position.

The boys woke up hungry as always, and she gave them each a bit of *Brötchen* and cheese from their knapsacks. The man next to them pulled out a small herring sandwich and ate his breakfast also. The smell made Regina ill, even though this was normally one of her favorite meals. She told herself she was simply too tired and nervous to eat. The boys began a restless game of Paper, Rock, and Scissors. She was thankful they were subdued for a change.

Passengers were dependent on what they had brought aboard. The train moved much more slowly than Regina had planned. Would the clothing and food they had brought be enough?

At least the boys already understood the shortages of wartime, she realized, though she would have preferred them not to understand so much. She remembered other such shortages.

Regina had noticed bright posters in Königsberg after 1942, asking women to donate warm clothing and to knit long stockings for Germany's soldiers by unraveling old sweaters and blankets. With the war on, they could no longer find any new yarn. She and Elli knitted stockings every spare moment, and even had some success in teaching Willi to knit small squares that could be joined to make blankets for the hospitals. Rainer helped unravel and rewind the yarn. Thinking of all their men in the snow of Russia without adequate winter clothing made it a duty.

In the German patriarchal society, women were allowed few skills outside the household. But they learned to fill in for absent husbands in businesses, and factories, cope with bombings, garden and farm, keep children safe, fix whatever needed fixing, and control their fear and loneliness. They were also feeling the results of clothing and food shortages.

Ships bringing wool, cotton, and everything else to Königsberg's port became scarce, and everyone was wearing old and patched clothes that certainly were no longer fashionable. Regina and Elli were young enough to still care how they looked. One day Elli was to attend a church supper and was discouraged. She could find nothing to wear.

"Here, Elli, try my pastel blouse. It will go with your dark blue skirt."

"That skirt has been worn out at the hem for months."

"Do we still have any lace in the sewing box? If there's enough to go around the bottom I'll help you sew it on."

But when they looked at the blouse, they found it was frayed at the collar as well.

"How about the scarf from my *Dirndl*? Will that match enough to hide the collar, and cover your shoulders?"

"I need a belt. I seem to have lost weight around the middle."

"Try this wide leather one...a narrow one won't hide the gathers." Regina removed the belt from her own waist and handed it to Elli. It was too small, so they moved the scarf to the waistband and switched blouses to another Regina had been wearing only a moment before.

They mixed and matched and did the best they could, but when Elli was all put together, Regina was down to her slip and Elli looked like a vagrant gypsy. They looked at each other in

Grandmother's mirror and laughed until tears ran down their cheeks. How very basic their wardrobes had become.

At that moment, Willi had walked into the bedroom with his homework, looked at his two authority figures in quite a disapproving manner, turned and walked out. They dissolved into laughter all over again. Elli went to the meeting in her everyday housedress with a scarf covering her ash blonde hair and found everyone else looked much the same.

They fashioned each old garment into something that looked new or draped something around their head or shoulders for a different effect. The two were forced to laugh at the result. It was better than weeping about the shortages. Regina had nothing left to remind herself of better days except the silver brooch she had inherited from her grandmother, her wedding ring from Gustav, and the dress he always said was his favorite, now folded carefully in her knapsack. She hoped to wear it again for him soon.

Longing for her husband, she caught herself in the act of turning her wedding ring around her finger with her thumb, and laughed.

Elli had once remarked, "You've made a habit of turning that ring whenever you start thinking too much, Regina. You must be getting absent-minded because you do it all the time."

Regina hadn't noticed the habit before. She did think of her husband often though and, in her loneliness, she had already worn the ring smooth. Her mind drifted away again.

It had been important for women to manage the clothing shortage as best they could. Thank goodness Regina had learned to sew during childhood as her mother sat by her side watching her progress.

"Do it right or not at all, Regina," her mother would chant like some ancient mantra. She could still hear the words. She hated to think of all the times her mother had forced her to pull out offending stitches and start over.

But, because of her mother's wisdom, Regina had been able to teach Elli how to cut down Gustav's old suits to make warm clothing for the boys, and to make smocks and kneepads to protect their scarce clothing. Willi and Rainer hated those kneepads and, boy-like, usually hid them as soon as they were out of the house to play. When they tore their short britches or knee socks, though, it was a tragedy, because they couldn't be replaced. The boys could never understand why both Regina and Elli became distressed with their carelessness.

Shoes had been another matter. They could pass Willi's shoes down to Rainer, and save Rainer's for little Franzi. But what could they do for Willi when no more shoes could be found for his growing feet? Bare feet were acceptable in the summer but finally he had to wear Regina's old gardening shoes in the winter to protect him from the frost. For a while he didn't really know the difference but, eventually, he did understand and became ashamed to wear ladies' shoes. In sullen defiance, he sometimes hid the shoes and walked in the snow barefoot.

"Why, *Mutti*?" he would cry when she tried to console him. "Did I do something bad? Am I being punished?"

It broke Regina's heart. The situation was the same for other families left behind. Even affluent mothers finally swallowed their pride and begin exchanging outgrown shoes with other families. They explained daily to their children that all these problems must be endured so *Vati* could be warm in Russia.

Food also became scarce as the war persisted. Even though the Wolff's had money to spend, there was little to buy. Enemy submarines had cut off most of the shipping on which Königsberg depended. All food was rationed. Having ration coupons didn't necessarily mean the markets had anything to sell. Regina would often spend almost the whole day buying a few slivers of *Wurst* or a small chunk of cheese because the lines would be so long.

When Regina had wondered aloud once about the families of their enemies having the same problems, Elli had countered, "Regina, you really are a dreamer. No one else would ever think about such things."

Perhaps Elli was right. To Regina, dreams were sometimes more comforting than reality. But the boys learned to say their prayers and thank God for whatever they did have to eat, and ask that everything else go to feed their *Vati* in Russia. Children in Königsberg no longer complained of their hunger and that, too, had become rather sad.

Whenever Regina watched her children play by the *Teich*, the small lake near their home, as children seem able to play even under the most difficult of circumstances, she prayed to God they would not remember any of the hardships and danger. But she could do nothing about her own fears for them.

Now, here she was on a train that seemed a target, with no shelter, little extra clothing, and no vegetable garden to draw upon. Regina feared there might be more hardship ahead for her children, perhaps even once they found Gustav.

She decided she must stop letting her mind wander so, and forced herself back to the task at hand--entertaining three young boys on a terribly long, cramped train ride that appeared to be getting even longer. She left her thoughts behind and joined the children's game.

The train dallied along with many stops and detours for another day, and it stopped each night for other trains to rumble by, or for prisoner groups to work on damaged track. Passengers felt no closer to Berlin. The restroom piled up in a disgusting manner and one had to hold one's nose to avoid the stench. The children grew restless and cranky. They could not even stretch their legs, or change their clothing, much less play. A few people tried singing to keep up spirits, but it was a weak and listless effort.

Rainer, Regina's curious child, called out to her, "*Mutti*, who are all those people?

On a road joining to parallel the train tracks, just after crossing a small river, were what looked like thousands of people dragging wagons, pushcarts, bicycles, and baby buggies. Each vehicle was piled high with belongings, as though the families were trying to take their whole household with them. Children clung to mothers' skirts and cried. Old people sat atop miserable, rickety wagons. Their voices blended in a collective hum audible even above the train's noise

It seemed impossible so many families could be on the road at once, all moving west, as far ahead as one could see. The people on board the train sat watching this slow procession in stunned silence. A few old cars, equipped for war shortages with wood-burning stoves to produce gas vaporization in the engines, were slowed among thousands of walkers. Pushcarts lost wheels and blocked the road, yet women grabbed what possessions they could carry, abandoned the rest, pushed the offending cart into the ditch, and moved back into this endless stream of ghostly people.

"Those refugees are fleeing to the west," said their knowledgeable seatmate, as they watched this terrible struggle. "The Russians must be moving north and west again. Non-combatants are all trying to get out of the way. They've probably lost their homes already."

"There must be thousands of them. Where will they go?" Regina asked.

"Oh, *Frau* Wolff," he said, "They will keep moving ahead of the fighting until they find shelter where the fighting has stopped. I heard a few days ago that the Russians were advancing north toward Königsberg and west toward Warsaw. Many of these people are Polish as well as German. They don't like us much, but they like the Russians even less."

He seemed so calm about this terrible sight. The children stared in stunned silence. Regina could not bear to talk about it further. She wept for all those poor people, never dreaming her own family would soon be among them.

Chapter 12

That evening, the train stopped in a rural station. No one paid much attention, since the passengers already felt trapped, going endlessly nowhere. They were now merely enduring whatever came with no way to influence their journey. Regina parceled out the remaining snacks to the boys in smaller portions, a bite at a time. She had assumed they could buy extra *Brot* and cheese in the village stations they passed, but no one had been allowed off the train.

Rainer, her heaviest eater, cried, "*Mutti*, my stomach is hungry, really, truly!" His words tore Regina's heart, but she could do nothing except hug him. Willi listlessly leaned against the seat. Franzi pestered him to do finger plays and guessing games and whined when Willi, tired of him, fell asleep on the floor.

Many soldiers sat around the station's platform, looking anxious and exhausted. The stationmaster and trainmen shouted at each other. Suddenly the stationmaster stepped up to the window and screamed, "Everybody out. Get your things and get off now."

"But we purchased tickets to Berlin," said the family's seatmate, startled. Others agreed. "I must get to Berlin for my business," he added, somewhat louder.

"Your business is not my concern," said the gruff stationmaster. "There'll be another train later. We need this one to take soldiers back to the front."

As people muttered and shuffled around in confusion, the stationmaster grew impatient. He wheeled suddenly, whistled, and several uniformed men came forward, pulling those nearest the door to the platform. An old man fell and cried out when his wife was pulled on top of him.

Realizing their protests did not stop the brutal guards, the remaining passengers gathered belongings together, donned knapsacks, and moved into the doorway. When the Wolff's turn came, their kind seatmate jumped off first and handed Regina down to the platform as Rainer passed her Franzi's awkwardly stuffed washtub. Willi and Rainer jumped down and Regina was barely able to catch Franzi before he could jump as well. They hurried toward the station, but found the doors blocked and the ends of the platform guarded. Passengers were confined to the open platform as they watched soldiers crowding into cars they had just left. Officers yelled orders and the train moved slowly backward toward the east.

Regina lost count of the hours they sat on the concrete. A cold rain fell while she sheltered the boys close to her side as best she could. It was hard to understand why they were not allowed inside the building where they could at least stay dry or purchase some food. The stranded passengers were unbelievably hungry. Regina also worried her forged *Ausweis* might be examined again if she had to board a different train. What could she do then?

Later, an engine towing a few dirty cattle cars chugged into the station. The stationmaster shrieked at the people trapped on the platform, "This is your train to Berlin." The passengers were puzzled. No one moved. Surely he could not mean humans were to travel in such a manner.

But with his screaming and the uniformed trainmen again pulling and shoving, the stranded passengers moved toward the cars, shuffling along in spite of their confusion. Guards boosted each woman up through the side openings, loading more and more people until they were jammed tightly together. Women who suddenly realized they were being separated from their men cried, not wanting to speculate what this might mean. The guards handed in a bucket for 'sanitary needs' and three buckets of water to drink. The sanitary bucket was whisked into a dark corner. Then the great sliding doors slammed shut and locks turned from the outside.

The sound produced a startled and momentary silence as the women in Regina's car realized they were trapped. Everyone began crying at once, begging the guards to unlock the doors. "We aren't prisoners!" screamed Regina. "What are you doing to us?"

Rainer asked anxiously, "*Mutti*, what's happening? It stinks in here. I want out?" The children were being crushed up against Regina, and she had no way of moving further back.

Franzi screamed, "*Mutti*, there's no room…no room. We can't stay in here!" He climbed up her side, clutching frantically at her neck and gulping for air, while tears streaked his face.

In the confusion, she had forgotten that Franzi was somewhat claustrophobic and feared closed spaces. Surely being jammed in under all the adult legs was terrifying for the little boy.

She held him tightly in her arms, crooning a lullaby to calm herself as well as the child.

One women screamed, "There may be strafing and we'll have no way out!"

After a hurried discussion outside, the guards unlocked the doors with the admonition they had to remain closed at all times. "You may only look out through the horizontal slats on the side of the cars," the stationmaster threatened. "Severe consequences await anyone trying to get off this train without authorization."

People settled themselves as best they could in the cattle cars, taking turns standing or sitting. There was no space to lie down, but no one wanted to lie down in the filth anyway. Even Franzi gradually became quiet. The train moved slowly out of the station. The lack of privacy was humiliating, even though there were only women and Regina's three children on board.

The boys had shared all but one apple and Rainer and Franzi were terribly hungry. But Willi refused to eat even a bite. He had been silent for some time and seemed dazed. When Regina felt his forehead, he was unspeakably hot, though shivering. It was only a few hours before he had diarrhea as well. The pail was already full, so several of the women helped Regina open the wide door and hang him out over the side of the car. The poor child hid his face in shame, but nothing else could be done. As Regina held him after each spasm and tried to bathe his unresponsive face with her share of water, she saw the look of terror on Rainer's face and realized it reflected her own.

"You remember when Willi was sick before, don't you?" she asked her middle son.

Rainer nodded, with tears running down his cheeks.

Only once before had Regina been this frightened for her eldest child. Shortly before the war began in Poland, in 1938, Hitler had been elated that so many of the previous territories taken away by the Versailles Treaty had voluntarily returned to the *Reich*. With his new *Kraft durch Freude*--strength through joy-- worker's vacation program, and better roads and railroads, more people were encouraged to travel than ever before.

This was particularly helpful to the Wolff family because they were forced to travel from East Prussia through Poland to place little Wilhelm in a *Kinder Klinik* in the Black Forest. Regina and Gustav had held hands tightly as the doctor told them the child had contracted a mysterious lung disease and that this cure in the southern mountains of Germany was Willi's only chance for survival.

Regina could tell her husband was as frightened as she was. As they prepared to leave for the *Kinder Klinik*, Gustav said brusquely, "Forget about all the proper packing, Ina. Let's just go!"

Willi was a very sick little boy, four years old at the time but, even so, both he and Rainer cried, not wanting to be separated. Rainer, only two, surely didn't understand what was happening, but he wailed and clung tightly to his brother. He sensed something was very wrong.

"Must I go, *Mutti*?" Willi had begged again and again.

It was hard to leave him at the *Kur Klinik* alone, but the staff insisted. Regina and Gustav had never been parted from their child before.

Regina cried all the way home on the train, and Gustav held her close and tried to reassure her.

"Willi's a strong child, Ina. He'll be all right." Once again, family matters had become more frightening than the politics invading every facet of their lives.

Gustav was right. Willi had recovered after a few weeks and, thankfully, they were able to bring him home shortly before Hitler mysteriously imposed a travel ban, apparently intended to keep all citizens in their assigned regions—a stupid order, Regina felt, and to what purpose?

Now, it was apparent that Rainer remembered that separation also. She gripped Rainer's hand tightly. "Please watch Franzi for me," she said, trying to divert his attention. She bathed Willi's hot face again. She was praying his natural strength would once again bring him through an illness that seemed severe. "He's never been this quiet," Regina said anxiously to a woman nearby.

The woman claimed to be a doctor. "He has either dysentery or typhus," she pronounced sagely. "He will surely be dead before we reach Berlin, and he'll infect the rest of us."

What did she want his mother to do--throw him off the train? Regina was so angry she wouldn't speak to the woman again. Instead, she held Willi tightly as he slept, wakened in delirium, and slept again, and she prayed. She knew nothing else to do. Rainer hovered over his big brother, but Franzi became oblivious to the scene when he found a young matron who would play his beloved games with him. Regina was grateful to the woman, because she couldn't keep Franzi under adequate control alone with Willi so very ill. She prayed any contagion would not strike her fellow passengers.

The train was forced by blocked and bombed tracks and stations to go forward, only to retreat and try another track. The torture continued, and all were finally forced to the floor with fatigue. Women cried out as the communal stench and the embarrassing effort to contain themselves took its toll. There was simply no way to stay clean or sanitary. Fear caused many to become sick to their stomachs as well.

Then, near a river, the passengers were again ordered off the train. This time they were told the cattle cars were needed to accommodate soldiers going to Berlin. Regina pulled Willi off the side of the boxcar with the help of another woman, and they laid him on the ground with his coat for a pillow. Rainer held tightly to his little brother. Franzi was in tears at yet another confusing change in their circumstances. Willi tried to struggle upright as Regina held him around his shoulders, offering him a drink of brackish water.

"You women can walk," shouted the train's officer, "Our soldiers are needed in Berlin to defend the Fatherland and the *Führer*."

By this time, Regina doubted anyone wanted to hear anything about the *Führer*, but all the women remained strangely resigned. No one voiced any protest. Had the terrorized and exhausted women become so conditioned to quiet obedience as their means of preserving safety that they no longer knew how to speak out?

Instead, the women gathered their boxes, climbed down, and began walking west--or at least what they thought was west.

They were in no danger of becoming lost, however. They were joining the mass of tired, dirty, and miserable refugees they had already seen stumbling down the road parallel to the railroad tracks. The long line meandered slowly toward central Germany.

Chapter 13

Standing in a confused cluster, the women were not sure where they were. Though they had been on trains for what Regina thought was about six days, it turned out they were barely into Poland. All agreed Danzig must be north of their location, and Regina was fairly sure they had passed Marienburg. Did that mean the riverside village ahead was Dirschau or some other? No one knew. Could she still get to Berlin and south to Karlsbad before her thirty day limit and, more importantly, before the Russians caught up with these thousands of refugees?

Regina would have given anything for a bath. The train's filth, Willi's illness, everyone in the same clothing for so many days--all had taken their toll on patience and comfort. She had never before experienced such circumstances, and she couldn't believe the stench of unwashed bodies, her own included. She felt sure Willi needed cleanliness and rest to get well. Even Rainer, who hated a bath under normal circumstances pleaded, "*Mutti*, if you find us a bathtub, I'll even be the last one and use cold water."

"I'll try, son. If you can keep going a little longer, I'll look for a hotel."

Willi was still very weak, but he insisted on trying to walk forward. Regina stopped frequently to let him rest, while hundreds passed them by. They soon trailed far behind the women from the train. At every bridge, Rainer layed aside the contents of Franzi's washtub, went down to the stream, and filled it with water. Then Regina bathed Willi's face, hoping to cool his burning fever. They moved slowly, at the best pace Willi could manage, and Franzi did his best to keep going, holding tightly to Regina's skirt. All through the morning and afternoon, they found themselves falling behind others who had been to their right and left.

Though the family loved recreational walks, walking continuously, under such fearful circumstances, and caring for a sick child at the same time, was overwhelming. Regina knew she dared not show her own fatigue, or the children would give up.

"Carry me, *Mutti*," was Franzi's constant plea. Regina finally realized she would have to do so, and tore off her petticoat to fashion a sling over her hip and shoulder. The exhausted little boy dozed off, becoming dead weight. She was already carrying the coats strapped to her opposite shoulder plus her own knapsack and Willi's. Rainer helped Willi along, and also struggled with the washtub and its contents. How long could they keep this up?

Even with a war going on, the flat countryside spread peacefully across their path during mid August. Such beauty was hard to reconcile with their desperate circumstances. The refugees spoke little, probably because of their fatigue, but they were not unfriendly. Most said they had come from Poland or East Prussia, south of Königsberg.

The column shifted and twisted, an anxious monster writhing along, as some people stopped along the road to rest, while others took their place. Most did not know their destination. It was simply west--anywhere away from the fighting, though many hoped to reach Dresden.

"Being caught between two armies is the worst thing that can happen," said one young girl of about fourteen as she trudged along beside Regina's family for a way. "My grandfather was killed, my mother was shot in the arm, and we can't find my little brother or my pet chicken. I think my brother must be in this line somewhere and my job is to keep looking for him. I imagine someone has by now eaten my chicken."

The child spoke in a matter-of-fact tone with little energy left for emotion. The effect was surreal, as though the people, their losses, and their fatigue were only foreground figures splashed against an artificial stage backdrop. Each person seemed to be playing a role rather than allowing any feeling of real grief. Regina hugged Franzi more tightly, thinking of the lost child.

However, she soon adopted much the same acceptance of the inevitable, though it was still hard to imagine her family trapped in this helpless trail of fearful and exhausted people. Nothing felt real to Regina except guiding her boys forward, one step after another. They were dirty and tired, but she realized they were also at another disadvantage. They had no supplies for camping outdoors or finding and cooking food. The other people had brought supplies for such a journey. Regina recognized the plight of the other refugees had been a longer one, since her family had more recently left a home providing shelter. But it didn't take long in a war for even the luckiest person to accept the inevitability of becoming a homeless refugee.

Finally a small town loomed ahead. Regina remembered her promise to Rainer from the morning and looked for a hotel. It was crucial that Willi have rest. He was faltering so badly Rainer could barely keep him steady. She and Rainer placed Willi between them where they could each help keep him upright. It was not a satisfactory arrangement. Regina was too tired to carry Franzi much further, and her feet, unused to long distance walking in street shoes, were already blistered. The first hotel was shuttered and empty, but she kept watching for a *Zimmer frei* sign, anyplace with a room to rent. Toward the end of the nearly deserted town, Rainer noticed a nondescript old hotel with someone moving around inside. They entered to inquire for a room.

"We're already packed and ready to leave," said the matron briskly, as she bustled around without even looking at Regina or the boys. "We have no time for all you gypsies."

"Please," Regina said, "my boys are very tired and dirty, and they need some rest. We can pay you in advance."

The woman's demeanor changed abruptly. "Oh, in that case, we might wait one more day and let you stay. Cash only, though. And don't expect any hot water. The heat and electricity have been gone for weeks."

"Cold water will do. And we can manage with a candle." Regina struggled to dig into her knapsack for some money while juggling Franzi, who still slept on her shoulder. She could not manage, so Rainer helped his little brother down, as Willi slumped to the floor. Franzi began to wail from waking up so suddenly.

"And don't you let those children cry all night either!"

Regina silently handed over almost twice the money she had been asked and suddenly, the woman was full of smiles and courtesy. She took Regina's knapsack and led the family up rickety stairs to a small room with an old double bed, a couch, and a sink.

"The toilet is down the hall. I'll have my husband bring you up a tin tub and I can boil you one pot of water to add to the cold before I put out the fire."

"Thank you so very much. Might there be anything we could buy to eat?"

"Not tonight, but I'll find something for a small breakfast."

Looking at the tired children, Regina realized they would be asleep before anyone could fix them a meal anyway.

"Breakfast will be fine," she told the woman.

Regina bathed Franzi first and put him into the sagging bed in his pajamas. The other boys bathed in turn and climbed in next to the sleeping child. Within minutes, all were breathing evenly.

Regina bathed as well, luxuriating even in cold water, washing her matted hair at the sink and soaking her blistered feet in Franzi's washtub. She put all their filthy clothes in one pile, washed everything by hand, wrung them out tightly, and hung them to dry around the room and over the windowsill. She covered the children as they slept, and fell quickly asleep on the couch. She could not have stayed awake a moment longer.

In the morning, the boys seemed refreshed. Regina gathered up the almost dry clothes she had washed, and everyone put them back on. Damp was, after all, better than dirty.

"Everyone sure smells better," Rainer ventured with a mischievous grin.

Even Willi was able to hold down the 'small breakfast' the woman promised. The ersatz coffee, a basket of dry Brötchen, and a tiny slice of cheese each was more than they had eaten for days, so they were ravenous. Each child stuck an extra Brötchen in his pocket for the day's journey. Regina knew the bread might have to last awhile with towns deserted, stores empty, and so many people on the road. She vowed to wash everything and everyone at each riverside opportunity, since she held out little hope of finding another hotel or restaurant open.

The proprietress and her husband had already packed their old auto with dishes, towels, and feather beds, so Regina knew she couldn't ask to stay another night. At those prices, she couldn't afford it anyway. Besides, who could know just how fast the Russians would overtake the refugee column, or how many more delays she might have in getting to Gustav? The train trip to Czechoslovakia that was supposed to be only four days had already eaten up more time than she could have imagined, and they were scarcely a quarter of the way to their destination.

Regina had been afraid of being left behind by the refugee column, but she needn't have worried. The number of people had not diminished during the night, since the line seemed endless. As the little family stepped into the moving stream, Regina tried to keep from thinking of her own situation by watching the others. How had these exhausted people managed to pull or push their belongings over rutted roads for days or weeks? She noticed the belongings they had saved appeared to be from blazing houses, most importantly, the down comforters used in every European home. These were often scorched, but they topped each wagon pile proudly-- symbol of a cozy room. Perhaps a chair, a cooking pot, or a small cage with a pair of geese was wedged into a wagon or buggy as family members tried to salvage remnants of shattered lives.

How different this was from the luxury Regina had known with her parent's and in her own home. Now she had difficulty believing she had once assumed Hitler was the great leader who would bring Germany to its rightful place in the world. There was nothing like half-herding, half-carrying exhausted children on sore feet to make her disillusionment and anger grow. She stumbled onward, challenging the boys to think of this trek as a parade.

She remembered another parade, in 1936. Hitler had come to Königsberg, and he seemed a hero at that time. He had stood up to those who had destroyed their economy. He had stated that since the Versailles Treaty was unfair and destructive to Germany, he would ignore its precepts.

The parade passed Regina's parent's apartment, and the Wolff family gathered there to watch. A sea of red and black flags floated by, hundreds of them, and people were screaming his name, "Heil Hitler, Heil Hitler," as he saluted from his open car. Regina held up two-year-old Willi on the balcony and proudly pointed out 'Our Führer.' They were witnessing history, and Regina's father taught Willi how to salute by raising his right arm.

Everyone laughed at the little boy shooting up his arm repeatedly and grinning proudly.

Her father had said, "Now, we're moving ahead."

Gustav nodded enthusiastically. It seemed the two men agreed on nearly everything by then.

Later, by early 1938, nanny Elli clapped her hands with joy whenever she saw photos of Hitler and she would say, "He's a man of the people and he understands those who must work."

His generous vacation travel policies for workers seemed to prove her correct. Now, however, Regina believed the policies were only an attempt to appeal to a wider group of supporters. In the name of jobs and security workers gave up freedoms of joining unions, bargaining for wages, and working reasonable hours. They were locked into their jobs. Much freedom had slipped away while the citizens cheered in ignorance.

One day, Regina's neighbor, who lived in the next row house, came running in excitedly."Turn on the radio, quickly. Listen to the *Führer's* speech," Annemarie shouted. The speech was all about the Austrian *Anschluss*. "The Austrians must be so happy to have joined Germany now," she said excitedly. "Listen to all the people cheering. Now Germans can have pride again."

Gustav's older brother, Paul, who was a lawyer, and later a judge, had joined the *Schützstaffe* or *SS*. Elli tried to suppress her excitement when she saw Paul in his uniform. "He looks so handsome. I wish he weren't married."

Regina thought Elli must have had a crush on Paul. She had to admit that he did look especially dashing. His uniform was much different from Gustav's. It was black, instead of field gray, and it had unusual heads on the collar.

Regina had asked her husband what it meant to be *SS*, and he explained. "The *SS* has special secret duties and they work directly under our *Führer* and Himmler. Paul will do well. My brother Walter has joined the *SS* as well." Gustav never mentioned the subject again and, it seemed, Regina was not to mention it either. Whatever secret duties Paul and Walter had, she had not learned until much later.

When the Sudeten Germans living at the edges of

Czechoslovakia demanded reunification with the *Reich*, even the British Prime Minister, Mr. Chamberlain, said there would be "Peace in our time." Was that not what everyone wanted? Germans rejoiced. Economics drove popular opinion, and economics were so much better than they had been only a few years before.

However, when the port city of Memel, as well as Bohemia and Moravia and the remainder of Czechoslovakia were also annexed, and this time *not* by their own choice, Regina began to wonder why Germany needed so much *Lebensraum*--or living space, as Hitler demanded.

In radio speeches, Hitler had emphasized this need again and again. Regina thought perhaps the country's leader knew something everyone else didn't know. Always idealistic, she had assumed everyone, even the *Führer*, at least tried to do the right thing. She also believed she hadn't the experience to understand politics as did, apparently, her husband and her father. She never thought to voice what she believed were her own naïve and unimportant opinions. Now, years later, she wondered if that silence had been wise. But, in her country, and in her family, outspoken women were frowned upon, and Regina had accepted that evaluation of a woman's place since childhood.

Regina and Elli had loved the cinema, especially the beautiful film on the joy of Olympian sport done by Leni Riefenstahl. It celebrated the German men and women Hitler described as 'new Aryans,' looking healthy and happy. Germans did, indeed, seem healthier and happier during the thirties, and even the public statues reflected that image, showing sturdy families working together, side by side. Most people seemed to like the image of sturdy families, and there seemed no reason to worry about it at the time.

By Hitler's orders, many young people had been sent to the countryside, especially in the newly annexed territories. They were to grow more food and live in a healthy farm environment, to spin and weave clothing by old-fashioned handwork, and to learn useful trades. Elli's younger sister was among them. Elli didn't have to go because she was already working in the Wolff home. She had commented wryly, "My sister is probably having fun and enjoying all the young men in her work group in Bavaria. But perhaps she is learning a trade as well." She seemed to concede this reluctantly.

Citizens adjusted to new circumstances thinking each change would be the last one necessary. Then, only a few months later, German troops invaded Poland, and nothing was ever the same again.

The Polish incident, as it was called, in September of 1939, occurred so quickly that Regina's friends didn't know what was happening until it was over. They saw soldiers rushed to the Polish border through East Prussia in all types of trucks commandeered from bakers and butchers. Regina was afraid because the *Führer* said there had been border incidents in which Poles had attacked Germans. Of course, everyone believed this, and the whole family gathered around the radio searching for news.

They couldn't understand why England and France took Poland's side and declared war against Germany. Both Hitler and Goebbels, the *Nazi* Propaganda Minister, announced in their loud speeches, which Regina didn't find so exciting anymore, "The Danzig Corridor must be in German hands where it belonged before the Versailles Treaty took it away. We cannot allow East Prussia to be isolated any longer from the rest of our homeland."

While this idea seemed logical and comforting to citizens of Königsberg, since they were the ones isolated, it also seemed strange when Gustav told the family that Polish troops were fighting with only horses and lances while German soldiers had tanks and planes. Surely the Poles would not have attacked Germans with such limited means. Regina thought something had seemed wrong about the radio's explanations. *Blitzkrieg* they called it--lightning war. Most people seemed excited by the quick victory, waving little flags in the streets.

Regina had pleaded a headache and stayed home to avoid all the flag-waving and boisterous approval. She secretly thought neighboring countries should work out their problems peacefully. But she also assumed her own ideas might be faulty, since the men in her family didn't share her concerns.

Delighted by the victory over Poland, Regina's father declared, "This will show we are again a great power and we cannot be intimidated. A show of force will clear away all remaining vestiges of colonialism by other powerful nations." Every statement he made had become a speech, but Gustav seemed to agree with him.

Regina thought surely Gustav was only trying to please her father. At that time, she could only wonder what the use of force might mean for her family and her dreams for their future.

Now she knew.

Cutting short her reverie as her blistered feet gathered more of her attention, Regina wondered where Hitler was now that half the people of Europe were trudging across the countryside to escape his enemies? She heartily wished he would march in this line and see the misery and hunger on refugee faces. Would it make a difference to him? There was a time when she had believed so. But now, in 1944, she felt sure he wouldn't care.

Her musings helped to keep her mind off Franzi's weight and their slow progress in the long line of refugees. The boys were no longer talking along the way. They only trudged onward, shuffling their bare feet in the dust after shedding shoes that blistered. Willi made no complaint, but Regina realized that while she had been absorbed in her own thoughts, he was getting far too tired. She knew he was still weak from illness. She pulled the boys down to rest at a quiet stream. Because of their exertion, the meadow seemed quite hot. They were all breathless.

They gathered in the shade under a small wooden bridge. Hordes of people clumped over it above their heads. Willi's fever had diminished somewhat, and he seemed a bit stronger. Regina let him rest a little longer, lulled by incessantly buzzing insects that seemed to accompany the refugees. Rainer was bathing Franzi's sweaty face and hands, when suddenly thundering roars and terrified shouts filled the air.

"Rainer!" Regina screamed. "Bring Franzi under the bridge with us, now!" For once, the startled child obeyed immediately.

"What's that noise, *Mutti*?" he cried, holding his hands over his ears.

At first, she couldn't tell what it was either. Then she heard the rattling sounds on the wooden bridge above, and she realized that planes were plunging out of the skies and machine-gunning the refugee column. Regina pulled the boys under her body as people jammed in next to them, huddling together in the noise, confusion, and fear. The planes came back again and again. One could see bright red stars on their wings.

"Ruskies," said an old man beside her, almost with resignation. "We've been strafed so many times in the last few days, I've lost count."

Rainer's eyes grew large. "Did anyone get killed?"

"Many," said the old man. "But perhaps that isn't the worst, since those unable to walk have been left behind."

Seeing the panic in the children's eyes, Regina huddled even closer over her boys and swore to them all, "No matter what happens, we are leaving no one behind, ever."

Lying beside her, Willi said, "I know, *Mutti*, 'cause you could have left me behind when I got sick, but you didn't. We're going to get to *Vati* somehow. Don't you worry."

He looked at her with those Gustav-like eyes, so serious and so grown up. Regina wanted to cry because he was only nine years old, and weak from illness, yet he was trying to reassure her. He was so much like his father.

When the planes seemed to have gone away, people disentangled themselves from the huddle, moving the dead and wounded. One by one, they pulled themselves back up to the road to evaluate the condition of their families.

The scene was a horrible rendition of Hell. The smell of burning flesh sizzled in Regina's nostrils. The air was still hazy from gunfire. Blood and dangling limbs, screams and muffled sobs demonstrated the futile attempt some had made to find shelter.

Regina had never seen such carnage. It was so immediate and personal. Her instinct was to send the boys back under the bridge so they wouldn't see the dead bodies, but she knew it was of no use. They were already gasping in shock. She realized with a mother's sadness that they would see more horror before this trip was over, and she would be helpless to stop it.

Franzi was sobbing and feeling the skin of his face, "Am I bleeding too?"

Willi knelt to hug his little brother and reassure him he was not. Perhaps he was also reassuring himself.

Newer refugees buried the dead and helped the wounded onto wagons, so the Wolffs' joined in silently. It took some time for the column to start moving again. Longer-term refugees were simply too weak and discouraged to do more than pick up the burdens from the dead, add them to their own, and carry on.

Regina could think of nothing comforting to say.

"May we pray for them, *Mutti*, even if we don't know them?" Willi asked softly.

"Of course. I think they'd like that."

The little family knelt in the road offering a quiet prayer as others walked doggedly on around them. All were silent. Some crossed themselves as they passed by.

The two younger boys were, she thought, too numb to fully comprehend what had happened. But Willi had apparently decided his duty was to help Regina get the younger boys to *Vati*. Wiping away the tears on his face, he suddenly warned Rainer and Franzi, shaking his finger, "You mustn't ever again be further than two meters away from Mutti and I!"

That seemed like a good rule, so Regina only nodded when the other two boys searched her face for some sign of disagreement. From that time on, Willi joined her at being in charge, and the two younger boys followed along as best they could, without argument.

One blessing, Regina realized, was that Willi now seemed much better, though he still was tired and frequently stumbled. However, he was determined to carry his own coat and knapsack again. The second blessing was that Franzi's washtub hadn't been a total waste. They redistributed its contents among their knapsacks and allowed Franzi to carry it by himself.

Two things were not blessings--the unmistakable fact that the countryside couldn't bear the hunger of so many people moving across it at the same time, and the certainty that the planes would be coming back.

Chapter 14

This region had changed political boundaries many times over the centuries, its flat, open vistas apparently conducive to battle. Most recently, it had been given to Poland after the Great War's Versailles Treaty, and taken back again by Hitler's Army. Many of its farmers spoke the German language or shared German heritage. Even the Poles living there were not without pity for the hungry wanderers at their doors. But all were angry that this retreat of German troops was bringing their farms and villages under the guns of an enemy. Caught in the middle yet again, they were no friends to Russia either. Truthfully, they didn't have enough food to help the thousands of refugees trekking endlessly across their countryside and gleaning their fields like a locust invasion.

The family's first night outside was an ordeal. Though Regina had been considered a gourmet cook at home, she had never cooked in the open, nor did she have utensils or staple foods to do so. She and the children searched for roots, wild mushrooms, turnips or beets, and ate them raw. But they watched more experienced refugees comb the fields all day, depositing their gleanings in their pockets. At night, with a tiny fire under a tin can, they cooked everything together with water from the streams.

"We can do that too," announced Willi.

After finding a can left by the road, Regina was ready to try this method. She still had her matches, and she tried boiling two stale turnips Willi had found. They were partially cooked, but edible. While the ground was hard and unforgiving to their bodies, such an open air bed smelled much better than the cattle train.

When they said their prayers that night, Willi added, "Thank you, God, that we're learning to manage, and that we're together."

Regina's "Amen" was barely audible through her anxiety.

The next Russian strafing came just after dawn. The planes roared out of nowhere, leaving no time for rational action. Regina and Willi merely shoved Rainer and Franzi into the nearest ditch and dove in on top of them. It was little enough protection, as they could feel thuds of bullets vibrate in the bank above their heads and were showered by dirt from the impact. When Regina dared to look up, the planes were so low she could actually see the face of one pilot staring down at the people. Surely he knew he was firing on helpless refugees. Regina's anger crowded out her fear.

She wondered if Russian harassment of refugee columns was planned to slow evacuation of German troops as well as to kill Polish and German populations. The constant diving into ditches certainly slowed the passage of this ragged file of people. The sporadic German troop convoys driving west down the road slowed as well.

As delays mounted, however, the soldiers screamed and cursed, pushing carts and people off the road with their trucks in their headlong rush to the west. These soldiers were their own countrymen. Could they expect any better if the Russians caught up with the refugee column? It occurred to Regina that if the German troops were in such a hurry, perhaps the Russians were closer behind than she had thought.

The next days were a blur of fear, hunger, exhaustion, and sleeplessness. The refugee column continued across open, flat country, roughly toward Bilton and Könitz. Fearful she would arrive in Karlsbad too late to see Gustav, Regina purchased train tickets at a small town, but the slow work train available only carried them to a village just inside old German borders. They gained two days, and some of the swelling and blistering of their feet improved.

But people in the endless refugee column they again joined were still subject to strafing. Regina decided it might be safer to strike out on her own. She led the children away from the crowded road, across the damp grass, and up a hill toward the forest.

"Where are we going, *Mutti*?" asked Franzi.

Rainer worried, "Won't we get lost if we leave the others?"

"No, we won't. We'll find a network of *Fusswege*, or paths, up there. Every German village owns a forest and has a *Förstjaeger* to protect the wild game and a *Förster* to protect the paths and trees. You know, like the forest paths we had at home."

"They have them here, too?" asked Rainer.

"Well, we're back in Germany, aren't we? These footpaths

are pretty well organized, and they go just about everywhere."

"Who made them for us, *Mutti*?" asked Franzi, trying clumsily to skip on both feet.

"Long ago serfs, I suppose. The paths have been here since feudal times. They may not be as well maintained since the war began, but at least the forest hides them from the air. We might even be able to find some wild mushrooms or berries in the forest, since there won't be so many people looking for food at the same time. I think this will be easier for us."

The boys didn't argue.

They waded in the grass until they found a path heading west. The family had always enjoyed long walks and Franzi had been pumping his short legs fairly well during the last two days. But now he became very tired trying to keep up, since they could travel faster on the less crowded path. Regina was again forced to carry him in the sling for an occasional rest. They moved ahead at the best pace they could manage.

"We aren't going to sleep alone here in the forest, are we?" Franzi asked as nighttime approached.

"You're not alone, Franzi," said Willi. "We're all here together. You and Rainer can sleep in the middle. *Mutti* and I will sleep on the outside."

Regina noted silently how Willi was taking charge at times, and smiled.

"I kind of like being alone better than with so many jillions of people, and I haven't seen a plane since we came up here," said Rainer. This was a new experience for them all, but Regina hoped they could adapt.

"Here, boys, let me cover you with our coats."

Just as Regina settled down, Rainer asked one more of his endless questions. "*Mutti*, there must be wolves or wild boars in this forest. Why can't we see them?"

Regina had always been convinced exhausted parents of seven-year-olds had invented the world's mythology. She imagined some ancient Greek parent making up wildly fantastic stories to answer unknown and unanswerable questions. The unending "Why?" She could not resist her own amusement when

Rainer continually confirmed her theory.

But for this question, she hated to admit she wasn't sure, nor could she think of a suitable story. Rainer had apparently read too many fairy tales about forest animals.

"I don't think so, Rainer," she finally answered, trying to sound convincing. Though Regina couldn't sleep now that she was listening for the rustling and grunting sounds of boars in the bushes, the boys were asleep when their heads touched the ground.

In the next few days, Willi and Rainer became experts at finding nuts, berries, and mushrooms, and Regina became fairly good at chopping them up with her pocketknife and cooking the roots and mushrooms in their can. She was glad her father had shared his interest in botany because Franzi, in his enthusiasm to help, gathered everything he saw in the forest. Regina needed to sort through it all to avoid poisonous contributions.

She also took advantage of at least one stream daily to wash out clothes and keep their bodies clean, feeling this was necessary for wellness, civility, and morale.

They came across a *Förster's* cottage a few evenings later, and the old couple living there invited the family in for a meal. It was not much different from what Regina and the boys had been eating, but the old man had shot a squirrel, and the woman had spices in her house, so they had meat for the first time since the bit of salami on the train their first day out of Königsberg. And the bed they made in the hay of the couple's barn felt warm and luxurious after sleeping in ditches and on muddy ground.

"Would you like to listen to the radio with us?" the old man asked. Regina hadn't heard any news since leaving home so, eagerly, after putting the boys to bed, she joined the couple seated by their radio. The news was not good.

"A disastrous bombing of Königsberg the week of August 24, 1944, caused a firestorm, and has killed more people than all previous bombings," said the announcer. Could it be true? What, exactly, was a firestorm? Regina could only imagine what it might mean, and she was frightened.

She wondered about her parents, Elli and her aunt, Magda, about their home on the outskirts of town, their business down by the harbor, and *Herr* Busch. Regina even thought about her old friends, the bears at the zoo, along with everyone else, quickly shaking her head at the strange thoughts that came with news like this. She suddenly felt guilty for being only hungry, scared of strafing, wary for her children's safety, and lonely for her husband. Things could be much worse.

Regina struggled to imagine a firestorm from what she already knew of other air raids.

She remembered one night of bombing that had brought a tremendous explosion near their *Keller*. Plaster and wood had rained down into the basement, terrorizing them all. Since the air raid sirens blared, Regina and Elli had been knitting in the dark, but now they could only clutch the boys frantically.

"How close was it?" Elli had shouted, through the noise.

"Close. It must be our house or Annemarie's. I smell smoke, but we should wait until we can determine the degree of danger from more bombs outside." They concentrated on calming Franzi who, by this time was wailing as loudly as the all-clear siren.

They emerged to see Annemarie's row house burning. Knowing her neighbor was alone with her daughter while her husband was gone in the Army, Regina ran next door to help while Elli held the boys close to their own house.

She could hear the two screaming inside, but the *Keller* door wouldn't budge. "I'm coming, I'm coming," Regina shouted, hoping they would hear her and not lose hope. She dug with her bare hands to pull away the debris, finally uncovering the door and jerking it open.

"Thank God," Annemarie cried as she pushed Christina out into the night and staggered out herself. Both collapsed on the ground, gasping for breath. Regina could see the inside roof of their bunker dropping flaming brands where they had been hiding and she suddenly felt weak thinking of what actually happened during a fiery bomb hit. She really had not dared imagine it before. Her hands were hot and shaking as she helped them up.

Both were smudged and frightened, but apparently unhurt except for cuts and bruises. They and Regina hugged each other and wept. With firemen busy downtown, the house was completely burned by the time neighbors could draw water in buckets from their wells or nearby water troughs meant for fighting fires. Annemarie and Christina spent the rest of the night with the Wolff's. Then they moved in with Annemarie's cousins across town the next day. Regina never saw them again.

After that raid, Regina had found two upstairs windows blown out by the blast. She tried to board them up with pieces of wood from the basement and Gustav's old hammer.

"You're supposed to hit the nails, not your fingers," said Elli as she and Willi held the wood in place and Regina hammered. All three boys made fun of their Mutti's bent over nail heads that refused to go in straight.

Soon Elli and Regina were hysterically giggling as they examined the crooked mess they'd made. But the wind would not blow in, and they had accomplished this all by themselves. Attempting to leave the room proudly, they got only to the door before one panel fell to the floor, and the two women started laughing all over again. Willi simply muttered something unintelligible and walked out, which started more laughter. The panel went up better the second time. They were still quite giddy with relief that no one in their neighborhood had been hurt in the bombardment.

Now Regina was far from her home and trying to imagine what kind of fire might be hundreds of times worse. The news broadcaster said the whole inner city had been engulfed in flame.

Could Elli manage alone? And were their mangled efforts at carpentry their last good laugh together?

"Where's your home," asked the old woman gently, as she noticed Regina's tears?

"There," she answered, pointing to the radio.

The woman patted Regina's hand, and her kindness was more than the young mother could stand at that moment. Barely holding back sobs, she thanked the thoughtful couple for the meal and the news. Then she ran out to the barn to be with her children. She could not tell them about Königsberg.

Chapter 15

As dawn cast shadows between the forest leaves, Willi helped Regina chop and stack firewood in appreciation for this old couple's kindness. They, in return, entertained Franzi and Rainer with Grimm's fairy tales. The children were delighted to hear their old favorites from a real woodcutter. Regina worked silently, thinking only of her home and family in Königsberg.

"Would you like a map?" interrupted their host. "Do you know where you are, or where you're going?"

"Berlin, and then Karlsbad," Regina answered. "A map would be wonderful. We've been staying in the hills and looking down to the road occasionally to see where others were going. It's hard to determine the route exactly, but I think we're going generally in the right direction."

"You were wise to travel on the footpaths this far, but you're getting closer to Berlin, and it'll be more difficult once you're in the city. Our daughter lives in Berlin and comes out to visit when she can get away from her factory. They're being bombed nightly, you know, and sometimes by day as well. The only way to travel through town safely is by subway from the east station. You might get there by afternoon if you can find a ride on a wagon carrying food into the city." The old forester scratched his head thoughtfully. Then a smile lit his wrinkled face. "I know someone in the village who might be going today."

Regina was so thankful she could scarcely speak.

The grandmotherly old woman gave each of the boys a precious dried plum, which they gobbled up right away, smiling their thanks. The man put on his heavy boots, his forestry cap, shouldered his gun, and the family followed him across the empty fields into the village with Franzi goose-stepping stiffly, in his own impersonation of a soldier.

The boys were delighted when they saw the wagon-like truck with a wood-fired boiler operating the motor. They immediately christened it the 'toy truck.' The trucker didn't want passengers, but when Regina offered to pay, he relented, and hoisted the boys up between his boxes of turnips, leeks, and moldy-looking kohlrabi.

The truck rumbled its way down the hill, swerving around bomb craters and straggling refugees in the road. They soon saw the plain outside Berlin with its two sturdy hills just to the northeast of town, heavily guarded by German tanks. Regina was troubled to see that so many buildings of the central skyline appeared badly damaged. Some were not standing at all.

Did Königsberg look as bad as Berlin? She wondered what she would find when she returned home. *Put it aside now. Concentrate only on the next step.* She had to be tough on herself to keep going forward. The children and Gustav were depending on her.

True to his word, the trucker stopped at a greengrocer's near the east station. Regina couldn't immediately tell it was a shop until she entered because the windows were broken, and it had only a single floor left at the bottom. Upper stories had been burned away or crushed into rubble on the street in front, but huge telephone poles braced against the sides held the façade in place. Business carried on as usual, with available food displayed on packing crates.

The *Hausfrauen* rushed in, searching the skies to the north and west as though expecting another raid. They needed to find food beforehand. Lines were long, with women already waiting for this meager delivery from the country village. Regina watched them, and tried to remember the luxury of shopping for plentiful groceries and going home to prepare them in a true kitchen. Before the war's rationing and homelessness, she had enjoyed shopping daily. At least she no longer cried to think of it now. There was no time for that kind of indulgence.

Time was more precious now than place. Regina had to find Gustav before the thirty days were gone. Otherwise, she wouldn't know where he'd be sent next time, and he wouldn't know where to find her. They could no longer turn back. The only choice was to go forward.

After paying the man in the 'toy truck' from the money she carried in her hem, and purchasing a few dried-up carrots from the greengrocer as soon as her turn came in line, Regina hurried into the nearby station and bought subway tickets.

She was surprised to find, despite heavy bombings, that the underground areas of Berlin were relatively intact, and the spirit of its citizens, who spent most of their nights in shelters, was not as demoralized as she had thought it would be. The underground *S-Bahns* were still running under the rubble of the streets above. And people were still going off to whatever work they had to do, once they crawled out of their bunkers each morning. Subway posters advertising musical or theatrical evenings were scattered among the pictures of a wild-eyed Hitler admonishing everyone to defend the Fatherland to the death. Few bothered to look. It was a great city under aerial siege, with little to see above ground. But work and courage among its people still existed.

Traveling across the besieged city, they twice had to get off the subway cars where bombs had scored a direct hit, go upstairs to the outside, cross to another line, and then descend again. But it was still a quick trip compared to all they had endured thus far. At least, their feet got a much-needed rest. Regina's shoes were disgracefully torn and dirty, and she tried to hide them under the seat in shame. She noticed that Willi was wearing some battered shoes she had not seen before. Perhaps he had gathered them from the rubble. *The child was becoming far too resourceful.* Regina didn't ask him about the shoes. She ripped up what was left of her underskirt to wrap strips around the younger boys' torn footwear to hold them together a bit longer.

During one detour, near Charlottenberg station and the *Tiergarten*, they saw that vegetable gardens had replaced the trees and flowers. Survivors were tending every millimeter of ground in central Berlin in their desperate effort to feed themselves.

Regina became uncomfortably aware that people were constantly staring at her children as they laughed and chattered with each other. One woman even came up to tousle Rainer's hair.

"My son is about your age," she said. "Please tell me your name."

Rainer was embarrassed, but he managed to mumble it out as politely as he could.

"When did you lose your front teeth, Rainer?" the woman continued. "My Ernst should have lost his front teeth by now, too. And are these your brothers?"

Willi spoke up to give his name and Franzi's, while Franzi huddled in his mother's lap.

The woman turned to Regina. "You can't know how wonderful it is to see children in Berlin."

"It does seem rather quiet here. I've been trying to think what was missing."

"We've almost no children left in the city. Most have been evacuated to Bavaria. I know it's safer this way, but I can still see my Ernst's face pressed to the train window as they took him away. He was sobbing so. It broke my heart."

"I'm so sorry," said Regina. "It must be dreadfully hard on everyone."

We Berliners miss our children, and I'm sure you've noticed how we all stare at yours. But we must work in the factories, and we can't leave the city. At least our children are safe."

"How did so many children get out of the city? Did each family take them to relatives elsewhere?"

"No," said the woman. "The government provided escort nannies when bombings of the capital became more severe. The children are placed at farms and homes out in the country."

Regina hugged her own littlest one more tightly as he nestled in her lap. "It must have been a traumatic experience for the children to be taken in by strangers. How will they all find their parents after the war?"

"The orders claimed there would be a system," the woman answered. "But I admit, we all worry about it. We fear our children will be lost and will never know how to find us again."

Regina could not even imagine the government taking her boys away from her, yet she understood that these people worked in essential industries. Hitler would not allow them to leave their jobs, so what else could they do except try to send their children to safety?

Regina gathered the boys to change subway trains, but she made sure all three told the lonely woman goodbye and shook hands with proper formality.

"I pray your child will be safe," Regina whispered to the woman. Then she helped the boys to the platform. The woman was still waving as Regina led them away.

Many buildings were still smoldering from last-night's bombing, and Regina wanted to get out of town before nightfall. She hurried the boys through the intense foot traffic to the next stop and charged onto the *S-bahn* toward Potsdam where she hoped they could catch a train southward.

They were not yet to Potsdam when the *Bahn* stopped for track damage. It was growing dark, so they got off and walked, hoping to find a more open place to sleep for the night.

They were on the outskirts of town, near a *Gardenplatz*--an area of small gardens owned or leased by city apartment dwellers where they could have a yard of their own. During peacetime, each little garden was required to have one-third grass, one-third fruit or vegetables, and one-third trees, so that each was a productive paradise for the family as well as a lovely view for those passing by.

But this was wartime, and the grassy areas were planted with vegetables. Each plot had a garden house where families normally came on weekends to work in the garden, fixing simple picnic lunches and storing garden implements in the tiny cottage. No one actually lived in them. But these seemed far enough from the city that only an occasional stray bomb fell, and Regina noticed many of the garden houses were now occupied.

As she and the boys walked by, trying to ignore the rumblings of their stomachs, a gray--haired woman noticed Rainer slowing by her gate as she pulled a few dried-up onions and leeks from the ground. She motioned him to come near and asked, "What are you running away from, boy?"

Rainer apparently didn't understand the question or was frightened, as he did not answer. But as Regina moved backward to take his hand and lead him away, the woman asked her, "Are your boys hungry? I have some soup cooking, and I'd love some company." Regina couldn't deny this straightforward question, and the woman invited them into her little garden hut.

Regina offered the remnants of the carrots she had purchased earlier, and the woman graciously added them to the pot. Regina wondered why she had been raised to think of soup as only a first course. Now, after years of shortages and hunger, soup seemed a feast all by itself. She could tell that the boys, especially Rainer, were only barely restraining their impatience. She kept silent when she noticed Willi hold Franzi's arm to keep him from sitting down at the table before an invitation. She was proud of how they were trying to wait politely as the wondrous aroma filled the tiny hut.

When the soup was finished, the lady brought out a few pieces of chipped china. "I saved these from my apartment in Berlin," she said. "They were a wedding gift from my mother."

"The whole block of apartments was burning," she said quietly, as though speaking to herself. "Some of the ceilings crashed in and I barely made it down to the *Keller* before another bomb hit. My old husband was out fighting fires, but he never came home that night." She folded her hands and touched her forehead to them, as though pushing away a bad thought.

Before Regina could comment, the woman's monotone continued.

"When the bombing was over, I climbed back up toward my third floor home and part of the stairway was just hanging there, waiting to fall. I wanted to save something from my family, something from my marriage, so I crawled up the hanging part to my apartment. Most everything had fallen through the living room floor, but I found these few pieces from my wedding china and wrapped them in a towel and brought them back down the hanging stairway."

Her mood changed suddenly, and her piercing blue eyes danced.

"And now, I can serve you, as my guests, on my fine china." She was smiling as graciously as if there were a banquet in a great hall with crystal and silver.

Regina was thankful the boys seemed to recognize this as a momentous occasion with a wonderful hostess and used their best manners without her needing to remind them. Rainer even helped Franzi when he spilled a little soup on his shirt.

Regina wanted to know about the fate of the woman's husband and about her life since losing her home, but she didn't need to ask. The woman continued without questions, almost, it seemed, through some lonely compulsion to speak.

"The authorities wanted me to move to a vacated Jewish apartment in the city, but I wouldn't do that for two reasons. First, I didn't like what I'd heard about Jews being forced to give up their homes, even their furniture, and about their being sent east to work in factories. They told me the vacant apartment had been the home of a teacher. Imagine, a teacher being sent to work in a munitions factory in Poland. How stupid of Hitler to send away so many Jewish Germans to the east and then cry about not having enough workers, and even importing foreign slaves to work for him in the local factories!"

Willi and Rainer both looked up at their mother with eyes popped wide open in alarm. Did they already understand the danger of telling one's feelings to others?

Though Regina agreed with everything the woman said, she realized she dared not answer. Children spoke too openly to be trusted with difficult political issues. Even though she knew hers wouldn't intentionally hurt anyone, it was simply not a good idea to talk too much during these tenuous times. She simply shrugged at the boys and hoped the old woman hadn't mentioned her ideas to anyone else. They wouldn't have been received kindly in some circles. Regina had discovered this almost against her will.

In Königsberg, Regina remembered her friend Magda warning her of such loose talk. Regina had expressed her fury at *Gestapo* men beating several Jewish people, a whole family, and forcing them from their house and into a truck. This scene enraged her as her *Strassenbahn* moved past. When she told Magda and said she thought they ought to go to the authorities and complain about this vicious treatment of the Jews, Magda had cried out in alarm.

"Regina, you must be crazy! Why can't you realize you mustn't be so outspoken? What would happen to your little boys if the authorities came and took you away to prison, or worse?"

"They wouldn't do that. I'm a German citizen and so are

those Jewish people."

"Regina," Magda said in that patient, motherly tone she always used on the young or the very stupid, "you're too naïve to believe. What do you think the *Gestapo* or *SS* does with people who complain about the government these days?"

Regina thought immediately of Paul, her brother-in-law, with his pregnant wife and four other children, and said, "Paul is *SS* and Gustav says he helps people. He wouldn't allow them to take me away merely for speaking out."

"You're such a child, Regina! Paul would have no choice. Even if he wanted to help you, or the Jews, which I doubt, he wouldn't be able to risk his own family or his own freedom only to keep you with your family. Just do me a favor and don't argue. Never mention your ideas to anyone again, not even to me. I don't want to know what you think about such things."

With that as her final pronouncement, Magda had stalked out to Regina's kitchen muttering to herself as she reboiled their shared tea leaves for a third cup. Regina had been so confused that day, because Magda's warnings had paralleled Gustav's before his departure. She could not accept the idea that such terror could come if she merely expressed her thoughts against violence. The whole *Nazi* thing was getting out of hand, and all personal freedom was gone. She had not mentioned the conversation to Gustav in her next letter. He would have worried. She didn't even mention it to Elli. What a terrible doubt Magda had placed in her head.

Regina shook away her memory when the old lady continued speaking.

"The second reason I refused to live there," she said, "is because my Friedrich would never know where to look for me. We've always agreed that if bombs took our home, we would stay here in the *Gardenplatz* where we've enjoyed working to make it calm and beautiful. Someday, he will come to look for me here," she added with finality and a firm nod.

The old woman seemed so confident, yet she had waited months now and her husband hadn't come. Perhaps everyone realized she was a bit crazy, so they ignored her outspokenness.

Regina thought her delusional and a bit foolish. But then, she wondered if she was hoping for a miracle as much as was the old woman. Regina worked hard daily to believe that her family would be together again in their home in Königsberg, just as they had been before the war. No changes. Was that delusional as well? She sighed. One believes what one must in order to live.

The woman rose after the meal was finished and Regina helped her carry the china bowls to a little pan she was using to wash them. "Where is your home?" she suddenly asked.

Shaken from her private thoughts, Regina told her, and then explained that they'd been on the road for some time trying to reach her husband in Karlsbad.

"Go through Dresden," the old woman announced. "That's the only rail yard our enemies haven't yet bombed, so there should still be a good rail line." She polished up the last dish with a flourish. "When I see what they've done to Berlin, and when I realize Dresden is one of our three biggest train marshalling yards for troop movements, I think it's only a matter of time until they bomb Dresden too. Be careful. You can get tickets tomorrow when you walk into Potsdam. You and your sons will sleep here tonight."

It was not a question, but a pronouncement. Regina wondered if she would be foolish to stay, but Franzi was already asleep on an old gunnysack in the corner and Rainer was leaning precariously from his chair. She shrugged at Willi and he nodded. They were all soon asleep anywhere in the tiny hut they could find a place to lie down. Again, Regina was grateful for their coats, as a tinge of autumn crept into the air that night.

Chapter 16

They woke to wailing sirens and bursts of light as the nightly raid commenced on Berlin. They all ran outside. The *Gartenplatz* seemed, as the old lady had said, far enough out of town that only stray bombs fell, but the spectacle of the beleaguered city was beyond Regina's belief.

This was the first time she and her children had witnessed a bombing raid while not in their bunker. She couldn't escape a horrid fascination. Regina wanted to turn the boys away, yet she could not. The sight was simultaneously beautiful and horrible.

More than a hundred bombers plowed the night sky with a thundering roar. Flak guns on the ground fired at them continuously. The planes frantically jerked to escape giant searchlights as bugs try to escape the collector's pin. Whistling and exploding bombs assaulted their ears. Like some shadow dance in Hell, fires silhouetted the central part of the city. The boys held on to their mother closely and shivered in the chill, but no one ventured back inside.

"See, see," the old lady chanted. "I knew they'd come. They almost never miss a night anymore. My Friedrich must still be fighting the fires."

"Probably," was all Regina could manage. Willi looked at her strangely. She made a face at him to keep him quiet, and they turned again toward the great city outlined in flame.

The mutual carnage continued far too long, as Regina stood first on one foot and then on the other in her anxiety. How could the bunkers protect everyone such a long time, and how could the plane crews stay in the air with all those guns firing at them?

Willi was totally silent, digging at the soft dirt with his toes.

But after awhile, Regina was startled to see Rainer and Franzi jumping up and down, cheering each explosion and imitating its sound as though they were witnessing a grand show.

"*Mutti,* look at all the big airplanes," said Franzi excitedly, pointing over the city. He spread his arms and dipped in circles, 'flying' across the garden.

"They're really noisy," added Rainer, his hands pressed over his ears. "Especially when one zooms down and hits the ground like a shooting star. Where are they coming from? Why is the whole sky so red?"

Regina was devastated by their reaction. *It's too far away for them to understand,* she realized. It seemed better not to comment. How could she explain to such young children that people were dying out there in the distance while they stood watching helplessly?

How senseless it all seemed. Regina found herself saying a prayer for both the men in those planes, someone else's husbands, and for the people trapped in bunkers and fighting fires below. She could imagine the courage and the fear of both.

Staring at the burning city of Berlin, Regina realized that in the face of such violence, she could do nothing except try to keep her boys alive one day at a time. Her heart grieved as her mind reluctantly accepted the challenge.

As the bombardment slowed and the planes turned back to the north, the raging fires continued unabated. They became more aware of the cold and tumbled back inside. In the quiet of the garden house, Rainer and Franzi quickly fell asleep for the remainder of the early morning hours.

Willi and Regina could not sleep.

"They thought it was all just pretty fireworks, *Mutti.*"

Regina could hear an echo of her own despair in his quavering voice.

"I know, son. They're too young to explain more now. Let them believe whatever helps them sleep a little." She reached out to squeeze Willi's hand in understanding.

Regina lay quietly, watching the flickering red sky in the distance. It was horrible. Was everyone just a helpless pawn in war? Was there a right side or a wrong side? Who would decide? She had felt of late that Germany might be on the wrong side.

She remembered when Gustav had come home on an early leave in 1939 rather discouraged. "Hitler's staff has made changes and they're becoming aggressive about furthering a war no one else wants!" he sputtered. She didn't have the impression that he blamed Hitler. Gustav seemed to believe bad or ambitious advisers surrounded Hitler, that his military staff did things without his knowledge, or that he was misled.

Others seemed to think the same. "If the *Führer* knew about this, it wouldn't be happening," became a repetitive preface to every discussion. No one wanted to believe Hitler would do anything wrong. By 1944, though, Regina felt Hitler must have been manipulating the outcome all along, and she wondered how long he had been planning this scenario of power. Was it fantasy that people could believe otherwise, even Gustav? Was Hitler not the only leader, now that the *Reichstag* had been reduced to rubber-stamping his every whim? . It seemed that at first, no one had believed Hitler could gain so much power and later, no one could stop his abuse of that power

Only now did she have a fleeting thought, wondering how Gustav might have known of any changes on Hitler's staff anyway. A normal soldier would have been at the front, wouldn't he? She dismissed the thought as coincidental and irrelevant to her current contemplative memories.

Since the beginning, there had been many dictatorial changes. People who muttered about changes they didn't particularly like began to disappear. The *Reichstag* had even rubber-stamped Hitler's proposal that he needed life and death control over each citizen's actions in order to keep order. How quickly everyone had adapted to not muttering about any concerns.

Teachers and preachers were called 'radical' and were replaced by more 'moderate' *Nazi* party members fairly early in the regime, but few paid attention. By 1941, Willi's schoolbooks were revised, as were their neighbor Christina's sixth grade books, which she brought over proudly to show to Regina. The *Führer's* speech said, "It is necessary for books to reflect more affinity for our Aryan history and our country's destiny throughout Europe. It is our children's future."

At the beginning, Hitler's men had burned books of writers and philosophers he considered radical. That had seemed a strange idea to Regina, too, because many were classics, but she had not protested. Doubting her own validity, she tended then to believe the government, and her husband, must have known best.

Were these new textbooks more than simply patriotic? Regina thought so, especially when she saw pictures in Christina's science book that compared the brains of Aryan, Jewish, African, and Chinese people. The Aryan brain was drawn much bigger, while the others looked shriveled. Her own childhood memories of science class had shown the human brain as only one size. These illustrations made no sense. Photos showed Gypsy and Jewish families in hovels, dirty and sullen, while blonde, cleanly starched Aryan families appeared smiling and robust.

Looking at the new book, Regina had felt a shiver of apprehension about her own eldest son. Willi's dark hair and slightly slanted eyes had already drawn comment from his new, 'less radical' teacher, and he didn't look at all like the Aryan models in the photos. She didn't want to draw further attention to him by voicing her feelings about the books' inaccuracies. Surely everyone else would also see them for what they were. But could children see through this attempt to influence their minds? Probably not, she thought. Yet if she contradicted Willi's teacher, she might be endangering him. She had finally made the choice to say nothing in order to protect her child.

Regina had not mentioned her fears about their son to Gustav, either, because he had said of the books, "Many changes are necessary for Germany to fulfill her destiny. We must support them." He was sounding more and more like the official radio's speeches. Regina had begun to realize there was more behind this war than she had known. That had been the first time she had ever disagreed with her husband. That fact had scared her more than anything else, so she had not told him. She dared not think about it anymore.

The flickering red sky was finally fading to gray dawn.

"Please God," Regina prayed silently as she had been doing nightly, "Don't let my sons remember this horrible night. Help me get them through one more day alive, and help me reunite my family. That's all I ask."

Chapter 17

The old lady's assessment was correct. A brisk morning walk brought Regina and the boys to Potsdam station. It was unfortunate her original tickets all the way to Karlsbad had been invalidated when the family was forced from the train. Now she again had to use her dwindling store of money to buy new tickets, never knowing whether or not a train would get them to their next destination. The ticket agent believed the track to Dresden had been repaired. "Dresden will never be bombed," he assured her, smiling confidently.

To her relief, Regina found people in central Germany were not so concerned with an *Ausweis*. No one had asked to see hers, and she began to relax her fear of being caught. Soon she started entering the bakeries and greengrocers to buy whatever bread and vegetables she could. Women pushed and shoved enthusiastically over each meager purchase. Her ration coupons were for the wrong area, so most stores would not honor them. But she ferreted out street venders who didn't care about such things. They only wanted cash in case they, too, would have to flee. Of course, they charged at least twice as much.

Milling crowds made Regina believe everyone in Germany must be on the move, though none seemed to know where he was going. Each seemed merely to be looking for what he thought might be a safer place than the last. Mass confusion resulted. The train to Dresden was crowded far beyond capacity with refugees, all of whom considered it the safest city in Germany. Some people clambered on to the outside of the cars, forcing the train to move slowly. Regina prayed there were no tunnels ahead.

With the boys trailing behind her, Regina peered in each compartment designed for six, now holding fifteen, and became discouraged. At each glass doorway, Regina asked politely if there were room for an adult and three children.

"We're too crowded already," said one man, fumbling to shove a valise below his feet. "Find someplace else. We don't need any crying brats in here."

Regina moved on, until finally a woman nodded and said, "Come in. We'll just have to move a bit closer together for the children, now, won't we?" Her seatmates grumbled rudely, but they moved themselves over and made room on the floor.

Gratefully, Regina settled her children and their knapsacks in the tiniest possible space, hunched together on the floor. Franzi napped on the luggage rack above the seats, between two stuffed and bulging suitcases belonging to the equally stuffed and bulging matron. Regina wondered how the matron stayed so well fed while others appeared lean and hungry. But the woman was kind and had generously offered her space to the children, so Regina sat on the floor near her feet. She rested a little. Willi and Rainer soon dozed fitfully as well, making up for their interrupted sleep the night before.

This train was in better condition, so the cars didn't sway as precariously. The monotonous clakity-clack set Regina to daydreaming, which she normally found easier than facing reality. But lately her thoughts were conflicted. They challenged what she had previously thought to be true. Hers were not easy, tidy discoveries. She felt foolish to have closed her eyes to changes surrounding her that signaled potentially dangerous events. What would the final result be?

Regina thought of the garden lady's comments about Hitler's stupidity in losing the Jews as a work force, just when they were needed most. When Jewish citizens were required to wear the Star of David in 1941, it had seemed a silly requirement. But it was another of many bizarre regulations, with different groups enforcing them. The *S.A.*, the *S.S.*, *Gestapo*, *Polizei* and Hitler Youth patrolled constantly, looking for citizens who would bring them notice at headquarters. No one could keep track of all of the rules whether one was Jewish or not. It seemed her country had lost all logic.

Jews, plus any Gentiles considered dissidents, were employed in munitions factories in Königsberg doing war work. The situation grew sinister when many were relocated to work in the captured eastern territories of Russia and Poland. Letters were received saying they were, "… safe and happy on a farm." No one knew where that farm might be.

Startled by a noise, Regina looked up to notice a good-looking, blonde young man of around sixteen walking through the hallway of the train. His uniform gave him artificial armor as he glared at everyone he passed. The people in the compartment looked away as though not to attract unwelcome attention. Regina wondered what kind of a boy he had been before the war... kind, thoughtful, amusing like her own boys? Goebbels proclaimed forcefully on the radio that the many uniformed personnel protected The Third *Reich* from radical thinkers, and must be obeyed. But most acted like young thugs, and these Hitler Youth behaved the worst of all. This young man wore the uniform. Teenage rebellion now had a sinister outlet?

How could she prevent her own boys from this evil when they were old enough that membership was required? She could tell others were afraid as well. If she voiced her thoughts this minute, would she be considered radical too? Who could protect good citizens?

Though East Prussia's *Gauleiter* Koch was a friend of Gustav's family, his power and the vicious behavior of his personal guards had spread terror within the region. Regina held no illusion that she could rely on his friendship should one of her family be accused of being radical, whatever that term had come to mean. She couldn't imagine why words had changed definitions almost overnight. She now suspected no one was safe from deportation, and wondered if Gustav had recognized her fear of his family's influential friend.

Not liking the course her thoughts were taking, Regina decided to talk to her neighbors in the compartment, though they had, thus far, all been silent. She turned to a middle-aged woman on her right and asked from where the woman was traveling.

"Potsdam," she answered stoically, but volunteered nothing further.

"Of course, Potsdam. But what made you decide to leave? Were you bombed out? Do you have family ahead?" Regina asked the questions in her most cheerful and friendly manner.

The woman looked around the compartment, glanced at

Regina's boys, and said, "Shh, the children might hear."

Regina knew children were under pressure at school to denounce their parents and, therefore, people had become careful not to discuss anything important in their presence, but she had thought her questions quite innocuous.

She sighed and became quiet again. Being afraid to speak one's mind limited even casual conversation. How might one's remarks be interpreted? Who could one trust with his ideas? Each person seemed alone with only his innermost thoughts for company. And sometimes Regina's innermost thoughts frightened her when she thought of their consequences. The woman was probably right to keep her background to herself.

It was 1941 when Regina realized she had become more careful discussing her fears even with Gustav, because he had seemed to defend Hitler. She prayed this had been just a phase, or perhaps she had been wrong about any perceived changes. It was a lonely time. Perhaps he had been as afraid to confide in her as she had been with him.

As she thought about it now, she realized individual speech had become unacceptable fairly early in their government when not only books were burned, but plays and movies had also become boring propaganda, and religious freedom was limited. She remembered Elli rushing in breathlessly one afternoon. This was before Franzi was born, so Regina thought it must have been perhaps in 1938 or 1939. Elli was a Jehovah's Witness, and she sometimes walked toddlers Willi and Rainer to outdoor meetings with her.

"I know they like to go along, but I don't think I can take them any more." Tears had rolled down Elli's face as she told Regina, "There were *Gestapo* men standing all around the clearing in the park listening to every word the speaker said. But we didn't think anything amiss." She paused to gulp in air.

"But when he preached about non-violence and how no one should harm their neighbors or neighboring countries, the men rushed forward, hitting people on the head until they reached the speaker. They tied his hands and dragged him away."

"Oh my," Regina had cried out, frightened that the boys had

witnessed such a thing.

"They even clubbed some of the worshipers who tried to help the leader. I had to run with Willi and carry Rainer to get them away fast enough."

The boys, of course, were flushed from the excitement of the experience. They were too young to understand what had happened, but Elli and Regina agreed they shouldn't go to any religious events until things calmed down.

Regina now realized she and Elli had not, at that time, understood the significance of the event. It never occurred to her to imagine it as anything other than some wild aberration.

Elli had started the usual mantra, "If Hitler knew, these things would not happen."

Regina wondered now if she should have been more alarmed? It had seemed, then, an isolated incident. She realized now she had accepted far too many things as isolated incidents. It was not as though she, as one lone housewife, could have done anything to stop all that happened--the lightning takeover of Norway, Denmark, Belgium, the Netherlands, and France, each within a few weeks. Nor could she have stopped the bombing of London or Berlin. But she did feel stupid that she hadn't identified the causes sooner, nor recognized that her fear was bred of propaganda. Had she believed it all?

"Hitler's radio speeches, which were announced by the music of Wagner, kept up a mantra of their own. "Our enemies only understand power. In order to retain our great German civilization and cultural heritage, we must crush them." Yet, now Regina realized that much of what had made Germany a great civilization with culture heritage had been destroyed or compromised by the *Nazi* government. And many of the so-called 'enemies' their leader wished to crush were their own citizens. Why were German citizens told something different on their official radio from what she heard at night on her clandestine British radio? Who was right?

Regina shifted her position and wiped her perspiring forehead, hoping no one in the compartment had noticed she was uncomfortable with her own thoughts. But some insightful ideas came together. It's a strange country indeed, she thought, which requires its citizens to listen to censored radio, and needs so many policing groups to enforce constantly changing laws no one understands. The proud German people seemed on a journey toward political chaos?

And more amazingly, she now could think about such questions without confusion? She was frightened that she might be committing treason, even if only in her mind. She had never before allowed herself so much freedom to question. This difficult journey now had forced her to crave answers and meaning.

The train slowed, and the jolting woke the boys. Regina again focused on the task before her. They chugged into Dresden on the beautiful Elbe River. What a relief to actually ride the train all the way to a destination and not have to get off and walk. She felt quite civilized.

Dresden was a gem-like city with no trace of bombing. Regina wanted to show the boys her favorite spot, the Zwinger, where their father and she had walked in the gardens hand in hand on their honeymoon. But she had no time to waste.

What would it be like when she and Gustav met again? She loved and missed him so much. But she was also beginning to think the war had modified his view of life, as she now was forced to admit it had gradually modified her own?

Chapter 18

Once in the Dresden railroad station, Regina hurried the children to a kiosk where one could purchase snacks without ration coupons. She bought the little bit of fruit and crackers available. The apples were bruised, but the boys were delighted with the juicy treat.

Tickets to Karlsbad, Czechoslovakia, however, were another matter. The ticket agent explained. "We can't use the shortest, most direct line anymore as it's being used by the military. We can only guarantee passage almost to Chiemnitz... perhaps only to Ebersdorf. From there, you might get into Chiemnitz on foot, or you might want to skirt around it since it's bombed fairly often. You may have to find another way to the south beyond Chiemnitz."

Regina counted her store of money. It was diminishing rapidly. Both train fare and food had become expensive for civilians trying to outrun the battle lines. And troop trains had first priority through Dresden's rail yard connection.

Fifty kilometers closer is better than nothing, she decided, so she and the boys waited for the train toward Chiemnitz. It was a relatively quiet trip as far as Ebersdorf with several stops on sidings while troop trains passed them hurrying east to meet the Russians. Then they had to walk again. The boys had rested on the train and didn't complain. It flitted across Regina's mind that the boys didn't talk much anymore at all. What were they thinking? It was one more thing to worry about... later.

Regina intended to circle around Chiemnitz. Considerable bomb damage was visible, and she wanted to avoid an air raid if possible. But she couldn't get completely out of this large city before dark. So, after eating the rest of their crackers and fruit, they searched for a public bomb shelter, hoping to rest in comparative safety for the night.

As predicted, there was an air raid near midnight, and the bunker filled quickly with anxious people. Each set up his tiny area with blankets, water, and an occasional candle, trying to snatch extra smidgens of space for the ordeal ahead. A few had brought food, especially those with small children. Soon the steady drone of large aircraft engines replaced the wail of sirens, and the bunker grew abnormally quiet. Regina hugged her children tighter, and noticed an old man nearby pulling his ragged coat closer around his frail body. All eyes focused in unison upon the ceiling.

But the bunker didn't seem to have adequate ventilation for so many people. At first, puzzled looks traveled from person to person, as each sniffed the air. But gradually, those suffering in the bunker started coughing and covering their faces with coats.

"I can't breathe, *Mutti*," Franzi screamed.

The little boy panicked and thrashed in Regina's arms.

"The air smells really funny," decided the more cautious Rainer.

"We can't go outside. The raid isn't over yet." Regina tried to think which would be worse. She heard bombs whistling down nearby. "Perhaps we can stay a little longer."

Something was definitely wrong. Air felt sucked from her lungs.

It was a terrible choice, between suffocating and being bombed, but by the time the next group of bombs fell, the air was acrid. Choice was no longer possible. Those nearest the heavy, iron door began banging on it, but the *Nazi* guards would not respond.

"Let's go now, *Mutti*," Willi yelled, grabbing her hand. Screaming and retching, the crowd lurched toward the door, knocking down the guards at the entrance.

Willi hoisted Franzi to his back, and Regina held tightly to Rainer's hand as they were swept outside along with the others. People nearest the door were pushed down when they didn't move quickly enough. Heedlessly, the panicked crowd trampled over them. Regina feared becoming separated from Willi and Franzi, as they were all spewed out into a nightmare of exploding bombs. But as her head cleared with fresher air, she quickly identified Franzi's coughs and cries and fought her way toward the sound.

They tried to keep together in the mob and move further down the only street seemingly clear of bombs. Regina hesitated. *Which way should they go?* It was her nature to ponder much too long before acting. An unbombed area could mean it was not targeted, or it could mean its turn would come next.

Willi had no such hesitation. He grabbed her hand and decided for all of them. They turned down the empty street and ran away from Hell.

As the family had almost reached the end of the street, bombs began falling where they had started. Regina glanced back and saw people and houses collapsing into the street. Clouds of building material and smoke folded down upon them. Surely they couldn't outrun the destruction.

Willi tugged at her again, yelling, "Run faster, *Mutti*, faster!"

The bombs chased them, rolling up the distance into a fiery ball. She stumbled on, dragging Rainer with her.

Burning embers fell around them, making smoking holes in their clothing and stinging their eyes. Reaching the next corner, they careened down a relatively clear alley, scrambling further into the outskirts of the city. They dared not stop.

They found an open space, a park, and tumbled into the dark shadows of a tree. Franzi screamed, "Willi hurt me! He's holding me too tight."

Willi was exhausted from carrying the youngster, and both collapsed in a heap. As Regina knelt nearby, she saw Rainer gasping for air and rubbing his wrists. She realized she must have hurt him by dragging him along so firmly, but he made no complaint.

Regina felt as though her lungs had been torn out. She feared the boys would be frightened too. "Are you all right, Willi? You were carrying the greatest burden."

"I don't think I can go any further right now, *Mutti*," he said between deep gasps. "Do you think it's safe to rest here awhile?"

Regina looked around. "Yes, this is probably as safe as we can find. Willi, you did wonderfully." She brushed the damp hair from his smudged face.

"I think I lost my coat, *Mutti*," interrupted Rainer. He cried in short gulps and tried to explain. "I had it over my arm, but..."

"It doesn't matter, *Liebling*... nothing matters. We're all here together." She hugged the little boy. The coat was nothing. She had her children, and grateful tears flowed down her face.

They huddled in the park to take their chances with the bombs. The sight of great fires, the noise of planes, and the falling of slower citizens were not things they could discuss, and the tired boys sat watching the chaos numbly, in stunned silence.

Would the children forget the happier times of their early childhood? Would they only remember flames and horror? Was there no way she could protect them from the brutality of war? Trying to calm herself, she vowed she and Gustav would create only happy memories for them, once they reached safety.

How many times now had she made this promise to herself, or to them? She'd lost count. Anyway, her good intentions for the future couldn't help her save them now. Even her decision to enter Chiemnitz had been a mistake. *One day at a time, Regina, one day at a time.* They could only be helped tomorrow if she could keep them alive today. She must not think further ahead than what she must do now, this minute. She squared her shoulders and forced a reassuring smile.

They huddled together around a tree in a park, in the middle of an air raid. As their breath gradually returned, she urged the boys to sing "Fal da ri, Fal da ra" to calm their fear. It was their favorite wandering song, having kept up spirits for the whole trip, and they sang it, tentatively at first, and then with gusto. Even though Christmas was a long time away, Franzi then requested "Oh, Tannenbaum." It was the song he had learned best last Christmastime, and he never lost a chance to show he remembered all the words.

Singly and in pairs, other people made their way out of the shadows and flames and noise into the open space, checking each other for injuries. They gathered around the family and joined in the singing.

"I know what," Rainer shouted. "Let's all sing louder than the bombs and airplanes."

Incredibly, these total strangers began singing at the top of their lungs at the child's request. *Was everyone crazy?* Yet it seemed the bombs and planes were turning away toward the northwest. Finally, they were gone, and the all-clear siren sounded.

"See, we drove them away, *Mutti*," piped up Franzi.

The crowd roared with laughter. For just a moment, they could laugh and pretend that by banding together and singing loudly enough, they had achieved a bit of control over their vulnerable situation.

Several people wished each other "Godspeed" and wandered away to find how their homes had fared. The park seemed the safest open place to rest, even with the fires raging in buildings around it. So Regina suggested the boys lay their heads on their knapsacks. She covered them with the remaining battered coats and they fell asleep, wrapped together, kitten-like, for warmth.

Regina woke shortly before dawn. She was reluctant to wake her peacefully sleeping children. Watching their faces, she wondered how much more strain they could absorb.

They were closer to Karlsbad now, but the trip had taken so long, Regina wasn't sure Gustav would still be waiting there. She wasn't even sure which day it was. Her exhaustion brought yearning for Gustav to take over the decision-making and allow her to be herself for a while. She was so tired. She knew she was never meant for the nomadic role she was playing. Perhaps no one ever was. She longed for release from this awful responsibility and to go back again to playing the happy *Hausfrau*.

Now that she thought about it, though, she didn't really know which role had been real and which play-acting. Nothing seemed real to her now, except her boys. They might not even have a house, or a business, or a family anymore. Was all this real, or a dream...or a nightmare?

Her sense of identity had changed so abruptly? She tried to remember when she had taken on this leadership role. Was it in 1939 when Gustav said he needed her to work with him and learn the import/export business? He had seemed to have confidence in her ability.

"You can do it, Ina, I know you can. You must. There's no choice, since I'll be gone more often with the Army. My partner Jakob is gone. There are many more regulations now, and we can't allow the business to fail for want of someone's supervision."

She had learned about purchase orders, sales, and had even

learned to drive their car to the surrounding villages. But she hated to make decisions. Their accountant, aged *Herr* Busch, was the one to whom Regina turned for advice when Gustav was away.

Though she felt particularly inadequate, she realized other women were also managing homes and businesses alone. Perhaps she, too, was stronger than she had thought. She had never dreamed of having to learn survival skills or leaving her home. How war had changed everything.

Regina had begun doing well at the business, even enjoying it, surprising both herself, and *Herr* Busch.

"I am amazed, *Frau* Wolff," *Herr* Busch said one day. "You have a head for business, even though you have never worked before. What will you want to do after the war?" He cackled in his high-pitched laugh. "You may not want to go back to cooking over a hot stove for your husband."

Remembering his statement, she chuckled to herself. Here she was, reclined in this quiet park in a strange city, and right now, she would like nothing better than to cook over a hot stove for her Gustav.

Chapter 19

"Wake up, son." Regina shook Willi's shoulder. Instantly, he rolled out to a standing position and began gathering their possessions. Rainer rose slowly, stumbling with eyes at half-mast, yawning and grumbling to himself. Franzi burrowed more deeply under the coats and whimpered as she lifted him to his feet. "Come now, Franzi," she urged.

Franzi whined, "Why can't we stay here?"

"Staying in Chiemnitz is futile," she answered. "The city's still smoldering, so no trains will run today. Perhaps we can find one going south to Karlsbad by the time we reach Marienberg. That'll be only a day's walk." She warily calculated the time.

Willi watched her closely. "You're talking out loud to convince yourself, aren't you, *Mutti*? That's a good idea."

Regina winked at him and laughed. He had her figured out.

She sought out a bakery on the outskirts, hoping for some *Brötchen*. None were left. Fatigue and hunger slowed their footsteps. She steeled herself to ignore Franzi's cries, "*Mutti*, when can we eat?" She could do nothing except herd the children to the next village, and hope.

Finding a stream, they waded in and bathed in the cold water, clothes and all. Their clothes would dry as they walked. With no remaining soap, their hair and nails were barely presentable.

How Regina longed for a manicure. Scarcely able to remember the days when a broken fingernail was a major catastrophe, she prayed for a hotel in Karlsbad with a real bathtub. She felt sure the greatest hardship of being a refugee, besides fear, hunger, and actual danger, of course, was always feeling dirty. Grit, sand, flies buzzing over everything, ant hills on the ground, streaks on her legs from a combination of sweat and dust... these apparently didn't bother the boys as much as they bothered her. She sought every chance to wash, while she was forced to coax and threaten them into the cold streams.

Many people still wandered on the back roads, pushing carts, endlessly walking. At one road junction, Willi and Rainer found a battered *Leiterwagen* in a ditch. Apparently, the owner had thrown it aside when one wheel broke.

"It's a big wagon, *Mutti*," announced Rainer. Its two wide planks of wood on the bottom were intact, as were the ladder-like, vertical strips along the sides. "We can pile it high, but not with little stuff because it'll slide out between the slats. No one wants it, *Mutti*." His eyes pleaded silently.

"I can fix it," Willi added his plea. "If we can stop a few minutes and gather some twigs, I can make a bracket or splint to repair the wheel."

Regina remained skeptical. "I doubt you can find enough. The trees, and even fences, have already been burned. It takes longer to find even enough wood to light our tin-can fire to cook a meal."

But the boys were excited by their discovery, and Regina didn't have the heart to object. She did her best to wrench the metal rim back into shape, pounding it flat with a rock while Willi and Rainer searched. Franzi napped on the fragrant grass nearby. Just as she was beginning to worry, the two reappeared with their treasures of twigs and a twisted piece of wire. Willi bracketed the broken parts with the twigs, wrapped the rim back around the wheel, and wired it all together.

"It's finished, *Mutti*," Willi announced proudly. "We can put in the knapsacks and let Franzi ride on top. We can take turns pulling and pushing. It'll be easier."

Though Willi frequently had to rewire his makeshift wheel together, they did seem to go faster with Franzi riding, still holding his precious washtub. They traveled the perhaps thirty kilometers to Marienberg in time to catch an evening train going south. It only went as far as Oberwiesenthal. So they rode that far and stopped in a field for the night, hoping to cross the Czech border into the village of Bozi Dar the next morning.

It was Willi's birthday. Regina had forgotten, but Rainer reminded her. Had the days and weeks really gone by so fast, or had the time been so filled with anxiety and fatigue she had lost track?

"I'm so sorry there's no party or cake like we had at home." Regina was near tears as she hugged her eldest son. She was pained that she could provide nothing festive.

"It doesn't matter, *Mutti*," Willi reassured her with tired eyes. He had grown accustomed to having little, and the boys settled for some dried turnips boiled in their can.

Then Regina remembered the little tin of peaches they had saved for just the right day. The boys watched eagerly as she opened the can with her knife and speared out the bright, juicy slices. Each slice produced squeals of delight. There were thirteen slices, and all agreed the extra one belonged to Willi.

Rainer asked, "May we drink the juice too, *Mutti*?"

"Of course you may. Each of you can have a few sips until it's all gone. Then we can wash the tin in the stream and carry an extra in our pack." This was accomplished quickly.

"That was as good as a cake, *Mutti*," Willi pronounced as he patted his thin belly.

After their meager dinner, Regina watched the boys take turns racing down a nearby hill in the wagon, shrieking with the perceived danger of running into the stream below. How strange, she thought, that real danger and playful danger are so interchangeable in a child's mind. Perhaps this is a blessing, she decided.

Morning brought better spirits. Regina was thankful Willi had only turned ten. She prayed the war would be over before he was eleven because membership in Hitler Youth would be mandatory then.

"I'm glad too," Willi said, when she mentioned her concern. "I think they want more than just healthy stuff like the campouts and exercise they tell you about."

Hoping he would say what was on his mind, Regina added, in her most casual voice, "What makes you think so? I know you like the uniforms."

"They didn't like me...they chased me and wanted to fight me on the way home from school." The words came slowly with obvious puzzlement. " They said I didn't look like a German boy and that maybe I was a Russian or a Jew spy. What did they mean,

Mutti?"

"I remember you had cuts and bruises, but you always told me you fell out of a tree while playing. Why didn't you tell me?"

"Don't know." Willi shuffled his feet in the dust, then turned away to help Franzi put on his small knapsack and picked up his own. He walked ahead.

Boys, and men also, are not always communicative, Regina thought. She wished she had known sooner, though she was not sure what she could have done without, perhaps, making the situation worse for Willi.

Regina jogged to catch up with her son. "Next time something like that happens, would you tell me, please?"

He looked directly at her.

"You are as German as any of us, and those boys shouldn't have said such things," she added.

Willi was silent, but he nodded before turning away.

She dared not pursue his increased understanding further. How sad, she thought, that she could not be open with her own son for fear he might endanger himself within the hearing of an enemy. When will this be over? She followed her children along the road, lined with autumn-colored trees that reminded her of more peaceful days. Soon the terrain sloped uphill steeply.

Just before the border crossing, a farmer offered them a ride over the worst of the hills, *Leiterwagon*, and all--for a price, of course. Regina had little money left, but the trail rose steeply, and the family was so exhausted, she agreed. Once over the range of low mountains, it was downhill the rest of the way into Karlsbad. She paid the farmer and gathered their belongings.

Excitement to see *Vati* mounted, but Regina feared they might be too late. She didn't want to take the joyous anticipation from her boys, however, so she kept her anxiety to herself.

They tripped down the last few kilometers triumphantly, in spite of blisters and fatigue. The center of Karlsbad, or Karlovy Vary, as the Czechs called it, housed the *Kur* or spa hotels and hospitals near the river, while the centuries old fortress commanded the hillside.

The boys slowed as they approached the riverside.

Willi looked around. "It's like some kind of resort, *Mutti.* Look at all those people sitting around drinking coffee at cafes. Don't they have a war here?"

Regina was wondering, herself. Fashionably dressed couples strolled arm in arm under trees gradually showing brown, blood red, and yellow leaves. "These folks are probably recovering from some illness," she said. "Karlsbad is where sick Europeans come to use special mineral waters and hospitals. The waters are supposed to cure just about anything."

Willi nodded. "It feels like we wandered into a make-believe place, doesn't it? Like there's been no war at all. Did we imagine the whole thing, or what?"

Rainer asked, "What's the matter with all of them? Do they think they're in a movie?"

Even Franzi piped up. "How come they're not running away somewhere like everyone else? Isn't anybody mad at them?"

Regina and the boys could not help staring, and she had no answers for her sons.

The children seemed to sense they were out of place in the clothes they'd been wearing for almost a month because, at a nod from Willi, they dug their shoes out of their packs and put them on. Even with shoes held together with rags, they apparently thought they looked better than when they'd been barefoot. Regina stifled a smile.

After a few inquiries, she found which *Kur* center was being used as a military hospital. Combing her hair as best she could, and washing all their faces in the courtyard fountain, they entered, but Rainer insisted on staying with their wagon in the foyer.

Regina said, "It's unnecessary, son. None of these people behave like the desperate souls we've seen along the way. A patched *Leiterwagen* is the last thing they'd want."

But Rainer would not be moved and insisted on guarding their treasure.

At the front desk, a rigid old gentleman performed the usual straight-armed salute and the family returned it perfunctorily. He frowned as Regina gave her husband's name.

"Gustav Wolff cannot be seen this day."

"Where is he?" she asked quickly, as Franzi began to wail.

"There's someone important with him at the moment, a meeting, and I told you, he cannot be seen today. Come back tomorrow." The man turned away.

Regina persisted, "If I see him tomorrow, how long will we have, and where will he be going then?"

"Back to the eastern front in a couple of days, of course. We can't afford to keep soldiers in the hospital when they're needed at the front. Don't you know the Russians are coming?"

Regina sank to a bench, hugging Franzi, as she tried not to cry—an unsuccessful effort. But at least Gustav was still here. She had already accepted the possibility they might be too late to see him at all. What was one more day after their long trek? Regina smiled brightly at the children to reassure them, and perhaps reassure herself, as well.

"We can all see *Vati* tomorrow. I'm sure he's looking forward to seeing you boys. Right now, let's go find a hotel, have a real bath, and get a decent meal. All right with you young men?"

There were cheers that apparently disturbed the gruff old man behind the desk, but Regina didn't care.

Tomorrow ... tomorrow... she could think later about Gustav's having to go back to the danger of the Russian front. As the young woman struggled to accept this fact, she also rejoiced that her husband had not been on one of the eastbound troop trains passing them on the road, as she had feared.

She was curious as to who might be with him in the meeting that made it impossible for her to see him today, but it quickly faded into her relief and excitement for the morrow.

What was she to do now? She couldn't afford to stay in this expensive resort town, but she assumed Gustav would have money to pay for hotel and meals when she saw him the next day. They were all too tired and hungry for her to believe anything else, so they trudged up to a quiet hotel she knew on the side of the hill overlooking the hospital and the river. She and Gustav had spent many wonderful vacation days there. She could think of nowhere else to go.

Chapter 20

It took a moment for Regina to convince the skeptical owner of the hotel, *Frau* Beck, that the disreputable children and tired mother who presented themselves at her door were indeed of the same family who had visited in style and comfort only a few years previously. When she recognized Regina, however, her reaction was immediate.

"Oh, *Frau* Wolff. How sorry I am I didn't recognize you! You all must be exhausted. Come in, quickly. Are you all right?" As *Frau* Beck bustled around to make the family welcome and take their knapsacks, Regina explained her situation and asked if she could pay the bill after seeing her husband. She felt discussion of finances was impolite, and hated the necessity.

"My goodness, *Frau* Wolff. Don't give it another thought. Don't worry about a thing. Just rest easy. You all are most welcome here, anytime...anytime."

She muttered about the war and how it had changed everyone so, all the while setting aside blankets and clean towels. "I have dinner for the guests ready in the dining room. Please sit down, join us, and we'll talk."

Franzi squealed his surprise. "Oh look *Mutti*. It's a real dinner with chairs, and plates, and everything."

Regina's cheeks burned with shame. "I'm afraid it has been a long, hard journey. The boys have not had much to eat, and life has been...well...rather primitive along the way."

Frau Beck clucked gentle "tsk tsks," slowly shaking her head. "You just rest here for a week and we'll get you all fattened up again," she said, turning aside to wipe her tears on her apron. She fussed around the children through dinner, trying to give them second portions, which their shrunken stomachs could not tolerate.

Regina smiled when she noticed Rainer smacking Franzi's left hand and replacing it on the table when it dropped into his lap. At least he had not forgotten Elli's teaching on good European manners. It reminded her of a time before the war when she had watched a tourist in a restaurant smacking her child's left hand and replacing it in his lap, according to America's opposite rules of etiquette. At the time, Regina had been amused at the scene, but now she appreciated every mother's such peaceful effort. How easy it is to take such simple things for granted until we no longer have them, she thought.

After dinner, she and the boys soaked in the hotel's mineral pool and climbed into real beds. Such luxury relaxed them, but Regina couldn't sleep. Anticipation vied with anxiety after such a long period of her husband's absence and silence. Where had he been that he could not write, and how seriously ill or injured was he? Should she ask all her questions right away, or hope he would clear things up now that they would have sufficient time to talk?

And what would he think of her efforts to arrive here? She had made mistakes. Had she done all he had expected of her? Would he remember all he meant to her? Would he still love her after so long? She would try her best with callused hands and broken fingernails to slip into her silk dress and precious silk hose with the abandon of her days before the war, but somehow, her thoughts were still not peaceful. She slept fitfully at last.

The family looked very different when they ventured out to the hospital the next morning. Much care and attention had been given to cleanliness and grooming. Even Franzi's uncontrollable cowlick had been glued down with water. Freshly scrubbed and shining, Willi and Rainer chattered excitedly, while Franzi was unnaturally subdued.

As the four walked hand in hand to the hospital and waited what seemed an eternity in the lobby, Regina again noticed Franzi's concerned look. His face was very white.

"What's the matter, little one?" she asked. "Aren't you excited about seeing your *Vati*?"

Franzi hung his head and leaned against her. "Do you think *Vati* will know me now? I was only a baby when he saw me before. Will he like me as much as Rainer and Willi?"

So that was the problem. "Of course he will. You're a very special little boy."

"Will he know Rainer taught me ABC's and Willi taught me numbers and that I'm not a baby anymore?"

"You can certainly tell him yourself. Do you think you could watch for *Vati* to come down the hall and give him a big smile?" Franzi brightened. "Yes, *Mutti*. Do I look all right?"

Regina surveyed his tattered shoes, the shirt she had laundered the night before--clean but with frayed cuffs, and the jacket she had brushed as much as its fragile condition would bear. She nodded to the little boy with his shining face.

"You look just fine...now don't worry." She wondered how she looked, herself, with her battered shoes, and Gustav's favorite dress now hanging loosely around her emaciated body.

The two older boys were bobbing up and down, puppet-like, in their excitement. Regina didn't bother to quiet them. She felt her own set of butterflies and understood their impatience. At last a door opened down the hall and all rose expectantly, but only a man in a crisp uniform marched out and passed them in the hall. He barely glanced at the boys, but his eyes lingered on Regina appraisingly before he said, "*Heil Hitler*" and moved out the door to a shiny black car with flags on its front fenders. They had noticed the car upon entering.

Suddenly, from the same door, stepped Gustav. The two older boys ran toward him immediately, expecting their remembered hugs and roughhouse play. He held out his hands to stop them. They looked bewildered, but he explained.

"I'm not completely well, boys, so I can't pick you up right now." He tousled the children's hair and hugged them heartily.

Franzi cowered behind Regina's skirt, now and then peeking out at his father, then ducking again behind his mother. She couldn't even walk because he was hobbling her knees. Gustav came to where Regina and the child stood, and they stared at each other a moment. Gustav reached out and kissed her on the nose, and then the lips. Regina longed to melt against his huge frame, but Franzi was tugging at her dress. Gustav laughed and peeked behind her to see the little boy. Franzi backed around in obvious terror. Regina was bewildered.

"Franzi, you were so anxious to see *Vati*. What's wrong with you?" Regina felt herself blushing as the child continued to cry whenever Gustav came near. He climbed, spider-like into

Regina's arms to bury his face in her shoulder.

"Oh, he's just being a baby like always. Don't mind him, *Vati*," said Rainer.

Willi chimed in. "Who knows about him. We can't ever figure him out. But Rainer and I are really glad to be here with you after our journey. It took forever."

The moment of tenderness Regina craved was lost as the older boys chattered on about train rides, strafing planes, and bragged about how they were never scared, even for a moment. Gustav listened with one child on each side.

Regina stood there, feeling extraneous, holding Franzi. He continued alternately to hide on her shoulder and sneak peeks of his father. He grew hysterical whenever she approached her husband. This was certainly not the way she had dreamed of their first meeting.

As the boys slowed their chatter, Gustav said, "Ina, please come sit down. You must be tired carrying the child. Let's see if he'll come to me now."

Franzi wouldn't. He continued clutching Regina's dress with great tears running down his face every time Gustav tried to touch him. The scene was a calamity for Regina, who so much wanted all the boys to behave well for their first visit with their father.

Gustav finally gave up on Franzi and teased and played with Willi and Rainer, while Regina stewed in misery. He asked them to dine in the hospital's cafe and, of course, the older boys grabbed his hands while he led the way. Regina followed slowly carrying a reluctant Franzi. *What on earth could be wrong with the child? And how was she to find time alone with her husband?*

At lunch, the boys ate so ravenously Gustav realized they hadn't been eating well. "Was it very bad, Ina?" he asked quietly.

"It was hard, but it doesn't matter now that we're here with you." She tried to smile and take her husband's hand, but Franzi climbed into her lap to eat his lunch.

"I wanted you all safely out of Königsberg before the Russian offensive and the British bombers..." He stopped abruptly.

"You knew those things were going to happen? How?"

"You're safely away now, so it doesn't matter. Now you must go to your brother's home in Weida to wait until the end of the war. The Americans are coming from the west and the Russians from the east. We'll try to stop them from crushing us in the middle. Weida will be the safest place for you and the boys."

"But, we just got here, and we're all tired. We need some time with you before going anywhere else." The walls were crushing in and Regina's breathing was becoming difficult.

"I know, Ina, but I'll be called away soon."

"When?"

"Soon...they'll send a staff car for me and I'll have to go."

"Who'll be sending a car? Why? I wanted to talk...so much has happened...I didn't know what happened to you and..."

"I know...and I'm sorry for that. I've been under heavy Army demands. This visit to the hospital was merely another flare up of the gall bladder problem I've had for years. After this new surgery, I'm much better, though a bit sore yet. They're sending me back to the front."

"Please, Gustav, can't we have more time to find answers. I was hoping you'd go home with us to Königsberg."

"You must understand that a soldier has a job to do. Besides, there may not be much left in Königsberg, Ina. You can't go back there, at least, not now."

"What will I do in Weida? We have no money left after this trip, not even for the hotel."

"I assumed you'd be taken care of by the business, so I hadn't thought about your needing money. I'll come by the hotel on my way out and pay your bill for ten days so you can rest up. You'll need train tickets to Weida. I'll see to it, don't worry."

"That's not what I was worried about. I wanted some time alone with you, and I..."

"Ina, I have no control over the war. It's imperative I go back as soon as the staff car comes for me. Until then, I'll do what I can for you and the boys. When the *Reich* turns back our enemies, I'll come find you in Weida."

"And when will that be?" Regina hated it that her own voice sounded like the pleadings of a small child.

"I don't know, Ina...soon, I think. Things are heading to a final battle and we must win, or else." Gustav looked away for a moment. A shadow crossed his fine features.

Was it doubt, she wondered, or sadness? She couldn't tell. Then he met her gaze directly for the first time. "We may have a few days yet. I'm not allowed to leave the hospital overnight, but you and the boys can come each day until I go."

Before she could answer, Willi and Rainer's patience had run out. They grabbed their father's hands for a walk around the hospital grounds, skipping and laughing. Gustav told them stories, and Regina could hear them singing together.

She sat quietly in the garden with Franzi still clinging to her shoulder. He sobbed in fearful spasms. She wanted to throw the little boy aside and run after her husband. Why had she not held Gustav to her in some way? Why had she not asked the right questions and received the right answers? Why was he so determined to go back to the front when she had already seen many deserters making their way back to their homes?

But Gustav was no deserter, nor would she want him to be. *What did she want?* Obviously she wanted her husband by her side, decisions made together, and a more definite plan for now. If she were honest, she wanted to lie with him in the night and make love, and talk of their future together at home in Königsberg.

The idea of continuing on this precarious journey was terrifying. She craved sanctuary and rest. She didn't know if her brother had returned from the war yet, if he'd been wounded, if her sister-in-law had survived, or even if they had room for her. To Gustav, it was all so definite--go to Weida. Once again, she realized it had been an order, not a decision mutually agreed upon.

But then, what did she expect? Hadn't she said she wanted Gustav to take charge again so she could relax? But she'd been in charge of a business and a home and a terrible journey yet her husband didn't see her as a definitive individual. In his eyes, she was still only an extension of himself. *Was that what had just happened?* He will take care of everything, and I will go where he tells me, and wait until he comes for me, and everything will be all right. She felt angry without knowing exactly why.

Regina's thoughts were disturbed by a tug on her shoulder and she faced a tearful Franzi. "He scared me, *Mutti*."

"Why? He just wanted to play with you."

"I don't know... he's so big, and he scares me bad."

Regina put her head down and let the tears of frustration fall on the lap of her silk dress. Had Gustav even noticed it?

By the time he returned with Willi and Rainer, Regina had composed herself and persuaded Franzi to shake hands with his father while holding on to her dress tail. He flinched visibly at the touch of Gustav's hand, but he stood his ground.

Gustav still looked disappointed, but he smiled and tried to take the child upon his lap. It almost worked, until Rainer crowded in next to his father and Franzi quickly slipped down and escaped back to his mother. The two parents looked at each other and shrugged. What more was there to do with so little time to solve all the problems generated by their long separation?

The next day inched by with another visit at the hospital. Franzi seemed better when Gustav appeared in lounging slacks. Perhaps it was something about the uniform. Regina could not fathom the child's unreasonable fear. They had little time to talk. When Regina asked about his war experience or his job in the Army, Gustav answered vaguely that he didn't want her to worry her pretty head about anything. Where had she heard *that* before?

It was obvious from his comments that Gustav still believed in Hitler's leadership. He would continue his role in whatever capacity he was needed until the war was resolved, one way or the other. It was also obvious he wanted his sons protected and safe in Weida. While the three boys played in the hospital garden, Regina realized there wasn't time to debate either issue.

"Why do you think Weida is safer?" she asked.

"Why can you not take my word for it, Ina?"

"You've given me no reason. Perhaps Nürnberg would be safer for the boys. We could stay with your sister, Erna."

"You've never needed a reason for my decisions before. Why do you need one now? In my capacity in the Army, I'm positive Weida is the safest choice, and that's where I would like you to go."

"I suppose I never realized before that your decisions were actually demands. Now I'm more aware of that fact. I'm not sure how to react."

"Ina, I'm sorry if it sounds like a demand, but I was right about getting the boys out of Königsberg in time, wasn't I? Please trust me on this decision too." A pleading tone had crept into his voice that softened Regina's defensive stance.

"All right, Gustav, I'll trust you on this, but you must tell me how you know all these things with such certainty. Where are you getting your information?"

"You've changed, Ina. You've never questioned my duty or my decisions before. I can't tell you anything further. You'll simply have to trust my judgment."

"We've both changed, my dear. We'll need more time to sit down and talk about all this." Regina took a deep breath and fearfully plunged on. "You want me to trust you, but I would like you to trust me with the simple information about what you're doing in this war that you supposedly know all these things." She raised a hand to brush hair back from her eyes.

Gustav was silent... what did that mean?

"It doesn't seem too much to ask, does it? After all, I love you and we're supposed to be partners." She felt she had to say it, and she hoped now for the desired outcome.

Gustav walked away slowly with clenched fists. She could see he was trying to gain control of his anger. Regina had never before seen him this way, as though he had become accustomed to being obeyed without question. It was true she'd never questioned his ideas before, but then, she'd never been alone to think or take responsibility for their home, business, and children's safety before, either. Perhaps she *had* changed. Certainly she didn't want to go back to the insecurity of the road again without more specific information. What could possibly be so secret?

After a few silent minutes, Gustav came back and took Regina in his arms.

She felt wooden. The change was too sudden.

He spoke softly. "Ina, there are many things I can't tell you right now. So much has happened while we've been apart and I

don't want you involved. After the war is over, I'll explain
everything. But for now, will you please just take the boys and go
to Weida?"

His voice broke, and Regina realized with a start that he, too,
was distressed.

"I'll come to you in Weida as soon as I can, once this mess is
straightened out and there's a decision at headquarters. Please take
my word that there are some things you're better off not knowing."

"Is this about your work, Gustav, or that officer that was
here when we came?"

"Both, plus many other things I can't explain now. Please
just be my sweet Ina and go where I know you'll be safe." He
touched his fingers to her cheek. There were tears in his eyes.

She nodded in acquiescence. She didn't want to cause him
pain, but the mystery seemed deeper than ever. She had never
questioned Gustav's leadership in her whole life, and their time
together was too short to further question it now. She gave in.

"When shall I leave?"

"I'll pay the hotel for ten days so you and the boys can rest
up, but time is running out. Two enemy armies are converging on
our land, Ina, and I want you in Weida soon. We'll go tomorrow
and get your train tickets so you'll be ready."

But the next morning, the staff car with the flags was again
parked in front of the hospital. Regina and the children rushed
inside. She felt a stab of panic.

Gustav, dressed in a black uniform, walked down the hall
with two officers. He stopped to hug the boys, and handed Regina
a roll of money for hotel and train fare. He held her lightly in his
arms for a moment while he whispered, "Don't worry Ina. I'll
make it all up to you when we're together after we win this war. I
promise." He stepped away smartly and entered the car, which
drove off immediately.

Regina didn't realize she was running after the staff car
until Willi called to her.

"*Mutti*, where are you going? Come back, *Mutti*, Franzi's
crying again."

She dropped to her knees in the dust and sobbed.

Even though Franzi and his mysterious fear of his father had ruined her dream of reunion, Regina couldn't remain angry with the little boy. He was still so young, and couldn't possibly understand her needs and desires. She scarcely understood them herself. She dried her tears as she rose and walked slowly back to the boys. They all seemed overwhelmed by their father's abrupt departure and their mother's discomfort. As always, when remembering that she, alone, would have to set the tone, she straightened her shoulders and forced a smile.

"Well, boys, we're on our own again. *Vati* is going back to the war. But he'll be coming for us soon."

"*Mutti*, what kind of soldier rides in a big, black car when everyone else is walking?"

"I don't know, Willi. Perhaps *Vati* got a ride because he's been sick." But she wondered herself what it meant. She had found no answers during their brief reunion--none at all.

Regina tried to put eagerness into her voice. "We'll have a few days vacation here in Karlsbad and stay at the hotel and bathe every day in the mineral waters, and then we'll take a train to go see *Onkel* Hans and *Tante* Gerda. Would you like that?"

"Why can't *Vati* come with us?" Rainer was crying and she could see that none of the boys understood what had happened. Actually, she did not understand it either, but she couldn't alarm the children with her own confusion.

"He has to go now to win the war. He'll be with us sooner than you think. In the meantime, *Onkel* Hans and *Tante* Gerda will be so surprised at how big you've grown." Her chatter did not distract Willi or Rainer at all.

"Do you think he'll be in danger again this time, *Mutti*?" Willi's voice trembled.

"I don't know, son. I really don't know, but he seems to have done well thus far, so we will assume he'll be fine, and he'll come home to us soon."

"But it won't be at our real home, will it, *Mutti*? Something's happened, hasn't it?" She prayed Willi would ask no more questions, but this one was the hardest yet.

"Boys," Regina said, kneeling again in the dusty road with

her arms circled around them. "Your father and I don't really know what has happened in Königsberg. Some buildings there have been damaged, but we're hoping our home isn't among them. There were some bombs downtown, and much was destroyed. Your father doesn't feel it's safe for us to go back there right now. We'll have to go back after the war to find out what happened. For now, at least the four of us are still together and we're safe. We'll have a few more days' journey to Weida and then we shall simply wait until your father comes for us."

"But *Mutti*, I don't want to go on any more journeys. I want to stay here," Franzi wailed.

She could see Willi struggling for control of his emotions as well. Then, he looked into her anguished face and nodded firmly. "Come on, Squirt," he said to his little brother. "I'll race you back to the hotel and we'll swim in the pool."

Regina watched the three run up the hill before she braced herself against a stone wall and cried, alone. She had no idea exactly what had happened during this visit, but it certainly was not what she had expected. It was almost worse to have seen Gustav with no answers than not to have seen him at all. Why did it seem everything was stated in terms of 'after the war?' It wasn't just about nations winning or losing. It wasn't even about physical survival anymore. The war dominated every family and every marriage.

Could her family and her marriage survive it? She didn't know anymore. She wasn't sure what to care about most. But for the boys' safety, and for any chance at reconstructing her family after the war, she needed to go to Weida. And she needed to go quickly.

Chapter 21

Restlessness plagued the boys the next morning. It was apparent they were as disappointed as Regina that Gustav couldn't stay with them longer. None understood why their father couldn't go home with them. As a restful vacation, the time in Karlsbad was wasted.

"*Mutti*, if we have to go to Weida, why don't we just go now?" proposed Willi.

In his naiveté, he stated what Regina had already considered. She nodded.

"I'll pay *Frau* Beck, and check something at the hospital. You boys wait for me here. I'll be back in fifteen minutes. Willi, please watch Rainer and Franzi."

The boys were already packing their knapsacks. Regina was thankful she had resisted Gustav's plea to buy more clothing in Karlsbad. She knew trains thus far had been undependable, and she wanted nothing extra to carry.

She ran down the hill and stood again in front of the stiff old man at the hospital's front desk.

"May I speak to *Herr* Wolff's nurse?"

"I do not recall which nurse was his, Madam," he responded coldly to her question. Almost as an afterthought, he said, "You might ask the nurses on his ward."

"Perhaps they can tell me more about his condition," Regina said.

She followed the direction he pointed, and asked each nurse until she found the one who had been caring for Gustav. The woman smiled when Regina told her name.

"You were very late getting here. *Herr* Wolff assumed you would be here much sooner on the train. He feared you and the children might be dead." She looked at Regina's traveling clothes and sobered. "I'm sorry, it seems you had a hard journey."

Regina nodded silently. "My husband did not discuss his illness. I would feel better about leaving if I knew he was completely well. Can you tell me anything about his condition?

Was he really well enough to go back to the front?"

The nurse answered slowly, "He thought he was. He said his job didn't involve much physical effort, only flying and taking notes. He was anxious that you and the children go to your brother's home until after the war. I don't remember the name of the town, but he spoke of your being safe there. I understand it's a small town with little industry to attract bombs."

"My brother lives in Weida, near Gera, in Kreise Thüringen. We'll start there today. I'd simply feel better about going if I felt my husband was fully well. He left so suddenly..." She wanted to cry, but it wouldn't help the situation. She looked out the window. "I suppose my sister-in-law can take us in for a while, until the children recover from the trip."

A pat on her shoulder startled Regina. It was the nurse. "It's good you're going to a relative's. It'll be best to stay where *Herr* Wolff can find you. So many families are lost and separated these days. You must register with the authorities once you arrive there."

Regina nodded.

"You must be very proud. Your husband is very devoted to the *Führer*. Surgery and all, he was most anxious to get back to the east. A good man, I'm sure." She paused a moment, then added, "A woman, I think it was his sister, was here about two weeks ago. She was very concerned. He called her Frieda, I think."

"He has no sister named Frieda." Regina said automatically. She pondered why Gustav could still be so 'devoted' to the *Nazi* leader who seemed to have brought them so much trouble.

"Well, perhaps I was wrong about the name." The nurse smiled. "We get so many soldiers here."

Regina nodded and thanked the woman. She had been most kind, to both her husband and to her.

She returned to the hotel, gathered up her boys, loaded their wagon, said their farewells, and walked dejectedly to the train station. The few days rest had not cured the type of emotional exhaustion they all felt. The family had been struggling forward for some time on hope alone--the hope they could all remain together. With Gustav's departure, that hope was gone.

So Regina turned practical. She studied the train station's

maps on the wall because she now knew all trains do not necessarily lead to where one wants to go during a war. Her own map did not go far enough west to show Weida. There were, of course, no trains going where she needed to go, but the stationmaster said, "There will be a farm train coming after midnight that stops at every village. You might take it to Prague and then get another to Chiemnitz."

Regina wanted to scream at him, "Prague is east." And she certainly didn't want to return to the bombs of Chiemnitz. But she thanked him with controlled courtesy and said she needed to go northwest toward Zwickau and then Weida.

"Not many people are going back into Germany these days," he commented. "Most are going south. If you really must, you can take the train west to where it turns north. But you'll have to walk across the old border and pick up another train going north at the first German village.

Regina quickly purchased tickets to the border, feeling almost apologetic that she should be going in the opposite direction from everyone else. The stationmaster took her money, closed the window abruptly, and turned back to his boxed lunch.

Regina told the children stories while waiting for the train west, trying hard to keep their spirits up. With little enthusiasm, they climbed aboard the train and slouched in the seats. She was not surprised when the train stopped a few hours later, quite a way before reaching the Czechoslovakian border. A uniformed official walked through the car.

He said, "All passengers are required to detrain here and walk to the last station we passed. You can take another train from there back toward Prague.

"Going backward won't help us at all, " Regina explained anxiously to the official, while the other passengers moved toward the door in silent obedience. "How far are we from the border if we walk to the forward station instead?"

"I would not advise that," he said. There was an edge to his voice. "The border is not far, but the road is uphill. There will probably not be any more trains for several days until the bridge ahead is repaired. And besides, it's against regulations."

"But there is a road, isn't there? Is the river a big one? Is there any difficulty in crossing the border on foot?" Regina was embarrassed at her impulse to disobey the instructions of any official, but she had great concern to continue in the correct direction. She was firm in her determination not to go backward to the east.

The official hadn't expected either questions or defiance. He answered with a note of disgust, "There's a road following the tracks, the river has a boatman who might be hired. There are only German border guards, so unless you're escaping from something ..." He paused and looked directly at her, his eyes boring into hers.

She was angry with herself for conveying embarrassment. She stared straight into his eyes. "I think we will go forward, thank you."

"But you cannot go against regulations."

Regina motioned to the boys to gather their belongings. She herded them to the end of the car and lifted Franzi down the stairs. She stepped firmly up to the baggage car and asked its attendant to hand down their wagon. The boys piled it with the knapsacks and Regina lifted in Franzi. They began walking northwest.

The official grew irate as she moved away along the tracks, and he shouted after her, "Remember Czechoslovakia is part of the Third *Reich*. You cannot simply go where you wish!"

She did not answer.

"*Heil Hitler! Heil Hitler!*" He screamed at her. "You should be returning my salute!"

Regina did not look back

The man continued to demand loudly that she turn back.

She saw Rainer's frightened face as he kept peering back over his shoulder. She gripped his hand tightly and walked faster, until they had rounded a bend out of sight. There, she relaxed a bit. She was shaking, but she would not give in to panic. Regina was concerned about setting a bad example for her boys by disobeying authorities, but she also felt justified. She couldn't let them see her frustration, either. This lengthened trip must seem a further adventure, or they might become too discouraged to continue, and she certainly couldn't carry them all.

She had let them, and herself, slouch along for too long. She forced herself to stand tall, smile brightly, and talk about getting something to eat soon. The children trudged on without comment. She could feel them watching her warily. She didn't think she'd been very convincing in her show of defiance.

At the next village, they stopped at a bakery and a greengrocer, but the fancy little pastries the boys craved were too expensive, and the same was true of vegetables. Meat was out of the question. Regina settled on four *Brötchen* and a slice of cheese. They broke the cheese into four pieces and ate along the way.

Suddenly, Franzi yelled, "Stop!" He climbed down from the wagon, and plopped down beside the road, screaming at the top of his lungs, "I want to go home. We came all this way to see *Vati* and *Vati* went away again. I want to go home and see Nanny Elli. *Vati* can come for us at our own house. I'm not going another step. Not one!"

Franzi folded his arms and scowled. His blubbering continued, but he quieted a little to watch his mother's reaction. He rubbed his eyes with two grubby fists. Dirt mingled with his tears.

Willi and Rainer looked at their mother helplessly. She didn't know what to say. She had just explained to the children yesterday. Could Franzi not remember what she had said, or was he simply too tired to listen? How much could she tell the children that they would understand? Was she expecting too much of them? They were still so young to be traipsing across the countryside like vagabonds.

She tried again to explain, slowly, choosing her words carefully.

"Franzi, I told you. We can't go home now, not until the war is over. We don't even know if our house is still there. There's been a big air raid, and much of the city was burned. Don't you remember what it was like with bombs falling in Chiemnitz?"

"*Mutti*," began Willi, "I know you told us about not going home to Königsberg until later, and I understand that. But how do we know Nanny, and *Opa* and *Oma* Reh, and *Opa* and *Oma* Wolff are safe? What about our bears at the zoo?" His chin was quivering.

Rainer chimed in. "What about our house at the beach and all the seagulls? Can't we go there, or is everything in the whole world gone?"

Rainer and Willi both started to cry.

Franzi was again inconsolable. "*Mutti*, you didn't even bring my sailboat. What if all our friends and toys are gone?"

Regina put her head in her hands, fighting back tears herself. Perhaps she was doing this all wrong. Did she have a rebellion on her hands? She didn't know what to say, except the truth.

"I can't tell you any answers, boys, because I don't really know any answers myself. We can only hope those we love are all right and that our home will be waiting for us once the war is over. I fear the Russians may already be in Königsberg, or at least they're very close. Your *Vati* feels we'll be safer in Weida with *Tante* Gerda and *Onkel* Hans, so that's where we're going. *Vati* promised he would come for us there, as soon as he can."

Regina paused for a moment, hoping her words would be understood. "I'll tell you if I find out anything more, all right?"

The three kept watching her, their eyes seeming to search for more comfort than she could give.

She added, "I'm sure our family in Königsberg will be fine. They've been through air raids before."

Not like this one, she thought to herself, but there was no point in scaring the boys further. "So, that's why we can't go home right now. *Vati* wants us to go to Weida, so our job is to go to Weida. Do you understand?"

"Yes *Mutti*," said Rainer and Willi in unison.

Franzi was still blubbering, but he rose slowly and climbed back into the wagon.

"If those Russians get my sailboat, they better not break it!" he said, with an air of having had the last word.

Chapter 22

The weary family traveled as far as they could by day, taking turns pulling Franzi in the wagon. They gleaned any discarded vegetables for their meager evening meal. But the road led uphill, and the hillside farmers seemed to have used all food themselves. The deformed, dried out, or even rotten potatoes and turnips sometimes found along the way, had disappeared.

They stopped one night in the forest near a village called Nijdek, camping on the banks of a small stream running northwest. But Regina had nothing to boil in the can that night.

She could see how thin her boys had become. There was unmistakable evidence of malnutrition. Her own dress hung loosely on her shapeless body as well, but it was the pain in her children's eyes that forced her decision. Leaving the younger children in Willi's care, Regina walked to the nearest farmhouse. Though she had never before resorted to begging, her children needed something to eat. She burned with shame.

A large wooden farmhouse loomed in the growing darkness. It was attached to the barn in the fashion of the *Sudetten Deutsch.* Regina could barely make out the ramp slanting up to the barn's second floor where hay was normally stored so it could be forked down easily to the animals waiting underneath. The animal warmth, in return, helped to heat the adjoining house. She had never liked the pungent animal odors in such a farmhouse, but the residents never seemed to notice. This farmstead looked as though it had existed since the Middle Ages, with its thatched roof extending out to cover an outdoor privy and washstand.

I hate doing this, she thought, forcing her feet to march on, nonetheless.

When Regina knocked on the door, she heard rustling footsteps and a door slamming. She knocked again. A woman near her own age opened the door a crack and peered at her.

"What do you want?" she asked.

"We've been on the road for over a month and my children are terribly hungry. Do you have any food at all that I might give them? I've only a little money left, but I'm willing to work for you. I can cook or cut wood."

"We don't want anyone poking around here, and we don't have any food to spare, either." The woman started to push the door shut, but an older man appeared behind her and forced it open wider.

"Where are your children?" he asked. A sly sort of smile played around his lips.

"Waiting for me by the river." Regina answered, warily. Something was strange about this pair. From the rustling noises at her knock, she suspected they were hiding someone, perhaps an army deserter.

"Come out to the barn. I can give you a few potatoes if you'll pitch some hay. You look healthy, if a bit skinny."

The woman looked at him strangely, extending her hand to his arm as though trying to restrain him. She looked alarmed. "Joachim, we must have enough for the others."

"Hold your tongue, *Frau*," he ordered, pushing her hand away. "We can find a little extra if she's willing to work."

"Come on, Girl," he said, motioning Regina to follow him.

The woman stood watching from the doorway for some time before she sighed, and closed the door.

Regina noticed he used the terms 'girl' and '*frau*' as though they were proper names.

Once in the upstairs barn, he kicked aside some hay and pulled up a floorboard. A large tub of potatoes was hidden underneath. He held out three withered potatoes but, as Regina reached for them, he pulled them back. "You said you'd work. There's the pitchfork." He pointed to the tool leaning in a corner.

Regina picked up the pitchfork. "Where would you like the hay moved?"

He pointed. "Over there, you pretty little thing." With a smirk on his face, he moved between Regina and the barn door. "You can have the potatoes when we're through."

The hair on her neck prickled some primitive warning, but she needed those potatoes. She also knew her waiting boys would soon be getting frightened. Determined to hurry, she lifted the hay from one part of the barn floor and heaved it to where the farmer had indicated. Regina could see no reason why the newly indicated spot was any better than the old one, but it was not her barn. Her muscles strained from the unaccustomed action of pitching heavy forkloads.

Regina could feel the man watching her intently. Glancing warily over her shoulder, she saw him edge around toward the door. She kept working, but she could sense his motion. Suddenly, he grabbed her from behind and shoved her into the pile of hay. Instinctively, Regina fought, scratching at his face, kicking and pushing him away while trying to crawl backwards. The man grabbed her legs. She kicked him again and struggled to her feet. He pushed her against the wall, cutting off her escape, and knocked her down again.

Regina thought of the pitchfork. She rolled over toward where she had dropped it, kicked him again, and managed to swing to her feet in one fluid motion. The man scrambled to a crouched position. Regina pointed the pitchfork at him.

He laughed. "You won't use that thing on me. I'll tell the authorities you were trying to steal our food, and they'll lock you up. I'll bet you don't even have papers for this part of the country."

"Of course, I have papers," Regina lied, hoping she could bluff him. She wasn't sure she could actually stab anyone, and she hoped this vicious man wouldn't force her to find out.

"Come on, my little one," he cajoled, all the time maneuvering her around the floor. "Give me that pitchfork. Lie down on the hay, and I'll make you happy. I'll bet your man has been away for a long time now." He leered at her again. "Or is he already dead?" His voice was revolting, wheedling, suggestive.

She knew he was trying to distract her. Her eyes followed each move he made.

The man circled slowly around her, inching closer.

Regina moved around also, trying to keep the pitchfork between them to gain some space. When she had positioned herself in front of the door, he lunged toward her again. She could wait no longer. She swung at him hard with the flat side of the pitchfork to knock him off balance, then pushed the points straight at him.

He yelped and grabbed his side.

Regina hurtled out the door as he fell. She might be faster than he was, but she needed those potatoes. She ran down the ramp and hid behind a water barrel, shaded by the overhanging roof.

The man burst from the barn, cursing loudly, and limped in the direction of nearby trees where he obviously believed she had run. She could see him still holding his side.

Upon reaching the trees, he called out, "Where are you, Girl?" When silence was his only answer, he returned more quietly as though searching in the dark for some clue.

Regina was unsure whether to run, which would give away her hiding place, or wait for him to go away. Endless moments ticked by as she crouched with the farm team's harness hanging over her head. Torn between the two actions, another option swayed her decision--those potatoes. She stayed still.

The man stumbled around rattling implements in the tool shed and cursing loudly. A lantern appeared at the door of the house and the woman's voice called out, "What are you two doing out there? Get back in here, Joachim. I need you, now." There was a definite emphasis on the 'now.' With a final curse, and much muttering under his breath, the man walked toward the house, clumped across the porch and entered, slamming the door.

Regina couldn't suppress her giggle, as she realized this lout of a man was afraid of his wife. She could hear them screaming at each other. While they argued, she slipped back up the ramp, through the barn door, and picked up her three potatoes. She hesitated, then lifted the floorboard and took three additional good ones. It serves him right, she assured herself.

As Regina worked her way back downstream, she could already hear Willi hooting at a nearby owl. The owl kept answering back, and the two sounded almost alike. She smiled, realizing he was trying to distract the younger boys who were both afraid of the dark.

Rainer and Franzi were up a tree with Willi, waiting with solemn faces. Willi had kept them from following their mother, first by holding them down with force, then by making them climb the tree. Regina proudly held out her apron in front of them. They squealed with delight at sight of the potatoes, and shinnied down the tree in mere seconds.

For reasons she did not explain to them, Regina moved their camp further away from the farm before lighting their little fire and cooking finely chopped potatoes in water from the stream. The boys ate every bit of her potato soup, and pronounced it excellent.

Only after she had boiled the can to clean it did Rainer ask, "What did you have to pay for the potatoes, Mutti?"

Regina giggled. "Oh, nothing really. I just had to do a little work with a pitchfork." This time, she did not feel guilty about stretching the truth.

The boys soon fell asleep. Only then, did her uncontrollable shaking begin, as always, *after* danger had passed. What could she have done had the man been stronger or younger? And what would her husband have thought about her stealing the extra potatoes?

It was strange, but she almost felt she didn't really care what Gustav thought at this moment. His opinion shouldn't matter now because she was only out here alone because of him. She was sure he wouldn't have seen the humor in her ridiculous situation, either. They hadn't laughed together much before his final trip to the front. He had become so serious about everything by then.

Letting her mind roam to calm herself in the darkness, she remembered especially his reaction when she and Elli had discovered Operation Barbarossa, quite by accident. Gustav hadn't been amused at all.

During the spring and summer of 1941, Hitler had constantly proclaimed his satisfaction with his pact with Stalin, and touted benefits of the long-standing friendship between Germany and Russia. With their pact, they apparently had hoped to prevent intervention by England and France while they divided up Poland and other eastern countries. The ruse had not worked. Both England and France had declared war, though little had happened for some time. But Hitler must have already been secretly preparing to double-cross his former ally, because it happened so suddenly.

Elli and the boys had gone to the family's Cranz vacation house by the sea. Regina was to join them on the weekend so Elli could take a day off to see her family. On this occasion, Elli's brother was on leave from the *Luftwaffe* and accompanied them, so Elli decided to stay at the seashore with the boys. She took many photos of the boys with her heroic brother in his pilot's uniform. The children thought he was quite wonderful.

When Regina arrived by train the early morning of June 21, 1941, Elli told of her surprise to find thousands of German soldiers at Cranz also, camping on the quiet tourist beaches with all their equipment, tanks, and trucks.

Elli was a pretty *Fraulein*, and Regina noticed immediately, how many young men approached her. These soldiers talked freely about invading Russia.

"But Hitler said the Russians are our allies," said Elli.

One soldier explained. "Since the treaty, Russia has taken Bessarabia, Estonia, Latvia, and Lithuania. Hitler knows this territory in Russian hands threatens our growth to the east and to the oil fields we need. So...no more treaty." He dusted his hands together as though ridding them of something unpleasant.

This plan was apparently no big secret, as even the most common foot soldier seemed to know German forces were now gathering all along the border, a thousand mile front from the Baltic Sea to the Black Sea, all to betray their former ally. This particular group bragged they were crossing the three Baltic states and would, "...erase Leningrad from the earth in three weeks."

Elli was indignant. "Regina, hasn't Hitler read about Napoleon? I refuse to believe we'll ever lose a war again, but I have to say, this is not a smart move to start war in the east."

"I've never seen so many troops in one place," marveled Regina. "Surely whole divisions are lining up."

Suddenly, Elli grew pale. "What would happen if the Russians should discover this German concentration of troops before the attack begins?"

"They'd most likely start shelling our troops...wouldn't that be the logical thing to do if they felt threatened?"

"I think we should go home immediately, Regina. My brother said he would be going back to his unit shortly too. This whole thing really scares me."

"You're right. I'm amazed civilians were even allowed into the village or the beach. Why weren't there signs or warnings for us not to come here?"

"Maybe the generals thought the Russians might suspect something if there were not the usual vacationers."

"Doesn't it seem odd, though, that by keeping the beach normal-looking with so many people, they were putting those people at risk? This whole thing smells funny. I think we're being used as camouflage."

By this time, Regina was already moving to pack up the children's things. Elli gathered infant Franzi's diapers from the clothesline, still damp and unfolded, and stuffed them into one suitcase. With Regina carrying the baby and Willi and Rainer holding on behind the suitcases, the two women hurried to the station and took the first train going away from this newly activated eastern front.

Both Regina and Elli had been silent on the way home, gazing solemnly at the fortresses surrounding the city on the way. All seemed heavily manned. They heard the guns of Operation Barbarossa only a few hours later, during the dark early morning, as German soldiers once again raced with *Blitzkrieg* tactics through a country that had suddenly become an enemy. Regina didn't understand, and was afraid to ask why this was happening. It seemed so unrealistic to attack yet another country. When would it all stop?

When Gustav arrived home on leave, everyone told him the story simultaneously in a babble of excitement. His reaction had also seemed unrealistic to Regina.

"You don't seem surprised," she said, trying to make her voice sound natural. "We thought it laughable that the troops should have been so open and verbal about their plans."

"No, I'm neither surprised nor amused. I expected as much," he said calmly. He sent the boys with Elli to get ready for bed.

"You don't think it was strange that no one was warned not to go to the seashore? We could have been trapped there. I'm sure some people were."

"Surprise must be maintained at all costs, for these types of operations to be successful. The attack is already going well, and that's what matters."

That seemed all he intended to say on the subject and, for an instant, she wondered if surprise for the German invasion mattered more to him than his family. But she quickly dismissed that idea as unfair. He had always been loving and protective of his family. It was surely some type of coincidence.

By that time, Regina was beginning to think there was something odd about Gustav's work in the German Army. Most of the other men were gone all the time except for an occasional leave. But Gustav was gone for only a few days or weeks at a time, then home, then gone again. He frequently received telegrams, which he promptly burned. Mysterious visitors came, but he never introduced them.

He responded to Regina's questions by saying, "These men are doing special work for the *Führer*. Don't worry your pretty head about it, and don't ask foolish questions." Touching her nose gently with his finger and flashing his disarming smile, he seemed his usual, loving self.

Regina stopped asking questions. She didn't want the husband she adored to think her 'foolish.' But his secretive behavior worried her. What was the meaning of it?

Like other German citizens, Regina had believed Hitler's statements that war was inescapable, a necessary way to negate the Versailles Treaty. But invading Russia was, she felt, foolishness. Had she been naïve to think Hitler was a good leader because of his positive economic actions? Hitler's avowed dream to restore Germany's former glory now seemed a euphemism. Was it really only a dream of conquest? If so, she believed, it was becoming ugly.

But she had kept her opinion to herself that year. She was beginning to fear that Gustav didn't share it.

As the country became mired in war with Russia, citizens were persuaded to believe only their *Führer* could bring them through the crisis. It was proclaimed their duty to keep silent and support their Army, no matter what they believed personally.

Of course, no one wanted a repeat of the crisis caused by loss of the first war, but Regina wasn't sure German leaders were right this time, either. Sadly, she had doubts not only about her country's leadership, but also about her own husband's views as well. She was more confused than ever, and longed to talk everything over with Gustav, as they had done before the war. But he no longer shared his ideas.

Now, as she lay shivering on a stream bank in 1944, staring into another night without her husband, she felt almost angry for his having placed her in this situation. She wondered anew, why had he not trusted her with more information? Was she not supportive enough? Would things have turned out differently if she had understood more or asked more questions? Even now, she didn't know.

Regina was surprised at the intensity of her emotion. She let her salty tears run down her face to the earth since the boys were asleep and could not see. How could one deal with this kind of confusion, she thought, except to keep silent, protect her children, and hope for the best?

She realized now that her husband had known more than a common soldier should have known. How had he known for her to get the boys out of Königsberg just before the terrible firestorm bombing? How had he known the Russians were only a few kilometers away? He had not answered these questions, even in Karlsbad.

The mysterious letters and numbers on his original telegram must have been some type of code. The *Bürgermeister* had certainly assumed something from them or he wouldn't have been so rattled, she felt sure, nor would he have given her the *Ausweis*. What role had Gustav played? Did she really know her husband anymore?

At least, Regina thought, trying to cheer herself up, she was no longer afraid of her own shadow. After her pitchfork adventure, she knew she could defend her boys, and herself, if she were forced to do so. As for the rest, she no longer would believe all she was told. She wondered, however, if becoming skeptical was a good thing, or a bad.

Chapter 23

October brought colder weather at the altitude they had attained. In the morning, the damp mist frosted their coats and the surrounding grass. Regina led the boys in exercises to warm up stiff muscles before starting out.

The next two days they climbed toward the fortifications marking the old border. Most people had evacuated from this hilly pass after Germany annexed Czechoslovakia in 1938. Occasionally, Regina or the older boys asked Franzi to get out of the wagon and walk. Light as he was now, they were also weak. He wanted to pull the wagon too, but he couldn't manage. Rainer stumbled and fell more often, and Regina feared his strength was failing. None of the children chattered, sang, or even complained-- a bad sign. She knew she must find more nutritious food for them somehow.

Water rushed past as they followed a stream toward the mountain village of Graslitz. Regina worried whether her dead reckoning was correct, however, as the peaks were steeper than she had anticipated.

Rainer was the first to ask. "*Mutti,* are you sure we're going the right way? I'm tired of going uphill all the time."

"It does seem pretty steep, doesn't it?"

Willi asked, "We just have to get back into Germany, don't we?"

"I think so, son, because once in Germany there'll be more roads, and one of them should take us to Weida."

"This mountain seems a sort of long ridge. Do you think we could just go left at this level instead of climbing? Perhaps we can go around the ridge rather than over it."

Regina stood still a moment, shading her eyes to peer in all directions. She had last seen a map in the railway station in Karlsbad, but it hadn't shown elevation obstacles, only towns and roads. She wondered if she'd made the wrong choice in avoiding the return to Prague by train. It was too late now. Whatever the future held, they were committed to getting across the border.

But Willi might be right. If she remembered the map correctly, the border should curve to the south soon. Should she continue over the ridge, or try his suggestion? Evaluating their fatigue, she decided they'd have a better chance detouring west to avoid further climbing.

"All right, Willi. Let's try your idea."

Staying at roughly the same altitude, they gradually worked west around the worst of the peaks. Toward the end of the day, they saw the old border sign into Germany. They saw no border police. Had they deserted their posts as many other soldiers were doing?

Regina felt sure the river heading northwest into Weida was not far ahead. But the slanting light meant they would not make it to Marktneukirchen in time to find a train as she had hoped. They would have to camp outside yet another night.

"*Mutti*, can we stop?" asked Willi. "I can't go on right now. My feet are sore from the rocks again." He panted deeply.

Regina noticed they were all walking gingerly. Her own feet were swollen and bloody as well. But this is unlike Willi, she thought. He's normally the one who pushes the rest of us onward.

"Let's stop here, then," she answered. They all dropped their knapsacks and sat down wearily.

"But *Mutti*," said Rainer. "We didn't find any vegetables for dinner today, and we only found a few little berries at lunch time." The child's hunger burned in his eyes.

"I know, Rainer. It's because of higher altitude and cold. Nothing much grows up here. We'll be in a town tomorrow and we can buy some vegetables then."

"But I'm hungry now," whined Franzi. The little boy put his chin in his hands and sobbed.

"I know, dear." She didn't know what to do. "We haven't seen any farmhouses, either."

Regina was still wary of approaching farmhouses, even though they were again in their native land. She tried to distract the two older boys by having them help her look for mushrooms in the nearby forest. No one found any.

"It's no use, *Mutti*," said Willi. He leaned against a tree with a big sigh. Rainer and Franzi were both in tears.

Regina's desperation increased. She hoped it wasn't apparent to her exhausted boys.

"Rainer, go get a can of water at the stream," she ordered. "Willi, bring whatever twigs you can find, quickly." When this had been accomplished, Regina doled out one of the last matches from her carefully wrapped packet, and lit the twigs.

"Here, Willi. You watch the fire. I'll be right back."

She slid into the forest beyond sight of the boys. Relying on her father's botany lessons, she searched for a tree with thin bark. With her knife, Regina peeled off several strips of the bark and filled her pockets with leaves and grass.

Returning to the fire, she placed her gleanings into their cooking can. As the concoction heated, she stirred busily. She wanted to avoid the children's questions.

The boys waited, listlessly grumbling at each other near the edge of the fire while Willi bathed and wrapped Rainer's blistered feet.

When the leaves had boiled to the consistency of tea, Regina removed the bark strips from the can and quietly let them drop into the fire. She hoped they had at least provided some flavor. Then she served her boys what she called 'bark soup.'

"You may have as much as you like," she said with a sigh.

Regina guessed there was no nutrition in the bark broth or grasses, and she also suspected Willi didn't believe her ruse. He said nothing, but he watched her closely as though she'd lost her mind. The children sipped the green broth rather carefully, but their hunger kept them eating. At least it gave the younger children the illusion of having eaten something. After a while the boys dozed off under the coats, but they shifted around restlessly. Rainer whimpered in his sleep.

Crawling away behind a tree where the children could not hear, Regina knelt on the soft earth and sobbed. When there were no tears left and she at last lay quiet, she looked up at the sky. The stars blinked brightly and the world seemed deceptively peaceful.

"Dear God," she whispered. "This is the worst day of my life. Forgive me that I cannot even feed my children properly. I'm a failure, inadequate for this task." Her tenuous confidence had faded. Never in their previous life had she envisioned existence as they were living it now.

"What should I have done differently?" she asked softly. "What have I done wrong? My boys have endured cold, hunger, disappointment, and fear in silence. Please, God, make them forget it all. If you can do that, I promise I'll never mention this journey again."

"And please, God," she added, "let the war end soon. It doesn't matter who wins. Just please end this horrible killing. Give my children the strength to get to Weida. And please guide my husband back to us soon. Amen."

She looked again at the stars. Nothing had changed.

"Gustav," She whispered, "I need you. Where are you now, and what are you doing to help us?" Silence met her words. Not even a breeze rustled the leaves. She wondered if somewhere, he also, was looking at the stars and trying to encourage her.

She sat against a tree, hugging her knees and remembering that he'd been trying to help her one of the last times he had come home to Königsberg. It was after the German attack on Russia in June of 1941. Gustav was putting all their business papers in her name that fall. She had wondered why.

"It's merely a safer business practice," he'd told her, "in case anything happens when I return to the eastern front."

Regina had felt sad and angry that he would have to leave again so soon. "There shouldn't even be an eastern front," she said. "This whole war is stupid!"

Gustav looked at her sharply, recoiling, as from a blow. "Where did you get such radical ideas, Ina? You're not to question authority or get involved in anything against our government."

She heard distance in his voice, and glanced up at his face, fearing she had said too much.

His frown signaled conflict. But suddenly, as though by force of will, the frown flickered away and he crossed the room to put his arms around her. His tone shifted warmly.

"I need you, Ina. I love you. I'm only trying to help you and keep you safe. Promise me you'll concentrate on the boys, our business, our home, and speak publicly of nothing else. Someone might take you away. These political things are not for you to worry about." He kissed her and held her close. But he also seemed to be waiting tenuously for her to agree.

His strong words of concern brought her promise of silence, though she didn't feel her opinion had been radical at all. But her spirits soared with his kiss. His warmth always melted away any doubt that might nibble at the edges of her mind.

Their quiet moment ended when the boys entered for their usual bedtime romp with *Vati*, and the children's shrieks and shouts could be heard all over the house. Gustav played *"Hoppe, hoppe, Reiter"* holding tiny Franzi's hands while joggling him in time to the ancient nursery rhyme. The older boys sang along and waited impatiently for their turn to 'fall down' over their father's joggling knees. This was their favorite entertainment and, seeing her husband with his boys, their laughter had washed away Regina's remaining concerns about his political views.

The army was still advancing rapidly on the Eastern Front with Russia, then, so Gustav had taken pains not to let her worry. "All will be well, and we are winning," he assured her, as always, with loving kisses and generous attention for his family.

Regina had believed his words, and counted the weeks until he would be home on another leave.

But no leave came until a few short days at Christmas. Gustav brought some warm Russian boots made of felt as presents for the two older boys and little Franzi, who was barely trying to walk then. He also brought the portrait of Willi--the same one Regina now carried rolled in her knapsack. He said he'd been on temporary duty near Riga at the Russian prisoner-of-war camp. He'd given her no explanation of his role at the camp.

Regina's father had insisted on hosting a Christmas party while Gustav was home. She thought it mysterious that so many high-ranking officers came. She had known none of them, and had felt an instant dislike that was probably unwarranted. After all, they seemed to be friends of both her husband and her father. Watching them all greet each other, she had noticed how much her father and her husband were alike, especially in their political views.

Her mother had made a special holiday dish, *Rouladen*, meat rolled with pickles and spices inside, served with red cabbage. Regina helped with the painstaking work of beautiful terraced cookies filled with jam and frosted, *Terrassen*, as well as other family favorites: *Linzer Augen,* and *Sterne.*

But Regina knew *Gauleiter* Koch was increasingly strict about rationing procedures. So it seemed strange for her parents to have had meat, butter and sugar when no one else did.

"*Mutter*, where did you get all this food?" Regina asked, while they toiled together in the kitchen.

Her mother only put her finger to her lips. "Shh. You mustn't worry yourself about it, *Liebchen*. Your father has connections for food supplies to entertain the officers."

No one answered questions anymore. It seemed to Regina that everyone she knew was patronizing her as though she were a child--her father, her husband, and now her mother as well. She kept busy in the kitchen, but she couldn't help listening through the open door to the parlor.

The officers sang, drank, and ate for hours and Regina could hear them asking Gustav all sorts of questions. "Hey, Wolff, what's the thought at headquarters on how effective we've been at Leningrad?"

"We moved swiftly," Gustav had answered, "until we reached the gates of the city. But since early December we've been bogged down in the mud and snow and we'll have to wait for next year to get rolling again. No one expected it to snow in early October. Those moving toward Moscow and Stalingrad have been forbidden to retreat, even just to regroup."

"Heads will roll—especially Prussian heads," said another man quietly. Several nodded.

"They already have. Rundstedt resigned in November and there may be drastic changes in high command. Guderian may be next."

One very tall officer said, "Let's choose another topic. That one is too depressing. Wolff, you're a lucky man, flying all around the front lines in that special little plane. And what do you think we should do with the Ruskies interned at Riga?"

Regina strained to hear Gustav's answer, but raucous laughter of the men met his response. It chilled her blood, though she could not have said why.

"Next time you fly to Berlin, tell them our troops haven't received proper clothing for the Russian winter. Even fires don't keep us warm in that God-forsaken steppe. I dread going back."

"With so many generals getting relieved of command, not many in Berlin seem concerned about warm uniforms. When you go back, you'll find that even the oil in the Panzers is thick from the cold, so be careful." Regina heard Gustav laugh in a strange, disgusted tone.

Regina wondered why these men wore various officers' uniforms with medals and insignia, while Gustav wore a uniform that held no rank or insignia at all. He was only a common soldier, yet these officers all accepted him as an equal. She thought common soldiers did not fraternize with officers, especially these fellows of high rank.

Another disconcerting idea entered her mind as she groped for answers. Why was a common soldier flying anywhere at all? And what was her father's connection to this group that they all came to his party so eagerly? They seemed to hold him in high esteem. Regina wondered why. There had been no time to ask questions since she and her mother were wholly occupied with serving these military guests.

Her father brought in his new movie camera and recorded the party. Willi and Rainer played with the officers' hats and Russian medals the men had captured for gifts to their children. When the men began the *Horst Wessel Lied*, a famous *Nazi* song, the children sang along, goosestepping to the lively music, copying the officers. They stood with upraised salutes.

Regina felt uncomfortable to have her boys accepting the attention of these militaristic men. The music was stirring, but as she listened to the words, *"Die Fahne hoch die Reihen fest geschlossen, S.A. maschiert,"* she shuddered, and ran forward to get the boys out of the living room. She didn't like the boys hailing the dreaded *S.A.* and its counterparts, the *S.S.* and *Gestapo*, no matter how popular the war-like marching song. "Lift colors high, close ranks" and such—it was too much like the war mongering which already threatened her whole world.

"Here, boys," she intervened. "Why don't you come with me into the kitchen. I'll get you some cookies."

Gustav moved between her and the little boys. "Ina, they're fine here. I'm sure our guests are quite pleased with their behavior." He squeezed her hand, expecting her to understand.

"Let them be, Regina," said her father, laughing at their antics.

Regina retreated, thinking that her father must have prepared her carefully to be the wife of her husband—always obedient. What was their connection anyway? She could hear the officers laughing as they lapsed into drinking songs.

Regina watched as one of the officers called Willi to him and presented him with a beautiful Russian medal. It was in the shape of a huge, sparkly blue star.

"For keeps?" the child had asked.

"Of course, for keeps," replied the jovial officer, shaking the child's hand formally. "The Ruskie will no longer need it."

Willi had loved the attention as much as the medal.

Regina felt resentful these officers were taking away the dwindling time she had to spend with her husband. She rattled the dishes forcefully, hoping the guests would take the hint and leave. But they chatted with Gustav and her father late into the night.

When she and Gustav were finally alone, she voiced her hurt feelings and discomfort.

"I didn't want a party, Gustav. I wanted to be at home, alone with you. We've had so little time together."

"I know, Ina, I wanted to be with you also, but this had been arranged for quite some time." He lifted her in his arms and carried her gently to their bed.

"Why didn't you tell me? And who were all those people, anyway? Both you and they had strange things to say." She tried to remain focused until he should give her answers.

Gustav put his fingers over her lips. "I beg you to be patient, my little one. You must forget anything you heard. This party was... important. I promise I'll make it up to you." He had kissed her and pulled her close to his warm body.

She had quickly become silent and loving. Neither of them wanted to speak of this being perhaps their last night alone together. How could a wife ask questions that might start an argument when her man was going off to war? If she did so, and he never came back, how could she cope with such guilt?

Ironically, in 1944, it was no longer any secret that mud and snow had ruined the German Army's offensive in Russia and now the Russians were coming to Germany in retribution. Regina thought now that perhaps Hitler's refusal to allow the great generals to retreat and regroup as necessary may have contributed to this defeat.

The breeze of the forest quickened. Sitting on the cold ground, Regina tightened her shawl around her shoulders. The stars were beginning to fade, and she was still trying to find meaning in everything she remembered about that last Christmas together. She felt a twinge of anger that she was dragging her children through a war and a wilderness purely at Gustav's request, and she still didn't understand his motives or his secrecy.

She rose and walked over to check on her sleeping boys. She tucked her coat more firmly under Rainer's shoulder, where he had tossed off the cover.

Regina's mind now searched all possibilities. She wished she had understood Gustav's army job. Why he was in so many places. How had he known so much about the war so early? Was he in procurement, as he had said, perhaps for all the battlefronts? Was he some type of courier for the army or in some secret intelligence unit?

Up until now her fears were only of how much danger he might be in. Now she felt something almost sinister in the mystery of it all. *No, that could not be! Push that thought away.* He had assured her his work was important, but not worthy of discussion.

He hadn't told her enough about his job for her to understand it. Why not? Why couldn't he have given her real answers?

Perhaps she'd been afraid she might endanger him in some way if she'd asked more questions? A cold chill caught her by surprise, and she shivered. Was there something about what Gustav was doing that he didn't want her to know?

Regina realized now, almost without fear, perhaps she hadn't really wanted to know the answers before. She'd been so afraid of everything in those days.

His decisions had impacted every corner of her life, and the children's. Yet she had simply accepted everything he said at face value. Had she been wrong to love him so much and trust him so completely?

Regina looked down at her children sleeping on the ground. How could she ever explain to them what had happened during this awful war, when she had no answers for herself?

"Stop this!" she told herself abruptly. "It does no good now." She tried to block her own constant analysis of things impossible to analyze, to push down her doubts. She felt numb and exhausted from the effort.

Regina finally stretched out on the ground beside her children. Nothing matters now except finding the children some food in the morning. She lifted her aching head. "One more day, God. Please just one day at a time."

Chapter 24

The cold woke Regina early, but sunlight sparkled everywhere, bouncing off dewdrops on the frosted grass. The day promised accomplishment and determination. She brushed off her dress and breathed deeply to fortify herself with the brisk fall air. Perhaps Weida, their new destination, really would be the safest town in Germany as their wartime enemies closed in from all sides. She clung to the thought.

The boys woke reluctantly and complained of stomachaches. Regina assumed it resulted from her bark soup. Suddenly they jumped up and were all three violently sick. But once they had rid themselves of the vile concoction, they seemed a little better. At least they had slept, and they had heard no enemy planes. Forests and fields still felt safer than cities and villages.

They needed to hurry to the next town, Marktneukirchen, so Regina could buy food. They found a road and walked beside it, hoping for a ride from a passing farmer. The sun climbed high overhead. A boy of about twelve came along on his bicycle and offered Franzi and his washtub a ride on the back. Willi, Rainer, and Regina could then move a little faster.

Franzi was waiting expectantly for them in front of the first bakery inside the town. Though she had a few *Pfennigs* left and hoped to buy a bit of cheese and bread, the town was larger than she had anticipated. She still felt some nervousness about getting caught without papers in a larger town. Regina also feared the larger towns wouldn't take her Königsberg ration coupons anyway, so she hustled the boys along to the next small village, Adorf, at the best pace their tired legs, vocal complaints, and empty stomachs could manage. Thankfully, it was only a couple of kilometers further.

A gaggle of housewives had formed a line for Adorf's grocery store, gossiping as they waited. "Where are you from, and where are you going?" one called out, as the others gathered around the newcomers. While they were curious about Regina's arrival, they seemed relieved to hear the young mother and her

children were moving on instead of staying in this village.
Regina was to find this attitude prevalent along her journey
into central Germany.

One woman, apparently the self-appointed spokeswoman for
the group, said, "Forgive us if we're not being particularly
hospitable. We've been flooded with refugees from the east, and
they'll soon start coming from the west as well."

Another added, "Our enemies are closing in on us like
pincers from both sides. Crops are scarce, our men are gone, and
there's been disruption from the bombing. Women and children
have done all the planting, tending, and harvesting. They should
get the food."

Regina nodded in understanding, and started to say again
that she and her children would be moving on, but another woman
interrupted.

"This season's food supply is almost gone. We've little
stored for the winter because we're already using our reserves
feeding all these extra people." She sounded resentful.

"You understand?" the first woman asked plaintively.

Regina did understand, even though it didn't help her
immediate situation. Surely the women could see for themselves
the condition of her children, but they said nothing.

Regina reminded them for the third time that the family was
moving on to Weida. When she found, as she had suspected, that
her food coupons were not accepted in this town either, she felt
dejected. But four women consulted together. Then they
contributed *Brötchen* so each of the travelers had a piece of bread.

"We can't let your children starve," said the spokeswoman,
dismissing Regina's tearful thanks.

The young mother was able to buy a potato from a street
vender outside the bakery, and she cut it in three pieces for the
boys to eat with their bread rolls. They were ravenous and couldn't
refrain from gobbling the raw food far too fast. Regina feared they
would be sick again. "Eat slowly," she reminded them, and forced
herself to eat her own *Brötchen* slowly as well.

"If you take the northeast road to Ölnitz," the spokeswoman
continued, "and then go on to Plauen, that's only about eight

kilometers from here. Then it's only about another twenty
kilometers the rest of the way. Just follow the river. There's a
bridge across the river that will lead you into Weida, if you go
parallel with its bank. At least the bridge was still there a week
ago," she added with the usual wartime skepticism.

Finding they were at last on the right road gave both Regina
and the children a burst of energy. To encourage the boys, she
drew a rough map in the dirt so they could see the worst part of
their journey was behind them. As they left Adorf, one old woman
hobbled on her cane to the end of the street to point them onto the
proper road out of town.

The family kept to their usual routine, but walked directly on
the road. They hadn't seen strafing planes for many days. Regina
assumed this meant they were farther from the front. She still
pulled the boys into the woods to avoid any stranger that seemed
threatening. With everyone desperate to get away from the fighting
and possible capture by the Russians, many soldiers she believed
to be deserters passed along the road, taking whatever they could.

Regina and the boys moved in a direction opposite from
other traffic. Most people were traveling south in an attempt to
reach the rural Bavarian highlands where they felt they'd be safer.
All knew by now the cataclysm was coming. But Regina had a
definite destination, so she and the boys simply nodded at anyone
whose path they crossed.

In the late afternoon, they stopped to rest and picked some
late season, dry berries that Rainer had found beside the road. By
evening, they had passed through Ölnitz and were again in the
countryside. Rainer, who liked to wander off the road a little, came
back towing a skinny old cow. The cow was on the other end of
what looked suspiciously like his shoestrings, tied together.

"She followed me, *Mutti*," he insisted. "I petted her and she
followed me back. Can we milk her?" He sounded so sincere. Did
he really believe what he said was fact?

"She's almost bursting, *Mutti*," said Willi. "Don't you think
she's uncomfortable?"

The mother tried to rationalize. They might be doing the cow
a favor since she needed milking, and they could certainly use just

a little of her milk. But Regina would have been ashamed to steal milk in her old life, and she didn't want to add to her already impressive list of sins.

Yet, the expectant looks of her hungry children finally washed away whatever guilt she felt, and she decided to try her hand at milking. As a city girl, she had only a vague idea of how this chore should be done. The cow kept turning back with doubtful eyes to watch her. Regina squeezed and squeezed, but made little headway. She couldn't hit their little cooking can with the few drops that emerged.

She scowled at the boys as they tried to suppress their giggles. Finally Franzi brought his washtub. It was at least a bigger target, but Regina still could not get much milk out.

"Here, let me try, *Mutti*," offered Willi.

Rainer gloated. "Remember, *Mutti*, we went to camp on the farm in Bavaria a couple of summers ago. I bet we can do this better than you can."

Willi and Rainer took turns and were, indeed, better at the job. Finally, each of the four had some milk to drink with the hard bread Regina had saved from the last village. She removed the shoestring 'halter' and sent the cow back into the field.

After walking a bit further, however, the boys conspired gleefully about 'finding' another cow the next day.

Regina wondered how she could establish a moral compass for her boys to learn right from wrong, once they were safe again. *If* there is such a thing as safety, she thought. She would never again feel sure.

They came across a haystack on a small hill. The boys crawled into its side and soon slumbered contentedly. It was hours before Regina could sleep, and her thoughts, as always, wandered away from her present condition. She wondered if everyone else took their life and safety for granted when no war threatened them.

Gustav should have reached the front by now, she thought. Everyone knew the eastern front was now a debacle, folding in on itself from the determined Russian onslaught. The German soldiers were losing ground fast, and those captured were shipped to Russia as prisoners. Was Gustav still alive? Was he even now lying wounded in some hospital to the east... or worse? She refused to consider that they'd had no time to resolve questions in Karlsbad. They would need to *make* time later, after the war.

Regina shifted her thoughts to others. Were her parents still able to live in their downtown apartment now that the city had been bombed so severely? Where was Elli? Had she been able to escape alone? Regina wanted to turn off her mind and shut out all the bad thoughts and questions, but they wouldn't go away.

Had the Russians already taken their lovely home and destroyed their cherished possessions? Could they ever go home again? Regina tried not to think beyond her next move--one step at a time. But even in this seemingly peaceful setting, it was hard to believe that anything would ever be the same as before.

The roar of airplanes high in the dark sky brought her back to reality. They were coming from out of the west, and too high for a nearby target. She tried to imagine where they might be flying, and who might be the recipient of their terror tonight. How long could this go on? Regina consciously prayed the war would end soon, though she realized the only way this could happen was if Germany lost. Even another Versailles-like treaty couldn't be worse than this chaos and uncertainty.

Worst of all was what the war was doing to families--not only her family, but other families as well. It was time to end it.

Regina must have unconsciously spoken the words out loud, because Willi was suddenly at her shoulder. "*Mutti*, what should we end?"

"We're almost where we can end this journey, son," she fibbed, not wanting to frighten him by sharing her thoughts.

"Dawn's almost here, *Mutti*, and I don't think you've slept yet," said Willi. "Let me stand guard so you can sleep a little."

He was growing up much too fast. But Regina did actually doze off for nearly an hour and felt more rested when she opened her eyes. She could see Willi still watching with a determined look, as he wrapped his coat around himself tightly. Bless him, she thought with both sadness and pride, as she rose and roused the two youngest boys.

As they reached Plauen, Regina found a small

Lebbensmittel--or food store. The unfriendly owner seemed not to trust anyone and wanted something tangible for her scarce produce. Regina regretfully bartered one of the family's beautiful silver pieces for food. The boys helped their mother select what food might equal the value of the silver ladle, but the woman obviously didn't think it was worth as much as what they'd selected.

She shrieked and howled, "The enemy is coming and my family will starve with what you want to trade."

Regina refrained from stating the obvious fact that her own family was already starving without this trade.

"We'll put some of the produce back," she said, "though I know our silver is worth much more."

Reluctantly, the boys returned the few carrots, leeks, and potatoes to the shelves, keeping only two of each.

Regina felt cheated. She knew that the silver was worth more, but it was already gone now, and there was no use arguing with this woman. Sometimes, Regina thought, hardship brings out the worst in people, and sometimes the best. With this woman, it was definitely the worst.

As the family walked away with the few vegetables, Willi commented, "What a strange person. We've sure had some scary times considering this trip was only supposed to be a short train ride."

"Yes, I'd assumed we'd arrive in four or five days. If I'd known how this trip would turn out, we might not have come." To herself, she admitted she had brought her children into this situation solely on faith in her husband. And now she was painfully aware he might not have been right, after all.

Regina wasn't sure of the date, but she knew it was beginning to crisp up for winter. Willi had chosen a field across a footbridge for them to stop for the night. When they awoke, a sprinkling of early snow had fallen atop their old coats. They rose and shook it off wearily. Regina knew they needed to hurry now, yet they'd been moving slower and slower. Fatigue wracked her whole body.

None of their shoes or clothing was adequate for cold

weather, and the boys continually shivered. Since Rainer now wore Regina's coat dangling down his legs, she wrapped herself in a shawl. But nothing seemed warm enough. The children still didn't complain, though their faces seemed pinched. Franzi had a strange rash on his legs. However, Regina and the older boys walked doggedly on, taking turns pulling Franzi in the battered wagon.

So far, Regina felt they'd been fortunate with only hunger, cuts, scrapes, blisters and Willi's illness. But she knew this extra dampness and cold would bring chills and perhaps another severe illness. They must find shelter soon. But how could they go faster with everyone so weak?

Shortly ahead, the main, paved road veered off to the north at a crossroad. They started along this northern road, but Regina speculated that only the dirt trail angling off to the left was aimed at Weida. Another dilemma. Should they continue along the main road, which again crossed the river and circled around Weida before turning into town from the north, or cut across the countryside on the dirt lane, seemingly the most direct route to the south end of town?

The skies, gray as usual for this time of year, offered only more cold and snow. Rainer was sniffling and had the beginnings of a fever. Regina knew she had to take the most direct route, even though walking would be more difficult on the small, rougher lane. It also was less likely they'd encounter a ride on the more deserted path. She hoped the church spires in the distance might be those of Weida. They turned down the loneliest trail.

Less than half an hour later, an old couple came along in a farm wagon with their equally old, tired dog and a small child. The little girl of about three or four, Franzi's age, called out to ask her *Opa* to give the group a ride. The couple at first scowled, then conferred, shrugged, and stopped to help the family and their wagon up behind the seats. The two sway-backed, skeletal horses stood on first one leg and then another, swatting flies with their tails.

Once the farm wagon was moving and civilities were exchanged, the children immediately were laughing and chattering with each other. Regina wondered if she'd been worrying too much. Perhaps children were far more resilient than she could tell. She was putting adult worries upon them when perhaps they were accepting everything as simply part of life. How she wished she could make it a better life.

"Well, you're on the shortest path for Weida," said the old man when Regina named their destination. "You'll arrive on the southern end of town. It sits on a bend at the junction of two rivers."

Regina said, "I'm trying to remember what Hans and Gerda wrote me about their home sitting in a small valley. I assume it wouldn't be far from one of the rivers."

"I hope your brother and sister-in-law are still in Weida," said the woman. "Some homes were destroyed in two recent bombing raids and people moved away."

"I thought Weida was too small to get bombed."

"The raids were probably accidental," the man answered. "We've seen bombers simply dump their leftover bombs on what must look like unpopulated areas below. There hasn't been as much damage in Weida as in larger cities. You can get information on all remaining residents at the *Rathaus*."

Regina hadn't considered the possibility Gerda might no longer be at home. She had dragged the boys so far. Surely such a devastating idea couldn't be true.

The old couple helped Regina and the boys from the wagon where they turned into their farm, and the woman gave each of the boys a raw turnip. Franzi and little Irmgard, the couple's orphaned granddaughter, giggled and waved to each other, as her family drove off.

Children recover, Regina thought, praying it was true.

They weren't far from Weida now, but the evening was cold and rain was again starting to fall. Regina didn't want to sleep outdoors again tonight, so they pressed on, walking as fast as they could to keep warm. Franzi cried most of the time, as he complained of the cold. Even Willi and Rainer wore strained, silent looks as they tried to keep up, or even set the pace, tucking their hands under their arms when they weren't pulling the wagon. Rainer was still feverish.

Regina knew they dared not stop. It seemed they might soon have to abandon their wagon, because of both the roughness of the lane and their fatigue. Regina carried the sleeping Franzi one last time so the other boys could pull it more easily without his weight. The wagon might be important to them later, since they had little else. Regina remembered when Franzi had been a chubby little boy with rosy, fat cheeks. Now he was such a thin child, yet he felt unbearably heavy, curled against her shoulder. She tried to keep a steady pace.

"Please, God," she prayed, "Please." She had no energy for the rest of her prayer. God already knew their needs.

Chapter 25

The family entered the southern end of Weida shortly before midnight. A watchman challenged them, growling, "You're violating curfew." But when he saw their fatigued condition, he helped them to a nearby public bomb shelter and handed down blankets from an upper shelf. The floor was damp and cold, but the boys fell soundly asleep, curled up on benches.

Regina collapsed in relief. It was the end of their journey. She no longer needed to worry about wild animals, marauding deserters, or analyzing her own confusing thoughts. And best of all, Gustav would soon come to find them in Weida.

When they awoke, townspeople were already walking to work at a small spinning mill down the valley. Perhaps they *would* be safe here, Regina thought. If there were such things as spies, she hoped any lurking in Weida had reported it as an inconsequential town.

They walked to the *Rathaus* to register their arrival. The authorities asked not only who Regina was looking for, but also who in Königsberg might be looking for her. It gave her hope that the ingrained German system for *Ordnung*—order, even in probable defeat, was still helping lost refugees find their loved ones. She listed every family member and friend she knew.

The clerk looked up Hans and Gerda's name on his list and said, "Your brother's house has been partially destroyed. Your sister-in-law is living in a *Baracke* near the town square fountain."

Regina had noticed these barracks-like, pre-fabricated buildings springing up all over Germany. As families were bombed out, survivors gathered together in these temporary shelters with a communal kitchen. Like permanent houses, they were painted with the strange dull gray paint Hitler had assured his citizens was 'invisible to bombers.' Regina knew of no one who was convinced the paint worked.

She followed the clerk's directions to her sister-in-law's building and found her room.

"Regina!" Gerda cried out as they clung to each other. "I was afraid I'd never see any of our family again. And look at these boys...how big. How did you get here?"

Regina promised to share their story in the evening because Gerda had to leave for work. She seemed happy to share her tiny room, no matter how crowded. Later in the day, a matron came to give them access to a vacant room next door, so the family had two rooms by the time Gerda arrived home.

Gerda told Regina of Hans' army service on the western front. "The Americans are marching across France," she said. "Our German troops have fallen back. But in his last letter, Hans said his unit was making an entrenched stand in the Hürtgen Forest and causing many casualties among the enemy." Her voice rose shrilly. "He said they were ordered to defend the *Führer's* cause to the death." Tears ran down Gerda's face.

The boys listened with wide, frightened eyes.

Regina held Gerda's hand and tried to comfort her as she sobbed.

"I can see no logical reasoning behind such an order. Surely the war will end before that happens," Regina said, hoping she was right.

Hills surrounded three sides of the town. On the hill west of their Baracke an elite group of tankers and artillerymen, the Waffen SS was entrenched. Any enemy air raids on Weida were undoubtedly to bomb this Kaserne or army base, but it was well camouflaged. It was never hit.

After many weeks with no news, Regina was again in daily contact with a radio. She hated the *Führer's* constant exhortations that everyone should fight to the death. Why? How would the sacrifice of their citizens help anything at all beyond Hitler's own pride? He was now asking old men and boys to take up pitchforks and shovels to go fight the enemy who had guns and planes. It sounded insane to the young mother as she anxiously watched her own little boys.

Gerda remarked, "You heard, didn't you, about the military men who tried to kill Hitler?"

"Yes. I heard the attempt was at Wolf's Lair. That's not far from Königsberg." Regina realized the previous news on her clandestine BBC radio had been accurate, but she wasn't yet sure she could trust Gerda with that information.

Gerda said, "It's almost as though this has happened too late for anyone to be much concerned."

"I've not heard anyone expressing outrage or sympathy toward either the *Führer* or the accused, except on the radio."

" I don't really care," said Gerda. "The only thing worrying me is when Hans will come home and whether or not we can find another day's food."

Regina laughed, glad her sister-in-law might have feelings similar to her own. "The *Führer* would call that a 'defeatist' attitude, but I doubt anyone cares anymore." Regina believed most citizens were simply too tired of haranguing and lies, though they would have been afraid to say so out loud.

Because of her business experience, Regina was assigned work with the registering agency at the *Rathaus*, keeping track of people leaving and refugees arriving. Gradually, the family settled into relatively normal living, at least for wartime conditions. Willi watched the two younger boys while his mother worked a few hours each day. She received a small wage and new ration coupons for Weida. Between Regina and Gerda, they were able to provide meager meals of whatever happened to be available. Of course, it was never enough to completely satisfy three growing boys, but it was, at least, better than being on the road with no provisions at all.

They were all lean, but life was more stable. Rainer overcame his fever once he was again living indoors. Clothing was scarce, but piles of second-hand, discarded clothing and shoes arrived at the *Rathaus* occasionally. No one knew where the shipments came from, but it helped outfit the women and children for another cold winter. With little for sale, and less money, townspeople were reduced to bartering for their needs.

Regina and the boys took the wagon further into the woods each day to gather sticks for firewood. Forests around the town were picked clean, and many evenings they came home with only tiny, damp twigs that smoked up the kitchen when lit.

When Regina's workday was over, she asked Willi, "Where did you go this morning?"

"Oh, just chasing frogs down at the river."

Or some days it was "...digging for frozen turnips in the fields near town." But Willi always saw to it that he and the younger boys were cleaned up when Regina and Gerda arrived home. Sometimes this must have been a difficult task, she thought, judging by Franzi's ears, which were frequently dripping water where Willi or Rainer had scrubbed them bright red.

Regina never questioned them further. She realized Willi was doing the best he could.

There were communal toilets in the back yard, but bathing was a luxury. The *Baracke* didn't have running water so it was carried from the town's well. Cold sponge baths in Franzi's little washtub were most common. Standing in line for their turn to draw water, or washing clothes with the other women in the street near the well were Regina and Gerda's only social occasions. With their heads bound in kerchiefs, the fashion statement of women at war, they listened eagerly as daily gossip was exchanged. Talk was never of politics, but of daily problems or of their men at the front. Letters were so scarce that anyone's news became everyone's news.

"I wonder if there's any way to celebrate the coming of Christmas?" Gerda asked one day while the boys were playing with other children in the square. "There doesn't seem much reason to celebrate right now, but for the boys..." Her voice trailed off into silence as she stared into the pantry, almost empty since food rations had been cut yet again.

"We always had a visit from St. Nicolaus at home in Königsberg." Regina said, remembering happier times.

"Who was it? Gustav?

"No. Gustav wasn't always home, and even when he was there, the boys would've figured it out if he disappeared when Santa arrived. But Elli would pretend to go to her father's home for the holidays and the boys would wave goodbye. Then she would sneak back into the house and appear in a Santa suit, complete with beard and all."

"Did the children ever guess?"

"No. Elli could even make her voice low, and the beard

always fooled them."

"I wish we could do something nice for them this year, but we have so little."

"We'll manage something," Regina assured her. "My worst fear is that we've heard nothing from either Hans on the western front, or Gustav on the eastern. I keep wondering where they are and what Christmas will bring for them." Loneliness haunted her every day's activities.

The evening radio news was never good. Goebbels had previously promised a massive offensive to drive back the Americans to the west. Regina feared the casualties would be heavy on both sides. But this night, the broadcaster had not mentioned the great offensive at all.

"Since they aren't mentioning their western battle across the Rhine to retake Belgium, I presume it has failed," she said.

It was the wrong thing to say. Gerda began again to cry.

"Don't worry," Regina tried to console her, "Hans will be all right. He's my brother and I know he's tough. Perhaps he'll be home by Christmas."

She tried again brightly. "The boys will manage to make Christmas interesting, and we still have a chance to sing. The *Bürgermeister* is promising a traditional midnight church service, no matter what happens."

But the conversation forced Regina to recognize the thought she'd been avoiding--that they'd be spending yet another Christmas alone.

Regina had written to her parents, *Herr* Busch, and Elli soon after the family's arrival in Weida, hoping they would still be safe. It was almost Christmas before she received an answering letter from Elli. She read it out loud to Gerda.

Elli's news was not encouraging. Their house in Königsberg was intact, but the business was not. "The big enemy raid in August caused a firestorm that destroyed almost everything. Most all the buildings in the harbor area are gone," she wrote. "Nothing but smoky sticks rise above the docks, with all those old iron cranes guarding non-existent businesses.

"*Herr* Busch came to say he'd saved your money from one

bank by transferring it to a Nürnberg bank before the raid. He hopes you or Gustav can gain access to it should you reach there. The account number is enclosed," she said. "The rest was lost when the other bank burned. The bank gave out promissory notes (enclosed) to be honored 'sometime after victory.'"

"Well," interrupted Gerda. "I guess we know what that means."

"I suppose so. It doesn't seem to me 'victory' is possible." Regina continued reading.

"*Herr* Busch also said he can send a few pieces of your household goods to Weida on business shipping invoices he was able to save, as long as the freight trains are running. He said he would choose the pieces himself if he didn't hear from you soon. He took his own salary and left mine here. He and his old wife are planning to get out of Königsberg this winter and he advised me to do the same, but where would I go? This is home."

Regina sighed. "I fear Elli is too stubborn to face the facts of defeat, and I know she won't listen to anyone about this."

"It's probably too late, anyway."

"But dear *Herr* Busch." Regina held up the letter as she spoke. "How many employees would be so honest and thorough under such terrible circumstances?"

Gerda only nodded, urging Regina to continue reading, as they were both hungry for news from home.

It was growing dark, and Regina called the boys to clean up. She lit the lamp and began reading again, hurrying to finish before they came in for dinner. "The university and the *Schloss*—the palace--and most all of downtown were destroyed. Even the *Dom* cathedral's roof fell in and burned, though the tomb of Immanuel Kant, adjoining the cathedral wall, wasn't damaged at all. Isn't that strange?"

Regina couldn't help but laugh. While Hitler's philosophy of threatening people was being bombed out of existence, Kant's philosophy of never using others for one's own purpose seemed to have remained intact. She wondered if it was her imagination, or was there not some tremendous irony in the contrast?

The next paragraph of the letter, however, sobered her

completely.

"I took your mother to the train. She's coming to live with you and your brother," Elli's letter continued. "Her home and the drugstore were both bombed out, and she's been staying here with me."

Regina found no mention of her father at all. What could that mean? Had he stayed behind to fight, or had he been hurt? He was too old for the Army. Surely he wouldn't stay behind and allow her mother to travel so far alone. Had something happened to him? And if her mother's journey was as difficult as her own had been, Regina felt sure the older woman couldn't survive it. Would she lose both her parents to this awful war?

Gerda interrupted her thoughts. "When will she come?"

Regina glanced quickly at the letter. "Your mother should be there by Christmas if the railroad tracks are still operative. She'll tell you all the news. Since the Russians keep trying to overrun the one remaining rail line west, the one next to the Baltic Sea, our soldiers are defending it fiercely, and have repaired it quickly when it's damaged. It's Königsberg's only route out now, unless we try to go by sea, and that route may be dangerous because of Russian submarines. The rail line must remain open! The radio reports our *Führer* has appointed a brave, new general named Lasche who will defend the city, and Hitler has new secret weapons coming any day now. I'll be safe here because I know Germany will still win. Don't worry about me."

The two women sat silently when the letter was finished, immersed in thoughts neither could verbalize.

Finally, Regina couldn't refrain from speaking any longer. She needed to confide in someone. "Poor Königsberg--and poor Elli," she said. "Elli has never lost her faith in Hitler. She can still believe in all those so-called 'secret weapons.' All along the way as we've traveled across Germany and Poland, I've seen the condition of the people, persecution of religious groups, hungry refugees, and cities and villages flattened after repeated bombing raids. I can no longer believe in anything political. Especially not that our military can turn the tide of war."

"Shh, Regina," Gerda said, startled. "You mustn't say that

out loud. Your boys might hear you and repeat it."

"I'm tired of all this. I don't care anymore—I just want the war to end."

Both women wept.

As the boys bounced into the room, Regina wiped her tears with her apron and tucked the letter into her pocket.

Only a few days later, on the morning of Christmas Eve's Day, and true to Elli's prediction, Regina's mother arrived by train. She carried a small cardboard box containing a smoky-smelling brown blanket, her only remaining possession. She was brought first to the *Rathaus*, where a co-worker ushered her into Regina's office. It was an emotional reunion. Regina took her mother home immediately, and sent for Gerda to meet them there.

The old woman seemed dazed as she collapsed in tears, exhausted from the trip. However, Elli had been right. The northernmost track to Berlin had been fiercely defended and kept open. Since *Ausweis* papers were no longer required in the chaos following the firestorm bombing, her mother had no legal difficulty in escaping from Königsberg.

At Berlin, the train had been rerouted around the city. But, once in Potsdam, another train traveled south to Leipzig, and she had arrived in Weida on the work train, without having had to walk. Though the trip had been slow and tiring, Regina was relieved to see her mother at all, especially after the dark thoughts that had come with Elli's letter.

"*Alles wek*--everything is gone," her mother repeated hysterically. Regina could not get a word said or a question asked, not even to ask about her father.

Her mother cried and clung to Regina's arm. She described the firestorm bombing and her intense fright. "The whole city was burning. We had no time to save anything. We grabbed two blankets to cover our heads, and all of a sudden we couldn't breathe anymore. It was as though the fire had sucked up all the air and everyone was gasping and falling and burning." Her sobs made her words hard to understand.

"I don't know how we got to the lake near Münzstrasse.

Your father dragged me by the hand and I couldn't tell which way we were running through all the fire. It was everywhere around us. Then he jumped into the lake holding the blankets and dragged them back up to me, wet, and ordered me to cover up and lie down. He crawled under his blanket next to me. But then he suddenly gasped and clutched his heart. I screamed and screamed, but no one came, and he died right there. The strain was too much for him." She put her face in her hands and sobbed.

Regina was crushed. Her wonderful father dead? She couldn't believe it. Why, she could still see his face with its old-fashioned mustache. She could even still hear his voice. She paced the floor, not wanting to accept the cruel words as true.

Regina's pain consumed her, and she wanted some time alone to grieve, but her mother continued talking as though she were in a trance. Tears streamed down Regina's face as she tried to listen, and Gerda grabbed her mother-in-law's hand.

"Others were all around us on the bank, some dead and some barely alive with horrible burns, but no one could breathe such hot air. I was crying under my blanket. I saw a young girl staggering toward the path and I screamed at her to get under the wet blanket with me. A policeman crawled to us and urged us into the shallowest water, and we lay there with only our faces out of the water. Sometimes we dipped them also, to cool the burning.

"It was only when I raised my head to get air, as I was facing the university and inner city, I could see there was nothing left. The Kneiphof was gone. I could see the Börse building far away through the smoke because all the buildings in front of it were gone. The fire had destroyed everything from the *Altstadt*-- the old city, and the smoke curled up high above the Pregel River, miles into the sky all around us."

Regina looked at Gerda, stunned. "The University Island has all those narrow streets criss-crossing the Kneiphof with thousands of people and apartments packed together."

"If Mother was able to see the Börse...it's horrible...all those people."

Regina wanted to shut out the picture she was seeing in her mind, but she couldn't. Neither could her mother seem to stop talking.

"The whole sky was orange and black," she continued. "We could go nowhere else. I wanted to die with my husband, yet I hadn't the courage to go lie with him. The heat kept driving me back into the water."

Regina's mother seemed compelled to tell it all, whether Regina could bear to hear the words or not.

"The buildings burned for hours, and smoke covered the whole sky. When the wind changed and reduced the heat a little, the policeman helped us out of the water and led us away. I wanted to stay with my husband and I cried to do so." She wrung her hands and pulled at her collar, almost turning it inside out.

"But... but the policeman checked your papa's pulse and said he was dead. The policeman dragged me along with the others and supported me with his arm. He made us hold hands so no one would be lost in the smoke, and he took us away to the other side of the river across the only bridge I could see still standing. It was the one across from the old university, but the university and all the homes on the island were gone... gone, nothing left but fire."

Regina moved closer to her mother and put her arm around the broken old woman's shoulders. "Go on, *Mutter*," she said quietly, though her heart was breaking and she wanted to cover her ears so as not to hear any more. She was thankful the boys were out playing and would not hear their *Oma's* terrible story.

"We stumbled along such a long time. My knees aching and my lungs burning but, at least, I wasn't alone." She turned toward Regina, nodding. "You know I'm so afraid to be left alone. Finally we came to an aid station in a church. Then the policeman disappeared back into the smoke. The city burned for days, and smoke lingered over everything."

"Later, Elli came looking for me and took me to your house. She was very good to me. She dressed my burns and then later helped put me on the train to come here. She felt I'd be safer with you."

Regina hugged her mother, reassuring her that she was where she needed to be.

"And so I lived and your *Vati* died. I'm so sorry," the old woman concluded abruptly, with a deep sigh that tore at her throat.

Regina tried to tell her mother that perhaps her father would have had a heart attack even without the raid. But the sobbing woman remained convinced he had died trying to protect her, and she felt terrible guilt. Regina marveled at how much guilt people piled on themselves for things over which they had no control.

When the boys came in, they were delighted to see their *Oma*, crowding around her noisily.

"Where's *Opa*?" asked Willi. Regina flashed him a signal to be quiet, as her mother started crying again. Willi looked quizzically from one to the other, then slowly nodded and took Rainer and Franzi to the kitchen.

Regina persuaded her mother to lie down by asking her to help get Franzi to take a nap. While the two rested, Regina and Gerda prepared the most festive meal they could manage--cold potato pancakes and a bit of *Herringsalat*. This fish salad was the favorite Christmas Eve dish of all the men in their lives, and Regina thought of Gustav, Hans and her father. She felt they could only recover from tragedy if they clung to their family traditions. It was all they had left.

Even on this cold and sad Christmas Eve, they managed to create their traditional Prussian evening. They all dressed up in their cleanest and least-patched clothing. When the boys sang their favorite carol, *"Oh Tannenbaum,"* as they stood in a circle and held hands, even Regina's mother began to calm herself. The older woman then led the family in *"Stille Nacht, Heilige Nacht."* She sang it as though it were a prayer. Indeed, that night, Regina also felt it was a prayer, for all their loved ones, the living and the dead.

The children had only practical gifts—scarves and socks their aunt and mother had knitted. Each also had an apple the two women had purchased. But the boys had not expected anything at all, so they were delighted. At midnight, the family walked to church near the *Rathaus*. They prayed for absent family members and for the war to end soon. As the tears rolled down Regina's cheeks, she believed, in spite of the news of her father's death, that the Christchild was near them, and it truly was Christmas.

Chapter 26

Enemy bombers came again a week later, probably looking for the *Waffen SS* tank troops on the hill. They bombed the church instead.

Dust and chunks of concrete fell on family members as the community bunker shook and rocked like a bucking animal. When Regina cracked the door inward a little, she quickly slammed it shut. She felt the heat from the burning timbers outside. More thuds of exploding bombs followed, but she waited until the all-clear signal. Debris from caved in buildings blocked the entrance. The women and children inside had to wait until air raid wardens came to dig the stairs free.

The church's ceiling next door was so badly damaged the soldiers knocked it down, but they left its bell tower standing with precarious, gaping holes. Willi joked that it looked like the empty teeth of Rainer's smile. The tower became a temptation to neighborhood boys for climbing and burrowing. Regina forbade hers to go there, but with little else for them to do except get into mischief, she worried during the hours she worked at the *Rathaus*.

Her mother offered to watch them in hopes of preventing further tragedy, but *Oma* Reh seemed preoccupied of late. Frequently she seemed to forget where she was and why the boys were with her. She even appeared in the kitchen occasionally in a disheveled state. This was not like the meticulous woman, and Regina worried even more. She also longed for schools to reopen and wondered how much her sons' education would be set back by the war.

A wooden crate arrived from *Herr* Busch in early January. It contained a few silver pieces and their Bible from among Regina's family heirlooms, a wooden sideboard, some sheets, towels, and cooking pots.

His note said, "*Frau* Wolff, I have picked these items that would fit into the last business shipping allowance. I know it is a great loss to not have more things from your beautiful home, but the Russians will have it soon, I fear. My wife and I will leave

Königsberg by ship shortly. We wish you well. Farewell until better times."

The note was accompanied by scrupulously stamped records and shipping documents.

Dear *Herr* Busch, Regina thought--reliable to the end. Though she regretted the loss of her beautiful home and furnishings, she didn't fret over them. Elegant living was gone forever. Food and bombings were more pressing problems. The household items *Herr* Busch had wisely chosen were of little monetary value, but useful and much needed. She had become quite practical.

One day in February, Gerda rushed in, breathless, "Dresden was bombed! I can't believe it. It's never been touched before."

Regina was shocked as well. "It was considered the safest city in Germany because of its cultural reputation. Lots of refugees we met on the road were heading to Dresden. How bad was the bombing?"

"Well, it didn't turn out to be the safest city. The bombing turned into a firestorm just like Königsberg. News reports are sketchy yet, but it seems the city officials of Dresden were so confident they wouldn't get bombed that the *Gauleiter* hadn't even ordered bunkers for the population. Do you think that can be true?"

"If so, it was a terrible mistake." Regina paused, remembering. "But an old woman we met near Berlin insisted Dresden would be next. I thought she was a little crazy at the time, but it appears she was right."

"It's horrible! The news said they buried thousands in mass graves. They'll never be able to identify them all, will they?"

Regina shook her head sadly, thinking of all the people killed and the beautiful old buildings she and Gustav had so enjoyed as young lovers, now gone forever. And the sordid description of firestorm made her ache also for her home in Königsberg, knowing it had fared as badly.

Regina received another letter from Elli in late March, written from west of Berlin. Regina was relieved to find she was with Gustav's brother Paul's family.

Oma Reh and Gerda gathered around to hear Elli's news as

Regina read the words aloud. "Your brother-in-law, Paul, came February 23rd and begged me to escort his five children (Inge had her new baby boy at Christmas) out of Königsberg. The rail lines had been closed off by the Russians. But on February 19th a counterattack had reopened the railroad to a seaport where Paul hoped we could ferry to safety, beyond the Russian advance. He felt this train would be the last to get out. The enemy was just outside the city's southern gates, and Paul said we must go that very day. I was to meet them at the train.

"I didn't want to leave, but Paul said the Army couldn't hold off the Russians much longer. It was rumored they'd been raping all women, young or old. He wanted his wife and children out. Inge was still too weak from childbirth to care for all the children alone. I agreed to help them, if he would buy me a round trip ticket because I intended to come back. My aunt evacuated to her sister's in Würzberg, but my brother in the *Luftwaffe* was reported shot down over Poland. I didn't want to leave in case he should be found, or escape back to German lines.

"Paul said if I insisted on returning to Königsberg, I should stop first in Berlin at an address he gave me. He said it was a safe place to get information about whether or not the rail lines were still open."

Regina's mother gasped and her hand flew to cover her mouth.

Regina immediately stopped reading. "Are you ill, *Mutter*? Can I help you?"

Her mother shook her head and became quiet, though her hands fluttered aimlessly.

When nothing further was said, Regina resumed reading. But she was puzzled, and watched the older woman more closely.

The letter said, "I had a terrible time finding Paul's family at the station because there were so many people fighting to get on the train. Just like at your departure, people were climbing through windows. I was mortified to find one of Paul's daughters carrying a chamber pot. Imagine! I objected to getting on the train with such a thing, and Paul said, 'Look at that crowd on the train, Elli. Just how do you think you can get the children to the toilet in that crowd?' Embarrassed as I was, I had to admit he was right.

"We could hear the rattle of gunfire ahead, and the train could only inch forward a little at a time. The whole countryside was frozen and the few windows with glass in them were totally frosted over. Some babies and old people froze to death along the way. Inge and I took turns putting baby Guntar inside our blouses for warmth, and we hugged the others close. Everyone looked blue. I think this has been our coldest winter in many years. But in spite of difficulties, we arrived at the port, and after hours of waiting, took a short ferry ride across to waiting wagons that carried us to a Berlin-bound train. We walked across the city...there's almost no transport anymore...until we found a train to Hannover from a suburb.

"We had the address of a man and his wife living in the country near Hannover, and that's where I'm writing from now. Would you believe this man was a deserter that Paul, as a military judge, set free to go home, provided he would prepare a safe place for Paul's family? I didn't know *SS* judges ever let anyone go, but Inge said Paul had acquitted several men in those last months in Königsberg. He allowed them to try to get home to their families. I always said he was a good man as well as handsome. Paul had somehow obtained work and travel papers for this man. The man was very grateful, and agreed to guard Paul's family as he would his own."

Regina paused, remembering something she had never understood. Elli's letter cleared up a mystery. It was an encounter with Paul in the early summer of 1944. He had come to her harbor business office with a bedraggled stranger whom he said needed a job with the family business. Paul was quite insistent, even though she told him she had no money to pay a helper.

"Don't worry about paying him, Regina. You must simply fill out papers registering him as an employee on official business to travel to Hannover to sell tobacco goods for your company. The man will leave on this business trip immediately."

"But we have no business in Hannover."

Paul frowned. "It has already been decided, Regina. Just fill out the paperwork!" He had said it almost menacingly. "And be sure it is stamped with the firm's official stamp." He waited while Regina performed this task, and the stranger left with the papers in his hands.

It was obvious she was to ask no questions. Brother-in-law or no brother-in-law, Paul was *SS* and, by then, Regina knew one didn't argue with *SS*.

Paul had then turned brotherly and asked her, "Have you heard from Gustav?"

"No, I haven't. I'm terribly worried about him at the eastern front."

Paul scolded, "Regina, you mustn't think of Gustav as groveling around in a foxhole somewhere. He's an aristocrat, he's well placed, and he's not in *that* kind of danger. You should know that by now."

Was that supposed to be encouraging? It was certainly mysterious, especially since Regina had not heard from Gustav for two years. Did Paul know something? Regina had wondered then, and still wondered now, what she was supposed to have known. What kind of danger had Gustav been in, and from whom? But, though Paul might have prepared a safe exit for this unknown workman, he hadn't been willing to answer further questions regarding his own younger brother.

From Elli's letter, Regina could now solve the mystery of who the man going to Hannover had been, but it certainly magnified the mystery of her own husband.

Gerda interrupted her reverie. "Regina, you're daydreaming again. For heaven's sake! Quit thinking and go on reading. We want to hear the rest of the letter."

Regina blushed and resumed the narrative.

"After getting Inge and the five children settled in this man's attic over the barn, I helped her obtain registration and ration books. I took the train back to Berlin alone, so I could go home to Königsberg. Regina, here is something you won't believe. When I stopped at the 'safe' address Paul had given me, I found it was an apartment belonging to Gustav!"

Mother Reh flinched and put her handkerchief to her mouth. Gerda looked up suddenly. "What's that?"

Regina's voice faltered in disbelief. Why would Gustav have an apartment in Berlin? But, though fearful of any answer, she needed to hear Elli's observations in hopes of understanding this new mystery. She took a deep breath to steady her voice, and resumed.

"I was quite shocked to find Gustav in Berlin as your letter had said he was back at the Front. I envisioned him somewhere in eastern Poland. I had not seen him since he mysteriously appeared a few weeks after the bombing of Königsberg and helped me get your mother on the train to come to you in Weida. I forgot to tell you about that in my previous letter, with all the confusion. He had disappeared immediately afterward."

Regina gasped. Gustav was in Königsberg as well as Berlin. But why hadn't he written to tell her? How had Elli forgotten something so important? And why had her mother not mentioned such information? She glanced sharply at her mother.

The older woman said nothing, but turned away sniffling into her handkerchief.

Regina sensed her mother knew something about this mystery, but her immediate concern was more information from the letter. She would try to ask her mother for details later, when the older woman was less distraught.

She continued reading the letter. "Gustav said he'd been sent back to Berlin on military business and would remain there a few weeks, or until he was sent out again. He gave no indication of what he was doing for the Army. In fact, he wasn't even wearing a uniform when I saw him, but a black business suit. I was puzzled, but I didn't ask because I had the feeling something was very secret.

"Gustav told me Königsberg was almost certainly lost forever, and he wouldn't allow me to go back there, as there was no longer a way out. He said refugees trying to escape by ship on the Baltic Sea had perished from Russian torpedoes, and many hundreds crossing the ice of Frisches Haff on sledges had broken through and died in the icy water."

Regina couldn't take in all this information--Gustav traveling all over the country without notifying her, and Königsberg lost?

Tears came unbidden and she almost crushed the letter. Then she suddenly remembered old *Herr* Busch and his wife had intended to leave by ship. The isolation of East Prussia from the rest of Germany by the Versailles Treaty was certainly a sad entrapment now. She said a silent prayer that the Buschs' had escaped safely and weren't among the torpedoed victims. People were dying! Had she been selfish to worry about her own confusion?

She tried again to read Elli's letter through her tears, desperately hoping for some logical explanation for her husband's presence in the capital city when she had not been notified.

"I told him you and the boys were in Weida after he sent you there from Karlsbad, and he seemed relieved you had arrived safely. By the time the air raids came that evening, Gustav had convinced me not to go back home. I went to the bomb shelter while he said he must 'report to his unit,' though he still was not in a uniform. He was dressed like one of those *Gestapo* men, in the black suit and a fedora, but he didn't volunteer any information.

"When he returned in the morning, he took me to a station outside Berlin and put me on a train back to Hannover. He said I should stay there and help Inge until Paul could get out of Königsberg. But he added, '...*if* he can get out at all.' It all sounded quite hopeless.

"I know you're now as puzzled as I was, but apparently, Gustav is doing some kind of secret work and travels around frequently. He seems to have a sort of 'base of operations' in Berlin to which he keeps coming back. That's all I know. But I knew you would at least want to know he was alive when last I saw him."

Regina laid down the letter and tried to think. What kind of soldier's job would take Gustav from the eastern front back to Berlin, to Riga, to Minsk, to Karlsbad, back to the eastern front, to Königsberg after a bombing, and back to Berlin? And those were only the trips she knew about. There were undoubtedly more about which she knew nothing. Surely Elli was wrong about his looking like a *Gestapo* operative. Gustav surely would have nothing to do with them. What was going on? Why hadn't he told her about all this in Karlsbad? And why had he not written her in Weida?

When Regina's mother had heard the whole letter, she didn't comment. She pursed her lips tightly, wrapped her shawl around her frail body, and walked away to the bedroom, closing the door behind her before Regina could ask any questions. The two younger women watched her go in silence.

"That's strange," said Gerda. "Usually *Mutter* Reh is a bit of a busybody and has opinions about everything and everybody. I thought she might have added something to the letter."

"I'm disturbed about that myself," said Regina. "But then, *Mutter* hasn't really been herself since she arrived in Weida, has she? I've assumed she was grieving the loss of my father and their home, but now I wonder if something more is bothering her."

"You seemed as surprised by the letter's contents as I was. At least it's news of Gustav, Regina. He appears to be safe. What do you think it all means?"

"I'm not sure. I need to think about it and try to see if *Mutter* knows something more than she's saying." Regina dabbed at her eyes. What on earth could Gustav be doing that required him to have an office, or an apartment, in Berlin? Nothing made any sense.

But she couldn't ponder over the mystery because, once again, the air-raid siren sounded, and she needed to gather up her family and go, as required, to their assigned community shelter behind the *Rathaus*.

The children ran in from the yard and Rainer commented, "I know how to find our shelter faster than I know how to find our *Baracke*. Why do we have to go in there when the planes are probably just flying over us to bomb some big city?"

"Just a precaution," his Aunt Gerda answered him. They all grabbed their ragged knapsacks and ran down the street to the damp shelter. The raids were now so frequent that they felt sure something big would be happening soon.

After the all-clear siren in the late afternoon, the family spread out into an adjacent field to gather wild wheat to pound into rough flour. Suddenly an airplane came into view.

Gerda stopped gathering, lifted her hand to shade her eyes, and stared. "That one is awfully low, and it's not one of ours. It has circles on the wings."

"Everybody get down," Regina screamed, as she grabbed Franzi into her arms. "He's going to crash."

At that moment, the plane's machine guns began firing. The bullets thudded into the earth and rattled against a nearby shed. Then the plane disappeared over the hill's crest, and they braced for the explosion. But instead of hearing the expected crash, they heard the roar of gunned engines as the plane flew rapidly upward.

All had flattened themselves to the ground at Regina's warning.

"Come quickly," Regina called. "Is everyone all right?"

"I'm awfully dirty," said Rainer, as he dusted off his kneesocks.

Franzi wailed loudly in his mother's arms, more frightened by the suddenness of the event than by any understanding of its danger.

Willi ran to help his grandmother to her feet.

"No one's hurt," announced Gerda, as she examined her skinned elbow. "Perhaps we've got enough wheat for today. Let's go home."

No one argued.

The next day, as Willi played outside on a slope behind the house, a fighter plane could be heard approaching again, firing its guns with engines screaming down in a dive.

Before Regina could get out the door to him, Willi ran in breathlessly. "*Mutti,* that pilot was aiming straight at me. Why are they coming so often?"

Gerda answered the child. "Pilots wouldn't bother shooting just at you. Perhaps they were aiming at the German tanks parked above you on the hill. Or maybe they just wanted you to stay inside, like we told you to do." She waggled her finger in her best 'I told you so' manner.

Regina hugged the boy. "You're right. They've been flying over more often lately. Something must be happening. We'll all stay inside until we find out what it is." She added firmly, "Do you understand me?"

Willi studiously examined his shoe tops.

"Perhaps the flights are a warning," she added.
Finally the child nodded his agreement. Regina sighed, hoping he would obey.

Only days later, warnings became unnecessary. It was an afternoon like no other.

The *Waffen SS* troops from the tank park on the hill scurried into battle positions in confusion, screaming orders, and fired their artillary rapidly toward the western hills.

As sirens wailed, Regina rushed the family into the bunker with others from their street. She heard rumbling tanks as the German troops retreated across the valley to the hill on the east side of town.

"They're firing the 88's. They can cut right through any tank's armor," Willi called out above the din.

"How do you know that?" asked Gerda. "And who could they be firing at?"

"Those are the loudest and biggest guns we have," answered Willi. "One of the soldiers told me so."

"It sounds like they are firing toward the west," said Regina. "I thought our enemy was further away."

As the afternoon wore on, shells came one right after another, and every shellburst brought new speculation. "It sounds like a different type of firing is coming from the west too," added Gerda. "I don't like being in the middle. Either side's guns can fall short, right on top of us." Gerda held tightly to Rainer on one side and her mother-in-law on the other.

"Should we try to get out of here?" It was a neighbor woman who asked.

"I don't think we can right now." Regina answered the woman's cry as deafening bombardment shook the bunker again and again. "Where else could we go? We're better off in here than out in the open."

They remained huddled in the bunker, drawing closer together with each new concussion. Franzi buried his face in his mother's lap. Other children screamed incessantly. All through the rest of the day and into the night, they were hammered again and again without interruption. What might come next?

Toward morning, another of the women called out, "Doesn't it sound as though the German artillery is getting further away? Surely our soldiers wouldn't leave us."

Regina's mother broke her customary silence and spoke into this new panic. "They wouldn't abandon civilians to the enemy while they retreat away from the town?"

The plaintive cries made everyone apprehensive. According to frequent German radio broadcasts, Americans and British were labeled cannibals who would rape women and eat their children. While the tales may have been quite preposterous, these women of the countryside believed them, and they were terrified. They held their children closely and prayed for rescue. Surely their own German troops would come back to help them before this horrible enemy could find them.

Suddenly, the doors to the bunker crashed open and several armed men in unfamiliar military uniforms burst inside. They slammed the door behind them. In the candlelight, Regina could see they were unshaven and disheveled, and one was bleeding from the shoulder, while another had burns on his face and neck. The men wore goggles on their foreheads and looked as though they had experienced something terrible from which they had sought shelter in the nearest bunker. They had their rifles pointed straight at the women and children.

The civilians were trapped and terrified. Regina was sure they'd be shot immediately. Some women began screaming and crying while she held her three boys tightly. The obvious leader of the soldiers paused, pointed his pistol around the room, then laughed and slipped it into his holster. With his motion, the other men slung their rifles onto their backs.

These men were black as the night and had great white teeth. Regina had never before seen a black man. Her only knowledge was from pictures in a nature magazine of wild men in some exotic place who shrunk heads and practiced ritual cannibalism. She could tell the other mothers thought of the same thing, because from shrieking in terror, they had suddenly become quiet and were shrinking against the wall of the bunker, trying to hide their crying children behind them.

Shelling continued to impact outside, but the roar of the 88's sounded further away. These strange dark men in the bunker kept grinning and grinning. Their white teeth flashed as they spoke to each other in a strange language. Surely the radio stories about Americans being cannibals were true.

There was a silent stand off as the women cowered on one side and the grinning, big-toothed, black soldiers stood on the other.

The women became further frightened and confused as the soldiers began pulling mysterious packages from their pockets and holding them out to the children with coaxing words and eating sounds and motions, all the while smiling broadly. No one knew what to do because these packages were undoubtedly poisoned.

Willi and Rainer apparently decided that perhaps the things being offered were food. Before Regina could grab them, they ran over and tried to take one of the little packages from a huge black man. He smiled and tore it open for them and broke it in two, giving half to each boy. Women gasped as the boys bit into the dark-colored bar and smiled.

"*Süss, Mutti, Süss,*" Willi exclaimed. The rest of the children rushed forward to claim these strange brown candies as the soldiers handed them out. The men just kept on smiling and digging into their pockets for more.

One of the women shrieked, "You fools, they're trying to fatten your children so they can eat them. They're cannibals! You all heard it on the radio." When the children didn't listen to her, and the other women only seemed more confused, she broke out of the door, screaming, "I'm going to get the *Bürgermeister.*"

The men didn't try to stop her. Instead, they kept smiling, as they dug deeply in their packs to find little tin cans of food and began handing them out to everyone.

Regina realized these soldiers were not trying to hurt them, but only trying to feed the emaciated women and children they saw in front of them. Soon, even shy Franzi was grinning back at the strangers and chomping on something rubbery that chewed and chewed and never dissolved. It was christened *Kau-gummi* because the children resembled cows chewing their cud, but the men kept repeating "chewing gum," and finally the children gleefully parroted the words.

So this was their enemy!

The women could see now that the soldiers were friendly. Regina and Gerda took rolled linen bandages from their knapsacks and made signs to the two injured soldiers that they could bandage their wounds. One allowed Regina to fold a cloth over the hole in his shoulder to staunch the bleeding, and then use the long strips to bind it around his chest. Gerda bathed the burned soldier's face and arms with water from her canteen, and then wrapped them gently.

When the first woman burst back into the shelter with the *Bürgermeister* behind her, brandishing his old hunting rifle and intent on freeing his villagers from the 'cannibals,' women stood in front of the soldiers and told him to put his gun away. He looked from invaders to his neighbors and back again, obviously unsure of his ground.

As the all clear sounded, the leading soldier tried to communicate with the Mayor with only an occasional word anyone could understand. But one word they all learned quickly. He was shaking the *Bürgermeister's* hand and saying, "American, American, it's OK, the fighting for this town is over!"

Chapter 27

The *Bürgermeister* struggled to interpret the faltering words and sign language of the American soldiers, and to help the women understand. The German troops were gone. Regina and Gerda clasped each other and cried. Could it really be true?

The soldiers invited everyone outside into the dawn. The boys gasped at the American tank still burning and smoking in front of the bomb shelter. Regina understood in an instant the breathlessness and injuries of these men who had invaded the bunker so abruptly.

More men and equipment arrived by trucks and little square cars called 'jeeps.' Muddy tanks rumbled in, occupying the open space on top of the bluff where the *Waffen SS* tanks had been parked before the battle. Civilians stood staring, bewildered by all the activity. While some soldiers set up tents, others dug and manned a defensive perimeter on the eastern hills where the German soldiers had last been seen.

The townspeople had no idea what to do in their defeat.

Regina's mother ordered the family, "Get your knapsacks. We'll have to leave town. This enemy Army will burn the town, and we'll be refugees."

But as they gathered belongings, an American officer motioned the people to return to their homes. Soldiers accompanied them to unblock damaged entrances. Other soldiers set to work helping the townspeople remove rubble and glass that cluttered the streets, vestiges of battle from the night before. Great energy replaced the lethargy of the town.

Regina laughed as she swung Franzi up on one hip and hoisted her knapsack to the other. "Is this the enemy of whom we've been so frightened? I don't see any need for fear, so far," she said to Gerda. This idea was bewildering to them both.

By noon, the soldiers had erected a huge tent called 'the mess.' A few soldiers dressed with aprons over their uniforms prepared fires under huge pots. A truck driver pulled in a water tank on a trailer and parked it next to the tent, apparently for food preparation. The townspeople gathered around to watch, from both curiosity and hunger.

Soon a big soldier stepped out of the tent and, amazingly, invited the civilians in to eat. Children were herded into a line and allowed to fill a tin tray with food first, followed by the adults. Smiling soldiers spooned out chunks of square meat, scrambled eggs, hot biscuits, and melted cheese mixed with macaroni. The hungry villagers gathered at long tables slowly, not quite believing their good fortune. They had not seen so much food in years.

"Look, *Mutti*," said Willi. "These stirred up yellow things taste like eggs, but they sure don't look like them."

"Obviously these heathens don't even know how to prepare eggs properly with a timer, and serve them properly in an egg cup," said his grandmother. She turned up her nose at the eggs and nibbled gingerly at a biscuit.

Willi caught his mother's eye, slapping his hand over his mouth. Both struggled to contain their giggles so *Oma* wouldn't see. It was a shared family moment, a rare moment, a memory of how families could interact without war.

"You know you're hungry, *Mutter*. Please try not to be ungrateful," said Regina, gulping down her laughter.

"This is good." Rainer tasted some brown stuff spooned onto his biscuit by a passing soldier. The man had ladled it out from a huge tin.

"Pea-nut but-ter," said the soldier, emphasizing each slow syllable.

"Pea-nut but-ter," parroted Rainer. "I really like this stuff." He grinned back at the soldier.

The Americans seemed happy everyone was eating hungrily, and offered second servings before they, themselves, sat down to eat.

Over the next few days, air raid sirens sounded with less frequency. The *Waffen SS* troops and their tanks seemed to be entirely gone. The townspeople gradually relaxed, no longer startled at every sound, and smiles from these foreign soldiers were timidly returned.

Regina was glad. Though the war wasn't yet over, not in

Berlin or in the east, she felt sure she and her children would now be safe with the Americans occupying Weida. She questioned her sense of confidence that she now counted on safety with Germany's enemies. But, after her initial encounter with Americans, the smiling black men, and with the kindness of these soldiers helping civilians, she felt more secure than she had in a long time.

Regina's boys, still having no school, joined the other children of the town in visiting the perimeter of the soldier's tank park daily.

The first time Rainer entered the house triumphantly carrying a tin of peanut butter, his mother accosted him at the door. "Did you get this food the same way you borrowed the cow that needed milking when we were on the road?" She wanted her boys to grow up as honest citizens, in spite of the war.

"It's all right, *Mutti*," Willi intervened for his startled brother. "It was quite different from the cow. The big *Ami* soldiers leave things along the fencerow on purpose, so we'll find them. We can see them smiling and motioning for us to take the food." He grinned sheepishly as he brought out a tin of square meat from behind his back.

It had been so long since the family had eaten meat, even a square kind, and they loved the peanut butter, so Regina hadn't the heart to make the boys return their treasures. The whole family felt they were feasting.

However, she followed the boys the next day and realized the off-duty soldiers really were placing food along the fencerow where the town's children could find it. It became a primitive game of international hide and seek that both sides enjoyed playing. Regina laughed while dabbing her eyes. She truly believed the worst was over for Weida.

When the American soldiers weren't on guard, she watched them gather up old scrap parts and put together a bicycle. In the evenings, they taught the children how to ride the bike, as well as how to stand in line so each could have a turn riding. A big sergeant taught them silly '*Ami*' songs that made noises like 'Old Farmer McDonald' and the 'Choo Choo train of Chatanooga.' The children joined in on the claps and hoots of the train whistle and they all laughed together while the soldiers helped them paint the bicycle Army green. The bicycle became their favorite thing, a community toy. Even Franzi learned to ride.

The Americans posted translated news on single sheets of paper at the *Rathaus*. The townspeople gathered daily, hoping to find out how their family and friends were faring in other areas falling to the Americans, the British, or the Russians.

From these broadsheets, Regina learned news of Königsberg and hurried home to tell Gerda and her mother about the German General Lasche who Elli's letter had said would save their city from the Russians. "The General wasn't able to break out of Königsberg, and he couldn't save the city, either. But he did manage to defend the corridor next to the Baltic long enough for nearly 100,000 civilians to escape to Pillau and then ferry to the mainland."

Gerda was excited by the news. "Perhaps some of our family and friends were able to get out of the city."

Mother Reh had tears in her eyes. The older woman had rarely spoken or interacted with the rest of the family since the last mysterious letter had come from Elli. Regina had stopped asking questions since they seemed to upset her mother so much that she became irrational.

Regina was pleased so many people had been able to escape her home city. However, she had some bad news to share, as well. "One group of escapees was shelled by Russian Kalyusha batteries on the night of April 9th. There were so many casualties General Lasche surrendered the rest of Königsberg when the Russians promised to spare its remaining civilians. But then Hitler branded him a traitor and ordered his family arrested. I can't believe it! Imagine, he saved all those helpless people."

Gerda was shocked. "The war is already lost most everywhere, and it certainly was already lost in Königsberg. What did Hitler expect him to do?"

"I suppose he wanted him to fight to the death and take all those civilians down with him in a blaze of glory. I'm afraid that's what Hitler plans to do everywhere else, too. It's like some horrible Wagnerian opera. Such injustice against the General's family, though, is stupid. I don't understand it. I just want the war to end and for Gustav to get out of Berlin safely." Regina couldn't help wondering if Gustav was even in Berlin anymore, but she did not mention her private thoughts to anyone.

By mid-April, the townspeople were recovering more every day with the support of their occupation troops. However, the posted news said the President of America had died suddenly in a place called Georgia. With so many soldiers clearly grief-stricken, Regina concluded that, in spite of all they had heard on Hitler's broadcasts, Roosevelt must have been a good man after all.

The Americans set up a temporary government composed of citizens who came forward to help. As soon as the *Amis* were convinced people were not *Nazis*, they asked each person to go back to the job they'd held before the collapse of the local *Nazi Gauleiter*, and to help reestablish services as best they could. Shopkeepers removed the boards from shop windows, farmers brought in what little produce they could find so the shops could reopen, trash collectors began the clean-up process, the linen mill reopened, and life began drifting back to normal.

Regina's job in registration became more demanding as Weida's former citizens who fled as refugees wandered back. Disarmed German soldiers also began returning home from western areas the Americans had already captured. They trickled in by truck, wagon, or on foot. All were exhausted, many injured, but every day a few more came home. In each case, Regina tried to match them with the location of their families. Sadly, many of their families couldn't be found among local lists of the living or the dead. These men wandered the streets searching, or set off to a new location within the area the Americans had secured, hoping to find some family member alive, much as Regina had done. She recognized the pain in their tired faces.

The reverse side of this sad situation was the women who waited for men who failed to come home. More women daily were seen in black, as they received telegrams of their husband's death, or a name was sent for the lists. Some simply succumbed to hopelessness. Regina refused to give in to widow's black clothing.

Gustav will come home after the war, she told herself constantly, and she continued to reassure her sister-in-law, Gerda, as well.

True to her hopes, Regina's brother, Hans, finally returned by ambulance wagon. Willi, who had started watching all comings and goings near the road, was first to spot his uncle and run to his Aunt Gerda's workplace with the news. She wiped her hands on her apron and ran after the procession of women who rushed to meet all new arrivals, hoping their man would be among them. Regina was waiting with the others as the wagon stopped in front of the hospital. Gerda stepped up quickly to help as her husband was handed down. Hans had been seriously injured, and he couldn't walk alone. Another soldier passed him his pair of crutches.

Those families who saw their missing relatives sobbed with relief. Others returned home dispiritedly to wait for the next wagon, or the next group of former prisoners straggling home. Regina and Gerda half carried Hans home with one on each side. Willi ran ahead to tell his *Oma* her only son had returned, alive.

"There was an American doctor reporting to his military unit here in Weida," said Hans, as the women settled him into a chair at the *Baracke*. "He gave the injured a wagon ride and took care of all the soldiers, German and American alike. A machine gun got me in the thigh at some old bridge, and I guess I was lying there a long time while the battle raged on. There was screaming and dying everywhere. The noise was terrible and I couldn't get into position to fire my gun. It was bad. There was no help, or painkiller, and not even any water, until the whole battle was over. But after the Americans captured us, I was well treated. The doctor operated at an American field hospital to fix my leg, and he thinks it will eventually be almost good as new. He just wants to watch that gangrene doesn't set in." He turned to his wife. "There, there, Gerda, old girl. Stop your cryng. I'm home now. It's all over."

Regina crept out quietly and returned to the *Rathaus*, asking her mother and the boys to walk along with her so Gerda and Hans could be alone.

The town then had a real doctor because this American didn't seem to mind helping sick or injured German soldiers, foreign laborers, or families, along with the American soldiers. His first act was to put up proclamations in German that citizens should use only the treated water provided by the Americans in the water tanks on wheels. It was for cooking and drinking until the soldiers could get sewer and water systems back to their prewar condition.

His next project was to line up all the children for injections. The women laughed to realize they had come to trust the Americans. They no longer believed the injections could be poisoned. Though the children screamed loudly, they were thus made safe from various diseases that come in wartime. The doctor announced that the civilian adults would be given this medicine when his next shipment arrived. He even gave Regina a salve that cured Franzi's long-term rash. Franzi was not alone. Nearly all the town's children had rashes, picked up from dirt, malnutrition, flies--no one knew for sure. But the doctor treated them all.

In early May, the *Bürgermeister* tearfully announced that the war had ended, Germany had been defeated, and Hitler had committed suicide. For Regina, it was a somber moment to think the war had been lost after all the bravado, promises, and privation, but she also rejoiced that Hitler was, at last, really gone. By war's end, she and her children, along with the rest of the townspeople, were healthier and felt free to start rebuilding their lives.

Walking with the children among the newly-leafed larch trees of bright spring green, Regina decided that if this was what peace was like, she could not believe why there had been war. She prayed silently to thank God for answering her prayers for bringing her children through it all safely. The news of capitulation also meant that German men could come home from battle lines and prison camps. People could reunite with family members who had survived.

Now she only needed to wait for Gustav. She knew he would come for his family soon.

But weeks passed, and she heard nothing. Was he perhaps dead after all? She refused to believe such a thing, even when her mother unexpectedly offered to help her sew a black dress.

"How can you suggest it, *Mutter*?" Regina cried out. "I

won't believe Gustav is dead."

"My child, you must face up to facts now. It is time for your mourning, too. It's better this way." She reached out her hands to enfold Regina's.

"I love you, *Mutter*, but you must never say such a thing to me again—no—there is no possibility that I will wear the dress of a widow." She pushed her mother's hands away. "I refuse to mourn. My husband is alive and he is coming home to me soon."

The old woman turned away, muttered something unintellible, and retired to her room. She did not come out for supper, though the boys had tried to waken her.

Regina hoped her forceful denial of Gustav's death had not wounded her mother further.

From her job, Regina knew reunions took time. Returning German soldiers often told her their stories. One had hidden without food in a bombed out Berlin basement before finally escaping to the west. One had tried to climb down a waterspout so as not to be seen by maurading Russian soldiers. He had been injured, and captured, but had escaped again as soon as he was able to walk. She consoled herself that Gustav would surely come to Weida soon with such a story.

Each German soldier was required to meet with American officers who 'de-nazified' him by asking questions to see what his rank and duty in the German military had entailed. If the *Amis* determined he was not a *Nazi*, he was released to go home. The procedure usually took a few minutes. Only if the soldier was suspected of belonging to the Third *Reich* hierarchy, the *SS*, or *Gestapo*, or thought guilty of war crimes, was he placed in confinement pending further investigation. The healthier men who had been cleared were soon employed to build pre-fabricated housing from materials provided by their former enemies.

During the last days of the war, many men arriving from the eastern front said they had deserted their units and run west to escape the Russians, surrendering to the Americans instead. There had been unabashed fear after word-of-mouth testimonies about Russian failure to tend wounds, and mistreatment or deportation of prisoners. In the chaos, many soldiers had simply scrambled to what they felt was the better of two enemies. Regina didn't think the families she helped reunite really cared how their men arrived home--only that they did. There were far too many who did not.

However, one morning in late July, just when Weida's villagers felt they were returning to a somewhat normal post-war condition, the boys returned from their daily play at the *Kaserne*-- the military base--with strange news. "*Mutti*," declared Rainer, "the *Ami's* are packing up their equipment on trucks and going somewhere."

"Did they say why?"

"I asked that big sergeant why and he said he didn't know— it was just orders to report to *Hof Kaserne*."

Franzi chimed in proudly, "My tall American friend threw me his square meat and I caught it."

Regina couldn't believe it. The men had been such a help to their town and had provided safe food and water. Grain and seeds to plant a winter wheat crop had also come from the *Amis*, along with additional seeds for backyard gardens to supplement their diet with vegetables. Why would the soldiers desert them so soon?

"It's true, *Mutti*, they're leaving," said Willi. He kicked the dirt and frowned. Willi was well known at the *Kaserne* and had managed to learn a few words of English from the friendly Americans. He even had learned where some of them were from, and reported strange names like 'Kentucky' and 'Ohio.' The soldiers frequently joked with him, and they saved their cigarette butts for him to take home to his mother. She could empty out the leftover tobacco into paper scraps and roll a cigarette for herself now and then.

Regina was puzzled. What did their departure mean? Could the provisional government continue without the Americans? Who would be in charge? But later in the afternoon, the trucks rolled out of town in a convoy to the west with the soldiers waving and tossing cigarettes, candy, and food. Regina and the rest of the townspeople shook hands with them while running along beside the slowly moving trucks, and the soldier named 'Ohio' handed her a large block of cheese. "For your boys," he said. Regina cried. They were losing trusted friends.

That evening, Regina heard the creaking of old horse-drawn wagons and carts, and the firing of rifles into the air. Once again, she accompanied other citizens into the street to see what was happening. In contrast to the crisp, clean-shaven *Amis* who had left in well-equipped trucks, she saw bedraggled, dirty Russian soldiers entering the town on the eastern road. Their Army immediately set up a barbed wire perimeter around the *Kaserne*, and took over the *Rathaus* for their officers.

A loudspeaker blared out that townspeople were to go home to bring any food they had in their houses, and assemble in the square. Each family willingly took a tin of food, assuming they would share with the Russians, though they hated the idea of giving back precious food they'd been given by the Americans.

As townspeople drifted into the square, a soldier standing at the fountain shouted brisk orders. "Drop that food in the pile and line up here in the street to be identified." This 'identification' required citizens to stand miserably in a light rain, while officers inspected papers for each of Weida's citizens. Those who had none were escorted away at gunpoint.

Regina was thankful she had provided careful paperwork for every refugee who had come to her office, including her own family.

"Quiet! You are not to speak," the Russian soldier kept repeating gruffly, shaking any child who became restless, and poking his rifle at anyone attempting to get out of line. Frequently, other soldiers poked people. "You have more food than that. You'll be punished if you don't bring enough."

Frustration and fear grew rapidly. Regina noticed tears running down Franzi's face as Rainer held the child's hand.

Regina thought this seemed too much like *Nazi* tactics, and she became wary.

A well-dressed Russian officer, clearly out of place among the other scruffy soldiers, walked back and forth in front of the lines, frequently stopping in front of her while smacking his hand with a riding quirt. Her skin prickled, as she shifted from one foot to the other under his steady gaze. She wondered what could be in his mind, as he continued to pace, apparently sizing her up for some purpose. Once he actually touched her face with the handle of the riding whip, and his lips curled in an insinuating leer. She could feel Willi stiffen beside her. He clenched his fists and bristled. Regina knew her son, and felt him gathering to spring if she were touched again. She squeezed his hand, hard, fearing he would move or speak. Willi apparently got her silent message and remained staring straight ahead, but she knew his obedience was only temporary. What was this officer doing, Regina wondered, and how could her ten-year-old sense danger as soon as she did? She strained to stand still and cause no further notice.

After hours of such inspection, the villagers were allowed to go home in the dark, while soldiers gathered up the pile of food into wheelbarrow loads and disappeared into the *Rathaus.*

Regina reported to her office the next morning to find that these ignorant Russian peasant soldiers didn't know what to do with normal plumbing. While the American soldiers had been in Weida, they had helped repair pipes in all the buildings. Most bathtubs and toilets had been restored and were operational again. Where there was too much damage, clean, temporary community bathhouses and restrooms had been constructed.

But now these Russians used the bathtubs and showers as toilets. They seemed to think the flushing of a toilet was some type of explosive weapon, and they destroyed many of them before being stopped by their officers. In one public restroom, soldiers washed some small potatoes in a toilet and flushed, apparently thinking they would be rinsed. When the potatoes disappeared, they became enraged and tossed a grenade down the toilet. It blew out the side of the building as well as destroying the plumbing. Regina couldn't even imagine how these men must have lived in their homes in Russia, that they should be so stupidly primitive.

The Germans who worked in the *Rathaus* were disgusted with their new 'guests' and felt quite insecure with the way they looked at women. The townspeople were required by the soldiers to bring to the *Rathaus* all watches, radios, and cameras, on penalty of death. Most complied, since they had no choice. Everyone waited fearfully for what order might come next.

Though Willi stayed aloof and watchful, Rainer and Franzi

tried to make friends with the Russian soldiers, apparently assuming they would be like the American soldiers they had considered their own. Rainer offered to help two of the men stack wood near a building when he came upon them working. But the soldiers pushed him away, knocking the sticks from his hands and calling him a *Nazi Kind*—a *Nazi* child. He ran home and hid behind the stairs. Regina found him there when she returned home. The men rebuffed and ridiculed any child who came near them, and the children stopped going to the *Kaserne*

Even in the streets, events spun out of control. As Franzi was riding the old bike the Americans had constructed for the town's children while others waited patiently in line for their turn, a Russian soldier grabbed the bike right out of Franzi's hands, and attempted to ride it. When the soldier couldn't stay up and fell over, even after several tries, he became enraged and shot the bicycle to pieces with his machine gun. The children gathered around the wreakage in tears. The soldier motioned them away with his gun pointed at them. Thus, even the children became confused and frightened of these men, and their outdoor play was ruined.

When Regina arrived home from work shortly afterward, the younger boys were crying and Willi was furious.

"They took it all, *Mutti*," he declared. "I tried to stop them, but they knocked me down and took all the food we had in the house--even Franzi's square meat and our peanut butter and *Kaugummi* chewing gum."

Regina searched the house and found Willi was right. All that had been overlooked was the cheese from 'Ohio' she had stored in a glass jar and hidden. Their new conquerors had stripped the town clean and, instead of having a big mess tent for everyone, as the *Ami's* had done, they each sneaked off into a corner and wolfed down whatever food they had managed to steal from citizens. Regina was humiliated and sickened.

And that night, once the soldiers had eaten, the screaming chases and rapes began.

Regina's mother listened at the door, and in a rare moment of lucid interest, turned to Regina and Gerda and demanded, "You girls are not to go outside again until this danger has passed."

"*Mutter*, what do you mean? We must go to work. We cannot stay inside forever," Regina protested.

Gerda clung to her husband shaking. "What is it *Mutter*?"

Hans nodded at his mother and asked his wife and sister to do as they were told.

"Quickly," her mother said. "Don't argue...I know about Russians." She gathered together her old woman's baggy clothes, and told the two younger women to put them on right away. Then she roughed up their hair and rubbed ashes on their faces to make them look ugly.

"There!" She stepped back, apparently satisfied with her work.

Regina remembered the Russian officer's unwanted attention of the first day, and her uneasiness with his touch of the riding whip, and she suddenly understood her mother's fear. Though she and Gerda tried to go to work the next day in their ridiculous disguises, they both arrived home convinced they could not return. The tales from frightened young women were on everyone's tongue. Drunken Russians had invaded several homes to search for women. Their mother had understood the danger. The two made no attempt to go out again for weeks.

Several days later, without refrigeration, even the hidden cheese had turned moldy and had maggots on it. They scraped off the insects and ate the cheese anyway. But someone would have to go out to find food soon. *Oma* Reh and the boys foraged in the empty fields and forests, just as the children had done while on their long journey. But they usually found the Russian soldiers had been to the farms first. Even the rotten potatoes were gone.

By September, Regina was sad to realize they'd been away from their home over a year. After several weeks of Russian occupation, Gerda, Hans, *Oma* Reh, and Regina were again emaciated scarecrows. They had all begun giving their own scarce share of food to the boys, but the children remained pitifully thin. Rainer and Willi no longer even had energy for mischief.

During one meager supper, Gerda was the first to comment, "We're all losing weight again, even with Willi shopping for whatever he can find. It seems the only women in the village who aren't getting skinny are the ones who are 'overly friendly' with the Russian soldiers. Of course, that means the soldiers have already picked out those girls and are more or less leaving the rest of us alone now. How long are these Ruskies going to stay here?"

No one had an answer.

Hans still had a pronounced limp and some pain from his war injury, but had otherwise recovered. He and several other men had been forced to work for the Russians at hard labor. Instead of moving heavy timbers by bulldozers, as had the *Amis*, the Russian soldiers forced the town's surviving men to carry them up to the *Kaserne* for their new, permanent-looking buildings. Hans came home exhausted nightly.

But sometimes he had news, always only by word of mouth and rumor. "A guard told me Germany's been divided into four zones. The Americans captured Weida first, but it had already been promised to the Russians at some big conference, so the Americans were ordered to leave. Now, we Germans living under Russian occupation aren't allowed to pass from one zone into another."

Regina asked, "Does that mean we're trapped again on the wrong side of some battle line? And, if I understand you, this time the division is between those who were formerly allies against Germany. That's a strange way to win a war."

Hans answered, "The worst part is that we're stuck in the Russian zone, and the borders between the zones are being fortified. I don't even know how far away the borders are. Some of the workers claim they were ordered by the Russians to put in minefields, trenches, guard towers, and razor wire on the Russian side of the border. They think it will soon be finished."

Gerda asked, "Regina, how will Gustav be able to cross this new border to come find you?"

"I don't know. I'll need to find out how one goes about reuniting families divided by this border. There must be a way. Surely other nations couldn't make this division permanent with people caught on both sides of it." She fought back a wave of panic.

"I don't think there is a way," said her brother, shaking his head. "There've been only rumors to go on because the Russian authorities withhold information just like the *Nazis* did. Even letters are censored."

He glanced around the room before continuing his answer. "No, Regina, I've heard of no one getting out legally. And German soldiers who've been cleared and sent home by the Americans have been disappearing. Some say they're being sent to work camps in Russia. No one knows for how long since there's been no accusation or trial. I think I'll be spending my time inside until we find out what's going on. I don't want to end up in Siberia."

Gerda took his hand and nodded her agreement.

"I'm not surprised," added Regina. "Have you noticed the Ruskies have taken wagonloads of valuables, even desks from the *Rathaus,* plumbing pipes and water faucets, and sent them to Russia as 'war reparations?' Why would they do that? There won't be much left in Weida, at the rate they're going."

Within the next week, the Russian soldiers also removed many railroad cars, engines, and trucks, even though Hans was certain the German equipment was not compatible with Russian railroad tracks.

"What can they possibly use them for? This situation is getting serious, but what can we do?" Hans shrugged. "They're stripping us of anything they can steal, whether they know how to use it or not. I imagine we'll have to stay here, though, and put up with it. Perhaps they will leave us alone once they have everything they want shipped to Russia. I'm wondering about Gustav? Do you have any idea which side of the border he's on now, Regina?"

"I still don't know if Gustav's alive or where he is. Elli last saw him in Berlin during February, supposedly heading for the Russian Front, but I've heard nothing since. We do know many were killed in the final battles for Berlin in May, so I hope he wasn't there by then. But his name hasn't shown up on the list of those dead or captured either."

Regina sighed and walked to the window, turning suddenly to express another idea. "The refugee roster in my office shows many German soldiers are prisoners of war in the American Sector in Bavaria. Perhaps Gustav is among them because that would mean he's well treated. But if he's there, he won't be able to get back across this new border to find us."

By facing this grim fact, Regina began making her own plans.

Her mother noticed during a lucid moment. "Daughter, I can see that determined look in your eyes. You must not do anything illegal. Wait patiently here in Weida. Things will get better eventually," she pleaded.

"The children can't wait, *Mutter*. They're starving. We all are."

Gerda said, "If you're thinking what I think you're thinking, Regina, don't! It's too dangerous, for all of us. What if the Russians found out?"

"Then you won't let them find out, will you? At least I can try to find out how to get across the border." Regina left them and walked to work.

She began listening more carefully to the refugees coming into her office. Piecing together their rumors, she determined that if the fortified border separated families, they could be reunited, but only if relatives in another zone were willing to sign papers to that effect. However, to get papers signed to go legally to the west, one had first to cross the border secretly and illegally to find the relatives and procure those signatures. Rather a dangerous undertaking, but one Regina knew she would have to risk. She confided her plan first to her brother.

"Gustav's sister, Erna, lived in Nürnberg before the war. That's now in the American zone. She can sign such documents for me, if I can get there."

"Regina, we don't know if she s survived the war, or if she's been bombed out and moved. You might not be able to find her."

"She's been my friend since we were children conspiring to tease her brother. I know she'll help me get the boys to the American zone legally. They'll be safe there and can start a new life. Erna may even have had some news of Gustav, if he's still alive. I must go there."

"You're not listening to me, Regina. Running that border illegally will be dangerous—impossible. The boys could be killed."

"If you think I should, I'll leave the boys with you until I return. But there's no choice. I must risk the journey. When I return with the documents, we can all travel legally to the American zone."

"Of course, the boys will be safer with us, but Regina, I'm your brother and I forbid you to do anything so rash and dangerous. You mustn't go. You must wait for Gustav to come."

"Gustav may be dead. Our boys are hungry. I can't stand by and do nothing, and you'll not forbid me something I must do, Hans." She stared straight into his eyes until he turned away.

By October, more weeks had passed, and Regina knew she could wait no longer. This time, she told her mother, trying to make the woman understand why she needed to cross the border alone.

"I'm afraid for us to part again if you try to leave," her mother cried. "You'll have no shelter, no coat, no money, no man to help you. How will you get by?"

"I've been without shelter, money, and my man before, *Mutter*. I can manage, alone."

"Regina, please reconsider. If the Russians catch you, they'll send you to a work camp in Russia, or shoot you. It's already snowing in Russia. You've always been my delicate child." The old woman drew herself up forcefully. "I cannot allow you to leave the safety of Weida to do something so illegal."

"*Mutter*, whatever I was before, I am no longer. The term 'delicate' has no place in our thinking, either during a war or an escape from the results of war." Regina took a deep breath and rushed on, unaccustomed to argument with her mother. "I must do what I can to restore our family and save you and the children. Weida is no longer a safe place to do that."

Regina's mother began to sob and stated her worst fears, "What shall we do until you return? What if you are caught? I have already lost my husband."

"He was my father, *Mutter*. It was a loss to me as well. And I don't want to lose my husband or my children because I fail to take action. I must go."

Regina wrapped her arms around the frail old woman and tried to comfort her. "Hans, Gerda, and the boys will be here with you, *Mutter*. Don't worry. I'm stronger than I look, and I must attempt the crossing now. I can't simply wait for Gustav to find us while our children starve. I must try to save them myself, and find my husband." Regina had already decided, alone, that escape was the only possibility. Her mother turned away and began mumbling to herself something Regina could no longer understand.

They had very little accessible money left for a train ticket, so Regina asked a former colleague from work if she could borrow money for food. He agreed to lend her some money in return for her wedding ring and promised she could buy it back whenever she had money again.

When the day arrived, Gerda lent her a sturdy dress, shoes, and sweater and, once more, Regina made plans to travel. She told her children goodbye with no explanation, but with many tears and hugs. She took nothing with her except a change of underwear in her worn knapsack and a few *Brötchen* to eat on the train.

Thus, the days during late October of 1945 would become some of the most frightening of Regina's life.

Chapter 28

Regina must have been in a daze as the train rattled toward the south, because when she got off several kilometers from the new border, she had companions—an engaged couple in their twenties, from Leipzig. Regina had only met Sepp and Agathe as they rode through the hills north of Hof and Coberg, the border area rumored to be the only one not yet strewn with land mines or equipped with gun towers by the Russians. The pair had guessed Regina was also going to the border to escape, and had invited her to join them.

"How did you guess?" she asked, bewildered.

"It's written all over your guilty face," Sepp said. But his smile was friendly.

The young girl tossed her blonde hair and gestured for Regina to sit with them while they planned their escape.

She had no choice but to trust them.

Sepp took charge. "Since none of us are quite sure where the borderlines start, we'll get off the train before the border town appears. That way we won't attract as much suspicion as if we went to the end of the line. Until dark, we'll say we are out for a picnic."

Regina and Agathe nodded and all got off the train at the next station.

The three hiked into the gathering darkness, stumbling in the general direction of the border through fields and woods to avoid people on the nearly deserted roads. Regina and Agathe were frequently left lying in the wet grass, shivering in the dark while Sepp scouted out a safe passage ahead of them. They splashed through gullies and waded a small river on Sepp's orders. Hours later, he found what he was looking for--a guarded path with a nearby sentry shack. They crept forward slowly.

It had to be the border.

Sepp helped them over some barbed wire and silently motioned them to press down into a muddy ditch, though they shivered with cold. Two Russian sentries walked back and forth above them on the path, their outlines barely visible in the dark. But Regina recognized the shape of guns above their shoulders. Her heart thumped against her ribs.

She was conscious of the clothes she had borrowed from Gerda, wet, dirty, and probably torn as well. But now only one thing mattered--focusing on every move the sentries made. She carefully counted out the time it took them to walk away from each other, reach the end of their perimeter, and return to pass each other again going the opposite way. Sixty-seven, sixty-eight, sixty-nine…the sentries took ninety seconds to reach the end and return. The three escapees agreed it was ninety.

Sepp whispered, "That'll give us almost forty-five seconds to run across the path, through the open field, and into the shelter of the trees while their backs are toward us. If you stumble on barbed wire, you'll have to get through it. We'll go one at a time, so if anyone gets caught, the others will have a chance to get away. Don't make any noise."

Regina trembled, hoping the other two wouldn't notice. She recalled feverishly the rumors that Russians would shoot, while Americans would not. Sepp hadn't seemed to believe they'd be safe on either side of the border. But she must go. Only this one last barrier kept her from getting her family safely to the west.

Still, Regina wondered if she had the strength for this. The trees looked far away. And hadn't she broken enough laws already? She felt only an indentation where her wedding band should have been. Since she had traded it for escape money, she missed its comfort. She vowed again to buy it back later. "For you, Gustav," she whispered to herself, trying to gain courage.

But too much thinking increased her fear. Whatever had possessed her to attempt crossing this hostile border between Russian guards and American troops? *It was insane.* She was torn between wanting to go back to her boys and needing to go forward to find her husband. What would be the consequences of the next two or three minutes…prison…death…freedom?

The deep mud became a welcome hiding place in the dark, feeling freshly turned as though something might finally grow after the years of war. However, Russian soldiers had plowed the fields to show footprints so they could catch fleeing refugees more easily. Somehow their misuse of God's earth for this purpose made it all the more important she get across the border, yet her legs felt as though they belonged to someone else.

Sepp put his hand on Regina's shoulder. It was time for her to go first.

She froze. She simply couldn't force herself to get up and move forward. He immediately tapped his fiancée instead, and Regina heard a soft rustle as Agathe disappeared into the darkness. Regina held her breath and felt ashamed of her fear.

Sepp whispered in her ear, "We've all come too far for you to drop out now. If you panic, it could mean Agathe and I, plus escapees coming later, will be caught. Remember *why* you're going, Regina." She nodded wordlessly, brushing the tears and mud from her eyes.

It would soon be Regina's turn again and she breathed faster, trying to develop the needed courage one more time. Telling her mother she had strength and actually drawing it together now, in a crisis, were two different things. But then, what more could she lose?

When Sepp tapped her shoulder again, Regina rose and ran crouched across the road and into the dark field, praying silently as she ran. Not since she was a girl had she run so hard. In those days, it was only pride that made her try to win first place from her friends, Gudrun and Erna. But now, it was a matter of life and death that made her wish she could run more quickly, instead of like a clumsy *Hausfrau*.

The ground was uneven, and ruts in the plowed soil were impossible to see in the darkness. She strained to run faster. Suddenly, her shoe caught a deeper furrow and she stumbled to the ground. A sharp pain pierced her leg. She tried desperately to remember the count. Where was she—at thirty-three seconds, forty-four?

Regina's head burst with questions. Should she try to get up and keep running? Should she wait longer? If she were to get up too soon, or too late, the guards would see her and shoot. She realized at that moment that Agathe must have made it safely to the trees since she had heard no shots or commands from the sentries. "Oh, God," she whispered. "What should I do?"

How far out was she? Could she crawl back and find Sepp? Perhaps he had already passed her in the dark and hadn't known where she was. Would they wait for her, come back to find her, or abandon her? Could she trust them? Her throat burned with the aching urge to cry out.

Regina knew too much time had gone by. She must try again. As she started to rise, something hurled itself at her and she fell to the ground again, hard. A rough hand clapped over her mouth, and the weight of a body held her down. She felt sure she would soon be dead.

Sepp whispered angrily, "You fool! You're off count. They'll see us if you get up now. Lie still."

Regina made no pretense of knowing what she was doing in the middle of that field. She waited passively for Sepp's hand on her shoulder as he again counted and, finally, at his signal, they rose to run blindly toward the trees. One sentry called out to alert the other Russian. The fugitives dropped to the ground and froze. The guards were apparently listening for something. Regina noticed a loud pounding sound and several seconds ticked by before she realized it was her own heartbeat. She became aware of something sticky on her leg, but she dared not move to investigate.

Sepp and Regina began crawling slowly, testing each move on the uneven ground as they inched forward. Suddenly, Sepp grabbed her hand, dragging her up to her feet as they ran for the trees. A fusillade of shots rang out behind them. Perhaps the guards were firing at them or perhaps someone else. They didn't wait to find out.

The forest smelled damp from the previous rain, but it was silent and, thankfully, dark. When they were sure no one had followed, Sepp whistled softly for Agathe, and she stepped out from her hiding place to Sepp's embrace. Each leaned against a tree to rest. Regina felt sure the whole world could hear her gulping for air. Her lungs constricted in pain and she felt faint. Gratefully, her glance at Agathe and Sepp revealed they, too, were gripping their knees and breathing hard from the exertion.

Running her damp hands across her forehead, Regina reminded herself this wasn't a good time to fall apart. She felt her shin and found the sticky substance was blood. She must have cut herself on something when she fell. It didn't matter anymore.

After a few minutes, Agathe whispered, and Sepp grabbed Regina's arm.

"We must push on to find the Americans," he said. Regina yearned to sink down in the mud, but they had no time for rest, or tears.

As the three of them ran through the dark forest, it seemed every tree had eyes. Not really knowing how wide the 'no man's land' was, or in which direction to find the Americans, they felt seriously in danger of somehow doubling back on themselves and re-crossing the Russian lines. After many minutes, they saw the flickering of a campfire ahead. They stopped abruptly in the shadows to listen to the strange voices.

"Those are Americans," Regina whispered excitedly. Though she did not know the words, she recognized the rhythms of speech used by the American soldiers who had been in Weida.

Sepp held up his hand to stop her from running forward. He had not yet gained such confidence in the *Ami* soldiers.

"How should we approach them?" he whispered.

"Let Agathe and me go first because they won't harm women."

Sepp was not convinced, and Regina didn't want to wait, so this time, she took the lead and simply stepped out of the bushes and called out the few words she knew, "Hallo, *Ami* GI, friend, OK. *Nicht shiessen*—don't shoot."

Three soldiers sat in the clearing near a small bonfire. They were smoking cigarettes, and didn't seem at all surprised to see her. One man rose and walked toward Regina with his gun hanging loosely at his side. She had an impression it was attached to his hand permanently, but that using it was rarely necessary. She felt no fear as he approached and said in very bad German, "*Vieviel*—how many? *Habe kein Angst, alles* OK—have no fear, all is OK."

"*Drei*" Regina answered, holding up three fingers in answer to his question. The other two soldiers got up and advanced carrying blankets. Her comrades stepped cautiously out into the firelight. The three were wrapped in blankets, led to the campfire, and offered hot coffee, cigarettes, and soup that had never tasted so good. Regina wrapped her cold hands around the tin cup and breathed in the warmth as the three rested by the fire. The soldier with the broken German began to ask questions quietly. This was certainly not the intense interrogation they had expected.

"Where are you coming from? Are you refugees? Are any friends coming to meet you?" These questions were interrupted by one soldier refilling their cups of coffee from a huge thermal pot on the back of the truck while the other brought them each a double-sided sandwich and an apple from a huge square metal box beside it. Regina realized she was really hungry. These soldiers acted as though they had been waiting for them to come. What a wonderful welcome!

There were more questions. "Were you seen or shot at by the Russian guards? Where do you have relatives?" The soldier stopped and looked at each of the three intently. Though his German was very hard to understand, his soft voice and concerned look made it obvious he was trying to help them. "Where do you want to go," he asked.

"Fürth, *bei* Nürnberg," said Sepp. The soldier shook his head sadly. "Not Fürth," he said. "The Bavarians don't seem to want escapees there. You must go elsewhere in West Germany."

Regina looked up, startled. She had not known her country had been divided permanently—enough to have a separate name—'West Germany.' She also realized sadly that rumors the Bavarians wouldn't take in more refugees must have been true. She'd been told to ask for a town other than Nürnberg. A sad joke even stated that the Bavarian farm wives had already received fur coats in exchange for food needed by the desperate Prussian refugees, so now they wanted no more Prussians among them.

Animosity between Prussians and Bavarians, the red and the blue, had always existed from many centuries of conflict and royal succession. Regina supposed even a long war against mutual enemies couldn't erase all of that history.

Her brain raced as she tried to think of some place near

Nürnberg she could ask for that would be north of Bavaria. She didn't want to travel far from her Bavarian destination. If they said no to Fürth near Nürnberg, she knew they would certainly say no to Nürnberg itself.

"Dieburg" she volunteered. "Dieburg would be good."

"How many kilometers to Dieberg?" the soldier asked, apparently trying to determine if she knew where the village was located.

Regina's surprise at the question told him she didn't know exactly where Dieburg was, and she was caught. But the soldier only smiled, not in any menacing way. It was obvious these soldiers received many refugee 'guests' like these three crossing the border each night.

"I'm sorry, Ma'am," he said. "We have orders to send refugees to process in at Frankfurt *am* Main, and you can go where you like after that." He must have noticed their disappointed sighs because he added, "Don't worry. You won't have to walk. We have transportation for you."

The soldier who had brought them food motioned the three to follow him. Warmed and comforted as much by the friendly reception as by the hot coffee and blankets, they willingly followed him three hundred meters to a road where a truck pulled over and stopped at his signal. It had flip-down benches on each side in the back and a canvas cover over the top. About ten other people, also wrapped in blankets, were seated inside with a boy on a stretcher on the floor. Agathe and Regina were lifted up and Sepp scrambled in by himself. A low metal gate was closed across the back, and they were on their way to Frankfurt, many kilometers west of their true destinations.

Chapter 29

Though no one knew quite what their future held or where they were being taken, the mood was almost jovial. The escapees chatted as the truck rumbled through the night. They shared their stories and found they had all expected to be treated with great suspicion, but it had not happened. They were relieved they had escaped safely to the *Amis*.

The refugees were from a variety of towns in what they were now calling 'East Germany,' and the truck had picked them up from several welcoming campfires along the border. They were surprised that the Americans seemed to have been expecting them.

How did they know we would come? Regina wondered.

One woman had come two nights before with her twelve-year-old son. Her boy had made too much noise crossing an open field and had been shot in the leg by the Russians. She had crawled back to help him, while the Russian guards searched for them.

"The trees were only about ten meters away," she said, "but they might as well have been a hundred since my son couldn't get up, and I couldn't leave him there. I was mentally trying to prepare myself for capture or death, when the strangest thing happened.

"This huge figure came barreling out of the woods, clasped my son's arms together, and dragged the boy into the tree line. I followed as quickly as I could and was bewildered to find a big American soldier with mud all over his face putting his finger to his lips in a gesture for silence. He was smiling. He used a belt to wrap Luis' leg tightly to a small tree branch, hoisted him across his shoulders, and set off through the trees at a run. I could barely keep up, and I feared where he might be taking us.

"The man spoke into an oblong box hanging on his uniform and soon a small military-looking car with no top on it met us."

"A jeep," Regina intervened, proud she had learned the name of the vehicle. The woman nodded and continued.

"The driver stopped, the big soldier put my boy in the back, hoisted me in beside him, and placed my hand on the side of the car. I suppose he meant I should hold on tightly. He nodded, grinned again, and disappeared back out into the night before I could get my wits back to thank him for saving us."

Her new companions were all listening intently. "The driver took us on a bouncy ride from the border to an aid station in a tent. It was near an old German cavalry barn by the town of Hof. The doctors fixed up my boy and kept us there for two days until he could travel. We were the first ones on this truck for Frankfurt."

The woman still felt sorry that she had not been able to thank her rescuer, especially after a German doctor working at the American hospital tent told her the soldier wasn't supposed to leave his post to save anyone under the new diplomatic rules. Refugees had to reach the trees by themselves before the *Ami's* were allowed to help them. This soldier had simply happened to hear the shot in time to see her plight, and he had taken it upon himself to break international policies to help her son.

The boy was lying on a stretcher on the truck's floor with blankets and pillows tucked around him. "I'll have a story to tell my *Vati* when I see him!" He laughed. The woman silently shook her head. How could anyone be sure they would ever find his *Vati*?

By morning, the truck had arrived at the refugee center in Frankfurt. Red Cross ladies in charge of the shelter squirted the refugees with a disinfectant powder and then directed the men and women to different barracks where they could shower and choose anything they needed from among boxes of clean clothes. Regina chose a sweater and some sturdy shoes, since Gerda's had been ruined by mud and her own blood. A Red Cross lady lent her some trousers and a shirt while Regina washed and mended her dress, but they felt strange and not at all feminine. She vowed she would never again wear trousers once her dress was dry.

Registration brought a few questions to establish their point of origin, their destination, relatives or friends that might be looking for them, and who they hoped to contact in order to get the signatures they needed. Each escapee was given the proper family reunification papers, a temporary travel authorization, and transit food coupons. They were told to check in again with the Americans before they returned to the East zone with their legal *Ausweis*. In Regina's case, as with most of this particular group, that point of entry and departure would be the *Kaserne* near Hof, not far from where she had entered the American zone. Although Sepp and a few other men of Army age were held while they were checked to see if they were former *Nazis* masquerading as refugees, they, and the rest of the group were soon free to go.

Agathe and Sepp shook hands firmly with Regina in farewell. She felt tears of gratitude and wished them well. She didn't feel she could have escaped successfully without them.

At the train station, though Regina needed a ticket to Nürnberg, she had only enough money for the night train to Ansbach, about thirty kilometers short of her destination. Upon her exit from the Ansbach station the next morning, she felt lucky to get a ride, first with GI's in a jeep, followed by a farmer in a wagon. She soon arrived at the western outskirts of Nürnberg.

Regina had visited Gustav's sister and her husband several times before the war, but now landmarks were unrecognizable in the ruined central city. She looked around in confusion.

Rubble was piled so deeply it leaned against building facades, forming hollowed out bowls. Distorted beams and wires hung from the few remaining walls, and roofs were rare. Only a meter-wide path had been clawed through the middle of each street to connect it up to the next ruined block of buildings. The paths were crowded with roughly clothed people searching for whatever might be of use. Most were women dressed in the black of mourning. She noticed few men in the city.

American military trucks provided water, much as they had in Weida. Where they had survived the bombings, old medieval wells had also been opened, cleaned out, and pressed into use.

Identifying the still damaged street signs was almost impossible, so finding the way to the *Hauptbahnhof* at the center of the city was difficult. Regina knew the way to her sister-in-law's house from that train station, if it was still standing.

Everywhere was the tap-tapping of hundreds of women with hammers. These were the *Trümmerfrauen*, the women who knocked off old mortar from any reasonably good bricks they could find in the rubble. These were stacked in *Leiterwagons* like the one Regina's boys had rescued, or in wheelbarrows. The bricks would be used again to rebuild. The women's clothes were dusty, and battered kerchiefs covered their hair. It was almost as though they were wearing a uniform. Regina noticed their chafed, red hands torn from the rough work. But the tapping made almost a synchronized melody as she walked through the city searching for a familiar street. She found herself walking to its rhythm.

It took until afternoon to get to the center of town. Regina came upon what was left of the *Altstadt*--the old town square where the *Kristkindlmarkt*--the Christmas market--had been held for centuries in celebration of a Plague's end during the Middle Ages. The Sebalduskirche, the church adjacent to the square, thrust a forest of girders above its roofless top. The Frauenkirche directly on the square was also simply a shell.

She was stunned to find that statues had somehow survived better than buildings. Freshly-washed laundry, which in normal times would never be visible, was now hanging anywhere two walls were still standing that could support a rope between them.

A group of twelve circus performers had rigged a tightrope wire high above the ruins. They walked, balancing long poles, above the crowd watching down below. After their daredevil stunts, they passed a hat among the crowd hoping for *Pfennigs* that would help them get by. Regina was saddened to see these talented stars destitute, working in the open air under such dreadful conditions. The circus was one of the few performing groups allowed to function throughout the war for morale purposes, and they had once been among a privileged class. She wondered what kind of life German people would have now, in defeat?

Regina could see the beautiful castle up the hill with its centuries-old moats and roofs smashed like some child's toy. Could it ever be rebuilt properly, even with today's modern tools?

From the castle's position in relation to the market square, Regina found her bearings and turned around to cross the old city wall to the *Hauptbahnhof*. Even with almost nothing left of this infamous wall, ladies of the evening still plied their trade in its sparse shelter that evening, as they had done for centuries.

Regina reached the train station and huddled overnight in its partially ruined shelter. It was a cold, miserable night, as she had no blanket or coat for cover. Half dozing, she remembered noticing the opera house, just opposite, had sustained damage also. It had been home of the famous Nürnberg '*Meistersinger,*' an opera Regina had enjoyed on former peacetime visits. The ancient city was in ruins. How could life go on in these circumstances?

It would have to go on, she reminded herself…there was no viable alternative, unless one were willing to be a quitter, and die.

In the wan light of morning, Regina pointed herself to the northeast and started walking toward the suburb of Erlenstegen, hoping it had not been damaged as badly as the inner city.

It occurred to her that if Erna was not there or her family had been bombed or scattered too, her whole trip would have been in vain. But she couldn't dwell on that thought for long without panic, so she put it out of her mind and kept walking.

Bomb-damaged railroad and street bridges forced detours, but Regina made good progress. As she got into the suburbs outside Nürnberg she saw that many private houses had escaped damage.

It was late afternoon when she found the correct street and excitedly broke into a run. Her heart pounded and she felt short of breath as she found the house and knocked on Erna's door. Rustling and banging noises preceded the sound of heavy footsteps running up the inside stairs. Then Erna opened the door, carefully patting her hair and apron to be sure they were in order, a characteristic gesture Regina remembered with joy.

"You!" Erna said, alarmed. She was obviously taken by surprise and her face registered a host of emotions simultaneously as her jaws worked hard to form some kind of statement.

"Yes, me," Regina answered. She was smiling with excitement while Erna only looked confused. Had Regina hoped for more elation in their greeting? It had been such a hard journey to get here. Yet now, her dear friend and sister-in-law, whom she had counted on to sign papers to bring her boys safely to the western zone, looked as though she had seen a ghost.

"May I come in, Erna?"

Erna closed her gaping mouth and stuttered several false starts before she mastered her usual sense of courtesy. "Of course,

Regina, forgive me. I was so shocked. I wasn't even sure you were alive, and I certainly didn't expect to see you here." She opened the door wider and stepped back for Regina to enter, shaking her hand in the formal Prussian style.

Regina felt the woman's discomfort and it increased her own as she sat rather reluctantly on Erna's immaculate white settee. This behavior was not like the friend she had always known. Erna offered a cup of tea and even had sugar for it. Regina was amazed. There had been none in the east, even with ration coupons. It was also odd that the tea was already prepared, as though Erna had been entertaining someone. A second teacup sat abandoned on the low table. Clenching and unclenching her hands nervously, Erna made Regina more ill at ease with each moment.

Finally Erna spoke, blurting out, "How did you get here? Where did you come from? Where are you staying?"

"I had rather hoped I could stay here with you for a few days and have you sign some papers to bring my boys over the border. And I prayed that perhaps you had heard something from your brother. I've not heard from Gustav in some time. The registration people traced a few men from Berlin to a prisoner of war camp in Bavaria, but his name was not on the list, nor was he registered anywhere else I could find."

Erna seemed close to tears as she stammered out, "Lots of men have been found and interned. He could be any place...dead, in prison. I...I just can't...I cannot imagine."

At that moment, Regina heard the sound of footsteps at the top of the stairs and looked up to see a man's form in the shadows.

"It's all right, Erna. She will not give me away, will you, Ina?"

"Gustav," she whispered. "You're here?"

"Yes Ina, you've found me."

Chapter 30

Of all Regina's most romantic dreams of how their meeting would be, this was certainly not it! She was not supposed to be tired, wearing a tattered dress and someone else's shoes instead of the flowery, romantic dress, high heels, and perfume Gustav loved for her to wear.

She was not supposed to be tongue-tied either, yet words would not come. Her tears came first and wouldn't stop, from relief he was alive, that now her journey was finished because Gustav would take charge, and from shame for the way she looked and the confusion she felt.

Regina couldn't have told her feelings at that moment, except they were all wrong... not at all what she had planned. Her impulse was to run to Gustav, yet she felt rooted to the spot. Was it shock? Reserve? Apprehension? Something didn't feel quite right.

Her mind refused her bidding to relax. If Gustav had been here all along, why hadn't she been notified through the Red Cross and International Refugee registrations? If Erna knew he was here in the house, why had she seemed so rattled, and why had she hid him, and lied? Why did Regina feel unsettled instead of rapturous as he walked down the stairs toward her? She had waited so long for this moment. Why did she now feel an icy chill creeping up from her toes?

"You're very thin, Ina," he said calmly, as he took her hands, brushed his lips to her forehead, and led her to the settee. Settling himself in an armchair, he asked Erna to bring another cup of tea. It was so dream-like, in horrid slow motion. Regina could not find any words.

"You see," he explained quietly, "I'm hiding here. The Americans captured me, but I escaped from a train carrying several prisoners-of-war to a camp for interrogation and de-nazification. I was able to get to Erna's home at night by hitching a ride under a coal train. I've been here since." With a casual flair of his hands, he stirred the sugar into his tea, as though this whole scene were not so utterly bizarre as Regina felt it to be.

She finally found her voice in a flurry of questions.

"I don't understand how you got here to Nürnberg. At the hospital in Karlsbad, you said you were going back to the eastern front. Then Elli wrote that she had stayed in your apartment in Berlin. How does a foot soldier have an apartment in Berlin and commute there from an eastern front foxhole? We heard Berlin was destroyed and our captured soldiers marched off to Russian concentration camps. Most haven't been heard from since. How did you get out of Berlin and arrive here?"

Regina couldn't stop the flood of questions, blurting out the vague suspicions that had tormented her thoughts for months. She also wanted to ask why he had come here without stopping to get his family in Weida, but the words jammed in her throat. She was suddenly afraid of the answer.

Gustav laughed. "Ina, this sounds like the interrogation I was trying to avoid from the Americans. My job was never in any foxhole. I was still more or less in the sales business, going from one battlefront to another to see what was needed. I procured armaments, checked on prisoners, carried out special orders of the *Führer*, all for the Army." Gustav paused for a moment and then chuckled. "Why you could almost say I wasn't really in the *Wehrmacht* at all, but…"

"Then why didn't you tell me that? Why were you never home after our last Christmas together? Where were you while we were in the bunkers in Königsberg, or while the boys and I were struggling across Poland and Czechoslovakia as refugees to find you, or fighting our way to Weida? Why was there no word from you?"

She was angry now, in a way she didn't quite understand.

Gustav casually lit a cigarette from the package in his velvet smoking jacket pocket and gestured to ask if she wanted one. He took his time, as though waiting for her questions to go away. He seemed so regally patient, a fact that left Regina feeling all the more exasperated.

Even though she desperately wanted a real cigarette, she wouldn't let him distract her from her quest for answers. She waved his hand away. He sighed and resumed explaining.

"Ina, I had to go wherever the *Führer's* orders sent me. There were many special jobs I was ordered to do. I did go back to the eastern front before I was recalled to Berlin. But while the bombing raids pulverized Berlin and the Russians closed in on the city, the whole front dissolved. The goal of both the military and civilian population was simply to get out of the city and try to get west to surrender to the Americans, instead of the Russians.

"Of course, I had hoped not to have to surrender at all, only to slip away to the west. But the Americans caught me swimming the Elbe and put me on a train to Frankfurt, and then on a cattle train to Ingolstadt for interrogation and internment. I was afraid of their court system, so when I found some loose slats on the car, I kicked them out. Perhaps ten or fifteen of us jumped out and rolled away from the tracks into the darkness. I came here to hide until things become quiet again, and until the authorities stop looking for me."

"You mean you deserted from your unit in Berlin?" Regina asked, suddenly incredulous. Even though she had no love for the leaders of the Third *Reich*, win or lose, it would never have occurred to her that Gustav would have run away. This did not seem like the man she had married almost fifteen years before.

"Ina," he said flatly, "I'm a salesman by trade. I've always been a salesman. I'm what the Americans call a 'wheeler-dealer.' What good would it have done had I stayed in Berlin and ended up in a Russian prison for ten years while they took their time separating the *SS* from ordinary *Wehrmacht* soldiers?"

Regina had a sudden flash of understanding—something had indeed, been unusual about his war service, his missing uniform— and something was, indeed, unusual about this escape and his hiding from the American authorities.

She knew ordinary soldiers had been released to find their families and restart farms and businesses after the official end of the war. There had been two-week amnesties for them to turn in their weapons and go home. At least, that was the case in the American sector where Gustav had apparently been captured. If he had turned himself in properly, and had been adjudged innocent, he would have been released and sent home many months ago. Why, then, would he have been anxious about the American court? From what or from whom had he been hiding?

But as Regina was trying to phrase her next question, Gustav interrupted her thoughts by changing the subject.

"At least I'm glad you and the boys are well. Where are they now—in Weida? When will you go back to them?"

He did not say, "When will 'we' go back." Regina was heartbroken by the omission.

"The boys are hungry—starving in fact," she answered. "The Russians took all the food for their own troops. I'll be going back as soon as you sign my papers saying we'll be reuniting a family by coming here. Then I can bring them safely and legally to the west."

She was suddenly calm now that she realized she would be going alone. She accepted that she must persuade her 'wheeler-dealer,' deserter, mysterious, escapee husband to do whatever was best for her boys, regardless of her own disappointment.

Regina rushed sturdily on before she could lose her nerve. "I'll also need money for train fare and clothes and food once I arrive in Weida. I presume you'll have your status cleared up and have a place for us to stay by the time we return to Nürnberg."

She said it as coldly and evenly as she could manage. It was a statement, not a question. She had never spoken this way to her husband before, and a sick, empty feeling came with the words. Did her voice betray the determination she had decided to adopt, or did she sound like the little girl's tearful helplessness she truly felt?

She must have sounded determined because he only replied, "Of course." Then he added, "I can't sign the papers since I'm not here legally myself, but Erna can sign them for you and I can give you money for the round trip now."

He disappeared for a few minutes and returned with several rolls of *Reichsmarks*. Another mystery--where would an escaped prisoner get money? Regina dismissed it from her mind. Her boys needed safety, a home, food, and a father, and she intended to see they got them, no matter what she had to do to arrange it.

"Here," he said, as he laid the bills in her palm. "This should take care of your expenses." Regina pocketed the money without comment.

Erna then called them to dinner and explained, "The children are spending the night with their grandmother Hess. She still lives in her old home across the street." Then she added, "You can sleep in the guest room tonight since you'll no doubt wish to start back to get the boys tomorrow."

"No doubt," Regina answered briskly, and they sat down to eat. Of course, after such a difficult trip, Regina had hoped to rest a few days. But the old familiarity of the house now dripped with tension and questions. She only wanted to get out of it as quickly as possible.

A strange meal followed. It seemed Erna's home had sustained no damage, as though a war had never taken place. Not a sofa pillow was out of place, and no shortage of food seemed apparent on the table.

Gustav and his sister made trivial small talk while Regina silently tried to put all these dissonant thoughts into some logical order. Who was this man for whom she had waited a lifetime, for whom she had become a wanderer with her children across a war-devastated land, yet who now seemed some aloof person she didn't know?

She silently burned away her long-treasured dreams. Only ashes remained.

After dinner, Regina bathed and retired to the guest room, saying nothing, expecting nothing. She was crushed and exhausted from her efforts to reunite with Gustav, and with all that had brought her thus far. Now they were again together, yet she felt more alone than ever. Had it all been for nothing?

Some part of her still hoped Gustav would come to her room and they could reconcile in all the ways of which she had dreamed. But, though she heard his footsteps stop a long time at her door, she also heard him sigh deeply and shuffle on up to his hiding place in the attic.

Should she have rushed to open the door and fling herself into his arms? Would such an action have prevented the heartache and painful decisions to come? She didn't know. Perhaps Gustav didn't know either because she could hear him tossing restlessly all night above her room. She knew both of them lay sleepless.

The morning air was brisk and cold as the sunlight filtered into Regina's beautiful room. It was only slightly more in need of yellow paint than when she had last stayed here, under different, much happier, circumstances. Sitting on a lacy, handmade doily, one of a pair of figurines was all that appeared to have been broken. It was a smiling little girl sitting in an apple tree. Regina held it in her hand and could see it had been patched with glue. The matching little boy figure was unscathed by the war, as was the rest of the collection, the room, the house, the street, the lives. *Why was she thinking of this at all? Insane, that's what it was... she must have imagined the whole situation of the night before. Perhaps she could mend the problems, if she tried. But something still didn't feel right. What was she missing?*

She felt broken herself, only she feared no glue could ever again put her back together to form a complete person. Gently, she ran her fingers over the cracked place, caressing the figurine in her hand for a moment, as though the little girl could give her strength for the morning. Then Regina placed her back on the doily, facing away from the little boy. She had to get away quickly, now, before anyone could sense the terrible questions she was hiding.

She dressed hurriedly and returned to the living room, not knowing what she would find. Erna's two children, Gerhardt and Renee, were home from their *Oma's* house, and they greeted their *Tante* Ina with enthusiastic hugs. Breakfast was set for five, but Erna was not there.

Gustav came down, well dressed, shaved, and handsome, as though he were a husband in peaceful Königsberg in 1935 rather than a fugitive in war-torn Nürnberg in late 1945.

He greeted Regina with a smile. "Erna has gone out to buy you and Willi some boots and jackets at the open marketplace down at the corner. She's using her children's ration stamps. We figured the two younger boys have already passed down Willi's. You must all have something warm to wear and I doubt there'll be much available in the Russian zone. Erna wanted us to go ahead and have breakfast without her."

Regina was not really listening and only nodded. *Why didn't*

he take her in his arms and make all the doubts go away?
Gustav talked on and on in his usual take-charge, practical way. Regina suddenly realized that for all the years she had prayed for him to take charge of the situation again, she now resented his doing so. It seemed an additional presumption.

He paused for a moment while he drew something out of his pocket, then said calmly, "Here's a checklist of things you can bring with you. I'm not sure if there are weight limits but, now that you'll be able to come across the border legally, you should be allowed to bring some baggage."

Regina sighed, shaking her head at the familiar act. Gustav had always needed a list for everything he did, and Willi was already doing the same thing. Was list-making hereditary?

The list included a few household furnishings from Gustav's parents, accounts from the business, and the silver pieces Regina and the boys had carried out of Königsberg in their knapsacks. She wondered for a moment how Gustav had known what had been rescued from their home, or what *Herr* Busch had shipped to them in Weida. It fell in the same mysterious category as how he had known she should leave Königsberg. Who were his contacts--his sources of information? Then she knew it didn't matter anymore. She nodded and tucked the list away.

At a joyful call from their niece and nephew, Regina and Gustav sat at breakfast. These delightful children she remembered fondly carried the conversation. It was a blessing, Regina thought, as neither she nor Gustav could think of much to say.

A long silence ensued afterward when one of them might have said something to soften the moment. Neither of them did. Then Erna bustled into the kitchen with her arms full of bundles, and the moment was lost.

"I have a coat for you, Regina," Erna said breathlessly. Every event was always an excited rush for Erna. Not even a war had changed her.

"It's nothing fancy. There's little available now, just thick cotton, not like any of your beautiful furs and clothes from before the war. But it seems warm, and I was rushing to find you something quickly at the marketplace. I still have all my clothes, so

I don't need ration coupons until next year. I found Wilhelm a pair of boots I think might fit, but there were no jackets his size. I'll send one of Gerhardt's and hope Wilhelm will not mind."

Erna seemed to realize she'd been rattling on and stopped in some confusion. She took Regina's hands in hers and said, "I'm so sorry, Regina. I know you have lost...everything."

The two had been friends since childhood, yet Regina could not find the words to share forgiveness. She could only squeeze Erna's hands and try not to cry.

Regina put on the cheap, plaid coat gratefully and stood in silence as Erna tied Willi's jacket and the boots into a bundle with a rope handle. Erna helped Regina put on her knapsack. It now contained money and the papers Erna had signed. She hugged Regina awkwardly with tears already trembling on her lashes and retreated into the kitchen.

Now came the part Regina had dreaded. How should she say goodbye to this husband she no longer knew? Was it this hard for all families to come together after the long separations of war?

Gustav made small talk about a *Strassenbahn* only a few blocks away, already repaired, that traveled to the *Hauptbahnhof* with only three transfers. He also mentioned how some men were drifting back home, but with terrible injuries, emotional as well as physical. Many had been interned in Russia, so the women were helping to rebuild the city. His talk was impersonal and carried no emotion. Regina could scarcely listen to the drone of his once-loved voice.

"I noticed the women coming here," she said into their embarrassed silence. She carefully kept her voice as casual and impersonal as his had been. "The tapping noise was everywhere. It must be hard for those *Trümmerfrauen*, but I'm sure they'll do the rebuilding, if they must. Women can do whatever they must."

On that inane comment, she turned to walk away. It didn't matter. What more damage could be done? Regina assumed there would be no further discussion between them, but as she reached for the door, Gustav grabbed her arm and turned her body to face him. Even then, she hoped for some sign of their long-ago love-- something hopeful she could cling to.

"Ina, you realize, don't you, why I can't go outside to see you to the train, and why I can't go with you to get the boys? I have no legal papers, and I could be arrested and interned at any moment."

Regina nodded, mute in a crisis, as usual. *Where was her tongue? Why couldn't she tell him how important this whole fiasco had been to her and remind him of her own lack of legal papers and her own illegal activities in trying to get the boys out of Königsburg? Why was his lack of papers and his safety the only thing important to him now?*

But instead of speaking her mind, she nodded silently, determined not to let tears fall in his presence. Her throat hurt from the effort. She needed to get out of the house and away from Gustav before she could think. She opened the door and he stepped back into its shadow. She looked into his eyes, wordlessly searching for some answers. There were none.

Suddenly, as she moved away, he grabbed her from behind, pulling her back against him with his arm across the front of her shoulders, pressing her against his long-remembered body. He whispered in a choked voice, "I know it's been hard, Ina. I know you've rescued our sons alone. I'm sorry I wasn't there, but I'm proud of you, and your strength. I knew you had courage all along. I promise we'll get the boys fattened up and happy again when you return. God will continue to protect you and our sons." She felt his lips brush her hair in a soft kiss.

Tears stung her eyes and coursed down her cheeks. Regina nodded, not daring to turn and face him. Pulling away, she ran down the steps and onto the street. She didn't hear the door close for a long time. The bundle slammed against her legs as she ran, and she was painfully aware of her awkwardness. But she ran as though possessed, chased by all her worst pain and fear.

Chapter 31

Regina chased her personal demons until she rounded the corner where she could lean against a tree and sob out her confusion and pain, unseen. She was not even sure what had happened between herself and her husband, but it felt devastating. Her throat burned from the effort to hold back sobs, but now they came uncontrollably, shaking her whole body and, she truly felt, her whole soul. She could feel the clammy dampness of tears against her hot skin where they trickled down the open coat front.

Unconsciously, she had dropped her bundle and was rubbing her fists firmly in her eyes like a child. She was unaware of how much time had gone by, but the street was filling with people, perhaps on their midday rest period.

A wrinkled old man in a battered hat and a patched coat shuffled by slowly, dragging an empty burlap bag behind him. To Regina's embarrassment, he stopped before her on the walk.

"May I help you, *Fräulein*? Are you all right? You look faint. Here, sit a moment on the bench and catch your breath."

Before she could protest, the stranger led her gently to the bench and seated her as though she were some grand dame and he, a swank *maitre-de*. He then retrieved her bundle and sat politely beside her on the bench. It was very unusual, given ingrained German restraint, for one stranger to intrude upon another.

Embarrassed, Regina tried to straighten herself up-- readjusting straps on her knapsack, twisting her hands in her lap, waiting for him to go away and leave her alone.

Instead, he began speaking quietly, almost to himself. "My old wife died in the very last bombing of the war while I was on duty as air raid warden. She cried every time I went out in a raid, saying I was too old, and the job was too dangerous. I never got a scratch, yet she died when the bunker under our building collapsed." He paused a moment, and resumed when he saw Regina couldn't help listening in spite of her own grief.

"I'm glad she didn't live to see our defeat and everything we'd saved, gone. She would not have had the strength to start over. She couldn't have withstood the loss. I'm glad she's not suffering now, but I do miss her."

Regina didn't know what to say. She remained silent.

"I'm 89 years old, and I can't rebuild under another new government, but I think losing this awful war was the only way to save ourselves from ourselves. Now Germany can start over.

What's the best thing to happen to you today?" he asked suddenly, catching Regina by surprise. "The very best thing? Don't consider the worst for this moment, only the best."

It was hard to think of anything good through all the painful things. But the old man waited quietly for her answer as though he had all the time in the world and no place to go.

Finally, Regina did see a best thing. Why had it been so hard? "I obtained legal papers to bring my sons safely out of the Russian zone," she blurted out, smiling for the first time. Had this not been one of her major goals all along? Had she not risked everything for this, to keep her children safe? Half a dream is better than none, she realized suddenly.

"Congratulations on your outstanding accomplishment." The old man saluted elaborately. "My name is *Herr* Arnold. And how may I address you, my successful young woman?"

Regina answered with her name, accepting his outstretched hand. His hands were gray and gnarled, with crooked, arthritic fingers. She feared her handshake would hurt him, but his grip was surprisingly strong. His face crinkled with a calm, intelligent demeanor, in contrast with the clothes and gait that marked him as poverty-stricken.

"And now, *Frau* Wolff, compared to your best thing today, an outstanding achievement indeed, would you care to tell me your worst?"

Without another pause, Regina stated it plainly as she could. "I'm confused about the status of my marriage. Something doesn't seem quite right, and I'm not sure what it is."

He cupped his hand around his whiskered chin and said quietly, "War does terrible things to people, all people, of all countries, but especially to those where the war is fought on their own soil. Brutality and nobility both come to the surface. People change, and families grow in different directions under the strain. Many are lost in the battle. My wife and I had a young friend, a Jewish lad from among my university students. He came to hide with me, his useless old professor, after his parents were rounded up by the *SS* and sent to the death camps.

Regina gasped, "Were there really death camps?"

The old man nodded.

"Then Hitler lied! In Königsburg we heard the Jews were taken to work camps. We thought that was already terrible enough." The pain in Regina's chest returned thinking of the people she had seen forced into trucks. Now she had a new image, one much worse. "The Jews were treated so badly in the streets. We heard rumors about brutality of the *SS* and *Gestapo* after the war ended, but no one wanted to believe such things. One cannot trust news in the Russian zone now any more than we could trust news from the *Nazis* during the war. I can't believe this. Surely it's too dreadful!" Her hands shook.

"Believe it," *Herr* Arnold said firmly. "Thousands were exterminated in various camps. Auschwitz was probably the most infamous. Euthanasia also took place in Grafeneck, Hartheim, and other places. The *Nazis* killed the helpless. I suppose we should have known Hitler's intentions had we read his book, *Mein Kampf*. Though it was a best seller because we were all expected to have it on our bookshelves to avoid being branded as dangerous, it was so boring. I think no one bothered to read more than a few pages."

Regina was devastated by this news, realizing she was one who had not read the book either. Should she have known?

Herr Arnold resumed his narrative. "Though my wife and I knew the risks, we grew to love this bright young scholar like a son and were more than happy to keep him hidden and share our ration stamps. After all, we didn't believe Hitler would last so long."

"I suppose none of us did."

"Of course, Benjamin felt terrible guilt because his parents perished while he had survived. Since he had no papers, he wouldn't go down to the bomb shelters. He feared he might bring danger to us. We told him we were old and didn't care, but he feared the *SS* would take us away, too. He hid in the bathtub during raids because the bathroom had no windows. When the building sustained a direct hit, however, my wife was killed, and Benjamin was killed as well. Two and a half years he hid there safely, a beautiful young life, and then he died anyway, in the very last raid. Now I'm a surly old man, and I'm left to mourn them alone. A war, you know, is full of irony." He shook his head as though to clear away painful images.

Regina could hear the pain in his voice. "I'm so sorry. You've lost so much. Are you still a professor, then?"

"I was considered by Hitler too 'radical' to teach, and now I'm too old to teach. It was hard to lose my place at the university. My ultimate question would be, did Hitler change because of the war, from one who rebuilt the German economy to one who destroyed our scholars, our gifted Jewish citizens, our country, and finally, himself? Or was he always bad, and not enough of us saw the evil lurking underneath all the promises? Perhaps we'll never know."

Regina was silent. It was a remarkable question. What about others besides Hitler? How many countrymen, she wondered, were willing to accept *Nazi* brutality because they believed in the man until it was too late to change, or until they were too afraid to say so? And how many let others take chances while they protected their own lives? Was Gustav one of those? Had he believed in Hitler, and done his bidding, even while his family was being destroyed? Had the war changed Gustav also, or had he always taken the expedient way and she had not seen it...or perhaps she hadn't *wanted* to see it? Had she been too naïve to believe the changes, even in her husband? It was a large problem to consider.

The professor continued, "I think now that all people are divided between those who build with whatever faith they can muster, and those who destroy. Those who stick to the status quo don't count. They neither add nor detract from the equation. They simply bounce along coloring within the lines, protecting themselves, interpreting things the way they want them to be, and ignoring facts that do not fit their chosen pattern. Now, is your husband dead?"

This old man had a way of startling Regina with a direct

question interspersed between his philosophical meanderings.

"No," she answered sheepishly. "And I think I may have been one of those people who stuck to the status quo and interpreted things in their own way. I never wanted anything in my life to change. I was happy before the war and I wanted everything to remain exactly the same afterward." She could feel the tears building again.

"Life always changes, sometimes in an instant," *Herr* Arnold announced firmly. "We can't stop the changes. We must adapt to them."

Then the old man caught Regina with another sudden switch of topics--a piece of advice.

"But now, my fine young woman, if your husband is alive, there is always hope. Collect your children from the Russian zone and bring them here to your husband. You are young and strong and have already left the status quo, whether you wanted to or not, or you would not be here now. You would have given up your life and your children's lives had you remained as before. You've already changed."

Regina was forced to think about this idea. Was it true?

"Rebuild a new home, a family, a safe life, in a new city, a new Germany, and give your husband time to determine if he is a builder like you've become, or a destroyer like Hitler. The status quo is gone forever. You must now choose, and it looks to me as though you've already chosen."

He smiled then, and Regina found she could smile too, even through her brimming eyes. She reached into her knapsack to retrieve the two extra *Brötchen* Erna had given her for the train, handing one to the professor.

"Let us break bread on it." She smiled, then, and meant it.

"To hope and to builders," the old man said, touching his bread roll to hers as though they were Bavarian beer mugs.

"To hope and to builders," she repeated, "...and to people who understand. Thank you." They shared their bread in silent, smiling communion.

He laughed out loud. "My, how I've rambled on. Once a preachy professor, I guess one is always a preachy professor...but

I still hate to see a pretty woman cry. Now, don't you need to catch a train?"

Herr Professor Arnold walked Regina to the *Strassenbahn* and waved goodbye before heading off with his empty bag to search for a day's living. Though farmers of Bavaria had food, those in the city still had lives of uncertainty, with needs for food, shelter, and a future, unmet.

The old man was right, Regina thought. There was no longer a place for the status quo, only for those who were willing to rebuild. Regina would stand by her husband to rebuild their children's lives. Somewhere in the process, there would be time for Gustav to choose also to be a builder--or not. She couldn't have known then that, for him, there would be a third choice.

Chapter 32

The return trip to Weida was uneventful by comparison to Regina's previous travels. She bought her ticket for an afternoon train to Hof and walked to the U.S. Army *Kaserne* near the border. There she filed her intent to go to the east zone and return legally, with her family.

She accepted the soldiers' offer of a warm dinner in the mess tent, though it was hardly German style. It still amazed her how only a few cooks could prepare huge portions for hundreds of troops, plus all the hungry refugees who came to their door.

Late in the evening, soldiers loaded trucks with refugees who had papers for a future return trip from east to west.

"Hide your papers somewhere safe," one soldier said in almost perfect German.

"Why?" Regina asked. "I thought we were legal now."

"That's in case you're searched by the Soviets at the border. Our latest intelligence gleaned from refugees and patrols shows the Soviets are lenient to people who go to their zone intending to stay. They aren't so kind to those who return with intent to leave again and migrate west, especially if they are able-bodied. It seems they don't care much about the old or disabled, but they'll keep those who can work in their zone, by force if necessary."

Everyone rustled around, searching for the best place to hide his or her papers.

Regina's papers joined her money under the false bottom of her knapsack, which she promptly sewed down,. As she worked, she heard others questioning the American soldier about the crossing. She listened carefully.

"What will the Russians do if they find our papers of intent to leave their zone?" asked another woman with trembling voice.

"They'd most likely confiscate your exit papers and demand a list of all your relatives so they can watch you and your family more closely. You all know the Soviets are hard on those they find escaping from their zone. One never knows what to expect. If they take your exit papers, you'll have to start all over and escape again to get new ones."

"Have many had to do that?" asked the same woman.

"We've had some folks come through Hof after running the border three or four times. We don't know what happens if they are caught again. But if you return to a legal border crossing point with legal papers, they can't stop your leaving. That's why they'll want those papers *now*, if they can find them. We feel you should know the risks before you go back. Hide your documents well."

Regina would guard her return papers with her life. She didn't want to risk another dark, panicky flight across this border.

A middle-aged couple excused themselves and walked away toward Hof. The young soldier spoke to them briefly.

"We're afraid to do it again," the woman said. "We were going back to bring our parents out, but they're already eighty years old and they wouldn't want us to risk so much just for them. We're going back to Würzburg and wait. Perhaps it will get easier for them to leave the east zone later." The woman cried.

"I hope so, Ma'am," said the young soldier quietly. He walked back to the group, shaking his head, and speaking to those who remained.

"We've found one border crossing where, if the right Soviet guards are on duty, they'll let you through with only a check of baggage and the naming of relatives and destination. So when they ask you, tell them you're going to stay in the east zone. If you can convince them, they'll let you walk ten kilometers to the nearest railway station and you'll be on your way."

"If the right guards aren't on duty, you can wait another night or you can try to get across without being seen through the woods, the way you came." The soldier surveyed the refugees to see if they all nodded understanding. "I'm really sorry there's no other way we can legally help you cross the border. Don't worry, though," the *Ami* soldier said. "We've managed to get lots of people through who were hiding their papers, and then seen them again in a week or two, crossing into the west zone legally."

On this particular night, Regina's group was lucky. The *Ami* soldiers found the lenient Soviet guards on duty. After a preliminary handshake between one of the guards and one of the

GI's who spoke broken Russian, the people got off the trucks and walked across the border. Two guards checked their packs. They didn't find Regina's money or her papers, and she was soon on the road to the train station.

Three desperate people were detained while the Russians confiscated their papers. They extracted from them a list of their relatives. They joined Regina's group later while they waited for the train to Leipzig. Even though they no longer would have a legal escape, the three were already plotting yet another illegal one. Hope! *Herr* Professor Arnold was right: Now that Regina looked for it, she saw it everywhere.

Even though she intended to redeem her wedding ring upon her return to Weida, given the mysterious circumstances of her marriage, she reluctantly decided not to. She was to regret the decision the rest of her life. But, at the time, the ring seemed an unimportant luxury when there were so many more important things at stake. She needed to get the boys safely back to their father, and away from the Russians while the border was still crossable. Regina's Family Reunification Documentation Permit was valid for only one month.

When her train arrived in Weida, Willi and Rainer were waiting near the station. They must have met every train, waiting for their mother's return. Regina cried, happy to hold her sons again, and they all trooped home singing and laughing. When the children asked where she had been, however, she told them only that they'd soon be taking the train to a new home with their *Vati.*

Regina selected and packaged some items her husband had on his list, the few kilos of household goods allowed, and the few pieces of wedding silver, mostly things *Herr* Busch had sent to her months ago from Königsberg. However, a minor emergency arose just as she thought they were ready to leave. She found Willi frantically digging in the back yard.

"I've got to dig up my Russian medal," he insisted. "*Oma* buried it while you were gone."

Regina's mother protested, "I was afraid the Russian soldiers would see it and…"

"But it's my favorite thing," argued Willi. "I carried it in my knapsack all the way from Königsberg. I'm not leaving it behind."

Regina remembered the beautiful blue, star-shaped medalian. "I didn't know you'd brought it with you."

"If the Russians see it, they will think we got it from some dead Russian soldier," insisted *Oma*. "We don't even know where it came from."

"But *Vati's* officer friends gave me the medal for keeps," said Willi. "I've got to take it."

"Perhaps your *Oma* is right, Willi. I'm beginning to wonder if those officers got it from a Russian prisoner of war. The Russians now guard the border we must cross. They might keep us from going to *Vati*. I think you must leave it behind."

He asked, "Can't *Onkel* Hans carry it? He was a soldier so he could have found it accidently."

"Willi, I'm sorry, but it might get *Onkel* Hans in trouble too. He was not fighting on the Russian front. Please cover it back up."

Regina felt sad for her son as he shuffled off again to the hole, dragging the shovel behind him, but she was afraid to take the chance.

It seemed they would have to leave even more behind. Her brother and sister-in-law decided not to join the family emigration to the west.

"But Erna included your names on the papers so we all could go to the west." Regina tried to persuade them. "Our mother is coming. We'll be together there."

Hans answered sadly, "We don't have your courage to start all over again. Things here in the east will get back to normal soon, and we don't want to leave our property, our furniture, and all the things we've worked for. We'll rebuild our house as soon as building materials are available again. After all, the Russians can't stay in Germany forever, now can they?"

Regina couldn't convince them to come along, yet she had a bad feeling about leaving Hans and Gerda behind. From what she'd heard in the West, she doubted the Communists would allow the couple to keep ownership of their home. Given the abrupt division of their country and the increasing difficulty of escaping the Soviet zone, they might never see each other again. The goodbyes were painful, but Hans and Gerda waved and blew kisses.

The boys loaded battered boxes in their precious wagon, and the family walked to the station, caught the work train to Gera, on north to Leipzig, and then transferred to a faster train south to the legal border crossing. The final walk through the border guard station was difficult for Regina's mother, but she seemed as determined as Regina to leave the Russians behind. Regina picked up Franzi to stifle quickly any comments he might be foolish enough to make.

The Russian border guards examined the papers closely, but could find no illegalities to hold the family back. They could not resist their final parting shot, however, "You know that if you leave, you will not be allowed to come back to the East, ever!"

Regina greeted that pronouncement with a stony face. She didn't want to give the Russian guards the satisfaction of knowing she even cared. She'd already been forced from her home, her culture, and her land, leaving everything behind, just to reunite with her husband and find some sense of freedom in the new West Germany.

Her mother stifled sobs as the two older boys led her through the checkpoint.

"Don't cry, *Mutter*," whispered Regina. "The *Nazis* and the Russians have already taken everything. It doesn't matter anymore if we leave." Regina was only intent on saving her children, while she still could.

After a short walk across 'no-man's land,' the Americans again met each group with food, medical care, and encouraging smiles, barely glancing at their papers. The boys wolfed down the dinner provided at the mess hall, and Franzi pronounced it, "The best food ever." He hadn't eaten a full meal in some time. Trucks soon arrived to take everyone to Frankfurt am Main for registration and further dispersal.

At a Frankfurt reception center, they were first deloused by being sprayed down their necks with powder.

Regina's mother was indignant. "How dare they think we have bugs!" she said, loudly.

"Many will be grateful for the chance to rid themselves of bugs," Regina softly hinted.

"But we've kept bathing, even when it was in cold water." Regina answered, "I know that, but at least you must admit everyone is being treated equally. It's already better than in the Russian zone where some people were sorted out for 'special treatment.'" Regina knew, to the Soviets, 'special treatment' usually meant confiscation of everything one owned, or 'protection' for females who had been selected to sleep with Russian soldiers. Should those women refuse, they were usually raped anyway, so it hadn't made much difference. She felt far safer with the Americans.

The five of them spent the night in a vertical bomb shelter, like none they'd ever seen. Floor after floor of this high round tower had circular rows of metal cots. They weren't particularly comfortable, and Regina imagined all the nights terrified people must have spent in these quarters under the heavy bombardment Frankfurt had received during the war.

"We can stand any discomfort for one night," she encouraged the boys in response to their complaints. "You've slept in worse conditions. At least it's out of the rain, and it's warm."

The children, of course, were buoyed by enthusiasm, knowing they'd soon see their *Vati*.

"He'll know I'm not scared of him this time," squealed Franzi.

The two older boys made their plans for having fun with their father again. Most involved things they could remember.

"He'll take us first to the zoo," announced Willi confidently.

"No, first we'll all go to the lake and go on paddle boats," added Rainer.

"We'll go skiing again with *Vati*, won't we *Mutti*?" Willi had loved skiing since he learned at four, well before the war.

"We'll need to wait and see what's available and what's still undamaged," cautioned their mother. "*Vati* won't be able to fix the whole city by the time we get there. You must be patient." Regina was nervous, too, not sure what the future would hold. It took her awhile to fall asleep.

Next morning, the authorities registered them legally for their new destination and gave out a month's temporary ration coupons. The family joined the crowds at the railway station and bought tickets for Nürnberg's *Hauptbahnhof*. Regina also sent a telegram to Erna's home so Gustav could arrange to meet them.

True to his word, Gustav was waiting at the station, looking quite dashing in a suit and tie. He helped his family load all their earthly possessions into the back of a patched up car he'd hired. How he had managed to overcome his problems with the authorities and leave his hiding-place behind, Regina didn't ask. He was there, and that was all she needed for the moment.

Strangely, Regina's mother became silent, and only spoke when questions were addressed directly to her. Regina assumed she was simply tired from the journey.

Willi and Rainer rushed to their father's arms with gleeful shouts. Franzi hid behind Regina's skirts and only peeked around at his *Vati*. For all his bragging about being five and fearless, when the moment came, noisy Franzi was again struck dumb.

But this time, it only took a few moments for Gustav to tease him out of his shyness, and soon the child allowed his father to lift him into the car with a big smile.

"Did you forget me, *Vati*?" Franzi asked. "Willi and Rainer said you wouldn't remember me because I was too little and too scared last time you saw me."

"Never!" said Gustav, in his old confident voice. "But you must never forget me, either. You boys are especially dear to me, you know."

Seeing her husband with his sons, as though he'd never been away, Regina began to hope that, between the two of them, they could somehow rebuild all they'd lost during the long separation.

"We'll be going to *Tante* Erna's for tonight," Gustav announced as he drove, "but I'll have a surprise for you in the morning."

Of course, the older children immediately began their endless questions with Gustav playing right along.

"Is the surprise a maple taple?"

"Not even close."

"Is it a slippo hippo?"

"No, guess again."

Apparently, Willi at least, had not forgotten the rhyming games, and Rainer quickly joined in the fun. Franzi made up silly questions that didn't rhyme well, and soon no one could stop laughing. It seemed as though, after all, there was the possibility of reuniting this war-fractured family.

Erna was waiting with a lovely dinner, and her husband was also at last home from the war. The family crowded into their home jubilantly. After dinner, all five children were to sleep on the floor in the living room, getting reacquainted as though it were a social slumber party. Young Renee and Gerhardt were excited to see their three cousins again after so long, and the children's giggling could be heard long after they should have been asleep.

Though Gustav slept in Regina's room to let her mother have his former hiding place, he stayed stiffly on his own side of the bed. Even had he approached her, Regina wasn't sure how she should have responded. All her longing was now wrapped up in both hope and doubt. It had been so long. She felt they both needed time to regain their former relaxed intimacy.

The next day brought the surprise. Gustav had found a house for the family. It was not fancy, but Because of post-war shortages, it was a miracle he had managed anything at all.

It was a prefabricated wooden barracks, much like what they had left in Weida. The family shared half of the building with two offices. This *Baracke* was built at the edge of a bombed-out factory yard, which had been hastily cleared of rubble. The factory fence remained-- a concrete structure six foot high, which surrounded the yard. The bombed-out factory sat silently brooding at the other end. It's burned and broken windows seemed quite menacing to Regina. She was searching for some reassuring sign.

As people in the Nürnberg suburbs dug themselves out of the rubble, with *Trümmerfrauen* cleaning bricks for rebuilding, each newly cleared piece of ground quickly filled with prefabricated homes. These would serve until enough refurbished bricks could be used to build anew. In most large cities of the western zone, this work was done cooperatively by women, to help pay for the family's use of the *Baracke*, or collectively for residents to rebuild their original home, apartment, school, or church. Regina knew that in the eastern zone, such brick cleaning was frequently done at the point of a gun as the Russians collected the clean bricks and shipped them back to rebuild Russia. Building materials were scarce everywhere in Germany.

Also on the factory grounds was an outhouse for sanitary purposes, a peach tree that had somehow survived the bombings, and another prefabricated building, a *Lebensmittel-Grösshandlung*—a grocery wholesale company--where Gustav was already an employee.

Regina soon found he was working for a Jewish man, *Herr* Wiesengrund, who had just returned from Switzerland. Their old friends and business associates, the Minslovs, had urged him to find Gustav's sister in Nürnberg and establish a potential partnership with Gustav, wherever he could be found. Regina marveled that a Jewish person wouldn't be afraid to return home, but *Herr* Wiesengrund had been out of the country a long time.

Ironically, it was now German soldiers who couldn't own businesses until they had been cleared by the military occupation forces. But the returning Jewish businessmen were able to get licenses immediately. Hitler's tables had been turned. It was about time, Regina thought.

Regina and Gustav settled into the small living room, two bedrooms, and a kitchen. Life still seemed strained. Their prewar love could not quite overcome this new wall between the two. Their long separation, its mysterious circumstances, and Regina's disappointment that Gustav hadn't come to Weida himself to find her and the boys, had taken a toll on the relationship.

Arguments disrupted their nights, over nothing of consequence. Regina supposed she had become more independent, from necessity, and this fact somehow seemed to bother Gustav. She could no longer accept everything he told her without question. Too much tension and distrust had come between them. Though Regina had vowed to be a 'rebuilder' as wise old *Herr* Professor Arnold had suggested on her last trip to Nürnberg, she didn't know how to bridge this gap. It seemed far too wide, and it was growing wider each day.

But they also had happy days. Gustav built a tiny one-person kayak from old canvas and wooden slats, and he took the family to the Regnitz River on Sundays. After a picnic, they all took turns paddling alone along the smooth edge of the river. Gustav warned the boys to stay out of the swift current in the center.

After everyone else had ventured out for a turn in the kayak, Franzi begged to try also. "Please, *Vati*, please," he whined. But when Gustav finally relented and gave him the chance, the little boy couldn't paddle straight in the smooth water.

"I'm going backwards. *Vati*, Help me!"

As the child kept paddling in circles, out of reach and sliding toward the river's center, Gustav shouted, "I'm coming, son. Stay where you are." The father jumped from the bank into the river and swam to the kayak, pushing it toward shore.

Everyone laughed uncontrollably as Gustav carried Franzi under one arm and dragged the kayak ashore with the other.

"What are you all laughing about," asked Gustav angrily, as the whole family dissolved in giggles upon his return.

"You forgot to take off your shoes, *Vati*." Willi announced to the world.

"You squish when you walk," added Rainer.

His soggy shoes sucked at the mud. After he glared at the two older boys, he looked at Regina for some sense of sobriety. She couldn't control her mirth either. Gustav then put down his squirming son, ran to his giggling wife, lifted her in a spin on the sand, and roared with laughter.

On such a day, Regina saw a glimpse of the old tenderness in her husband's eyes. Gustav might hold her at night, and sometimes they made love, but it still felt tentative. Regina wondered if other husbands and wives, separated by war, were having similar problems getting their lives back together. She wanted their love to be as exuberant and warm as it had been before Gustav went away to war. Perhaps, she thought, he wanted it too. Sometimes he would again place his fingers to her lips, call her pet names, and her broken heart would soar.

But the mysteries in his life still came between them. Gustav remained silent about his past activities. Perhaps, she realized, he was afraid to tell her, and she was afraid to know.

Regina began helping other women in the factory yard as a *Trümmerfrau,* hoping to speed the rebuilding process and keep herself from thinking. It was, indeed, just as hard work as she had presumed when she had first seen it, and her small hands quickly deteriorated to pulp and split nails. One evening, Gustav grasped her hands and caressed them as he had when a newlywed. Then he kissed them with tears in his eyes. What could have been in his mind? He remained silent. Within the month, however, Gustav found Regina a job in an office near the streetcar line downtown, and her hands began to heal.

It was not long before Regina's self-proclaimed 'wheeler-dealer' husband had his own business again--a wholesale chocolate outlet. Somehow, *Herr* Wiesengrund had cleared away all legal problems for Gustav, and he seemed again on top of things, at least, in business. But the arguments continued. The two were careful not to raise their voices in front of the children during the day, but they were both fearful they could be heard at night, when they tried to discuss problems together in the dark.

How long this situation could go on, Regina didn't know. She felt they were both trying hard, when Gustav was actually at home. But his wholesale business kept him on the road half the time. He would be in Nürnberg for two weeks and then off to his Munich office for two weeks.

Even though he kept his own financial records, and she never bothered to look at them, she noticed her budgeted household money seemed only half what he had earned. She thought this was strange. However, Gustav was still of the traditional German opinion that women had no place in politics, business, or decision-making, so Regina bit her tongue to keep the peace. She did not ask about the discrepancy. She was to wonder later at her complete trust and lack of suspicion.

Chapter 33

With both Regina and Gustav working, Regina's mother, *Oma* Reh, watched the boys. But soon, she seemed to become more forgetful, and increasingly lax about checking up on them. Of course, mischievous Willi and Rainer took advantage of the older woman' confusion.

War-torn Nürnberg was a child's temptation to trouble. Gustav built the boys bikes out of old parts they found. They became adept at the activity of 'scrounging,' a new term they had learned from the American soldiers. They were out daily, searching among the ruins to find old things they could rebuild and make nearly as good as new.

Willi and Rainer quickly made friends with other boys in the neighborhood, especially two their ages, Karl and Dolf. The four ventured out on their bikes from daylight until dark. Franzi's shyness continued to keep him close to home, usually 'flying' around the yard alone with arms outstretched, making bombing noises. Regina feared he was not as resilient as the others, and may have always felt a bit left out of the older boys' activities.

Of course, along with the useful items they found, the four friends also managed to find old, unexploded shells, dynamite sticks, bullets, and bombs in the rubble as well. Regina remained blissfully ignorant of where her sons went with these other two boys she considered so nice, until a day when the remaining chimney of an otherwise totally destroyed factory blew up nearby. Neighbors caught the fleeing boys and brought them home in disgrace.

Regina was shocked. "What on earth could you boys have been thinking?" Unaccustomed to seeing their tiny, mild-voiced *Mutti* so angry, all four of the older boys pressed against the wall, not knowing what to expect.

"But *Mutti*, they were all old buildings that were already bombed out," ventured Willi. "Nobody worked in them or wanted them anymore."

"You may not have meant to destroy anything valuable, but

you damaged property that was not yours, no matter what condition it was in. Besides you boys could have blown yourself up." Regina faced them squarely with her arms folded in front of her. "Where did you get the dynamite? Where have you boys been going?"

From the corner, Franzi snickered and pointed at his brothers and their friends.

"I did not ask you, Franz Josef Wolff!" snarled Regina.

Franzi quickly hid under the stairs. His mother never called him by his complete name unless he was in big trouble.

"Now, you!" she said, staring at the remaining boys.

The four culprits looked at each other in confusion. Regina didn't know which one of them to accuse first. Even Karl and Dolf, shuffled their feet, and all four stared at the floor. Never had they seen Regina so fired up as this.

"Rainer," she said, deliberately choosing the most sensitive of the group, "Where did you get the dynamite?"

"I…we…we found a lot of old stuff at the stadium. It was just lying around in the bunkers. We didn't steal it or anything. Nobody wanted it, so we decided to play with it. We've had it a long time, *Mutti.*"

The other three boys glared angrily at Rainer. He blushed.

Regina stood her ground. So, they'd been playing under the Nürnberg stadium where Hitler led his torchlight parades and speeches in the old prewar days. During the last battle for the city, the bunkers had been the scene of hard fighting between German and American soldiers. How could the children even think of going there?

"What else did you find in the bunkers?"

"Lots of old money and medals and powder and unexploded ammunition of all kinds," ventured Karl. We stored it in one of the bunkers. We just looked at it. We weren't going to do anything with it." He must have realized his mistake as his hand suddenly flew over his mouth.

"What kind of powder and ammunition?" demanded Regina.

"It's just some old black powder we emptied out of the shells and rifle bullets after we took off the tips," said Dolf. "Nothing important. We stored it in an old leather pouch."

This was not going to fly by Regina, either. "You removed the tips by yourself? Is that powder what you boys used to blow up the chimney down the street?"

"Yes, Ma'am," they all chorused.

"Tell me how you did it." Her voice had grown deceptively calm.

The boys looked at each other for confirmation. Finally Willi answered, stuttering a bit initially from nervousness. "We put some rifle rounds under the chimney and put a couple sticks of dynamite on them. Then we poured out the black powder in a straight line from the chimney to our dugout behind the wall of a ruined house, and lit it with a match. You should have seen the fire just run down that powder line, and then, Kaboom!" In telling his story, Willi no longer looked chagrined, but had become quite animated. All the boys grinned, apparently excited by remembering their adventure.

Regina took a deep breath before answering. She didn't want to scare them, yet it was necessary. She couldn't allow the boys to think they should be doing such things again.

"Don't you boys realize that the ordnance and powder you've been hoarding is dangerous?"

All of them shook their heads.

She suddenly realized the truth. "You've done this before, haven't you?"

"Well, a little bit, *Mutti*," admitted Willi. "But it's not dangerous because we're really careful with the powder and ammunition. Nothing ever happens except it makes a loud explosion and chimneys of old buildings fall down. They'll have to knock down the chimneys anyway before they can rebuild the houses. We saved them the trouble." The other boys nodded in agreement with his logic. They looked quite smug and pleased with themselves.

It was obvious to Regina the boys didn't believe they'd done anything wrong or dangerous. She had to make them understand. "You could easily have lost a hand or an eye in a careless moment. And you make everyone in the neighborhood nervous with these sudden explosions. Our neighbors have been through enough fear with the war. They don't need you boys frightening them all over again."

The boys might have gotten off with only this scolding had Willi not added one more comment, proudly arching his head. "But *Mutti*, I *never* make mistakes, and we *never* have careless moments, so you needn't worry."

That did it! Regina marveled at how much he had become like his father--just a bit too adventurous, too sure of himself, and perhaps slightly dangerous.

Willi and Rainer were ordered to their room until their father should come home later that day from Munich. Regina marched Karl and Dolf to their respective homes and made them repeat their indiscretions for their parents. All the parents expressed anxiety at the boys' lack of fear about such dangerous behavior.

Gustav confronted the children upon his arrival and scolded them about their adventures. His solution was to put the children on three days of bread and water, hoping they would be suitably contrite.

Regina didn't feel this punishment was appropriate. "They've been hungry before," she said after the boys had gone to bed. "This will not be difficult for them."

Gustav, however, felt sure the punishment was severe enough. Neither parent thought to confiscate the cache of weaponry, however, so the boys, especially Willi, gave both Regina and Gustav a good scare on several more explosive or fiery occasions.

Though the boys had promised obedience, there were always challenging new temptations. With so much rebuilding going on, builders needed a way to get rid of basement excavation dirt, and trucks were scarce. To serve two purposes, it was decided the dirt could be spread around on a lower level to fill in remaining bomb craters. A metal construction lorry was set up on a track to facilitate getting this dirt down the hill.

Willi, Rainer, and their two friends climbed into the lorry, cut its tethers, and hurtled headlong down the embankment toward the gully below. They had craftily set a large wooden stake between the tracks almost at the track's end, assuming it would stop them. It didn't. Fortunately, not quite trusting their makeshift 'brake,' the boys had jumped out in time and weren't hurt. But the lorry flew off the track at the bottom and flipped over into a small stream. The neighbors came running, with the police not far behind. Gustav had to pay for the recovery of the lorry, and the boys were back on bread and water.

By this time, they had won a reputation in the neighborhood as troublemakers. The *Polizei* began watching their house closely, dropping by at odd hours to check on their whereabouts. Gustav was still away every two weeks and, of course, the boys would always try some new prank during his absences. Regina never knew what would come next.

Whether setting afire piles of tarpaper in a bombed-out swimming pool bathhouse to see the thick black smoke that resulted, or invading the many unfinished houses deserted by the builders on weekends, the four managed to find ever more creative mischief. Sliding down third story roof rafters of such a house, dropping two-by-six beams from an open roof down unfinished stairwells to a basement, or baracading themselves inside 'forts' they built in new basements against boys from another neighborhood became tremendous fun. In one such neighborhood 'war,' the 'enemy' boys pelted their fort's windows and roof tiles with rocks, again costing Gustav and the other fathers for the damage.

"Those Wolff boys," neighbors would say with clucking tongues. "It's only a matter of time until one of them kills himself."

Regina feared the same thing, and the boys' ideas for adventure seemed unending. The whole neighborhood was relieved when schools reopened and all the loose children were gathered under a more rigid and structured schedule. Then, the boys could only get into mischief after school. Never was Regina more aware that saving her children from outside danger, like the war, was only part of her job. Saving them from their own adventurous spirits was proving almost as difficult.

The parents were working together to take care of their boys, but in their personal life, Gustav and Regina still had both good days and bad ones. Regina had become much more independent than Gustav wanted her to be.

"That's why I always tried to protect you, Ina," he said one particularly bad day, "...because you were the perfect wife just the way you were. You grew up in a protected environment, and women were never meant to make decisions. I loved it that you were dependent on me."

"But how can I go back to being dependent? You're gone so often on business, I'm still forced to make decisions and discipline the boys during your absences, and you seldom agree with my choices when you come home."

He turned his gaze away and became defensive. Why did he always become sullen if she mentioned his absences?

"Gustav," she continued in self-defense, "how did you think I could take care of the boys through the war without learning to make decisions for myself? You were never there."

"Simply by agreeing with me without asking so many questions," he blurted out, his dark brown eyes flashing. "You've changed!" It was an accusation.

"I don't think I can be that same helpless, mindless person anymore. I never *wanted* to change. I wanted everything the same between us as before this awful war came and tore us apart. But I had no choice. You were gone, our home was gone, our money and belongings were gone. There was no one else to take charge, so remaining helpless was no longer an option, if I wanted to save our boys."

"Well, you at least did that, and you did it well. But now, I'm in charge again."

Regina took a deep breath and added, "But you've never answered any of my questions or told me all I needed to know. You're no longer the same person I married either. I think we've both changed."

Long, painful silences followed such an exchange.

Colossal differences of opinion surfaced also in the political arena. Regina felt in her heart, though no one would talk about it, that the German people had been wrong to follow what she had come to believe was an evil leader. This realization had come gradually, over the several years Gustav was in and out of her life. It had come from watching the changes in their whole society in Königsberg--the distrust, the anxiety, the roundups of law-abiding citizens by *Gestapo* or *SS* thugs only because of their religious or political views, and her own inability to act against these changes out of fear for her children. When Gustav mentioned his disappointment that Germany had not won the war, her feelings overwhelmed her.

"Look, I saw first-hand what catastrophe the war brought on refugees of all backgrounds and faiths, and I had plenty of time to think about it while trekking across Europe to find you. Hitler's policies forced his own people into this catastrophe. Surely, you saw some of that in your travels, too."

"That's wrong, Ina. Women should not meddle in politics. Hitler did so much good in the beginning. He overturned the Versailles Treaty and brought us out of the depression. I owed it to him to follow him to the bitter end. He was a genius. You just don't understand because you never saw him in action."

"And you did?"

"Of course. I received instructions for my projects on several occasions. He was a strong man with great ideas. Unfortunately, he was misled later in life by bad advisors, but he never had any evil intentions of his own. We should preserve our leader's memory against this current trend to malign him by those who didn't do their duty for the *Reich*."

"And what was your duty, Gustav?"

"I can only define my activities in his service as doing whatever was necessary." He refused to say more.

"If Hitler did nothing bad, what about the Jews? We had Jewish friends. How could you think he was a great man while so many people suffered? Did you know many were killed?"

"Those tragedies in the news never happened. How can you believe our conquerors' propaganda instead of our *Führer*?"

"I believe he was always evil, and perhaps even crazy, and we just didn't see it because we were all happy for the economic progress Germany made at the beginning. "

"And I know the war may have brought about painful

necessities, but Hitler never intended any evil. You, and the rest of the world have misunderstood him."

The two of them argued on this subject frequently, since they each held strong beliefs.

Though Regina wanted the arguments to end, she was unable to stop feeling her analysis of events was the correct one. In desperation one day, she screamed, "Hitler is dead, Gustav! We lost the war! Why is he still controlling our lives and coming between us just as he did during the war? Why must we jeopardize our marriage because of these arguments? Can't we please just let the old *Nazi* cause die and start living a new life for our sons?"

To her surprise, Gustav replied soberly, "Do you believe our marriage is now a mistake, along with our disagreement over how and why we've come to feel these divisions?"

Regina wondered if he was hinting at divorce, something unthinkable in her family, in her culture, in her religious belief. She panicked. "Of course not. We can still work this out. Perhaps we just shouldn't discuss the past at all. Let all the old ideas die with Hitler. We have three sons to raise, and they need us."

Gustav said quietly, "All right, Ina, we'll never mention the political past again, but you're not as politically naïve as you used to be. I'm not sure you're any longer able to hold your tongue about matters and people you should know nothing about."

"I can," she replied. And she did.

But inside, Regina was aware there were far too many things the two could no longer discuss. She was beginning to feel she was trying to maintain a marriage for two, all alone. And perhaps it was only for the sake of her sons.

Chapter 34

And so the couple continued on, yoked together, at least during the two weeks out of each month that Gustav wasn't gone on business. They both worked hard through the rebuilding of their children's lives, the rebuilding of Nürnberg, and the new beginnings of Germany.

The Wolffs soon learned their business and home ownership documents, as well as their bank account vouchers, so carefully saved from Königsberg, were worthless. The Soviet Russians had seized all private property in the East Zone, and they refused to honor agreements between the former allies. Only the small account *Herr* Busch had transferred to a Nürnberg bank was available to the family, so they were starting over, financially, as well as in every other way.

The fact hardest to accept for the Wolffs was that they could never go home to Königsberg again. The Russians had forcefully deported all Germans from the city on trains to Berlin. Then they moved in Russian people from their inland steppe and renamed the city Kaliningrad, USSR--not even an occupied German city, but now a Soviet city. The harbor they loved had become a Soviet submarine base. The historic Prussian city of Königsberg no longer existed.

They also learned that Gustav's parents and a younger brother had died in the war. Regina and Gustav shed many tears together...and separately.

"I simply had to close the door and walk away from everything we ever owned, every friend, every stick of furniture. It really hurts to think of our lovely home and much of our family gone, forever." Regina told Gustav, as she cried in his arms at the reality of this news.

"We have our jobs, our health, and our children," he said, encouragingly. "We must work to start over again. It will simply be in this new city."

Perhaps he would become one of the builders instead of the destroyers, after all, Regina thought. In spite of their disappointment, her hope was rekindled.

The school children of Nürnberg were among recipients of little gray pasteboard Red Cross boxes filled with pencils, erasers, rulers, toothbrushes, toothpaste, and washcloths, which were gathered together by school children in America and shipped directly to the children of Germany. In many cases, the American children, instinctively knowing what's important even in adversity, had tucked a few wrapped candies under the obvious necessities. This kind act usually occasioned a letter written to the far-away class. Willi, of all the children, spoke often of going to see America for himself, perhaps even of becoming an *Ami* soldier.

Gustav's business gradually became more financially stable, and he had a prefabricated cottage built for the family in Erlensteigen. The day they were to move in, Regina's mother disappeared for many hours. When local police brought her home after dark, she didn't remember where she'd been. While the family had noticed more confusion, silence, and forgetfulness, they had assumed it was because of her losses during the war.

Regina became aware that her mother could not be left alone while she and Gustav were at work and the children were at school. They placed *Oma* Reh nearby, in a newly refurbished nursing home. Regina visited her daily, after leaving the office.

Before long, the old woman didn't recognize any of the family. But she kept talking. She talked for hours of her former life in Königsberg, of Regina's father, of their early years together. She even talked about the wonderful party the old couple had given Gustav and his high-ranking officer friends that strange Christmas in 1941. She was rarely silent. Even during sleep she rambled on, telling the unknown world her story.

One such day, while Regina knitted socks for the boys as she waited for her mother to have a lucid moment, the old woman suddenly became quite agitated. She began talking rapidly. "Why, he even came to me, to me of all people, and told me!" she cried out in an indignant tone.

Intrigued, Regina looked up. Who was her mother talking about this time, she wondered. Her mother had not recognized Regina for over a month, and most of her rambling talk had been gibberish. It was as though Regina were only one of the nurses, instead of her own daughter. But at that moment, her mother seemed quite animated and her words were unusually clear.

"Who told you, Mutter? What did he tell you about?" Regina asked in a conversational tone, hoping perhaps her mother's mind was becoming clear, and that a little encouragement might make her remember her family.

"Him," the old woman repeated, quite forcefully. "I told Elli, and she agreed it had to remain a secret or it would kill her."

"Elli?" Regina stopped. What would need to be a secret so as not to kill Elli? This didn't make any sense. "Mutter," she asked urgently, "Who would hurt Elli?"

"Of course, no one would hurt Elli," her mother stated, looking rather puzzled. She was silent for a time, and Regina tried to make sense of her strange words. If not Elli, then who?

Her mother suddenly grabbed Regina's hand with such force that it hurt. How could she still be so strong?

"It was after Father was buried on the hillside," the old woman said clearly. "He came home to see that I took the train to Weida. He cried and cried, and said Regina mustn't know, that it would kill her if she knew. He told me again and again how sorry he was, that he hadn't meant it to happen."

Regina's mother was weeping profusely now and had risen almost to a sitting position from her pillow.

"Mutter, Mutter," Regina screamed, her heart pounding in a dread she had never known. "Whom are you talking about? Wasn't it Gustav that put you on the train? Are you saying Gustav told you something? My Gustav?" She tried to keep her voice controlled, but it rose out from under her. Regina stood quickly, dumping her knitting to the floor, unheeded. She placed pillows behind her mother's back so she could sit up more comfortably.

"Mutter, do you know me? Do you mean these words for me?" Regina realized the woman looked confused whenever she called her Mutter, so she consciously stopped doing so.

"What did Gustav say to you?" Regina asked carefully, not wanting to hear what her mother had to say, yet not sure she could bear it if she didn't know this secret, now that it had been mentioned.

"He had another woman in Russia and another child." The old woman spat out the hated words.

Regina could no longer speak through the fog of pain that overwhelmed her. She gasped, and felt she was drowning in this room that now seemed an airless vacuum. *Was this what it felt like to die?*

Her mother kept right on talking. "Why, the child was already two years old. And he wanted me not to tell Regina. I refused. But when I told Elli, she said the same thing, that knowing would kill my own dear daughter."

By this time, Regina's mother was quite agitated and shrieking loudly.

"Did I do wrong?" her mother screamed," as nurses rushed in. The head nurse injected *Frau* Reh with a sedative to quiet her, while Regina watched, frozen in horror as though she were watching someone foreign speaking from a long distance away.

"Did I do wrong?" came the question again, plaintively. Regina could not understand what had happened, yet she couldn't let her mother become sedated without comfort.

"No, *Mutter*. You did nothing wrong," Regina said slowly. She sat motionless, holding her mother's hand as she drifted off to sleep. The old woman's conscience was apparently now clear.

Regina had no idea how long she sat at the bedside with her head buried in her hands. How could her mother have kept such a secret? And Elli had known also, yet she had said nothing in her letter. Her mother had come to Regina for safety in Weida, yet she had been keeping this knowledge to herself. Was this why she bit her lip silently whenever Gustav's name was mentioned, or left a room whenever he entered it?

Regina finally accepted that her mother had been silent to protect her, to avoid hurting her further. At whom was she angry? Was it at her mother and Elli for not telling her sooner? Would it have made a difference then? Probably not, as Regina had already left her home on Gustav's warning to get the boys away safely. He must have at least cared enough about them to want them safely away from the enemy.

Then, was she angry with Gustav and this other woman? Regina couldn't even picture her. Was she Russian? Gustav hated Russians. Regina had to ask herself the horrible question, "How could he have gone to another woman when he knew how much I loved him? He *knew* I was waiting at home, fighting to keep our family together until he could get back to us."

Her efforts to fight tears resulted in a terrible ache in the back of her throat, as though something were constricting the screams there. Finally the tears streamed quietly down in spite of her desperate attempts to remain controlled.

The child was already two years old. Why, that would mean this betrayal happened soon after Gustav had left her in Königsberg that last time. "But how?" Regina cried, realizing immediately that she had said the words out loud. He had been so sweet and loving that last night. Could he have been so false, so loving to her if he already had a woman in Russia he was going back to? Or had he met the woman *after* their last time together?

Again and again, Regina lingered over the little bit of information she had, trying to put pieces of the puzzle into place. She could find no logical answers. Though, if her husband had loved someone else, it would explain why he couldn't seem to get along with her now. Was he only staying with her because he realized how much the boys needed him? *But she needed him too! Didn't he know that?*

Her attempt at rational control collapsed, and she started crying all over again. A nurse came to ask if she needed a sedative to combat the stress of her mother's illness. Regina shook her head and ran from the hospital blindly, not even noticing the rain that poured down heavily.

What would she do now? Should she confront Gustav when he returned home from Munich? Should she leave him? Finally, unable to come to terms with this horrible information, she returned home, climbed the stairs wearily, and started a letter. "I need answers, Elli." Regina wrote, "I need the truth." Her tears fell softly in her lap as she sealed the letter.

Chapter 35

Regina waited for Gustav to arrive home on the next Friday as planned. He came in rather soberly, greeted his family, and they had dinner together. Food was becoming more available in the open markets to supplement the Marshall Plan items from America, and life, at least everyone else's life, was becoming more normal again. Regina's life during the week had been lost in the limbo of her own mind. She had accomplished every task in a haze, and she had talked with no one.

After dinner the family played games together. Then the boys took baths and got ready for bed. Regina waited another hour until she was sure the two youngest were asleep, then asked Willi to watch them for a while. She asked Gustav if they could take a walk together. He smiled, offered his arm, and they walked out into the late evening.

"Perhaps we can go to the outdoor cafe nearby and have a glass of wine," he suggested.

Regina did not feel like wine, but thought perhaps it would help her overcome her fear of asking questions. Did she really want to know the answers? What would happen to her family if Gustav would not, or could not, explain? Should she keep quiet and hope this awful information was simply the ranting of a confused old woman?

The couple settled at a quiet table on the square and ordered a glass of wine. Regina remembered the lovely evenings they had spent like this, at a café overlooking the harbor of Königsberg before the war. Couldn't they simply remain as they were now and hope to build a better relationship? *Not any more*, she realized.

Mustering her courage and hoping against hope Gustav might have some plausible explanation, Regina quietly mentioned visiting her mother while he had been gone.

"How is she?" Gustav asked, with genuine concern. He always had loved her mother.

"Not well, I fear," Regina said. "She still doesn't remember who I am, but in her delirium, she said some things I didn't understand. I want to ask you about them now."

"I think I know," Gustav said, almost inaudibly, "and I've wanted to talk to you for a very long time."

"Please, tell me now," she said, calling all her courage together. "I don't think I can stand these painful feelings anymore. I'm truly aching, in body and soul."

"I know, Ina, and I was wrong to keep secrets from you. You, of all people, know me best and love me most, and I want you to know I appreciate that your love for me has never faltered." He took her hands in his across the tiny table.

She was aware of the soft scent of lilac in the air. In the moonlit evening, she could not see the destruction of the old city. Everything seemed so normal, even as her world crumbled with his affirmation of her mother's statements.

"It was all my fault, Ina, not yours."

Aware they were sitting in a public place, acting like the lovers they used to be, Regina thought of the incongruity of this moment. She should have been screaming and crying. But, in her numbness after his first words, she could only nod at him to continue. She couldn't even find the strength to draw away her hands from his. She sat in stunned silence, feeling all her hope float away.

"When?" she asked. She really wanted to know "Why?"

"It was a few months after I left you that night in Königsberg, Ina. I returned to the Russian fronts at Minsk, then to Kursk, and then Smolensk on Army business. In Smolensk, I fell ill with the old gall bladder problem I've had so many times, and I became unconscious. I awoke in an Army field hospital near the front lines. The doctors said I'd be there a week before I could return to my duties. But, before the week was out, our hospital came under enemy attack and the Russians were approaching the front gate." He held her hands more tightly.

"There was... there was this young auxiliary nurse among the hospital volunteers who helped with the patients in our ward. As the Russians closed in on the front side of the hospital, she helped those of us who could walk out the back. She found a farmer's barn with a storage cellar where she could hide us.

"The battle raged back and forth for many days. This young girl, Frieda, crept out every night to find food, and brought water for us to drink, and to clean the more seriously ill. After awhile, I was feeling better and was able to help her a bit with the other patients."

Gustav stopped to light a cigarette for them both, then continued. "She was always cheerful, even with the fighting going on right over our heads. When the barn above caught fire from the shelling, she hauled each patient out and hid each in the underbrush several meters away, returning to the barn until all were safely rescued. She had great courage, great strength. I don't know when she began relying on me more heavily, but somehow she did." Gustav stopped abruptly and looked out across the square toward the lights.

"Did you love her?" The words felt torn from Regina's throat.

"I don't know, Ina. I think at first I felt indebted to her, as we all did. She had, in fact, saved our lives. She brought an energy and dedication to the task one couldn't help but admire. But love? I don't think so. I was always aware any feeling for her was wrong, and that you and the boys were waiting for me at home. I've always loved you, from when you were still a child. You know that, don't you?"

He again took her hand across the table.

Gustav searched Regina's face as though for a sign. She could not summon an answer.

He continued softly. "But then, during a concentrated push by the Russians, the situation grew so desperate I began to doubt I would survive the war to ever go home again, and she shared the same doubts. The bombardments were all around us and we couldn't do anything to defend ourselves. Somehow, in our desperation, we clung together, and..." His voice trailed off, leaving her to picture the scene for herself.

She didn't like the picture.

"What about the child? How could that have happened?"

"Oh, Ina," his voice broke. "I so underestimated her attachment to me and her lack of knowledge of the world. She was much younger, only twenty, and I should have known better. It was my fault. I had been so frightened myself, that I compromised this young girl."

Gustav seemed to search Regina's face for clues to her feelings. She could summon no words from her pain.

"Our German soldiers finally pushed back the Russian advance and we patients who were able to walk carried the weaker survivors back inside. We were ordered to fix damage so the field hospital could resume full operation. I was helping there for two months while getting treatment for my illness and a shrapnel wound I picked up in the woods.

"When I was ready to go back to my military duties in Berlin, Frieda came to tell me she was pregnant."

Regina couldn't believe Gustav could say this so calmly, yet she felt powerless. What could she say to her husband next? He continued on as though she should somehow understand these awful circumstances.

"I had assumed Frieda would feel as I did, that we had made a shameful mistake. The crisis was now over, and we would each go back to the old lives we'd been given back, and move on. But she was pregnant...pregnant!" He shook his head as though he could not believe it himself.

"What was my obligation then?" Gustav asked Regina, as though he really wanted to hear an answer.

"Frieda was still there when I was ordered back to Smolensk three months later, 'waiting for me to return,' she said. But she could no longer stay at the front. The officials were sending her back to her mother's home in Munich to await the child. Her father and brother had died in the early days of war in Poland and France, shortly before Frieda volunteered. She and her mother were alone.

"I felt so helpless. But I also felt obligated to provide her what money I could. I promised I'd send more for her and the baby every month. I was so frightened. I knew this whole episode would be such a blow to you, if you ever found out."

Regina dared not stir. She tried to imagine Gustav wrestling with such a catastrophe.

"I might have ended it there with only sending her money,

except I got a message from Frieda's mother later that she had gone into labor prematurely. The child was born sickly, and she asked me to come. I felt so torn. I knew I mustn't see Frieda again, yet I felt terribly guilty for getting her pregnant when I couldn't take care of her.

"I wanted to come home to you, or write and tell you, but I was so ashamed...so horribly ashamed. What could I tell you, my best friend, my only love, when you were bravely trying to keep our boys safe at home? What a horrible thing I had done to you, to her, to myself, to all of us!" Gustav shrugged his shoulders as he faced his wife. "What could be said?"

Regina could almost feel Gustav's pain. Finally, her voice came, as though from someone else, slowly, carefully, "Had you been a more callous man, you would have been able to send her away and forget any obligation. Because you couldn't, it made all of our lives much more complicated. But then, perhaps, I would never have loved you so much if you'd been a callous man. You must know it hurts terribly to listen to you, yet I know you need to tell it all as much as I need to hear it all, if we are ever to move beyond this moment."

Tears were running down Gustav's face as he clung to her hands. They had forgotten the wine altogether. Regina neither knew nor cared what other café patrons might have thought about the handsome couple so engrossed in their own conversation.

"I was able to get a flight to Munich that coincided with my Army duties, and I had a few days there to conclude my business. When I found her, she and her mother and this frail baby, Konrad, were living in a tiny basement apartment, and Frieda's mother welcomed me as though I'd been a prodigal son. They both acted as though I would now assume my place in their family and stay with them. It was impossible! I had Army duties of my own for the *Führer* and my own family at home. I knew I must leave them in Munich.

"But I was touched by her simplistic solutions to everything. She said that '...because she loved me so much, and because poor little Konrad had no one else, she was confident I would find a way to be with them.' I was beaten. She was so sure of everything, and

I was so torn with guilt. It was awful."

Gustav put his head down on their joined hands and Regina felt his damp tears. What could she say to this errant man whom she had loved all her life? No words came. The silence hung between them until Gustav again found his voice.

"Her mother was gracious and treated me as though I were the man of the family coming home. I explained that I had a family already, and that I wouldn't be returning. But Frieda's mother said, 'No one knows what the war will bring. Perhaps none of us will survive--perhaps some.' They kept telling me that perhaps you wouldn't be able to keep our boys alive either, and we must all wait until the end of the war to see what was meant to happen.

"When I left, I was quite confused. Frieda always knew where I was stationed because I mailed her some money each month. I knew you and the boys had the proceeds from the business and *Herr* Busch would not let you do without."

"Except without you," Regina said, her anguished voice muted.

"I know, Ina. It was a terrible dilemma, one in which I never intended to become entangled.

"On my next assignment to Dachau, Frieda hitchhiked from Munich, bringing Konrad, to visit me there. He was a beautiful little boy, and very cuddly and loving, but so fragile. She did the same again to join me when I was at Nürnberg, and even once at the hospital in Karlsbad. Each time, I told her she shouldn't come again, but she continued to expect we should be together. She thought I should be *glad* to see her and this baby.

"Gradually, the war was going so badly, near Königsberg and elsewhere, I began to feel that you and the boys could never travel so far, and that there was no way we could all survive. Perhaps I would never have a choice in the matter at all. When you were so late coming to Karlsbad, I gave up hope that I would ever see you again, so I allowed Frieda and Konrad became a part of my life too."

Regina gasped. Had her tedious and dangerous journey been a part of his decision?

"By the time you arrived, and I knew you were safe, I felt

too much pain to know what to do. We had too little time to explain and, with my meetings with staff officers taking so much time, we had no chance to talk. How could I ever explain this whole thing with Franzi scared of me and hiding behind your skirts, and with Willi and Rainer needing my attention? It wouldn't have been fair to tell you such news and then leave right away. The moment of confession slipped away from me."

Regina stroked his hands slowly. "I, too, felt terrible having no time alone together, and I found myself too shy to ask the questions left unanswered. It was a strained time in Karlsbad. The boys felt it too. They didn't even want to stay the extra days without you, and neither did I. We started traveling again almost as soon as you left with those men. I was frightened when we couldn't talk to each other then. And we've had such trouble talking all this time since we've been together again."

"I've been so torn, Ina. I haven't known what to say or how to tell you. It seemed easier to simply take care of two families until I could get the courage to do something about the mess I got us all into. Perhaps that's why I told your mother, almost hoping she would tell you since I lacked the courage myself. I'm relieved you know now."

It seemed strange to Regina that she felt closer to Gustav now, even after this horrible revelation, than she had in the last few months of their strained existence.

"You asked if I loved her?" continued Gustav. "Is it even possible to love two such different women? I feel so helpless in this dilemma, and I can't even think of it without pain and self-loathing."

"Are we so different, then?" Regina asked.

"As different as it's possible to be, Ina. You've always been my beloved, my delicate little bird, with graceful movements and thoughtful ways--so tiny I could carry you away to our room. Your voice was that of a dove, compliant and soft for listening. Sometimes, I only wanted to listen to the music of your voice and I didn't even care what you were saying. You were kind to my friends, courteous to everyone, and such a joy to have as my quiet, sweet wife. In my wildest dreams, I never thought any of that would change. Perhaps you were only giving in to my ideas then, instead of promoting your own, in order to be compliant. I don't know anymore.

"Frieda, on the other hand, is a sturdily-built girl, a bit noisy and opinionated. Your hair is soft, and always beautifully in place; hers is red, and wildly wind-blown. Where your complexion is pale cream, hers is ruddy and tanned. Her rough speech almost embarrasses me at times, but she was a dedicated Party member when her country needed her. Her hearty laughter kept my spirits up on many occasions when I despaired of ever finding you again. I'm not sure I know what I feel. I owe you both so much."

Regina's pain forced her to look away, leaning her head on the back of the chair. "I wish this would all go away," she said quietly, even as her heart was screaming the words.

"So do I." Gustav was silent for a time, then he sighed deeply. "Now, here I am, a man torn, compromised, beholden to two women and two families in two cities. You're so strong, Ina, stronger than you know, to have done all you've done alone. Perhaps that's why I bristle at your strength so much now. It makes me aware of the strength I lack. The boys are growing up so fast, but they still seem to need a father's guidance too. They've been through so much. I can't leave you with no help to raise them."

Then this affair of his is over, Regina thought, and he'll stay with us.

He kept speaking.

"But Frieda also has a child on her hands for whom I'm responsible, and he's frequently sick. If she lost him, I don't know what she'd do. She, too, depends upon my support, both financial and emotional. I may as well be completely honest now, before we make any further decisions. I see her and her son when I go on business to Munich, when I'm not here in Nürnberg."

Shock registered, as though artillery were pounding in Regina's ears. Yet, she realized the truth with sudden clarity. Why had she not seen this as a possibility? She knew he spent two weeks in Munich every month and she received only half what he earned. Why had she not even considered there might be another woman? Did she still trust him so much, then, remembering all they had once been together? She felt angry and yet she found herself feeling sympathy for Gustav's dilemma as well. What was she really feeling? She wasn't sure of anything except the pounding pain. She realized Gustav was waiting for her to say something.

"It must have been very difficult for you to keep two families in two places, and to feel compassion and responsibility for both. I had no idea. A lesser man would have simply given up one or both families. But, of course, this situation cannot continue, can it? You'll have to choose."

Gustav hesitated a moment without answering her statement, then nodded and stood.

"May we go home, Ina? I can't even begin to say how sorry I am, and I desperately want to find some answers with you. I truly don't know what to do next. I need you and our sons so."

Regina rose while Gustav called the waiter and paid the check, their glasses of wine sitting forlornly in the night, untouched. Gustav took her arm as they picked their way over the recently replaced cobblestones on their street.

She offered no resistance. What would she want him to do, after all? What a ridiculous question! *She wanted him to stay with her and tell this Frieda that he loves his wife and will never leave her. That's what she wanted him to do!* Her heart screamed the words inside, while her outside demeanor remained deceptively calm. She had always restrained violent emotion in the name of decorum, and now, when she desperately wanted to tell her feelings, nothing would come out. She wondered for a moment if Gustav thought she didn't care because she was too hurt to speak. Would that influence his decision?

They walked in silence for a way. "I wish there had never been a war," Gustav said suddenly, as though he could blame all their terrible misfortunes on a war that had torn their family, and many other families, apart.

"So do I."

Chapter 36

Weeks crept by as the once-loving couple tried to make life tolerable for each other. Gustav was very solicitous and spent their two weeks together doing as much as possible with the boys and Regina, trying to recapture their sense of confidence and fun. They didn't talk further about the decisions facing them. It was as though each was afraid a confrontation would force them to part-- or perhaps not to part. What was best? What was there to say? Pain consumed Regina, pain she struggled to hide.

Downtown Nürnberg held much excitement in 1946 and '47. The international war trials were underway to find and punish the *Nazi* leaders who had caused such evil to other countries as well as in their own land. The *Strassenbahn* that passed by the Palace of Justice, where these trials were held, stopped at one end of the blockaded street while guards got on and locked the doors. They kept everyone from getting off until they had passed through the gate at the other end.

Regina was never sure whether the military officials in charge were afraid someone might try to free the suspects, or to assassinate them. There were, of course, enough political activists on either side of the argument to make the precautions necessary.

Her two oldest boys thought all the intrigue very exciting and rode the streetcar past the Palace as often as they could manage, no doubt pretending to be spies or saboteurs or military guards. They had such wild imaginations, and they still didn't seem to discern real from imagined danger.

Willi and Rainer were quite vocal about what should happen to the *Nazi SS* and *Gestapo* leaders on trial. Their comments usually came at dinner, after each new atrocity was discovered and announced on the radio.

Gustav followed the proceedings with intense interest. It seemed he could barely wait for the daily newspaper. But he stayed strangely silent and never stated his views on the topic.

"I'm glad they're hanging most of those *Nazi* men, or at least giving them long prison sentences," said Willi one night.

Rainer added, "Me, too. They got us into a war and lost all our homes, for nothing."

"There's more to it than that," declared Willi forcefully. "What about all the people they killed in Russia and in the concentration camps? Those Russians were terrible to us, and I sure don't like them, but I guess they didn't deserve shooting after they'd surrendered to our troops."

Regina said, "The *Nazis* deserve those heavy sentences. They've disgraced Germany before the whole world. I sometimes wonder if anyone will ever trust our country again?"

"They said today that some of the *Nazis* got away, or they're hiding," Willi announced. "I think every one of them should be hunted down and hung."

"They'll catch them eventually, Willi," said Regina. "Don't worry, they won't get away from punishment any more than Hitler did. But discovering all that happened, and all these accusations, has been difficult for everyone. I keep thinking about the families of these men that probably didn't even know."

"The *Nazis* seem as bad as the Russians to me," said Willi, "and I don't want to know any of either bunch. I do like the American soldiers though. They've been good to us, haven't they?"

Rainer chimed in again, always wanting inclusion in the conversation. "I'll be glad when they find all those *Nazis* that are hiding, won't you, *Vati*?

Gustav silently put down his knife and fork, folded his napkin, rose from the table abruptly, and walked away to his office, shaking his head.

Rainer immediately asked, "What's the matter with *Vati*?"

Regina wondered too, but she said, "*Vati's* just tired tonight. He also wants to listen to the radio. Now, finish your dinner."

Though she would be glad to have the *Nazi* trials and accusations over, they didn't affect the family's immediate personal dilemma--at least, Regina didn't see any way that they could.

A week later, Elli arrived on a surprise visit from Hannover. A taxi brought her to the address, and she marched up the walk.

Both women were delighted.

"Regina, you'll never believe this. I drove Paul to the Hannover *Bahnhof*. He was supposed to report to Nürnberg for his required de-Nazification. At the last minute he seemed to see *Nazi*-hunters behind every bush and was afraid to take the train. He said he feared he'd be arrested before he could report to the American officers, and the common soldiers would hunt him down like a dog. He handed me his ticket and told me to come visit you."

"It's wonderful to see you after so long, no matter how you got here. But I cannot imagine why Gustav's brother felt so vulnerable."

"Paul felt he'd done nothing wrong except try to be a good lawyer and judge for the *SS*. He's always been such a good man."

"With the temper of the times, though, perhaps he felt helpless to defend himself. No one would want the disgrace of judgment, even if they were eventually judged innocent."

"Anyway, I was so glad to come see you," Elli said. "It was such a surprise. Paul saw guards around the train station and turned all white. That was it!" She laughed. "Look, I don't even have proper clothing with me because I left with no warning, but Paul gave me money and said I could buy something once I arrived. I've really missed the boys and you. I also feel so bad about your letter asking me for the truth."

Regina had mixed emotions, having felt quite betrayed at being the last to know of her husband's infidelity. But she guided Elli into the kitchen, pulled out a chair, and offered her friend some tea. Though the cups were second-hand, she poured as regally as she had always done in East Prussia, and waited politely for her guest to begin telling her story.

"Regina," Elli said, "I'm so sorry. But when your mother told me this awful news about Gustav and that other woman, she was terribly distraught. I needed to get *Oma* on a train and out of Königsberg after the firebombing and the loss of your father and her home. I knew I couldn't take care of her if the Russians came. Her only chance was with you. But she wouldn't leave unless I promised her I wouldn't tell."

Regina bowed her head trying to carefully frame her words.

Mustn't cry, she thought. It will change nothing. "I assumed as much, Elli. It's just that it was such a blow, and we've not yet recovered." The two women sat in an uncomfortable silence, each buried in personal thought.

Elli filled the void, "I had to get your mother on the train somehow before the Russians attacked again. I agreed with her that any such news would hurt you deeply. God knows that's the truth." Elli paused, remembering her confusion. "I just didn't know what else to do but give her my promise and get her out of Königsberg before it was too late. I'm so sorry. I dared not tell you."

Tears rolled down her flushed cheeks, as she continued.

"I just prayed that once the war was over, this would turn out to be some kind of mistake. I didn't want to believe any of what your mother told me because it was all too terrible. I knew you were doing your best with the boys in Weida, and your mother's arrival and your father's death would be surprise enough. I didn't want to pass on such a thing when it might be just a mistake, like I said, and you certainly didn't need further distractions while you were being encircled by two enemy armies." Elli rattled on uncontrollably, her face tormented in an obvious plea for understanding.

Regina reached out to take her hand. "I know, Elli. You and mother were both just trying to protect me. But I've been protected too long. Please... go on."

"Well, when I found Gustav in Berlin in February, he confessed it to me also, but I didn't know what to say. He had even shown both your mother and me a photo of the child he carried in his wallet, just as he still carried Willi's. That *really* made me angry, but I didn't want to write that news to you and have you upset as well. You already had enough worries. I kept hoping something would happen to change it all."

Elli paused for a moment and smoothed her skirt across her lap. "You know... it's strange to say, but I had the distinct feeling that Gustav also hoped something could happen to change everything. He left during the air raid before we could talk further, and he returned to put me on the train back to Hannover the next day. I never saw him again."

"Well, you won't see him here, either, Elli. He's in Munich this week and next."

"With her?"

"Yes, with her and Konrad and Frieda's mother. We've not yet decided how to tell the boys, or whether we should. Neither of us knows which way to turn. Perhaps we must just hang on until something further happens, or until the children are older, or until someone can't stand the tension any more. I cannot imagine what would hurt everyone least. But we can't go on like this."

"You're braver than I am. You must love him more than I ever imagined, for you to put up with this affair."

"I've loved him my whole life, Elli. He swears there is no longer any 'affair.' He says he goes only to help with the boy, and I need to believe him. It's hard for us both now, though we both seem to have trouble saying what we really feel. It keeps coming out wrong. Deep inside, I'm hoping he'll see how much I love him and give her up. Of course, he'll always have to support Konrad. He couldn't abandon a child. But sooner or later, I hope he'll tell her that he's coming home to stay with me...forever."

"Have you asked him to do that?" Elli was unusually subdued as she asked the question.

"No. I haven't. Perhaps I should, but I feel the decision must be his now, and it must be final. I think he's nearing a solution, and I'm simply hoping it will be the right one."

After this initial conversation, Regina sidestepped the subject as much as possible the rest of the week, and Elli didn't push her to talk about it. They concentrated instead on taking the boys to the park, the river, and to the scenes of Nürnberg's former glories. Most of all, the boys enjoyed taking the *Strassenbahn* down to the old *Marktplatz* to watch the rebuilding that was going on. More rubble was cleared from the streets and bombed-out buildings every day. New buildings were taking shape, and old ones were being restored. It would take time and patience, but the progress was enough to give heart to even the most reluctant observer. There were heavy cranes all over town hoisting building materials into the air and onto rooftops.

"The American soldiers say those cranes are our new

national bird," said Willi, laughing at the humor of their former enemies.

Franzi added, "I want to build huge buildings like that when I'm big, too."

"Well, I hope you can do it more quietly," Elli said, holding her ears against the hammering.

Regina and Elli laughed at the normal post-war problems of eradicating bed bugs and finding material for curtains. People were beginning to care again about such things after the long wartime period when they were helpless to effect any change for themselves. They also found themselves discussing friends and relatives who had not returned from the war.

Elli said sadly, "My brother was never found after his plane crashed somewhere in Russia. I really miss him."

"What about your younger sister?"

"She married a nice young man, a doctor, and they'll be living on his family's farm in Berchtesgaden. It seems Hitler put in place some kind of law that bound each family's oldest son to the land, and it's still in use. She wrote me that Hitler had confiscated much of the hilltop farm acreage to build his own home, *Gestapo* offices, and troop barracks before the war. He even had an underground system of tunnels in Berchtesgaden that she says he was going to hide in, if he got out of Berlin. The family is having trouble getting that part of the land back, even now that the war is over. Now, I don't believe Hitler had any knowledge of such confiscations and tunnels and all, but my sister's husband is still angry and fighting in the courts to get the rest of his property back."

Regina changed the subject, not wanting to discuss Hitler's confiscations of land, or Hitler at all, for that matter.

"Have you had any word of Magda since the firebombing? I've been worried because she lived right downtown."

Elli shook her head sadly. "I can only imagine what might have happened to her. There was nothing left in that whole area "

They both lamented the loss of home and friends.

When the time came for Elli to take the train back to care for Paul's family in Hannover, she asked Regina if perhaps she could stay on in Nürnberg to help with the boys. Regina tearfully replied that she could offer Elli no position until her own situation was clarified.

"If Gustav and I are together this time next year, the boys will be older and won't need so much care. If we're not together, I'll have no money to hire anyone at all."

"You know I'd stay with you for just room and board. I don't need much," replied Elli.

"But I can't let you do that, Elli. You have a good, dependable job with Paul's family now. They can afford to pay you, and their baby needs you. Besides, you'll want to think about finding someone with whom to have a family of your own someday."

Elli smiled shyly. Regina had never seen the younger woman act shy before.

"You've met someone, haven't you?"

"Yes, sort of, but I don't know if I'm ready to make a decision. I haven't known him very long. He was a submariner in the German navy, and he'll go to Canada soon for a new job. He wants me to come next year and marry him. I'm afraid to do that--a new country, leaving home."

"Elli, we've already left our home. Königsberg is gone forever. Perhaps Hannover is just a stopover on the road to your new future."

"I suppose you're right. At least I have the year to think about it. He's a good man. And I do want a family of my own, if I can have some boys as lively as yours--ours. I do miss their mischief." Elli said this with both a laugh and tears in her eyes.

"I wish you happiness, Elli. You deserve it. And I know you'll find it."

The boys and Regina accompanied Elli to the train station the next morning.

"Elli, I'll never forget you boosting us up through the window of the train from Königsberg," said Willi, as he hugged his nanny goodbye for perhaps the last time. "Never."

"We should boost her through the window now, just for luck," joked Rainer, as Elli started to cry.

Willi said, "Don't worry. Canada isn't very far away from America and I'll be going there soon as I'm big enough. I'll come see you then. I promise."

Everyone waved until the train was out of sight. Then the family slowly walked home, feeling somewhat diminished yet again.

Regina's mother passed away quietly in her sleep only a few hours after Elli left for Hannover. She died without ever remembering Regina was her daughter. Devastated, Regina wired Gustav the news at his Munich business office. He drove home immediately to help her make arrangements for the funeral.

"My poor mother lost her husband, her home, her memory, and even me," Regina sobbed in Gustav's arms.

He tried to comfort her. "I know, *Liebling,* but at least she wasn't in pain.

"I pray this illness isn't hereditary. I wouldn't ever want to forget my own family."

Gustav hugged her tightly.

"I'm not afraid to die. I've faced that possibility many times. And I wouldn't mind being able to lose some of my more painful memories. But it terrifies me that, with such an illness, I might unwittingly tell the boys of the catastrophe that has befallen us, as my mother did. They would then hate you, or me, or the world that caused them pain."

"War has wreaked havoc upon us, Ina, though most of it is my fault. Neither of us knows how to repair such damage. The children may never understand it, no matter who tells them."

"I know they'd never understand all the laws I broke trying to bring them to you, and they'd never understand your difficult dilemma of how to take care of all your little boys."

Gustav held her silently as they cried together.

He was a rock for Regina to lean on then. He didn't even become angry with the boys when Willi, Rainer, and their friends took a joy ride around Nürnberg suburbs in his old, battered Audi. He found the boys had push-started the car, and Willi had guided it all over town before crashing into their gate to stop, letting off the gas pedal, but misunderstanding use of the clutch pedal.

In fact, Gustav was mellow, relaxed for the first time in many months, and he didn't return to Munich at the end of his two weeks. The family settled into the new house in Erlenstegen, and Regina felt some of the tension lift from her soul.

She didn't ask about Gustav's intentions. She wanted to leave him free to make his own decision. She prayed it would be to keep their family together, just as she had always dreamed. Yet, her dream had already changed, and she was no longer sure he would be part of it.

Regina still loved him enough to forgive him his indescretion, as long as they could be together. She hoped being patient would bring the desired result rather than confronting the dilemma openly. Was that a mistake? She might never know.

Three months passed and Gustav was still with the family. He transferred his business affairs in Munich to another salesman and operrated only in and around Nürnberg. Regina began again to enjoy his presence. Though Gustav never mentioned the situation, she felt he was finally home to stay. Very gradually, even the old warmth of their lovemaking had returned.

But Regina's dreams were suddenly interrupted.

Once again, an unexpected letter was brought to her after work one day. Franzi announced solemnly, "*Mutti*, a letter came for you today."

"Thank you, dear." She added a big hug.

Hoping it was from yet another long lost friend trying to find her following wartime separations, Regina put aside her dinner preparations and opened it eagerly. Then she slowly realized she must send her son away while she read a disturbing letter in private, just as she had done before leaving Königsberg. Tears were already forming on her eyelashes.

"Run along and find your brothers, son," she told Franzi.

He dawdled on his way out, apparently waiting for a clue to her sudden mood change.

"Go on, dear," she added. He finally left, and she closed the door.

"*Frau Regina Wolff,*" the letter began. It was in an unrefined handwriting. Regina looked again at the envelope to verify her worst fears. The postmark was from Munich.

"I know about you and your sons, and I understand now that you know about me and my son, Konrad. Gustav must choose between us, but I want you to know that I will fight for him to the end.

"Perhaps I know more than you think I do," the letter continued. *"Did you know that Gustav was in the SS and Gestapo? His journeys were related to prisoner-of-war camps and all that went on there. He was also involved in many 'special projects.' If you didn't know, I'm telling you now that I have proof—letters, photos, documents--I kept them all.*

"Do not tell him about this letter. If you do, or if you fail to send him away so he can come live with me, I will turn him in to the authorities currently conducting investigations about such things. Then, neither of us will have him! It's all or nothing for me.

"I mean what I say! Think it over. You have until next Wednesday to be sure he arrives here. Should he not be back in Munich with me by then, I will act. Make no mistake. I'm desperate for my son to have his father.

"I know you will make the right decision as Gustav says you are a real lady in all circumstances. Frieda"

"Oh Gustav!" The words tore from her insides as she dropped to her knees. The letter drifted to the floor, unheeded. The decision was not to be Gustav's to make, after all. It would be her own. And now, his life could depend upon it.

Chapter 37

This unexpected letter became the final, painful blow to Regina's dream of keeping her family together. When her tears produced no insight except pain, she found the strength to rise, pick up the letter, and read it again and again, hoping some part of it could offer her a clue of what to do next.

The family had been doing well together in Nürnberg for the months since Gustav had come home to stay. Regina was convinced he had already made his decision—that they would support this little boy, Konrad, but Gustav would not see Frieda again. Now, she felt panic rising from her heart into her throat.

She tried to think clearly. The letter must be a bluff...a ruse to persuade her to send away her husband. *I'll just show it to him and he'll never want to see her again. Gustav will clear it up right away. The whole thing was preposterous!* But the letter sounded desperate and dangerous. Could this woman really publicly accuse the father of her own child of being part of the *Nazi* hierarchy when such an accusation carried deadly consequences? Did Frieda love Gustav that little, or did she love him that possessively? Would she rather see him disgraced or dead than lose him to his wife? Regina realized she knew nothing about the woman and couldn't judge her motives. If she judged wrong, it could be fatal to her husband as well as her marriage.

Frieda said she had proof, but what proof could that be? How could she prove something Regina didn't even believe happened?

Yet, she thought, Gustav had always been secretive about his position in the Army and his assignments, and certainly, they had argued about what Regina felt were his misplaced political loyalties. But she couldn't for a moment imagine he could be involved in the type of brutality she had seen in the streets of Königsberg, or in what she'd heard about camps from the Nürnberg trials. This woman was lying, or at least exaggerating or misinterpreting.

Regina frantically thought over all she knew about Gustav's military service. Surely he would be able to fight such charges and lies. He had been called into the Army--he hadn't volunteered to leave, while the *SS* and *Gestapo* had been volunteers. *That was one point in his favor.*

But while she had thought he was on the eastern front the whole time, he had apparently been flying around to various fronts. *What kind of common soldier flies around war zones?*

It was true that he had always been a businessman, so perhaps the Army simply took advantage of his procurement experience and had him visiting various fronts to determine what supplies the troops would need and then delivering them. That was, after all, what he *said* he'd been doing that painful day at Erna's. *Had he been telling the truth then?* But if he had hidden his relationship with Frieda in the first place, could Regina even be sure when he *was* telling the truth?

The mystery about his never wearing insignia like other soldiers had bothered her, yet perhaps he needed discretion when flying, in case he was captured. Or perhaps he had simply removed his insignia when he came home to keep her from knowing his unit. *Was it to protect her... or himself?*

What had Paul meant the time he said not to think of Gustav being in a foxhole like a common soldier? And who were the officers visiting him and carrying him away in a staff car from Karlsbad? And why did he seem so much a part of the highly placed *Nazi* officers' group at Regina's father's party? They had seemed to recognize and accept Gustav's job and his presence. *Had Gustav been one of them in some way she hadn't known?*

Was he in some type of intelligence work? If that were the case, he couldn't have told the family about his duties.

Regina's mind desperately grasped for every possible explanation. It circled back again and again, struggling to find an answer that would negate what this woman said in the letter. There had to be an innocent explanation of his wartime experience. *There had to be!*

Did she dare confront Gustav and show him the letter?

Regina considered that option for a moment. What would happen if she told him about the letter? He would know what Frieda had done, and he wouldn't go to Munich. But the woman would surely turn him in to the authorities and he would be implicated, nonetheless. He would either have to become a fugitive, or be detained and tried as a war criminal. *Neither was an acceptable risk, and either would destroy their children.*

Regina could not believe in her innermost heart that the Gustav she knew had ever done anything evil or heartless. Was not even their current domestic problem caused more because of his compassion than because of his cruelty? No, she was convinced he could never be cruel.

But then, she had to admit that sometimes he hadn't seemed the Gustav she had always known, either. Surely he couldn't have changed *that* much. Yet his political opinions had changed.

Then she thought of the mystery of the strange coded letters and numbers on the telegram Gustav had sent her in Königsberg. He had neither explained their significance, nor what was in the carefully hidden little green book, nor the reaction it had drawn from the *Bürgermeister*.

Frieda said she had evidence. Letters, photos, documents...could Gustav be accused openly and implicated in Third *Reich* schemes through his idealistic devotion to Hitler? Could he be prosecuted and imprisoned, or even executed? Some of the Nürnberg criminals had been hung, and it was certain more would follow. *My God, I don't want him to die.* She felt cold shivers in her spine, and her hands would not stop shaking. Was it colder in the room?

Regina tried to think good thoughts--of how much she loved Gustav. But the thought was too fevered, too aching.

Another idea—what if Regina should confront the woman directly? If Frieda loved Gustav as she said, perhaps she would back down and not implicate him after all. But the woman sounded determined to destroy him if he were not hers. Could Regina dare take that chance?

And what about the children? Regina's frantic mind switched directions to yet another problem. What would the boys endure in such a scenario? They had been through far too much already and were only just now beginning to trust people again. Regina could not let their father be charged and tried for some heinous crime, even when the charges were false.

There's no good answer, she thought, crushing the letter into a ball, and asking questions of the silent room. "Gustav, why didn't you tell me more about what you were doing during the war? Didn't you trust me enough? Didn't I seem interested enough? Did I fail you somehow? You should have told me so I wouldn't have been trapped by this letter. Now, I truly don't know what to think... or what to do." Her tears flowed freely.

She pulled herself into a chair, determined to analyze her dilemma. She tried to remember everything--*all* the clues. Her memories had suddenly become vital, a life and death matter. Actually, Gustav had always told her what he did was important, but that she was not to trouble her head about it.

But that could mean almost anything. He also said he had done several 'special' jobs, but he had never defined them. Had he kept her unknowing to protect her, or to keep her from asking questions? *Either idea could be logical.*

Or was his silence because he feared that, if she knew of his activities, she might someday be called upon to testify against him? He'd never wanted her involved in politics and, even now, he hated it if she expressed a divergent opinion. There had never been much opportunity for her to ask questions.

She rose and paced the kitchen floor, alternately balling up the letter and ironing it out between her hands. She tried desperately to think of any idea that might save her husband.

What would happen to Gustav if she told him of the letter and he fought the accusations in open court? Who could testify on his behalf and prove his innocence? She could not truly testify that he was innocent. Even the things she had observed for herself could possibly be construed as incriminating. *Could he hope to defend himself with no witnesses in his defense?*

Probably not, she concluded, reluctantly dismissing the idea. Though the *Nazis* had been gruesomely adept at keeping records and photos of every atrocity committed, they were not nearly so thorough at keeping records of those who were innocent. Should this woman have any so-called 'proof' at all, even if she manufactured something incriminating, Gustav would not be able to defend himself against her charges.

Of course, if he were accused publicly, even the knowledge that Frieda had betrayed him would not restore his reputation, his home, his children's belief in his heroism, or perhaps his life.

This realization was devastating. The sobs she could not contain brought shortness of breath and chest pain. It was as though she were losing Gustav all over again. And again she was facing decisions she felt ill-equipped to make.

Regina wanted to tell someone, to get advice, not to have to make this decision alone. But she had no one.

She finally had to accept that, in this postwar political climate, just being accused would destroy her husband, and her children, even if he were innocent. Why hadn't he given her enough information? Had he done so, she'd have enough evidence and confidence to ignore this letter.

Time was hurrying by, and Gustav and the boys would soon be home for dinner. In the automatic haze of practiced motherhood, she stoked up the wood stove and added her pared vegetables to the pot standing there. She knew she was using these deliberate actions to give herself time to think. As the pot boiled and the familiar aroma entered the kitchen, she forced herself to consider if there were any other options.

She could think of none.

She would do anything to keep her husband with her, and to protect him from any possible past indiscretions. *But if he stayed with her and the other woman accused him, he might die.* What could she do to protect both her husband from these accusations, and their boys from the shame if he were found guilty? Already she knew the children wanted *all* the *Nazi* criminals ferreted out and punished. And their comments had caused Gustav to leave the table. How would they react if their father were accused?

If Regina told Gustav of the letter, and the charges were false, the woman would still accuse him because he wouldn't want to go to Munich. If she told him of the letter and the charges were true, he wouldn't be able to protect their boys from knowledge of his wartime actions, unless he went to the other woman. Either way, he would have to go to Frieda in order to save himself and his family from shame, or worse.

She shook her head, realizing her thoughts were beginning to repeat themselves, and she still had not produced any safe options.

A more horrible thought suddenly entered Regina's confused mind. What if she confronted Gustav and he confessed Frieda's statements were true? For the first time, Regina wondered if she could continue to love him if she knew him to be guilty.

The scenes of *Gestapo* thugs terrorizing everyone into silence, throwing unsuspecting Jews and dissidents into the back of trucks going to...to where? My God! Some of them were going to their death.

If the accusations were true, she could not live with him. Not any more. She'd come too far, and there was no way to go back to the politically naïve little girl who had believed everything her handsome husband told her. She wouldn't want to know, or the boys to know. They could never build a life together with such doubt and lack of trust between them. Though she knew their political beliefs were incompatible, she had never before considered that he might have actually *acted* on his views in some brutal way. *No, he couldn't have...* her grief at the thought blocked all thinking for a moment.

Sobs tore her throat. She couldn't breathe. *What was she to do?*

It all came back to the same answer. Regina knew she would feel this painful heartache and loss forever, if she sent her husband away, but she could find no other option for his safety.

"Oh, God. Must I give him up in order to save him and to protect our sons? Please make this letter go away. Make this decision go away," Regina called out. Couldn't God hear her desperate cry?

She had to decide before Gustav came home for dinner. She'd only been given a week before the woman would turn him in to the authorities, and the mail had taken two days of that already. If she waited, it would be too late to save him. Besides, if this horrible dilemma tore at her for another day, she could not bear it.

Though Regina truly wanted to believe Gustav could do nothing cruelly wrong, she didn't know enough about his life to take the chance. He might not be able to explain away his confusing actions, either to her or to a war crimes tribunal. His silence and his marital disloyalty had left her with tiny, nagging doubts. It was enough doubt that she was afraid for him, for his life, for his sons, and for her love for him.

Could she take care of the boys alone? She knew it would not be easy to raise three rambunctious boys in a postwar world, but wasn't that essentially what she had been doing alone since 1942? She felt sure her own office job would not enable her to keep their house, but she could find a cheaper apartment. She assumed Gustav would continue to send money for supporting the boys as he had done for Konrad.

What would she tell the boys? Regina decided she would tell them nothing, *ever*--only that *Vati* had to go away to live in Munich. Perhaps they could go visit him when they were grown. Never would she implicate him in war crimes or infidelity. The children must always know that he loved them. She never wanted them to hate their father--she loved him too much. *Too much.* She began crying again as she made tentative plans for living alone…forever.

Regina sighed deeply and made her last decision. It would have to be final. It was an impossible situation. She remembered a Bible story with King Soloman trying to solve the problem of two women who claimed the same child. She realized that the woman who loved Gustav the most must be the one to give him up. All other possibilities were no longer viable. They would only bring further pain for everyone.

She also knew that she was the one who loved him most…who had always loved him most. She wished a hundred times over that she could have been more aggressive in telling him so. But it was not her way. It had never been her way. And now it was too late.

Regina strode to the stove, moved the pot of vegetables aside, and pried the stove lid open, exposing fire within. The letter fluttered in her hand as she pondered the possibilities of saving both her dream and her husband. Again and again, she pushed the letter toward the fire, only to withdraw it one more time. She had no options, and nothing further could be achieved.

Determinedly, and with a sigh that shook her small frame, she crushed the letter and threw it into the fire, pulling the stove lid and the pot back as the paper flared up. She quietly put both hands over her face.

And so it was that Regina burned her second dangerous letter. Her decision would bring change, which she had always hated. It would bring loneliness. But it would also save her beloved husband's life. Any other decision would bring death and shame to her love, and her sons.

Regina dressed carefully in Gustav's favorite dress, brushed her hair with considerable fervor, dabbed on special perfume, and finished preparing dinner. If it was to be their last night together, she wanted both of them to remember it forever. She lit candles on the table, folded the soft damask wedding napkins *Herr* Busch had sent long ago from their beloved home in Königsberg, and opened their only bottle of wine.

At twilight, Gustav returned from his office and immediately showed his pleasure at her efforts. It was a richly warm evening, and they both relished dinner and the tussle time and rhyming games with the children afterward.

Franzi seemed strangely quiet throughout the evening, constantly looking from one parent to the other, but he said nothing. Finally, the boys hugged both parents tightly and went off to bed.

Regina told her husband later, as they lay in their room holding each other quietly. "This will be our last time together, Gustav. You'll be leaving us soon."

He was stunned. "What do you mean? I'm not leaving you."

"You need to go to Munich. The boys and I will find a small apartment here.

"What are you saying, Ina?" he asked plaintively. "You can't mean you want to do this. Things have been going well lately and I know I can make a better life for you and the boys."

She fought to keep from saying her logical question out loud, "But what if you had no life at all?"

Instead, she said, "It will be best this way, Gustav. We can't be torn like this forever."

"Are you still angry with me because I lied to you over this whole mess? I beg you to forgive me, though I can't ever forgive myself."

"I've forgiven you already. You know I love you more than life itself."

"Then why, Ina? Why now? Are you doing this because you think you're making the decision easier for me, Ina?" he asked, but he seemed confused and hurt even as he asked the question.

"I don't know, Dear," she answered softly, struggling for the right words. "I only know this whole situation has been so painful. Something must be final, and I want no more hurt for you, for myself, or for our boys. I'm assuming you will keep a soft spot for them in your heart...and for me."

"But, Ina, I'd already decided I wanted to stay here with you. Haven't you realized that? Why would you send me away now?" He was trembling, even as he continued to hold her body near to his.

Regina bit her lip to fight the natural impulse to wrap her arms around him and tell him again of her love. She pushed herself away and rose to sit on the edge of the bed.

"Because I must. There have been too many secrets between us, and this is the only way we can all live with those secrets. Perhaps someday you'll know and understand. I love you too much to keep you with me if it means that you'll not be happy--or safe. We all need to live. We all need the confusion to end."

"I *am* happy here. Surely you can see that. Frieda and Konrad are out of my life. What has happened to make you so sure sending me away is the best decision? I don't understand."

Regina took a deep breath and folded her hands in her lap. She dared not look at him. "This must be my decision now, not yours. I've had to make it alone, Gustav. There can be no other."

She could feel her composure slipping away. She knew she must finish the discussion quickly, or she might endanger him by telling him her reasons. She couldn't let that happen.

She rose and moved away from the bed.

"But, I'll always keep you safe, Ina," Gustav insisted.

"I also want *you* to be safe. Our lives can never again be like they were before the war tore us apart."

"They can be. I'll make everything up to you, Ina, I promise!"

Regina's tears could be held back no longer. But she answered him the only way she knew. "The promises have never been kept. We need this situation finished and I need to know both you and our boys are safe, whether we are able to be together or not. Now I know we cannot be together."

"Ina, please tell me what brought all this on. I felt sure you wanted to remain together."

"Don't ask me to explain, my dear. I cannot risk it, for your sake. This decision breaks my heart, but there can be no other." She turned her face away so he would not see the pain registered there.

A long silence ensued, as both husband and wife tried to make sense out of the bizarre scene. Gustav finally broke the silence.

"What about the boys? What will you tell them? They need me, still."

"I'll have to make decisions for myself and the boys, just as I was forced to do during the war. I'll tell them nothing. You'll have to go away, for your own sake, and so that they will know nothing. Someday, you'll perhaps understand how much I love you. But for now, there's no other choice."

"Do you want me out of your life right now...tonight?" His voice quavered.

Regina could not tell if the question was in anger or despair. Shadows of the curtains mercifully blocked out their expressions from the moonlight. How she wished they could also block out the sound of her own words.

"Yes, my love, go now. Go and be safe. Please remember only the good times. Someday before our lives are over, I pray you'll know my heart, and understand."

Bewildered, perhaps somewhat angrily, Gustav snatched his clothes from the bureau and closet, forced them into his large suitcase, and slammed out the front door.

Regina moved to the bed and lay down quietly, one arm draped across Gustav's pillow, reaching for whatever warmth remained there. With her fingers, she traced the space where her wedding ring had once been. She scarcely noticed the tears coursing down her cheeks.

Epilogue – 1997 -- The Funeral

It was afternoon by the time German custom brought the group of mourners, family and old friends, to Cousin Renee's luxurious terrace overlooking the Regnitz River.

Bill Wolff stood at Renee's side, greeting each guest and mumbling politely in response to the usual inane comments and ridiculous small talk "'…She looked so natural,' '…At least she's not in pain any more,' '…It's too bad that, in the end, she could not recognize anyone, just like her mother' '…She had such a hard life all those years alone, but she was blessed with three successful sons,'" on and on.

"No one knows what to say," Bill whispered to his cousin. "Certainly not me. God, I'll miss her. Why can't I slip out of here and be alone?"

"That's easy. You're the eldest. Tradition, that's why you'll stay, Willi." Renee smiled.

No one but the German side of the family ever called him Willi anymore. His American friends and his wife used Bill, or just Wolff. But now, among family and old friends, he easily slipped back into his original nickname.

"It's kind of you and Horst to have this dinner for everyone who attended the funeral."

"She was my favorite aunt. She was always special to my brother, Gerhardt, and to my husband and me--as much as Uncle Gustav was always an enigma."

"Funny, I sort of regard them the same way."

"My mother died without ever explaining her anger at your Dad."

"But neither *Tante* Erna nor *Mutti* would ever discuss his life or his leaving. There are mysterious elements within this fractured family, aren't there?" The two nodded, smiled, and joined their guests

Bill surveyed the living room. Though most people had severed their ties with his father, Gustav, after his move to Munich, all had remained close to *Mutti*.

With Regina's passing, many had arrived from far-away places. Bill smiled as he recognized his old nanny, Elli, from Canada, and *Mutti's* brother and his wife from Weida. Uncle Hans and Aunt Gerda had only been allowed to travel out of East Germany after the Wall came down in 1989.

Of Regina's three sons, Franzi's family lived near her tiny apartment in Nürnberg, Rainer owned a *Konditerei* in Kempten, and neither of the younger brothers had ever left West Germany. As for Willi, as soon as he was of age, he left for America to become one of those *Ami* soldiers he admired so much. Between three Vietnam tours, much of his thirty years as a military pilot was spent stationed in his native country. This had enabled him to keep close ties with his mother, his brothers, and even his father and the new family in Munich, as well as his old teen buddies, Dolf and Karl.

How good to see them again, he thought, though Dolf doesn't look well these days.

Dolf, now arthritic and nearing retirement, smiled when he shook Willi's hand. "When I remember all the mountain climbing and mischief making we did together, Willi, I'm amazed we didn't blow ourselves up or get dumped in a crevasse somewhere.

Bill smiled. "We're lucky we survived, I guess.

"That's probably your mother's doing. She was a great lady," said Karl.

Dolf added, "Remember how your *Mutti* always invited us to eat, no matter how short of food she was?"

"I remember you were always hungry," broke in Rainer.

The rest of the mourners gathered around, joining in stories of Regina's culinary creativity.

"Do you remember all those cornmeal pancakes?" asked Karl.

"She must have had a million recipes for using that Marshall Plan cornmeal," said Franz. "I hated those pancakes."

"You liked the fritters, though," said Rainer, still teasing his younger brother though both were now in advanced middle age. "Besides, it was a lot better than starving, wasn't it?"

"And what about the cornmeal soup, the cornbread, and the

time she baked it like a cake and tried to fry it?" added Bill."Worst of all was the night she added cornmeal to the potatoes and turnips to make them go further?"

"Yeah," said Dolf trying to stifle his laughter. "That's the night Karl and I both showed up unannounced at dinnertime and she just put out two more plates, lit the candles, smiled at us, and ladled out this 'stuff.' None of us wanted to say what it tasted like after she was so nice to feed all of us at once, so we just shut up and gulped it down."

"Except for Franzi," said Willi. "Remember, he tried to scoop it out into his pocket when she wasn't looking, and she caught him? *Mutti* sent him to bed with no dinner at all. Come to think of it, he probably got the best deal, after all." They all broke into laughter again.

" And Dolf didn't even tell her he'd already eaten at his own house," said Rainer in mock dismay. "Hey, he always needed an extra meal anyway...never seemed to have enough. Look at him now."

Dolf patted his bulky midsection and grinned. "Seems like in the old days we could work it off climbing up mountains, skiing back down on those old homemade wooden skis, and scrounging the neighborhood on our bikes. Now it all seems to stay around my middle. It's been a long time since any of us thought of those hungry times."

"Regina never had the heart to turn anyone away," said Elli. Their nanny was now an elderly lady herself, but she had left her husband and grown family in Canada to fly to the funeral of her old friend and employer. "I remember when she told me to use the last of our potatoes to make soup for the Russian prisoners of war building bunkers in the back yard in Königsberg. She didn't even hesitate when she saw how weak they looked."

"I remember that," said Bill. He looked thoughtful for a moment. "You know, it's funny how I can remember so few things from those times. *Mutti* never talked about any of it and she changed the subject if we asked questions about the journey or the war years. I remember the look on her face in Königsberg, when she got a letter from our Dad, and Elli pushing us up through the windows of the train, and a lot of walking and being hungry, but that's about it." He glanced around at the others. "I don't remember ever getting a straight answer from her about anything that happened then, or any time since."

"You were only nine when you left Königsberg," said Elli. "What can you expect yourself to remember if Regina never talked about it?"

"I sure do remember you being sick on that cattle train, Willi," shouted Rainer. "You hung out…"

Willi interrupted quickly, " The less said about that part, little brother, the better. I don't have to remind you that I'm still older than you!"

Rainer raised his hands in terror, leaving everyone else to wonder about the long-ago incident. The laughter had died for a moment when Rainer turned serious and said, "I know *Mutti* must have been really strong to get us all through those bad times, but I could never understand why she sent our father away."

Cousin Renee stepped into the conversation at that point. "You really can't blame her for that, Rainer. She didn't have any choice, now did she? Uncle Gustav already had that other woman and another son in Munich. He left her--she didn't send him away. My mother cried about her brother doing such a terrible thing to *Tante* Ina for weeks."

Rainer turned toward Renee. "*Vati* never said he left her. When Franzi and I worked for him awhile, he said he didn't know why she sent him away. So which was it?"

"Frieda and Konrad were there when we visited Munich," said Franz in a quiet voice. "Even before I understood about the 'other woman,' I guess I thought it funny that Konrad was almost as old as I was."

Franz paused in reflection, refilled his coffee cup, then plunged on. "Actually, I also remember feeling there was something important about a letter from Munich that I gave *Mutti* from the post office the evening before *Vati* left. The look on her face scared me, but she wouldn't say who sent the letter, and she sent me away while she read it. I guess I was about six or seven then. I know she was crying and pacing the floor because I peeked through the window. I saw her burn the letter. The next day when I woke up, *Vati* was gone. She never saw him again. I always thought his leaving had something to do with that letter."

"You never said anything about it to us," said Rainer.

"I was afraid to ever mention *anything* to you two then. I thought you wouldn't believe me because I was youngest."

"Neither of your parents would have answered you, even if you had asked questions," said Elli. "Regina wrote that she was alone with you boys shortly after I traveled to Canada to get married, but she never said a bad word about Gustav. She always loved him, more than you boys ever knew. She would never have sent him away unless something was terribly wrong. You must not speculate on things they chose to keep secret between them. There must have been more to the decision she had to make than any of us will ever know."

Elli's quiet determination in her defense of Regina said more than her words. When she noticed everyone was looking at her expectantly, she merely added, "Regina never discussed things with you boys because she never wanted any of you to remember the hard times or think badly of your *Vati*. Let it be!"

For a moment, each of the three men remembered their nanny's firm voice when she had had enough of their boyish badgering. They knew she meant what she said and would say no more. Surprisingly spry for her age, her presence still carried a comforting authority.

Renee broke the silence. "Well, if it helps any, I was around when *Tante* Ina arrived in Nürnberg without you boys, after she had escaped across the East German border alone." Renee poured more coffee in her brother's cup while she continued. "Though *Tante* Ina dined with us many times since, she always changed the subject when any topic relating to your father came up. She was so gentle and loving. I never understood why she didn't hate Uncle Gustav and say bad things about him. but she protected him and retained her dignity, *and* her silence, for all these years."

"Hey, when was she ever in Nürnberg without us?" It was Rainer who asked the question. "I remember we all went to Nürnberg together and *Vati* met us at the train and took us to your house, then to a barracks apartment. But *Mutti* never went anywhere without us."

"And what's this about her running any border?" Franz said, "She couldn't have done that. She wasn't the type to break laws."

"Well," said Willi, trying to remember exactly, "she did leave us with Uncle Hans and Aunt Gerda and *Oma* Reh in Weida for awhile after the area was given to the Russians. When she came back, we packed up and moved to Nürnberg on the train, but she never said where she had been. It was sort of a mystery."

"I thought she'd gone back to Königsberg," added Rainer, trying to remember the exact timing of her absence.

"She couldn't have gone back to Königsberg. The Russians had already taken it over and were sending the remaining Germans they hadn't slaughtered back to Berlin. They renamed it Kaliningrad, and brought in thousands of peasants from the steppes to live in the surviving German houses...in our house too."

"How do you know that?" asked Franz, with his usual air of suspicion toward his older brother.

"Military history after a long Cold War in which I was on the American side, little brother. Plus, if you remember, when The Wall came down in '89, Amy and I got visas to travel to Kaliningrad to see what, if anything, was left. Between the bombing by the Brits in 1944, and the shelling and street battles of the Russian's fight with the city's defenders in 1945, there wasn't much. We wanted to take *Mutti* with us, but she said she preferred to remember it the way it had been before the war when we were all happy there."

He paused, wondering if he should tell them the rest. "She gave us her old map of the city and the worthless deed to the house. She'd protected them all those years since she brought them out in 1944 in her knapsack. The Soviets had changed all the street names and numbers, but we were able to find the house. It was really depressing. They had three families living in our one family home. And no flower gardens were left in all Königsberg. We had the feeling the Russians hadn't even taken out the trash since 1944, and nothing had been repaired. I'm glad *Mutti* didn't see her home and her city under Soviet domination. She would have hated it."

"We all would have hated it, I suppose," said Rainer. "Was our apple tree still there?"

Willi shook his head. "They apparently burned all the trees for firewood. Nothing but the stump was left."

He turned then to his cousin. "I don't know how *Mutti* could have escaped across the border in 1945 though, Renee. As far as I knew, the Russians had already fortified the East-West border as soon as they were given their zone of influence at war's end. It's hard for me to imagine *Mutti* tackling such a dangerous journey. She was always so gentle and quiet. It would have been totally out of character for her."

Uncle Hans broke his silence. "Regina did it all right! She felt running the border was the only way to get papers to take you boys to the Western zone and find Gustav. I tried to talk her out of it because of the danger, but she was right to go. I wish we had been brave enough to go with her. By the time we really wanted to come to the West, the borders had been irrevocably closed, and no one was allowed to leave. We could no longer own our home under the Communist system. We didn't see Regina again until we were both quite old, in 1989. We lost a lifetime."

"And it wouldn't have been out of Regina's character at all!" Everyone turned in surprise to hear Elli's forceful voice. "She could, and she did run that border to get you boys out of Weida, and she broke all kinds of laws in order to get you out of Königsberg in the first place. She may have looked all delicate, graceful, and perfectly groomed, but she could get muddy enough to fight for you boys when she had to. Someday, perhaps you'll discover just how strong your mother really became." It was apparent Elli was sure of her facts and would brook no argument.

Renee nodded. "You kids were starving under Russian occupation, and she just wanted to save you. She escaped the East zone and walked across Nürnberg to find my mom. But your Dad was there too, hiding from the Americans and…"

"What do you mean, '…hiding from the Americans?' Why would he have been there? Why would he have been hiding?" Rainer was indignant at the suggestion.

"I don't know, but he was. My mom said he had escaped

from a POW train taking him to interrogation. I remember that he never left the house and stayed in a locked room whenever Mother went out. He peeked around corners and through curtains all the time and we kids couldn't have friends over while he was there. He was definitely hiding from something. But he gave your mom money, and my mom signed the papers. *Tante* Ina left immediately to go back to Weida to get you boys.

"Why didn't any of us ever know anything about this?" asked Willi of his brothers. "Why didn't she ever tell us anything?"

"Your father was under sort of a 'suspicion,' or at least he thought he was, because of his job in the war," interposed Elli. "Your mother never wanted you boys to worry about it or to remember any of it. She wrote that she just wanted keep the family together and build a new home in Nürnberg. I really think it would be best if you all just let this alone. After all, if your mother and father kept it from you all these years, they must have had their reasons. They apparently felt it was best that you not know everything. What does it matter now? They're both dead."

Rainer asked, "What's this 'suspician' thing? All of a sudden, I don't feel like I knew my father at all, and maybe not *Mutti* either. Doesn't anyone know the whole story? We each seem to have just bits and pieces. Can we put it all together? Why did our parents really separate and what did he do in the war, anyway? I only remember he was rarely at home when we were in Königsberg, and *Mutti* missed him. I could hear her cry at night in her room."

"He was just an ordinary soldier, wasn't he?" said Franz. "Why would the Americans have been interested in questioning him…so much so that he would have to hide out? Didn't they give amnesty to ordinary soldiers that turned in their weapons? I don't remember seeing any weapons."

"He had a pistol," said Willi. "I came across where he had it hidden after the war, and he made me promise never to touch it or talk about it. But, now that I think about it, ordinary enlisted soldiers don't usually carry pistols…only officers. Was he an officer? I don't remember any insignia."

Franz said, "Do you remember when we saw him in at that

hospital? I think it was in Czechoslovakia, and I was about four. For me, it seemed like the first time I'd ever seen him because I was so young when he left. I thought his black uniform was eerie. One part of me was proud he looked so important, but the other part was scared to death. He was so tall and looked like that villain from Star Wars to a little kid. I wanted *Mutti* between us the whole time." Franz laughed at the fear he had felt then.

Several heads turned suddenly in surprise. "*SS* troops were the only ones who wore black uniforms, weren't they?" asked Renee's brother, Gerhardt.

"He didn't wear a black uniform in Königsberg," said Rainer, "but now that you mention it, I do think I remember that black uniform in Karlsbad. We only saw him about three times, but he looked all dressed up and in that big staff car. Was he really in black? Do you remember for sure?"

"I'm positive! It was the black that scared me so much."

"I'm trying to remember," said Willi slowly. "I think you're right, Franzi. It was black, but perhaps there could have been some other reason. I'm trying to remember what I know about uniforms and insignia of the German Third *Reich*. It just never seemed important to me before. Now, I'm wondering too. Did *Mutti* know something about *Vati* that she never told us? Was she protecting him, or thinking that she needed to?"

Elli again broke in with some degree of forcefulness. "I don't know why you would all be so concerned about the possibility your father was *SS* or perhaps working for them. Your Uncles Paul and Walter were both *SS*, and they never did anything wrong. Much of what everybody says about *SS* and *Gestapo* was American propaganda." She said this with such conviction that the others quickly glanced at each other with raised eyebrows.

"Does she really think that?" whispered Renee to her husband. He shrugged. Several occupants of the room looked rather puzzled, but no one dared respond to Elli's challenge.

Willi was not surprised. He had found that many older Germans didn't want to talk about their wartime activities, and they most always gave noncommittal answers if one asked about those days in the thirties and forties. Perhaps it had been just too painful to discuss.

Mercifully, Karl changed the subject. "I know your father worked for a Jewish man in Nürnberg after the war, so that alone would undermine such an *SS* theory, wouldn't it?"

"He had a Jewish partner in Königsberg too," added Willi, and I think *Vati* helped him and his family escape. I was really little, perhaps four then, but I remember playing with the couple's little boy who was a bit younger. When they didn't come around any more, *Mutti* said they had been forced to leave Germany. I never heard anything more."

"You left Germany too, as soon as you could, so you wouldn't have heard anything more," accused Franz. "*Vati* mentioned his Jewish partners many times while I was working for him in Munich when I was eighteen. Their names were Minslov."

"I can confirm that, on both counts," said Elli. "They left in 1938 and escaped to Switzerland. Your father sent them money from the business. Gustav mentioned their location when I saw him at his Berlin apartment. That was in February, 1945."

"But wasn't that after we were in Weida and after Königsberg had been all but destroyed?" said Willi. "Are you sure of the time, Elli? Why would he have had an apartment in Berlin when we were in Weida and the Russians and Americans were closing in on us from both sides?"

"Well, he did have one, because your Uncle Paul told me to go to that address if I was determined to return to Königsberg, and your father told me I couldn't go back because Königsberg was already lost. He told me to go back to Paul's family in Hannover, and I did."

"Do you have any idea what his job in Berlin was?" asked Willi. He was making an obvious effort to keep a quiet tone with his old nanny.

"And what kind of uniform he was wearing?" added Rainer

Elli answered simply, "He told me about the Minslovs' being safe in Switzerland, and he also told me about his other woman and baby. He had confessed to your *Oma* Reh before he put her on the train to meet you all in Weida, and he swore us both to secrecy so your mother wouldn't be hurt." She twisted her immaculate white handkerchief into a ball and dabbed at her eyes, remembering her helplessness. "About his job, he only said he was still in the Army and the job was important and made it necessary for him to stay in Berlin until the very end."

Remembering the original question, Elli added, "He was wearing a black business suit and hat, Rainer, not any uniform at all. I don't know what that would mean to you, but he went out 'on duty,' he said, when the nightly air raid started. When he returned in the morning, he took me to the train and sent me back to Hannover."

"Well," said Willi with a sigh, "that explains why *Oma* Reh acted so strangely when we were in Weida and lost her memory completely when we got to Nürnberg. She must have known what *Mutti didn't* know, and was torturing herself with it. In Königsberg, she always forced cookies on us between meals and pampered us all the time. When she arrived in Weida, she almost didn't seem to notice we were there—like a different person."

Rainer said, "You're right. *Oma* never did say much to any of us anymore, not even to *Mutti*. I thought she just was sad and missed *Opa*, but perhaps she was afraid she would give away the secret she knew."

"It still doesn't explain what Uncle Gustav was doing in Berlin or during the war, for that matter," said Gerhardt.

"Perhaps we would really be better not to pursue this any further," said Dolf, glancing at Willi's puzzled face. "What does it matter now after so many years anyway? Lots of people did jobs in the German Army that they weren't proud of, and no one cares to hunt them down now. Elli's right. It's over."

"After watching him be the indispensable man all his life, I could believe almost anything about him," said Willi. "He always got things done, whether anyone knew how he did it, or not. I guess I'm really not surprised if there was something mysterious...not as much as I was at first, anyway. He called himself a 'wheeler dealer' so who knows what or to whom he was wheeling and dealing?"

"I suppose he could have been in some type of procurement position, since that was his specialty in business before he was drafted into the Army."

"Or he could have been a spy."

"I think he was *SS!*" said Franz, positively. "That uniform was a dead giveaway…and that big car. He also said some things while I was working for him in Munich that sounded like he knew an awful lot about things in the war that I didn't think would have concerned him at all."

"But Franzi, you could have been mistaken about some things or jumped to conclusions, too. Remember you always insisted we stayed in that hotel in Karlsbad as long as six months too, yet it was only a few days before we started for Weida."

"Yes, but that was when I was only four and I think time always seems longer than it really is to little kids."

There had been nothing said by the next generation, Franz's and Rainer's young adult children, but now Friedrich stepped into the speculative conversation, "All I know about this is that your *Mutti*, my *Oma* Wolff, was crying for days when she found out *Opa* died in 1974, and none of you had even told her. She only found out when a lawyer sent a letter saying Opa had left her half of his estate. She was angry with *all* of you. She just kept repeating, 'I never got to tell him, he never knew,' until I felt really sad. It made me mad at all of you. I *know* she still loved him, even though they had been separated all those years."

Willi said, "That makes me feel really bad. I was with dad the day before he died, and even I didn't think to tell her. I didn't think she would care, since they had been apart so long. And he must have still cared about her too, if he left her an inheritance."

"We didn't think she cared about him or would want to know about him, since she sent him away for no reason," said Rainer. Then he added, "At least, I thought at the time that she sent him away for no reason. Now I'm not so sure about any of it."

"If *Oma* Reh had told *Mutti* about *Vati's* affair before she left Weida, I don't think *Mutti* would have taken us to him. So I presume *Mutti* found out afterward, and she would have asked him about it. *Mutti* would have known soon after we got to Nürnberg, wouldn't she?" Willi was trying to put two and two together. "He didn't leave until later, so she must have forgiven him."

"Yes," said Elli. "She knew. Her mother gave it away before she died. Regina had forgiven him. I'm sure he felt bad about having betrayed her. In Berlin, he cried when he told me how ashamed he was to have compromised the young girl who had saved his life on the Russian Front. But I'm not so sure he was only on the Russian Front," added Elli, shaking her head with the memory. "He could be pretty mysterious."

"And I know Frieda was not just a young girl who saved his life," said Renee. "My mom said she had been his secretary throughout the war and had flown all over with him. She had even shown up at our house."

"Then he lied to Regina!" said Elli, jumping up and waving her hands at the others as she spoke. "How could he have done that? She loved him so and was willing to forgive him for his mistake because Frieda had been young and they'd been in so much danger. He said they'd just stayed together because they thought they'd die any minute? Regina believed him, and he was lying. Her decision to save him was based on a false premise. Oh my God, she sent him away for nothing. He wasn't worth all her pain." Her sudden tears made it apparent she felt strongly about *Mutti's* fateful decision and suspected something she was not telling.

"Save him from what?" Willie asked the question, but Elli only shook her head and continued dabbing at her brimming eyes.

Gerhardt said, "I think Karl and Dolf and I may know something that might bear on whatever your father was doing in the war, although at the time we were not old enough or smart enough to put the ideas together."

Both Karl and Dolf looked puzzled.

Gerhardt continued, "Don't you remember when we were all listening to the radio after the war and some news came on about the Americans and British finding tons of gold in a lake in the south and whole tunnels full of artwork in Bavaria? Do you remember that Uncle Gustav had been listening absent-mindedly and playing chess with you, Dolf, and he suddenly went white as a sheet and we had to help him to the couch to lie down? He was shivering and we feared he was having a heart attack or something.

We wanted to call *Tante* Ina or a doctor, but he said for us not to mention it and he would be all right. Then, after he was able to get up, he seemed really agitated and frantically rummaged through his desk. He sent us all home quite firmly. Don't you remember?"

Dolf leaned back in his chair and thought a moment. "I remember the incident, but I never connected the news on the radio with his attack. I thought at first he was mad at me for winning, but then I thought, too, that he might be quite sick. He scared me."

Karl said, "Now that you mention it, it did seem like a rather sudden attack, and he did seem quite shocked, or perhaps scared, by the announcement...at least the timing does seem strange. Of course, we are looking at this with hindsight, too. I'm not sure."

"Why didn't anyone ever say anything about this before now?" asked Willi. He unconsciously smoothed his short military haircut in frustration.

Gerhardt sighed. "I suppose none of us were trying to gather clues before...and we were young. We didn't know it might all be part of a mystery we would someday want to solve."

"What does Frieda say about how they met and what he might have been doing for the Third *Reich*, Willi?" asked Franz. "You're the only one that forgave *Vati* enough to stay in touch with him and his new family until he died. Rainer and I didn't get along with either of them and never returned. Do you still see Frieda, too?" It was almost an accusation.

Willi squirmed in his seat and then admitted that he had seen Frieda from time to time. "She's just a lonely old lady now, like *Mutti* was," he said lamely, "and she must have loved him too. She took care of him when he became ill. Frieda said they met in Minsk, and she was struck by his exotic good looks. But of course, she insists *Vati* was only a common soldier and changes the subject if you ask further questions. I'm sure she knows something, but I know she'll never tell. I've always felt there was something more to the whole question of the separation. That letter from Munich you saw, Franzi, may be the key factor."

"How have you managed to forgive *Vati* and stay in touch with all three of them? Konrad, too? I've never forgiven any of them for splitting up our family," said Rainer.

"I don't think I forgave them until I'd been to war too. Difficult things happen to any family under such pressure. People in danger do what they have to do, but their relationship to their buddies or those who share the same danger is close, perhaps closer than to their families at home. And the constant separation from the rest of your family becomes a factor also." Willi was struggling to be fair.

"And *Mutti* had to take on so much responsibility while *Vati* was gone...she may have changed, as well. Both people change so much while they are apart, they just aren't the same people anymore--like living with a stranger. It isn't anyone's fault. So I guess I can't be too hard on any of them, and I can sympathize with all of them in some ways." He faced Franzi again.

"Of course, that's before I knew about the letter from Munich. It could have been some type of threat, if it caused *Mutti* to send *Vati* away so suddenly. But if it was a threat, say about his wartime activities or something, it was apparently never acted upon. He was never prosecuted, so everyone must have kept the bargain, whatever it was. We're finding out a lot of things here today. Now, I'm not so sure I could sympathize with *Vati* as readily." He paused and pushed away his coffee cup. "Yet I loved him. Perhaps I forgave him everything anyway. It's a long time back now. It's too late for anger. I'm sure they all did the best they could under difficult circumstances."

"I wish *Mutti* had spoken for herself and told us what she knew, and why she made the decisions she did. I think she didn't discuss any of it, thinking she was somehow protecting us, and probably our father, too."

"You're right, Bill," said his wife, Amy, as rested her hand on his arm. "*Mutti* confided to me pretty much what you all have been able to figure out for yourselves. I guess it isn't a secret from you anymore."

"You? She told you, even with your terrible German?"

Amy patted his shoulder and smiled. "*Mutti* had more patience with my language skills than you do. And we talked for hours while the rest of the family was out on those endless after-dinner walks."

"Why did she tell you when she didn't tell us?" Rainer apparently felt left out.

"I asked questions. She answered them all and, at that time, she still remembered everything. When I said I thought her story should be told for all of you, she made me promise I'd never do it until after she was gone. I've had my notes hidden at home since before she became ill and could no longer remember any of us.

"It struck me as ironic that in the end, when she became ill, like her mother, and couldn't remember anyone, she would still talk about her … 'three little boys playing outside in Königsberg, and how her wonderful husband would be home any minute.' At the end, she remembered only her happiest days in her own home, before the war and all the heartache ruined it all."

Franzi said, "We should have asked more and understood more, and forgiven more. Perhaps you should write it all down now."

"I guess I was wrong to judge them both, too," added Rainer. "I suppose they did the best they could to protect us. "I wish I'd known *Mutti* still loved him, and that she was so strong. I wish *Vati* had known that, too."

The others nodded, deep in thought.

Then Dolf added, "But Amy, if you ever do tell this story to anyone, you must change the names and actions to protect us guilty ones. I don't want you all remembering how much I ate in those days."

At last, with the tension broken and with a widened understanding, the family and friends of Regina Wolff sat down to dinner and spoke of her life with great love and laughter, just the way she would have wished.

"Do you remember the time when she…"

"I remember…"